THE GREATEST
MALAYALAM STORIES EVER TOLD

In the same series

The Greatest Bengali Stories Ever Told (ed.) Arunava Sinha

The Greatest Urdu Stories Ever Told (ed.) Muhammad Umar Memon

The Greatest Odia Stories Ever Told (eds.) Leelawati Mohapatra, Paul St-Pierre, and K. K. Mohapatra

The Greatest Hindi Stories Ever Told (ed.) Poonam Saxena

The Greatest Tamil Stories Ever Told (eds.) Sujatha Vijayaraghavan and Mini Krishnan

The Greatest Assamese Stories Ever Told (ed.) Mitra Phukan

The Greatest Gujarati Stories Ever Told (ed.) Rita Kothari

The Greatest Kashmiri Stories Ever Told (ed.) Neerja Mattoo

The Greatest Telugu Stories Ever Told (eds.) Dasu Krishnamoorty and Tamraparni Dasu

The Greatest Marathi Stories Ever Told (ed.) Ashutosh Poddar

The Greatest Indian Stories Ever Told (ed.) Arunava Sinha

The Greatest Punjabi Stories Ever Told (eds.) Renuka Singh and Balbir Madhopuri

The Greatest Kannada Stories Ever Told (ed.) Chandan Gowda (forthcoming)

GREATEST MALAYALAM STORIES
EVER TOLD

Selected and translated by
A. J. THOMAS

ALEPH BOOK COMPANY
An independent publishing firm
promoted by *Rupa Publications India*

First published in India in 2023
by Aleph Book Company
161-B/4, Gulmohar House,
Yusuf Sarai Community Centre,
New Delhi 110049

This edition copyright © Aleph Book Company, 2023
Copyright in the individual stories and translations vests
in the respective authors/translators/proprietors.
Introduction copyright © A. J. Thomas

The Acknowledgements on p. 423 constitute an
extension of the copyright page.

All rights reserved.

This is a work of fiction. Names, characters, places,
and incidents are either the product of the authors'
imagination or are used fictitiously and any resemblance
to any actual persons, living or dead, events, or locales is
entirely coincidental.

No part of this publication may be reproduced,
transmitted, or stored in a retrieval system, in any form
or by any means, without permission in writing from
Aleph Book Company.

ISBN: 978-93-90652-76-1

7 9 10 8 6

Printed in India

This book is sold subject to the condition that it shall
not, by way of trade or otherwise, be lent, resold, hired
out, or otherwise circulated without the publisher's prior
consent in any form of binding or cover other than that
in which it is published.

CONTENTS

Introduction	vii
1. Wooden Dolls KAROOR NEELAKANTA PILLAI	1
2. The Oath P. KESAVADEV	9
3. The World-renowned Nose VAIKOM MUHAMMAD BASHEER	29
4. Dhirendu Majumdar's Mother LALITHAMBIKA ANTHARJANAM	36
5. The Speaking Plough PONKUNNAM VARKEY	43
6. The Farmer THAKAZHI SIVASANKARA PILLAI	53
7. On the Riverbank S. K. POTTEKKATT	62
8. The Fair Child UROOB	66
9. The Shade Trees K. SARASWATHI AMMA	80
10. Chankraanti Ada T. K. C. VADUTHALA	92
11. The Omen KOVILAN	102
12. Fear PAARAPPURATHU	110
13. Allopanishad PATTATHUVILA KARUNAKARAN	118
14. Humans and Animals NANDANAR	126
15. Candle N. P. MOHAMMED	136
16. Lunch V. K. N.	146
17. The Hanging O. V. VIJAYAN	160
18. The Apology RAJALAKSHMI	167
19. Chidambaram C. V. SREERAMAN	173
20. The Death of Makhan Singh T. PADMANABHAN	178
21. Your Story (Mine Too) N. MOHANAN	190
22. Vision M. T. VASUDEVAN NAIR	198
23. Scent of a Bird MADHAVIKKUTTY	213
24. The War Ends KAKKANADAN	218
25. Dimensions ANAND	225

26.	Pempi P. VATSALA	238
27.	The Court of King George VI M. P. NARAYANA PILLAI	251
28.	The Society PUNATHIL KUNJABDULLA	260
29.	Photo M. MUKUNDAN	271
30.	The Mission SETHU	279
31.	It's the Gallows for Us M. SUKUMARAN	286
32.	The Dinosaur Baby E. HARIKUMAR	294
33.	We, Tomorrow Shame T. R.	306
34.	Mushroom for Breakfast MAYTHIL RADHAKRISHNAN	311
35.	The Garden of the Antlions PAUL ZACHARIA	318
36.	The Hook P. PADMARAJAN	326
37.	A Daytime in '53 VICTOR LEENUS	330
38.	Niravatthu Kayyaani C. AYYAPPAN	335
39.	Sweat Marks SARA JOSEPH	342
40.	The Twelfth Hour V. P. SIVAKUMAR	348
41.	The Fourth World N. S. MADHAVAN	355
42.	Civics and Physics Practicals MAANASI	366
43.	A Letter to a Friend Plunged into Despair U. P. JAYARAJ	375
44.	Two Historians and a Young Woman GRACY	380
45.	A Path in the Moonlight N. PRABHAKARAN	386
46.	Pomegranate Trees Blossom Still C. V. BALAKRISHNAN	391
47.	How Many Jennys Are There in Anthikkad? ASOKAN CHARUVIL	395
48.	Man-in-water AYMANAM JOHN	401
49.	The Ship of Butterflies THOMAS JOSEPH	411
50.	Reindeer CHANDRAMATHI	417

Acknowledgements   423

Notes on the Authors   427

INTRODUCTION

I

THE MALAYALAM SHORT STORY IN THE TWENTIETH CENTURY

Of the various literary genres in Malayalam, the short story is one of the most developed, and by certain estimates, some of these stories are deemed to be on a par with the best stories in any literature in the world. The Malayalam short story has reached a very significant phase in its evolution over more than 130 years of its existence.

The short story as a modern literary genre spread its roots in Malayalam literature and sprouted in the last decades of the nineteenth century, under the influence of Western literature. Important works of French and Russian masters; the plays of the Scandinavian genius Henrik Ibsen; and the works of Karl Marx, Friedrich Engels, and Sigmund Freud had been translated into Malayalam in the early part of the twentieth century, among those of other critical thinkers and writers. An encounter with modern thinkers in translation widened the horizons of literary sensibility in Malayalam. The modernist and after-modernist trends found in Malayalam fiction are traceable to the increasing Western influence on thinking, education system, and lifestyle in Kerala. However, the pioneering Malayalam short-story writers had not outrightly imitated the Western models; they had written truly Keralite short stories, although the influences of other literatures could be discerned in the evolution of their form.

Kesari Vengayil Kunhiraman Nayanar is the author of what is surmised to be the very first Malayalam short story that exhibited the essential features of the form. It was titled 'Vasana Vikriti' (Strange Stirrings) and appeared in 1891 in the literary magazine *Vidya Vinodini*. This makes this genre 132 years of age in Malayalam literature.

The Malayalam short story had begun as a loosely narrated, often verbose model, then moved on to the properly structured photographic-realist, socialist-realist, sentimental-romantic, romantic-realist, psychological-realist, dirty-realist modes shot through with naturalism. Next, it passed through the rigidly-structured modernist phase with its allegories, fantasies, and parables through the 1960s until the end of the 1970s. Then, it entered the phases described variously as 'utthara-aadhunika' and 'aadhunikotthara' in Malayalam, which I translate as the 'after-modern' and 'postmodern' phases, respectively. In the context of Indian literatures, it will be misleading to term anything 'postmodern' as it makes for instant comparison with the Western 'postmodern', which is an entirely different phenomenon.

The prevalence of centuries old storytelling traditions contributed to the development of the short story in Malayalam: this included classical forms like the *Kathasaritsagara, Panchatantra, Jataka* stories, and the tales of Vikramaditya and Betal in the larger Indian tradition; stories and sagas like the *Thekkan Paattukal* and *Vadakken Paattukal* (The Northern Ballads and The Southern Ballads), *The Arabian Nights*, and *Karalman Charitram* (a chavittu natakam—a play-story based on the legends about the Frankish emperor Charlemagne); the different traditions of *Prabhandhakoothu* (oral traditions of storytelling in the classical dance-drama koothu, differing in style from region to region); and the folk tales of each region, including myths and legends of the kind compiled in the grand compendium *Aithihyamala* (A Garland of Legends). In this process, the heritage accumulated over the centuries was drawn upon and assimilated; myths and legends found their place in the modern context, generating fresh meanings and levels of relevance.

The short story, especially since the modernist period, began to have a direct bearing on the cultural climate of Kerala. This evolution has reached the present times, and the stories of today are awaiting serious critical treatment. Thus, the short story has developed in Malayalam for the most part through an indigenous process of evolution and drawing on the healthy influence of Western literary trends and philosophical advances up to the present times.

In the nineteenth century, as the renaissance in the socio-cultural sphere had gained ground all over Kerala and India at large, newspapers and periodicals had begun to be published and circulated in large numbers and the story narrated in a short form appearing in them attracted a wide readership among common people who approached it as the best form of entertainment. According to M. P. Paul, the pioneering Malayalam literary critic who wrote the first critical treatise on the Malayalam short story, *Cherukatha Prasthaanam* (The Short Story Movement, 1946),

'Among the practitioners of this form, the most famous name was that of E.V. Krishna Pillai. MRKC (Kunhirama Menon) and Ambadi Narayana Poduval were also reputed as good story writers. There were only a few writers like Otuvil Kunjukrishna Menon and Vengayil Kunhiraman Nayanar, who could be considered as pioneers of this movement.'*

Sukumar Azhikode, citing M. P. Paul, observes that even the term 'cherukatha' (short story) was established only after 1932, as the first edition of his book was titled *Khanda Katha Prasthaanam* (The Short Tale Movement, 1932). In the prefatory note of the second edition of Paul's work, now titled *Cherukatha Prasthaanam* (1946), the author notes that 'the best specimens of short stories' in Malayalam were published after 1932. This consideration informed my decision regarding the time frame for choosing the stories in this volume. The stories in this selection were published over the last seven decades, post the independence of India, and can be considered modern classics.

The early short stories were loose bundles of narration, suggesting the lack of any concept of a definite form. However, in the hands of writers like Moorkoth Kumaran, C.V. Kunhiraman and others, it further improved. The short stories of E. V. Krishna Pillai and C. S. Gopala Panicker were a far cry from the early samples, marking an advanced stage in the evolution of the form. S. Rama Varrier, V.T. Bhattathiripad, M. R. Bhattathiripad, Muthiringotu Bhavathrathan Namboodiripad, and others wrote the earliest of the realistic stories, which served simultaneously as a catalyst and a mirror of rapid social reforms.

Following these realists, P. Kesavadev, Thakazhi Sivasankara Pillai, Malabar K. Sukumaran, Lalithambika Antharjanam, S. K. Pottekkatt, Vaikom Muhammad Basheer, and Karoor Neelakanta Pillai got established about this time—the early 1930s. Ponkunnam Varkey entered the scene towards the end of the 1930s. The short story had come to acquire its classical form by this time. Basheer, Antharjanam, and Varkey were instrumental in bringing about drastic reforms in their respective communities.

These authors were writing stories under the influence of Marxist ideology, following social realism, and were active in the Jeeval Saahithya Samithi (Living Literature Organization). According to Kesari

---

*Quoted in Sukumar Azhikode, 'The Short Story in Malayalam', *Indian Literature*, Vol. 20, No. 2 (March–April), 1977, pp. 5–22.

A. Balakrishna Pillai, 'Jeeval Saahithyam' could be roughly translated as 'Living Literature' or 'Literature for Life', which was literature so connected to human life that it becomes 'as useful to human life as a thing of nature to nature' and 'so beautiful that it generates immense joy'*. In 1944, the forum was renamed as Purogamana Saahithya Samghadana (Progressive Literature Association), which aligned itself with the Progressive Literature Movement at the national level. M. P. Paul was one of its founders. (In 1981, it was renamed the Purogamana Kala Saahithya Samgham—Progressive Art and Literature Association.)

Kesari A. Balakrishna Pillai had been propagating the latest trends in Western art and new ideas in philosophy and psychology through his incessant articles, which he continued writing into the 1950s. Masters like Maupassant, Chekhov, and Gogol were to influence Thakazhi. Thakazhi and Basheer made use of Freudian psychoanalytical approaches in their stories.

Though Basheer wrote realistic stories at first, he anticipated the modernists and even the after-modernists in his experiments in the language and form of the short story. Basheer wrote realistic stories inspired by humanism and socialist realism for a time in the early 1930s. Then, following his self-awakening experiences during his freedom struggle-related underground life, incarcerations, and exile, he undertook nearly seven years of extensive travels within the country and abroad, in Asia and Africa, before embarking on his experiments with language and structure, creating a style entirely his own.

Meanwhile, Kesavadev was too impatient in his social reformist zeal to adopt such an intellectual approach. His stories are marked by the spirit of rebellion and daring in leading a frontal attack on the establishment. Pottekkatt had no such ideological affiliations and was the exponent of 'pure' stories. With a well-defined plot and characters, quaint sense of humour, and romantic approach, his stories set him apart from the others.

Lalithambika Antharjanam was a pioneering female writer who firmly established herself in Malayalam modern fiction. Further, '[s]he disregarded "Womanly" norms of writing...as a young woman intervening actively in the gender politics in Travancore in the 1920s

---

*Quoted in N. G. Ardra, 'Is Ambivalence Progressive? Representation of Labour in Malayalam Progressive Poetry', *Indian Literature*, Vol. 61, No. 3 (May–June), 2017, pp. 71–85.

and 1930s and writing stories that fed into ongoing public debates...."*

Karoor Neelakanta Pillai, never confining himself to the flat one-dimensional approach of the realists, had dug deep into the complexities that modern short story demanded and had written stories in which the acme of perfection was reached using faint humour, irony, and understatement.

Next, P. C. Kuttikrishnan (Uroob), Paarappurathu, Kovilan, Nandanar Ponjikara Rafi, Pulimana Parameswaran Pillai, the well-entrenched K. Saraswathi Amma, and Vettoor Raman Nair formed an array of eminent short story writers. The stories written in this era were either realistic or romantic. The stories of P. C. Kuttikrishnan, Kovilan, and Pulilmana were noted for their lyrical quality.

It was K. Saraswathi Amma, alongside Lalithambika Antharjanam, who introduced fully developed female characters (as against those developed under a male gaze) in the Malayalam short story for the first time, heralding the advent of feminist literature.

Next came N. P. Mohammed, T. Padmanabhan, Madhavikkutty (aka Kamala Das and Kamala Surayya), Pattathuvila Karunakaran, V. K. N., and M. T. Vasudevan Nair. These writers stand apart from their predecessors (except Basheer) in that they introduced symbols and images in their stories, revealing the inner worlds of characters. The story came to be regarded as an independent artistic entity. Madhavikkutty anticipated the latter-day 'modernists', in the deft employment of images and structural innovations and in the total rejection of romanticism opting for a cruelly objective analysis of interpersonal relationships. Madhavikkutty, T. Padmanabhan, and M. T. Vasudevan Nair elevated their stories to the level of poetic realism.

Following them, modernists like O. V. Vijayan, Kakkanadan, M. Mukundan, M. P. Narayana Pillai, Punathil Kunjabdulla, U. A. Khader, Sethu (A. Sethumadhavan), Sara Joseph, Zacharia (Paul Zacharia), Anand (P. Sachidanandan), T. R. (T. Ramachandran), Padmarajan, V. P. Sivakumar, and many others captured the centre stage.

The main characteristics of modernist stories are as follows: disregard for the narrative element; rejection of the traditional form; the adoption of a mythical structure comprising symbols, images, and archetypes, giving expression to inner urges and the riddle-like existential problems of

---

*J. Devika, *Womenwriting = Manreading,* New Delhi: Zubaan/Penguin, 2013, p. 93.

the individual; fashioning of the story in a predetermined philosophical mould that is invariably dark; and an objectivity denying any room for the author's subjective intervention.[*]

Thus, the evolution of the Malayalam short story up till this point can be summed up as follows: after the action-dominated early stories, the short story was centred around, first, the specific outward expressions of life as in the social reformist stories, then the inner life of individuals, and, finally, the abstract plane of indirect experiences full of paradoxes involving a philosophical outlook. The form evolved from the bulky narrative structure of the early days to a well-organized plot, then to the employment of language to generate multilevel meanings, and finally to the deployment of symbols and images.[†]

Different phases, or stages in the evolution of the short story cannot be confined to the ascent or decline of specific generations of writers.[‡] There have been great writers like Karoor, Basheer, Uroob, Kovilan, Madhavikkutty, T. Padmanabhan, M. T. Vasudevan Nair, O. V. Vijayan, Zacharia, and Sara Joseph, among others, who left the indelible mark of their contributions in more than one phase or movement. However, it is pertinent to classify the stories when distinct characteristics separate some from an existing kind.

Even in adopting philosophical concepts from the West, like the absurdism of Camus, the nihilism of Nietzsche, and the atheistic existentialism of Sartre, the iconoclastic modernists of the 1950s and 1960s had been sadly limited in their selection. Although Kesari Balakrishna Pillai had been writing essays for a quarter of a century highlighting all leading European modernist trends in art and literature, most writers who were content with the compromised existence of the middle classes lacked a radical approach or an intense sense of history akin to Kesari's; as a result—with the exception of a Basheer or a Thakazhi—the vast majority of short-story writers did not try to engage with new ideas to help open novel worlds of perception in the literature of the 1930s or 1940s.[§] Thus, the continuity of the modernist evolution in the West was

---

[*]Azhikode, 'The Short Story in Malayalam'.
[†]K. S. Narayanapillai, 'Adhunika Katha' [The Modernist Story], *Katha*, pp. 78–79.
[‡]K. P. Appan, 'Chilakaaryangalil Viyojicchukondu' [Dissenting on Certain Points], *Kalakaumudi Weekly*, Vol. 690, 1988, pp. 23–24.
[§]M. V. Devan, 'Cherukatha "Hatao"' [Short Story Hatao], *Kalakaumudi Weekly*, Vol. 692, 1988, pp. 29–32.

lost, and the re-reading of Nietzsche, Marx, and Freud carried out by neo-Marxists and structuralists did not influence literature in Malayalam until the early 1980s. Meanwhile, the staple diet of modernist thought in Malayalam was based on the philosophical concepts of Camus and Sartre.

This situation improved subsequently, however, with the introduction of the neo-Marxian and post-structural theories and postmodern Western and South American fiction and poetry made available in translation to the cognoscenti and common readers alike through literary journalism, making writers and readers acquainted with the latest in the world of writing. M. Krishnan Nair played a decisive role through his weekly literary column 'Saahithyavaaraphalam' (Weekly Literary Horoscope) in three successive literary publications *Malayalanaadu*, *Kalakaumudi*, and *Samakaalika Malayalam* in introducing these writers to Malayalam readers, writers, and critics over four decades from 1969 to 2006 till his death.

There emerged an array of short story writers who started writing at the heyday of modernism. Their writing was characterized by the conscious selection of images and symbols, care for the time of action of each sentence, the awareness that a broken sentence would cause fissures in the plane of inner structure, predilection for factors like antiquity, and a sentence order that helped to portray the violent countenance of contemporary culture.* These stories mark a transition from modernism to the next phase. Many writers had kept open in their hearts the raw wound of the excesses committed on the so-called extremist youth during the Emergency. This 'generation of the lost spring' soon petered out in the early 1980s. Of these, K. P. Nirmal Kumar, N. S. Madhavan, and Maythil Radhakrishnan came back with powerful stories.

T. R. and Victor Leenus, though at two different ends of the same grouping of high modernism, too built back their story-worlds after gaps, but both met with untimely deaths and their careers were cut short. However, Aymanam John developed and thrived, growing into a major storywriter who, in his works, has deftly captured human beings, other living beings, and their environment, mostly based on his native village.

---

*Ashamenon, 'Abhimukheekaranathinte Ghadanakal' [Structures of Encounters], *Prathibhaasangamam [A Meeting of Geniuses]*, edited by C. H. Haridas, Kozhikode: P. K. Brothers, 1985, pp. 285–300; M. K. Harikumar, 'Naveena Kathayude Antharlokam' [The Innerscape of the Modernist Story], *Mathrubhumi Weekly Onam Special*, 1991, pp. 25–31; 151–57; Prasannarajan, 'Cherukatha—Prashnangalum Yaadhaarthyangalum' [The Short Story—Problems and Realities], *Kalakaumudi Weekly*, Vol. 698, 1989, pp. 35–36.

While most of the modernists were confined to the existential agony of the individual alienated from society and history, a line of progressive writers who were lonely voices but were committed to the social and historical aspects of existence came down from the late 1950s, through the 1960s, 1970s, and 1980s to the after-modern phase, and mainly till the mid-1990s and a few into the twenty-first century. Pattathuvila Karunakaran, M. Sukumaran, E. Harikumar, and a few others are the prominent names in this line.

Two writers who began writing in the mid-modernist era, Sara Joseph and Zacharia, progressed through the succeeding phases, each unique in their voices. While Joseph solidified feminist writing and later progressed into eco-fiction, Zacharia took the form and content of the short story to international standards.

A contemporary of the great American short-story writers Raymond Carver and Tobias Wolff, Zacharia independently developed in Malayalam his own brand of the short story abreast with them and in some cases ahead of them—but with a difference too. While the stories of the former were mostly bare, grim, and dismal in tone, Zacharia's were deeply ironical, steeped in black humour and often hilarious even in tragic circumstances. All three could be categorized as dirty realist if one followed their stories till the late 1980s. However, Zacharia has sailed past this stage and is already leading the youngest kids on the block—the twenty-first century Malayalam short story writers.

The group of short story writers who began writing steadily from the early- and mid-1980s would include names such as Maanasi, Thomas Joseph, N. Prabhakaran, P. Surendran, C. V. Balakrishnan, V. Vinayakumar, M. A. Rehman, Shihabuddeen Poythumkadavu, V. R. Sudheesh, Socrates Valath, P. F. Mathews, George Joseph K., Joseph Marian, S. A. Shujad, and some others who have been mentioned earlier, the actual translation of whose stories, incidentally, formed part of my M. Phil dissertation. These were the 'after-modern' or 'neo-modern' writers I presented. To this group could be added names such as N. P. Hafiz Mohammed, T. V. Kochuvava, Akbar Kakkattil, Asokan Charuvil, and a few others. Jumping from the previous high-modernist phase, Zacharia, Sara Joseph, and N. S. Madhavan were intensely active in this phase, as well.

Modernism broke through the stagnation of the romantic and realistic modes, and, in the process, rejected the function of the short story, of creating a world of human experiences. However, as time passed, this experiment repelled readers. The after-modern story reintroduces the main function of the short story, that of creating a world of diverse experiences, releasing the readers from the tedium of conceptual stories.

The diversity of themes representing lived and imagined experiences is the main feature of the after-modern story. Its various forms are in fact different approaches in giving expression to the complex contemporary experience. This may be better explained through the concept of the 'everyday' introduced by Henri Lefebvre.

> The everyday signals the advent of a new epistemology concerned with the representation of immanent objects rather than of a transcendent reality and implies the emergence of a new aesthetic that is geared to a radical understanding of culture. Lefebvre makes a distinction between 'Everyday' and 'daily life'.... The 'everyday' as he sees it, is what is excluded from philosophy, and it is this exclusion that accounts for its departure from elite responses and forms of thought, including art and literature of the esoteric kind....*

In effect, the writer and the artist can, in this scheme of things, write about immediate experiences in a fragmented sense, rather than giving it a framework, based on already existing philosophical formulations.

BREAKING UP OF THE MONOLITH: DIFFERENT VOICES

The grand narrative in Malayalam literature, or 'high literature', has tended to be led by the elitist, gentleman writer variety, dominated by the upper castes. However, with the advent of modernism and after, cracks began to develop in this monolith and the multiple voices of the different communities and sections sidelined or marginalized in literature began to emerge independently. This follows on the theme of the fragmentation of experiences in modernist times.

Feminist consciousness, reflected through women's experiences in the Malayalam short story, was established firmly right from the first half of the twentieth century. J. Devika, presently the foremost feminist critic and social and cultural historian in Malayalam, rightly places Lalithambika Antharjanam, K. Saraswathi Amma, Madhavikkutty, and Sara Joseph as

---

*Quoted in P. P. Raveendran, 'Introduction: *Bhasha* in Focus', *Under the Bhasha Gaze: Modernity and Indian Literature*, Oxford University Press, 2023, p. 4.

pioneering leaders in feminist writing in Malayalam, who wrested their rightful places from the bastion of condescension of the homogenous, all-male aesthetic power structure of Malayalam literature from as long ago as almost a century.*

Lalithambika Antharjanam began as a poet in the romanticist tradition but soon established herself in the short story in the 1920s and became the first woman reformer among the Namboodiri community. Devika views Antharjanam's writing, in sum, as 'a re-visioning of the order of gender beyond patriarchal reformist versions by a woman intellectual committed to speaking for Women....'†

K. Saraswathi Amma was Antharjanam's contemporary, who gave shape to her writings based on the debates in the literary public of the day, as well as the debates around the gender questions in the 1930s and 1940s.‡ However, unlike Antharjanam, she was a loner, who was marginalized, remained unmarried, and was 'fiercely independent'. She was suspicious of 'the valorization of motherhood...and the very space of the feminine domestic itself.... Her style was a strident sort of realism', leaving no room for romanticism at all.§

Discussing Madhavikkutty's writing, Devika observes, after subjecting her *Ente Katha* (My Story) to intense scrutiny from several angles that 'perhaps we must raise the question of a female modernism, afresh, from a *feminist perspective*, whether women authors in Malayalam created a "female or feminist modernism" and how it differs from the male version.' This is a serious question, which automatically leads us to Rajalakshmi Madhavikkutty's contemporary, who cut short her brilliant writing career through suicide in 1965 at the age of thirty-four. Devika writes,

> If Madhavikkutty's writing represents the disillusionment with the promise of harmonious conjugal love held out by community reformisms to women in the 1930s, in many ways, Rajalakshmy's writing is informed by a deep disillusionment with the promise held out to women by political forces in the 1940s and 1950s, that they would be freed by entry into employment and the public. In her writing, the spaces of intellectual debate, of politics and

---

*Devika, *Womenwriting = Manreading*, p. 10.
†Ibid., p. 99.
‡Ibid., p. 109.
§Ibid., p. 109.

the public, are incorrigibly male and inhospitable to women....
The women in these texts have no language to express desire....*

Progressing from those three early pioneers, through Rajalakshmi and P. Vatsala, whom the feminist critic Geetha describes as a modernist and many others term as a female representative of socialist realism, as noted by Devika, we reach Sara Joseph. She makes a kind of arrival with her style of feminist writing, which K. Satchidanandan deftly defined as 'pennezhutthu' (womanwriting) in a virtual comparison to Hélène Cixous's *ecriture feminine* in his introduction to her iconic story collection *Paapatthara* (The Platform of Sin).

From here, we reach Gracy with her starkly realistic and sometimes strident feminist voice, as well as Geetha Hiranyan, B. M. Suhra, Ashitha, Manasi, and Chandramathi. Of these, Chandramathi and Geetha Hiranyan resisted the notion of pennezhutthu, as Devika points out. She says that in an interview in 2010, Chandramathi 'reiterates her point that the discourse around critical women's writings ought to have been inaugurated by women themselves.' We have the 'post-modernists' in S. Sithara, Priya A. S., K. R. Meera, E. K. Sheeba, K. Rekha, Indumenon, and down to youngsters like Steffi (with one collection) and the younger generation of women writers, who reveal diverse worlds of human experiences in their writing.

The after-modern Malayalam short story significantly features expressions of Dalit experiences. The Dalit discourse in Kerala begins majorly with the history of the predominantly Pulaya agricultural labourers, who were enslaved under the feudal system of the Kerala princely states. In a gradual process that unfolded in Travancore, Rani Gowry Lakshmi Bai, advised by the Diwan Colonel Munroe (the only white person to hold the position in the state's history), influenced by Christian missionaries, issued a Proclamation in 1812 abolishing slavery; however, agricultural slavery continued until it was abolished through a royal edict in 1855. The British government abolished slavery in India in 1843, twenty years before the Emancipation of Slaves in the United States in 1863.† There is a counter-narrative to this, though.

---

*Ibid., pp. 132–33.
†V. Kavaskar and V. Ranjan, 'The Christian Missionaries and Abolition of Slavery in South Travancore', *The Journal of Emerging Technologies and Innovative Research*, Scot Christian College, Nagercoil, Tamil Nadu, 2018, Vol. 5, No. 10, pp. 386–91.

It says that it was anti-colonial historians who asserted it was through Christian missionary writings that the plight of the slaves first came to the attention of the British government. Although missionary writings have majorly contributed in this regard, the fact remains that it was the Malabar District Magistrate Thomas Hervey Baber (though infamous for hunting down the rebellious chieftain and patriot Pazhassi Raja to his death) who intercepted and punished a slave trader, the Scotsman Murdoch Brown and his Mahe-based assistant Hassan Ali, inquired into the whole affair, and wrote a series of articles about it as early as the 1810s which first brought the matter to global attention, leading to its abolition in 1943 in British Malabar, as Kerala Sahitya Akademi award-winning historian Vinil Paul states.*

Further, what happened in Travancore post the 1855 declaration was:

> [m]issionary initiatives and colonial legislation enabled agrarian slaves (who formed only a section of the Dalits) to move into plantations and factories as labourers and also into the education sector. In missionary documents, slaves feature as human beings, with emotions and bodies that suffer.†

In this context, Sanal Mohan posits that 'Christianity offered them a new language of the body, of interiority, of subjectivity'. Meanwhile, '[K. K.] Kochu points out that Dalits asserted themselves as agents in these processes and therefore the view that Dalits are eternal slaves is erroneous.‡

However, Dalits continued to be in quasi-serfdom through the landowner–landless labourer bond they had to follow; they still went on toiling in the field for a weekly measure of paddy as wage, through much of the first half of the twentieth century.

Concurrent to this century-long hiatus in the plight of the Dalit people, the revolutionary changes that resulted from the social levelling by reformers like Sree Narayana Guru, Ayyankali, Poykayil Appacchan, Pandit K. P. Karuppan, Sahodaran Ayyappan, and several others in the late nineteenth and early twentieth centuries were kicking in. This was

---

*Adimakeralatthinte Adrishyacharithram: The Invisible History of Slave Kerala, Kottayam: DC Books, 2021, pp. 38-39.
†K. Satyanarayana and Susie Tharu, 'Introduction', *No Alphabets in Sight: New Dalit Writings from South India*, New Delhi: Penguin India, 2011, p. 47.
‡Satyanarayana and Tharu, 'Introduction', p. 47.

happening contemporaneously with the development of the genre of short story in Malayalam. The reformers were followed on their heels by the Radical Socialists and Communists, and parallel to them, the camp-followers of Jeeval Saahithyam and the Progressives.

The communists who came to power in Kerala brought in policy changes that culminated in the land reforms of 1964, which ushered in revolutionary restructuring of the social and the agricultural sectors and brought most of the Scheduled Caste agricultural labourers outside their virtual bonded-labourer conditions. However, in none of these had the communists acknowledged the existence of caste. For them, it was always a class question.

George K. Alex and Elizabeth John have identified three distinct periods in Malayalam Dalit literature.[*] In the first period, as already seen, 'the depressed castes' (not yet referred to as Dalits) were in a state of slavery. Subsequently, fiction writers of the so-called Kerala Renaissance beginning with Thakazhi, P. Kesavadev, and Ponkunnam Varkey and reaching up to the post-modern ones, non-Dalits wrote stories about the Dalit experience. These writers did not accept the Dalit identity. Some of them were driven by ideology, rallying against what they acknowledged as class difference, oppression, and exploitation of labour. For others, it was 'the aesthetics of romantic realism and Renaissance egalitarianism', inherent in the general reading sensibility. They did not accept the Dalit perspective; nor did they accept any identity other than 'class identity'.[†]

The beginning of the second period was with the emergence of T. K. C. Vaduthala in short story at about the same time as the above writers of the romantic realist and modernist groups. Unlike the other writers, caste identity was what drove T. K. C. Through his stories, he acted as a reformer from the inside, explicating 'the very essence of caste/community identity'.[‡] Critic M. Dasan mentions that T. K. C's work 'was a celebration of Pulaya life and culture, with all its good and bad aspects. It also portrays Dalit rituals, beliefs, ceremonies, and superstitions'.[§] Most of his stories

---

[*] Quoted in George K. Alex and Elizabeth John, *Reinventing Identity: An Anthology of Dalit Writers from Kerala*, Mumbai: Vikas Adhyayan Kendra, 2008.
[†] M. Dasan and V. Pratibha (eds.), 'Introduction', *Oxford India Anthology of Malayalam Dalit Writing*, Oxford University Press, 2012, pp. 49–51.
[‡] Ibid.
[§] Quoted in Satyanarayana and Tharu, 'Introduction', p. 33.

are about Pulayas, some of the important ones being 'Jatheeyatha' (The Nature of Caste), 'Chankraanti Ada' (Sweet-rice Offering at Sankraanthi), 'Randu Thalamura' (Two Generations), and so on. Post T. K. C, there were his late contemporaries like Paul Chirakkarode, who wrote stories about the predicament of the Pulaya people who converted to Christianity, about their dilemma of the dual rejection they faced from their original community and the newly embraced one.

Another writer who adorns the pride of place in this context is C. Ayyappan (incidentally T. K. C's son-in-law), who stands out as one of the masters of the late modernist/after-modernist short story. His stories have carried out the subversion of the mainstream, conventional, elitist narrative beyond compare. While the mainstream modernists and after-modernists were in a search of identity and the dehumanization, alienation, and other problems of urbanization, Ayyappan filtered out the superficial attitudes of romanticism and realism and made visible Dalit life in all its intensity in his stories.

> Ayyappan chose to be different and initiated a dialogue between the discourses of modernity and the Dalit perspectives of writing.... Ayyappan constructed a Dalitness beyond and above mainstream aesthetics through his characters. By the skilful use of narrative strategies based on the likes of lunacy, possessed self, and soliloquy, he creates a counter-discourse of the downtrodden. He was able to rupture the sensibility of the mainstream writing by creating an element of magical realism in his writings.*

The third phase began with the Ambedkar birth centenary celebrations in 1991, which marked a rebirth for the younger, assertive generations of Dalit writers and literature, which has not looked back ever since. P. A. Uthaman is a major voice of this period of Dalit short story. His stories are collected in *Sundarapurushanmaar* (Handsome Men) and *Kavaadangalkkarukil* (By the Side of the Gateways). He won the Kerala Sahitya Akademi Award for his novel *Chavoli* (The Sound of Death). By employing caste-specific dialect and culture of the groups of people he writes about, he attempts to present them in their proper selves. His stories written during the Emergency, employing orality, highlight the invisible and muffled experiential world of Dalit people. The language

---

*Dasan and Pratibha, 'Introduction', pp. 49–52.

of his stories contains the language of indignation and anger, assertion, pride, and dignity.

P. K. Prakash and M. K. Madhukumar are the names that stand out in the context of the Dalit short story after P. A. Uthaman. They dealt with the vast body of non-Brahminic Dalit systems of knowledge available to them in the post-Ambedkar centenary era. They dealt with binaries like black/white, mainstream/marginalized, and modern/feudal from a Dalit perspective. Instead of the customary characters, in their stories, lived experiences or interpretations of constructs/contexts are examined.[*]

Thus, cross-cultural, multi-community, intrinsically political experiences in modern Malayalam fiction place it in a larger frame of reference, and processes of translation have historically played a prominent role in it. Besides, community-based nuances expressed through the creative language of the short story mark their identities as well. Translating such texts into English presents a very complex task.

The character of the literature of the twentieth century consisted not in explaining but in revealing. It is the incessant revelation of man's inner life. This becomes obvious when the subject of a short story becomes a link between imagination and reality.[†] This observation is relevant in summing up the development of the Malayalam short story from the modernist to the after-modernist and post-modernist/millennial phase.

II

ABOUT THE STORIES IN THIS VOLUME

Most of the stories in this volume form an arc from the works of the Living Literature/Progressive Literature writers to those in the after-modern phase. While the authors' names have been arranged chronologically according to their year of birth, some stories in the collection fall outside this periodic arc.

'The Farmer' by Thakazhi and 'The Speaking Plough' by Ponkunnam Varkey are both in the best tradition of Jeeval Saahithyam of their times, dealing squarely with the farmer and his use of the

---

[*]Ibid., p. 53.
[†]Pavese, *This Business of Living*, p. 142.

ox and the plough and the natural manure, keeping the earth fertile. The devotion of the female protagonist of Karoor's story 'Wooden Dolls' to her craft of creating wooden dolls also is akin to the Zen-like, reaching-to-the core of the two aforementioned farmers in their vocation. In 'The Oath', P. Kesavadev delineates the seemingly simple, but intrinsically complex personalities of two rural women characters. Basheer, on the other hand, resorts to biting satire to expose human vanity and the driving forces behind political and other power-centres, through his mighty hyperbole of a story, 'The World-renowned Nose'. S. K. Pottekkatt, standing at the crossroads of a romanticist–realist–naturalist narrative tradition creates a magical atmosphere with words in 'On the Riverbank'.

In Lalithambika Antharjanam's 'Dhirendu Majumdar's Mother', the mother emerges as the revolutionary heroine of two struggles—the Partition of 1947 and the Bangladesh Liberation War of 1971. In 'Shade Trees', Saraswathi Amma presents a Christian nun, meeting her Hindu lover, now a sanyasi, in a platonic set-up after several decades.

'The Fair Child' by Uroob is a fantasy that grows into an allegory. At first sight, it looks like a children's story, but deep down, human virtues and vices are delineated in the most phantasmagorical settings and language in this story.

'Chankraanti Ada' by T. K. C Vaduthala, is a pioneering story, full of reformatory vigour and positivity. The story is not about any zamindar–serf conflict, but life within the Pulaya agricultural labourer caste of a particular locality.

Kovilan, Paarappurathu, and Nandanar were pigeonholed as military fiction writers as they had served in the defence services and written of life in the barracks, the snow-clad mountains of the Himalayan ranges, the arid sands of the Rajputana desert, and the rainy forests of the Northeast, which most of the so-called 'homegrown gentlemen' writers could not even dream about. 'The Omen' by Kovilan, employs rare verve with the use of language, bordering on stream of consciousness. This story deals with a sthalapuranam (local legend) and the esoteric. 'Fear' by Paarappurathu, portrays the dread of the locals for Naini Devi of Naini Tal, and all attendant superstitions and mystery that swirled around the death of a British memsahib in the colonial times in a picturesque spot in the hill resort. 'Humans and Animals' by Nandanar narrates an unbelievably macabre incident from the Partition horrors.

Nandanar does not seem to relate the army with violence. Soldiers in the barracks are portrayed as gentle and humane. It is the Partition that spawns the real violence.

In Pattathuvila Karunakaran's 'Allopanishad' in a subtext, the protagonist comments on how caste-conscious the Kerala Marxists are and how E. M. S. abandoned the Naxalites. N. P. Mohammed's 'Candle' portrays the inner turmoil of the protagonist's mind, bound by his filial bonds to his mother and other family members, and by an equally compelling relationship with his lover, shrouded later by the guilt of forsaking her. V. K. N's 'Lunch' is from his famous 'Payyan Series'. Payyan is a sophisticated, adequately degenerate young journalist who strikes up friendships with beautiful women in the high society in the 1960s Nehruvian Delhi. Coinage of special phrases and expressions and language-magic are the specialties of his personalized style. O. V. Vijayan's 'The Hanging' brings out in a touching, serendipitous style the story of the little people. The narration is about the inexorable power of the state in the form of capital punishment brought upon a young man from a poor community who is too dazed on the eve of his execution when he meets his father face to face to remember whether he has committed murder.

Rajalakshmi's 'The Apology' ends in the dismissal of a bright student over a seemingly trivial matter involving the teacher, but which the teacher felt had mocked her existence as a woman. In the words of the apology, the student scribbles in a volume of Pushkin's poems he left for her as a parting gift before he leaves the college; in it, there is an allusion to his possible suicide. Madhavikkuty, in 'Scent of a Bird', draws in bold strokes the existential angst of a modern woman who wishes to make a career for herself. P. Vatsala's story, 'Pempi' describes the plight of the Adiyaar tribal women of Wayanad in the 1960s.

C. V. Sreeraman's 'Chidambaram' and T. Padmanabhan's 'The Death of Makhan Singh' are masterpieces located outside Kerala, in the larger Indian context. 'Chidambaram' has the Andamans and the temple-town of Chidambaram in Tamil Nadu as its locales and deals with the human predicament of weaknesses bringing in catastrophe. T. Padmanabhan's is a road story with a difference.

N. Mohanan in his 'Your Story (Mine Too)' writes about the cross-cultural ties and basic human exchanges between a Namboodiri youth and a poor Syrian Christian boy, which grow strong over the years. M. T. Vasudevan Nair, in his celebrated story, 'Vision', reiterates the freedom and liberated state of women choosing for themselves.

Kakkanadan's 'The War Ends' is an example of the modernist story in which the writer invokes primal archetypes and myths. In 'The Court of King George VI', M. P. Narayana Pillai lays bare the by-lanes of a madman's mind, structured by the atmosphere of esoteric rituals that he grew up with from his childhood. The living presence of native lore and sorcery are made to be felt. 'The Mission' by Sethu is about the clash between two worlds—that of a sage father and an ambitious but confused son, with a strongly esoteric vein running through the narration.

Anand's 'Dimensions' keeps the mystery and suspense of a night full of appalling events, involving life and death, and exploring destinies in the classical post-modernist mode. 'The Society', by Punathil Kunjabdulla, is an extended allegory but done in a realistic mode, sometimes the frames of the visuals a little frayed, creating a surrealist atmosphere. M. Mukundan in 'Photo', which is a study in cold-blooded child molestation, describes the nonchalant witnessing of a heinous act, like in many of his acclaimed 'Delhi' stories.

The beginnings of a stream of protest that rose amongst certain radically minded writers against anti-democratic tendencies can be discerned in many of the stories. M. Sukumaran's 'It's the Gallows for Us' is an allegory in which the state or the authorities in charge of keeping the moral, ethical, and social order are doing just the opposite, by executing the naïve protagonist for his good and meritorious deeds instead of rewarding him as he expects. 'We, Tomorrow's Shame' by T. R., is an allegory about absolute power, and in its wake, the powerlessness and sycophancy of the common man. Like Basheer, O. V. Vijayan, V. K. N., M. P. Narayana Pillai, and Thomas Joseph, T. R. too creates his own language style.

E. Harikumar's 'The Dinosaur's Baby' lays an elaborate trap for the victim–protagonist betrayed by the position of planets in his asterism, in an ironic symbolism of the so-called 'modern man's' predicament in the rat race of modern living. Maythil Radhakrishnan's 'Mushroom for Breakfast' is a postmodern story in the Western mode. The beginnings of a panic culture are portrayed by this pioneer of after-modern poetry and short story in Malayalam. Zacharia's story 'The Garden of the Antlions' reveals his deftness in dealing with language to bring about a freshness that was hitherto not experienced during the heyday of modernism. Feminine creativity based on care and nurture is given a beautiful illustration throughout this story.

P. Padmarajan, beginning as a romantic realist, progressed into the after-modern and even the post-modern in the treatment of his stories and screenwriting. 'The Hook' creates a rare atmosphere through the deft handling of emotions and choice of diction. Victor Leenus, in 'A Daytime in '53' employs the full ambit of modernist language to create an atmosphere of eagerness, anxiety, apprehension, and taut suspense. In 'The Twelfth Hour', V. P. Sivakumar uses heightened language to drive a premonition of death to a super-dramatic pitch. The story is autobiographical as the author, a cancer survivor who had a close call in real life, lived in the shadow of death, and finally succumbed.

'Niravatthu Kayyaani' by C. Ayyappan is part of his 'spectral speech' series, which includes stories such as 'Madness' and 'Pretabhashanam' (Spectral Speech). This story is narrated by the ghost of a girl raped and murdered by a landowner-capitalist Christian. Sara Joseph's 'Sweat Marks' analyses a typically Kerala Dalit situation—the politics of reservation at the higher echelons of 'caste' elites who come together to dupe a brilliant Dalit student, while a 'creamy layer' Dalit professor in the selection committee is compelled to remain a mute witness owing to his lower-caste-born fear to protest.

N. S. Madhavan's 'The Fourth World', written responding to an actual news item, was the hottest story of the time right after the disintegration of the Soviet Union when the space assets of the erstwhile communist giant were left orphaned, with no one to take responsibility for them. 'Civics and Physics Practicals' is a story that presaged the rise of the right-wing that unleashed violence on the minorities—in this case, a victim of regional chauvinism coupled with religious bigotry—that began to become apparent from the early 1990s. U. P. Jayaraj's 'Letter to a Young Man Plunged into Despair', deals with the underground life of the Naxalites of the 1980s or 1990s, their modes of operation, and how a real revolutionary leader turns out to be a father figure and a guide, led on by a sense of compassion and commitment.

In 'Two Historians and a Young Woman', Gracy makes an emphatic feminist statement employing the concept of rebirth.

'A Path in the Moonlight' by N. Prabhakaran appears to be a political story. The conflict arising out of ideal and practical approaches to an ideology and the ironic situation that results come out couched in the stilted satire of a political animation. C. V. Balakrishnan's story, 'Pomegranate Trees Blossom Still', like E. Harikumar's, deals with the cultural chaos brought in by westernization, which wrecked traditional mores and brought in the rat-race-level push of materialism.

Aymanam John's story, 'Man-in-water', is based on the author's childhood recollections of his village, its rivers, waterways, homesteads, farmhouses, the ordinary people, and their daily lives. Gradually, the story develops into a local myth of surrealist proportions. In Thomas Joseph's 'The Ship of Butterflies', what is actually, 'lost in translation', is the unique tone, mood, and atmosphere he achieves through the combination of his rare coinages and word-choices, which a translator finds hard put to bring into a language like English.

In Asokan Charuvil's story, 'How Many Jennys Are There in Anthikkad?', we encounter the writer's mind that reacts in a romanticist vein to the global collapse of communism via a theme with a Moscow-connection and the dual 'citizenship' of comrades of the locality with the archetypal belief systems at a primary level and later the dialectical materialism inculcated through the influence of the elders. Likewise, 'The Reindeer' is a Kerala-Russian story with a surprise twist at the end. Chandramathi poignantly portrays the disillusionment that is in store for the woman who ventures to dream, deftly using magical realist elements.

I leave you, readers, with the glittering array of short stories in Malayalam, which I have had the pleasure of sharing with you. Finally, I wish to express my deep gratitude to Aienla Ozukum for guiding me through different stages of manuscript preparation, for the meticulous and thoughtful editing and final execution; my sincere thanks also to Vidisha Ghosh for all the support.

Dr A. J. Thomas
Kaitharam, North Paravur, Ernakulam
16 August 2023

NOTE

The section up till 'Breaking up of the Monolith: Different Voices' has been developed based on my essay published in *Indian Literature* on the evolution of the Malayalam short story.* The English translations of all the in-text citations from Malayalam sources in this essay have been mine.

---

*A. J. Thomas, 'Malayalam Short Story after Modernism', *Indian Literature*, Vol. 36, No. 3 (May–June), 1993, pp. 174–81.

WOODEN DOLLS

KAROOR NEELAKANTA PILLAI

The enumerator stood in front of the courtyard of a hut whose walls and roof were made with braided coconut leaves. He said to himself, '312 Aashaariparampil' and then said aloud, 'Is anybody here?'

A young woman came out onto the veranda.

The enumerator looked at a paper in his hand, and said, 'Is your name Ummini?'

The young woman's wide eyes widened. She was worried that the man could be from the police station or the court.

'I am collecting the census data. How many people live in this house?'

'Right now, I am the only one in the house. Mother has gone to collect screw pine leaves by the bank of the stream. My younger brother has also gone out for work.'

'Who is Ummini?'

'That's my mother.'

'That's right. Is Ummini male or female?'

She let out a peal of derisive laughter. Yet, the laughter was beautiful.

'Mother and I are female. My brother is male.'

'Your father?'

'He's dead.'

'So, is Ummini a widow?'

'Yes, she's now a widow.' The young woman continued: 'When you go about collecting census data, don't you carry an umbrella? If you count the number of people standing in this blazing sun, the number would be one less soon. You may come in and sit on this bench.'

The visitor sat on the bench. The floor of the veranda was well polished with cow dung paste. He started to record all the details about Ummini.

'What is your name?'

'My name is Nalini,' she replied quietly.

'Age?'

'What do you think, looking at me?'

'I don't think anything.'

She smiled. 'Twenty-three.'
'Are you married?'
'Hmm.'
'Where is your husband?'
She felt perplexed, somewhat.
'He's not here now.... Have you collected the census details from the 13th Mile area?'
'Someone else is doing that. You do have a husband, don't you?'
'You may write there's one, or that there isn't one,' she said in a resigned mood.
'If I write that there's one or that there isn't one, the meaning would not be the same.'
'Then write that I have a husband in such a way that my marital status is ambiguous.'
'So, your marriage would just have been fixed with someone, right? Then instead of "Married" I would have to write "Unmarried".'
'No, it's not that way. I am married.'
She scratched the back of her head. Her long, dry, and unkempt hair fell loose on her shoulders.
'Your husband?'
'I have a husband, yet I don't.'
'He's left you, right? Then I have to write "Vibhartruka", Abandoned Wife.'
'I think you can write it down as I hear you say it. Once more, please. "London Wife!" Mine too is such a complicated case. But he hasn't abandoned me. If he had abandoned me, then why would he send his messenger to me every week?'
'Did you abandon him then?'
'Not exactly. I didn't abandon him nor did I beseech him to return. You may write whatever you like since you seem to know everything.'
'I do not know anything about your husband. I will write what you told me: that you have a husband.'
'That's good.'
'This book is not to write anything good or bad. This is for writing the facts, the truth.'
'What I said is the truth.' Saying that, she tied her hair up. He watched her pulling her hair from her face though it was not part of his official work.

'Have you given birth?'

'No boy has given birth; neither has any girl.'

'Have you had cchchidram, a miscarriage?'

'Needless to say! The chchidram began even before I completed six months in my husband's house. I haven't spent a single day without chchidram, a quarrel.'

'A chchidram every day?'

'That's why I came away.'

'What are you saying? I meant a garbhachchidram...a miscarriage. Have you had any miscarriages?'

'What shameful things are you asking? Good that my brother is not here.'

The enumerator was a bit irate. 'What if your brother is here? This is a government matter. Even if your grand-uncle were here, I would still have asked you what I had to ask you. And you would have to answer truthfully. It would be an offence if you provide any incorrect information. Whatever you say would be confidential, of course.'

'If you are feeling hot, you can fan yourself with this,' Nalini offered him a hand fan made of areca palm leaf.

'What I meant was I would have been embarrassed if you had asked these questions if my brother was here.'

'OK, go on.'

'No.'

'What no? That you won't answer my question?'

'No, no! Didn't you ask me whether I had a miscarriage? I am saying I haven't had a miscarriage.'

'What is your average monthly income?'

'My brother charges three rupees for a thachch.'

'I am not asking about your brother's thachch. What's your average monthly income?'

'I don't go out to work.'

'So, you don't have an income. You are dependent on someone!'

'Me? Who told you? Did Kaaththa who lives near the boat jetty tell you? I also have something on her to tell you.'

He laughed amusedly.

'Kaaththa? Said what, do you say? You are not listening to me. If someone does not have an income, that person lives off someone else's earnings. You don't have an income. So, someone has to spend money on your food and clothes. You depend on someone—your mother or your brother. Right?'

'This is like being cross-examined in a court!'

'Has someone asked you such questions in a court?'

'That terrible man caused me to suffer that too.'

'Isn't he your husband?'

'Is he a husband? Please write, I don't have a husband. I will give you something for doing that, oh dear!'

'Let it be. So, you don't have any income, do you?'

'I do have an income. I don't depend on anyone. I make at least fifteen rupees a month.'

'All right. What's your trade?'

'What all does this government want to know? My trade is not one but many.'

'Tell me about all of them. There is enough space on this sheet of paper.'

'I cook for the entire family. I clean the house....I scrub the floor of the veranda.'

'It's a fine work. The veranda floor shines like a mirror.'

'My panikkan—ha, he's no one to me now—used to say that my cheeks shone like a mirror. So, this veranda should shine just like my cheeks.' She laughed.

He, too, laughed.

Just then, a girl from the neighbourhood came to the courtyard and stood rooted there, staring at the enumerator.

'Did you see that girl staring at you? She is only ten. In a couple of years, she won't let men walk along this path.'

'Have you lost something, panikkatthi, because I looked at him? Oh dear! I am leaving!' Saying this, the girl walked away murmuring to herself.

Nalini said: 'Let her fly into a rage! If she so much as sees someone passing along, she rushes to my courtyard from nowhere!'

The enumerator was now feeling nervous about sitting on the bench.

'Now, you haven't yet told me about your trade.'

'Haven't I? I said I do all the work at home.'

'I want to know about the trade that brings you income.'

'Will you give me something if I do not have a trade that brings in earnings?'

'If you ask me whether I'll give you something....' he was reluctant to complete the sentence. He proceeded in a low tone: '...you'll give if I ask, won't you?' He looked around furtively.

She continued: 'One must be courteous to a visitor.'

He said suddenly: 'Did I say something ungentlemanly?'

'You didn't. It's I who didn't show courtesy to the visitor. You seem to be in the habit of chewing paan.'

Saying that, Nalini went inside the house. He could hear her rummaging through something.

A moment later, she returned with betel leaves and areca nut. He helped himself to a paan. He enjoyed chewing it. She went inside the hut again and brought out three wooden dolls. 'This is my trade. I need only one day to make one of these,' she said.

He took the dolls in his hand. They were female figurines, the length of a chaan. Each of them was perfect. Painted dazzlingly. Buxom and smooth. Beautiful limbs. High breasts. Heavy buttocks. Narrow waist. Long, abundant hair. Bewitching smile. Overall, enticingly pretty sculptures. He looked at them without batting an eyelid. Then he looked at Nalini.

'They are wonderful. All four are alike!'

'The wonder is that you see four of them, while there are only three,' she said.

He didn't reply.

'Do you cast these in a mould?'

'We are not bronzesmiths.'

'You would have made them in a lathe. Looks like Goddess Lakshmi who rose from the Ocean of Milk during its churning.'

'I never joined in the effort to churn the Ocean of Milk. Therefore, I haven't seen Lakshmi. I am merely showing you what my trade is. Why did you say four?'

'The three lifeless ones and the living one who makes them. Thus, four. The wonder is that all four look alike.'

'Does it mean that even the living one looks lifeless? There's no wonder about it. It's my fate!'

Her eyes flashed. She went back inside the hut once again. When she came out, her face was flushed. She was carrying another doll. She placed it before him. He picked it up and looked at it.

'Is it Lord Krishnan from *Kamsavadham*? Or, did you make some rogue take on the role of Krishnan? If it was bigger, it could be used as a scarecrow in a cucumber field. To ward off the evil eye. Or, if it were smaller....'

She intervened: 'I had been making dolls of Krishnan. People bought them. I used to charge three to four annas apiece. After I had made about fifty dolls, the dolls turned out to look like that of another Krishnan—my own Krishnan, my panikkan, once upon a time. Whenever I thought of him, I would fly into a rage. And when I made these dolls, they would somehow come out like my Krishnan. The doll's face would reflect my rage. Eventually, people stopped buying the dolls. Then I stopped making these male dolls. I decided to make figurines of Sri Parvati. I made female figurines and named them Sri Parvati. Have I seen Sri Parvati for that matter? I have heard that Parvati performed penance and had danced with Shiva. I have seen it in films, too. And they say Parvati and Parameshvaran even quarrel with each other sometimes. I started making the dolls thinking about all that. Sometimes, I looked in the mirror, mimed the various expressions of Parvati, and made dolls modelled on that. I did the work imagining that I am Parvati. In the end, all Parvati dolls looked alike....'

Before she could start again, he interrupted her: 'You and Parvati became equal to each other.'

'How can Parvati and I be equal to each other? Parvati began to resemble me! I started feeling shy about it. If I made my own form and began to sell them....'

He interrupted her: 'There will be a lot of people to buy them.'

'I have indeed seen that there would be many to buy them! The dolls were first-class. Those who bought them too began making fun of me, saying I trade in these dolls to show off my figure and to entice the males. Kaaththa whom I had mentioned earlier said so to my face. I shouted "pshaw" at her face with such vehemence that I thought her eyes would pop out. Then I thought to myself. How would I say "pshaw" if someone had said the same thing, but not within my earshot? If another woman did what I had done, I, too, would have maligned her.'

'That may be true. But your expertise in making a figure modelled on yourself so accurately is amazing, indeed!'

'You are merely flattering me. If I make one, can't I make several more copying from that one? I made the first one by looking at myself in the mirror. That's not a big deal, either.'

'That's true.'

'Most of my neighbours used to say, "that's true" to whatever I say. I was afraid of all of them.'

'Now, you are not afraid of me, are you?'

'No, I am not afraid of anyone. I do not even think that there are people other than me.'

'Many practitioners of art feel like that.'

As they were talking, Nalini went back inside. He said in a low voice: 'It's called the artist's ego.'

She placed before him four more figurines—her own image displaying compassion, fierceness, wonder, and enticement. 'If I say these are exceptionally beautiful, will you make fun of me and call me a flatterer?'

'No, but why do you say that they are "exceptionally beautiful"? They are not for sale. I work on them for keeping off sleep during the day. They might be of use someday. I am sure when these dolls reach the hands of those who do not know about me, they will not scoff at me saying that these are exhibits of a harlot.'

'You know a trade; you are excellent at it. It's a pity that you are not able to sell them! Why do you fear scandal? Let people say whatever they want. Any blind man will give one rupee for one of these dolls. You can have an independent source of income. I am going to write your trade as "Sculptor".'

He wrote it down along with other details about her and her brother. As he was writing his report, she took all the dolls inside the room except one.

He made another paan and started chewing it. 'Didn't you say that these dolls were not for sale?'

'I don't eat them, obviously. Neither do I put them in the hearth to burn them down.'

'Do you have many of these?'

'Is that question also a part of the census survey?'

'I shall move on. "Husband quarrelled"....?'

She broke in: 'Haven't we finished discussing my husband? Can I say anything more about my husband to a stranger? He is a beast. He drinks to blankness. Then he is like a mad dog, picking a fight with anyone he meets on the way. Then he gets beaten up. Till the booze in his stomach fizzles out, he lies in the police lock-up, until the morning.

One evening, the head constable sent a policeman to fetch me. He told me that I should go to the station and take my panikkan out on bail immediately. I said it would be all right if they let him out the next morning. The head constable told me if someone came to my home and committed some outrage knowing that my panikkan is not at home, then I should not go to the police station with a petition. I said for someone who tries any outrage here, I have kept ready under my pillow, the veetuli, the broad chisel. He went away. After about two hours, my husband staggered in. I did not say a word to him.

'The next morning, I said: "I am going to my family home."

"Why are you going?" he asked.

'I said, "If I continue to stay here, I may kill someone with the veetuli. Therefore, I have to leave."

'Pat came the reply: "My hands won't stay idle if someone tries funny business like that."

'I replied, "I am not ready to live with you, you beast."

'I walked down the road, got into a bus, and came here. There are many more such vulgar stories but I flinch at the thought.'

When she stopped, he got up. 'You can keep this,' she offered him the doll.

He accepted it and looked at it happily. It was the doll with a fierce mien. He thanked her. He put down a sheet of paper in front of her and said: 'Take a look.'

She looked. He had drawn her figure perfectly on the paper. She looked at it closely.

'It's such a wonder that while talking, you drew this picture so well! Give me back that doll I gave you.' Saying this, she went back inside and returned with a bigger figurine of Parvati doing penance and gave it to the visitor. He accepted it happily.

'Now be on your way,' she said and got down into the courtyard.

He walked over to the next house. His heart was reverberating like the strings of a veena.

THE OATH
P. KESAVADEV

Nani bought an uruli, a big, flat bronze vessel, at Ochchirakkali, the annual temple festival dedicated to Brahma. She had managed to buy at rupees three and three quarters an uruli whose actual price was four and a half rupees. She bought some dates and crispy vaamurukku for the children and kept them inside the uruli. She also bought a winnow and placed it over the uruli. Then she hoisted the uruli on to her head. She felt immense pride and joy as she walked towards home carrying on her head the uruli and her other purchases in it.

As Nani approached her house, she saw her neighbour Kalyani spinning coir ropes, and pretending not to have seen her. Nani stole a glance at Kalyani, just to check if she had noticed the uruli that she was carrying on her head. Kalyani had stopped her weaving and stared at the uruli as Nani walked past her.

'Did you buy that uruli from Ochchira?' Kalyani asked.

'Yeah,' Nani replied, without stopping or addressing Kalyani properly.

'How much did it cost?'

'I got it for free!' Nani replied sarcastically.

'I bet it was your father who gave it to you for free,' Kalyani replied.

Nani turned around, 'Pah! Actually, it was your father!'

Kalyani flew into a rage. 'Pah! Who are you to take my father's name? What makes you think you could be so arrogant? Just because you bought yourself an uruli, huh?'

Nani stood her ground. 'Why, you are jealous of me because I bought an uruli.'

'Hey you, I am not jealous! Not even my dog would want to have your uruli.'

'No! Come! I'll give it to you!'

'I too can buy an uruli, if I care to.'

'Impossible! Not even if you and your man tried to buy it together.'

'Pah!' dropping the coir, Kalyani got up and advanced towards Nani, 'if you take my man's name, I'll have your....'

'What'll you do if I take your man's name?' Nani too took a few steps towards Kalyani.

'Do you want to know what I will do? I dare you to repeat what you just said when my man is around.'

'I will, not only he, but even if his father were to be here as well, Nani will speak her mind!'

'Hmmm. You'll speak! Keep that wish to yourself!' Kalyani knew she was beaten. 'I'll show you that I too can buy an uruli!'

'You'll never be able to! It costs five rupees!'

'Oh, oh, did you think I'll be scared if I hear you say five rupees?'

'Then go and buy one! Have you ever seen five rupees?'

'Oh, yes! You just watch me buying it!'

'As if I'd watch it happening! The day you buy an uruli, I'll come before you as a man!'

Kalyani's pride was wounded and her eyes filled with tears as she reflected on her exchange with Nani who had said that even if she tried, she would not be able to buy an uruli. That she had not ever seen five rupees in her entire life!

Just then, her infant son, Kuttappan, awoke from his sleep and began screaming. She rushed to pick him up and breastfed him sitting in the courtyard.

From afar, Kalyani saw her husband, Gopalan, wearing a lungi, a netted vest, and a towel wound around his head walking towards the house, smoking a bidi. He has spent the whole day with his friends drinking tea at the tea shop.

Two years ago, Gopalan had quit his job as a coolie in an estate in Ceylon and returned to the village. He had returned from Ceylon wearing a shirt and jacket and twirling an umbrella in his hand. He had one trunk and in it were two or three dhotis and a couple of shirts, four vests, three bars of Vinoliya soap, a bottle of perfume, a comb, and a mirror. He had told everyone in his village that he worked as the writer—clerk, accountant, and personal assistant rolled into one—of the planter, a white man. After returning home, he dressed up in his shirt and jacket, combed his hair, rubbed his skin with unguents and went around visiting the houses in his locality, extolling Ceylon and his life there. As he rambled on, he also looked out for marriageable young women in the homes he visited. He boasted to his friends that he had managed to catch the attention of several young women. This went on until one day when the brother of a young woman smacked him across his face, and his loose talk stopped forthwith. Finally, he found favour with Kalyani and courted her and they got married. By that time, he had spent all the money—forty-three rupees—he had saved from his daily wages working as a coolie in Ceylon and what was left of that amount after paying for his fare back to his village from Ceylon.

Gopalan then borrowed money from Kalyani's mother who had twenty rupees that she had invested in a Ponzi scheme. He had convinced her that he had money deposited in a bank in Ceylon and would return her money as soon as they sent him that money. Soon the twenty rupees also was over, and Kalyani had become pregnant.

Kalyani's parents took care of the expenses incurred during the delivery of the baby. They also took care of Gopalan hoping that the money he had deposited in a bank in Ceylon would arrive soon. Finally, they got frustrated waiting for the money. Her parents had now spent all their savings. As the family descended into a state of impoverishment, tempers begin to rise. Grumblings turned into full-blown quarrels.

Gopalan and Kalyani with Kuttappan left Kalyani's family home. They arrived at a dilapidated house next to Nani's house. They repaired the house and started living there.

In order to take care of household expenses, Kalyani started processing coir—soaking coconut husks in water and beating the husks in order to extract fibre and spinning coir. Gopalan began his day cadging money from his companions or swindling them for the day's tea and bidis. If he did not succeed in his endeavours, he would come back home, quarrel with Kalyani and snatch from her half a chakram or one chakram from the meagre amount she made selling coir.

On the day Nani had flaunted her uruli to Kalyani, Gopalan came home after having a good time with his friends sharing jokes over endless cups of tea bought with the one chakram he had taken from Kalyani.

As soon as he entered the house, he said, 'Hey you! Is there something to eat?'

'Yes! There is! Rice and meat!' The pent-up anger and sorrow began to burst and rush out of her like floodwaters.

Gopalan came towards Kalyani and asked, 'Why are you crying?'

'Because I feel like it. Who are you to ask about it?' Her rage shot up.

'You spent the last coin buying yourself tea and snacks and you have the nerve to ask me if there's something to eat!'

'Why are you being so aggressive?' Gopalan too was incensed.

Kalyani replied contemptuously, 'No! I won't be aggressive! I will cherish and nurture you then!'

'Hey, mind your words or I'll knock off your head!'

Kalyani was shaking with rage. 'My...O! I will blurt out something now!'

'What will you blurt out? Go on, say it!' Gopalan approached her with raised hands.

Kalyani did not budge an inch from where she was sitting. 'Come on! Hit me!'

Waving his palm in her face, Gopalan said, 'If I whack you once, you'll be finished.'

'Finish me off! You have to raise me for that! I get my food by beating coconut husks and spinning coir.'

'Look here, you! I'll teach you a lesson!' Saying this, Gopalan left the house.

'Go away! Let's see who teaches what and whom....' Kalyani shouted back.

She got up and placed Kuttappan on a tattered rug on the veranda and began to spin the coir.

'What was the quarrel about....?' Madhavi, one of her neighbours, asked.

'Matavi, this morning he took the last coin to buy bidi and drink his damned tea. Then he came and asked me if there was anything to eat! Don't you know how I manage here? Am I not the one who toils and feeds three mouths here? I married him because I was enamoured by his stylish dressing, enchanting conversation, and good looks. Look at me. I don't have anything to eat, anything to wear. Have I looked like this, ever?' Kalyani's eyes filled with tears.

Madhavi replied sympathetically, 'How beautiful you were then, Kalyani chechi. Absolutely stunning! My brother had said at that time that no one should give a girl in marriage to that dandy!'

'That gentleman of the Pulimoottil house had been after me, then. My folly! What else to say! I said no, then. After that, he married the daughter of that fatso Kochchoonj. He cherishes her so much that he doesn't so much as let her feet touch the ground. The other day when I saw her all dressed up walking along the road, I felt a searing pain in my heart!'

'He is quite well off. They are very happy together.'

'This is my fate, dear!' Kalyani sighed. 'It's been almost twelve days since the Ochchirakkali commenced. I haven't been able to go and make my offerings to the deity. I used to go every year.'

'Why haven't you gone yet?'

'How can I? Do I have anything decent to wear? Don't I need a chakram to offer neyvilakku? I had sworn that I'd buy the effigy of a leg and offer it to him when my child fell ill. Don't I need one chakram for that, too? I will need at least two chakrams besides, won't I?'

'That's true. When we went to Ochchirakkali last week, we spent two and a half rupees to buy things for the house and to meet other expenses.'

'You people are quite affluent, aren't you? I am not like you. This is my fate. I feel like weeping when I see women coming from Ochchira after buying things for the house. Today, as I was standing here, spinning the coir, I saw Nani returning with an uruli. I asked her the price of the uruli. She abused my parents and walked away haughtily. She didn't have her feet on the ground and had her nose up in the air after purchasing that uruli.'

Madhavi replied, 'She's a haughty one indeed! The other day, I asked her if I could borrow her frying pan. She refused outright to my face! Don't we know when and why she became such a show-off?!'

'Don't we know, indeed! The lice-ridden one! Now she pretends to be a rich bitch. I swear on Ochchira Bhagavan, I too will purchase an uruli!'

Just then Madhavi's mother summoned her and she ran to her house.

⁂

Kalyani was determined to buy an uruli on the next Ochchirakkali. She planned accordingly. From that day on, she saved a half chakram from her daily earnings from her coir spinning and hoarded it beneath the hearthstone. Within a week, she had saved three and a half chakrams.

She got to know that a baby chick was up for sale in Deaf Velu's house. Its price was two and a half chakrams. She took out two and a half chakrams from beneath the hearthstone and bought a chick—a black chick.

That evening when Gopalan returned home after loafing around, he saw the chick. He asked, 'Where did you get the money to buy this chick?'

'I picked up a chakram from the wayside.'
'Then give some to me too.'
'Go and pick them up yourself.'

Tending to the chick became Kalyani's most important task. When she bought rice, she would first set aside the chick's share. When she cooked rice, she would first serve a morsel to the chick. Kalyani would rake up the refuse heaps for the chick to forage for worms and bugs. She would guard over it like a mother hen when crows or kites hovered around. If the chick wandered away from her sight, Kalyani would summon it with her sonorous 'Baba…babbaba' call.

Watching the chick pecking at the insects and worms in the courtyard, Kalyani would say to herself, 'She taunted me that she'll come before me in a man's form if I manage to buy an uruli. I will watch her turn into a man.'

One night, after supper they retired to bed. Kuttappan was sleeping in the middle between Kalyani and Gopalan. It was past midnight. Everyone was sleeping soundly.

'Koozha…koozha…' Kalyani shouted and sprang up from the bed.

'Hey, hey, what's it?' Gopalan too arose with consternation.

'Ayyo! The kite has swooped down and taken my chick away!' Kalyani wailed.

'Kite? What kite? What are you saying? How can a kite come at night?'

Kalyani didn't say anything. She realized it was just a bad dream.

Gopalan was beside himself with ire. 'You and your chick! I will kill you all and dump you in the bushes!' he roared.

The chick thus grew into a healthy hen and began to lay eggs. Kalyani picked up the first egg and touched her eyes with it as a mark of thankfulness to the deity. She was beside herself with happiness. She called out to Madhavi, 'Hey Matavi! My hen has laid an egg!'

'Feed her raw paddy. She will lay eggs regularly,' Madhavi replied.

That evening, Kalyani went to the market to sell the coir rope she had spun during the day. She did not take her usual route. She took the one that went past the ripe paddy fields. After selling the rope, she bought rice, tapioca, salt, chilli, kerosene, fish, etc., and hastened back home just as dusk was falling.

Kalyani descended into the paddy fields, carrying on her shoulder the basket containing the provisions she had bought. The ripe paddy ears were swaying in the breeze in the evening sun. Evening lamps had been lit in the homes on either side of the paddy fields.

Kalyani slowed down her gait and looked around. Making sure that no one was around, she stretched her arm and plucked a couple of paddy ears and put them in the basket. Again, she looked around. No one was in sight. She left the mud bund that lined the fields and stepped into a field. She hurriedly plucked around fifteen paddy ears and put them in her basket. She looked around again. There was no one. She got on to the mud bund and quickly walked towards her house.

Thus, she began feeding raw paddy to the hen regularly. The hen obliged by laying eggs daily. Within ten days, there were ten eggs. Kalyani put some paddy husk in the basket and arranged the ten eggs on it; she then placed the hen over the eggs to brood.

Several days passed. One morning, Kalyani was woken up by the sounds of chirping from the basket in the corner. Tiny chicks had crawled out of all the eggs. Kalyani's expectations were blossoming one by one. She lifted each chick and examined them closely. 'Let all of them be hens, my Ochchirapparadevare!' she prayed fervently, joining her palms.

May all of them become hens, enabling me to sell all the eggs and make money—and so, on the next Ochchirakkali....

'Hmm...by Ochchirapparadevare, I won't rest until I give it back to her in full measure.' Vengeance reared its head through her bliss!

As she let the hen out along with her chicks, Kalyani's anxiety increased. Will the cat catch the chicks? Will the crows and kites swoop down on them? These thoughts haunted her even while she ate and slept. If some stray cat ventured in, she would beat it and chase it away. If crows alighted near them, she would drive them away by throwing stones at them. If she spotted a kite circling the sky above, she would cover the chicks with a big basket.

One day, Kalyani was spinning coir, while proudly watching the mother hen raking up the trash and feeding her brood titbits. As she watched them, she saw many things as if in a vision. Nani's words when she returned with the uruli on Ochchirakkali. Her oath that she would buy an uruli on the next Ochchirakkali; all her chicks growing up and laying eggs; selling those eggs and earning a lot of money; going with that money for Ochchirakkali; buying an uruli and parading it before Nani....

Her reverie was interrupted by a commotion at the base of the mango tree. 'Keeya, keeya, keeya....'

Kalyani sprang to her feet shouting 'koozha...koozha' as she ran towards the mango tree.

A chick was squealing, hanging from the talons of a kite, flying up and away.

'Ayyo...damn it!' Kalyani rushed towards the direction where the kite was flying. She screamed 'koozha...koozha...koozha' to scare it away.

The fence suddenly loomed up in front of her. She collided into the fence and, along with it, collapsed to the ground.

Nani was standing watching it all. She clapped her hands and laughed, as Kalyani fell down on her face.

Kalyani got up quickly. She had lost her face and lost the chick too! Filled with sorrow and anger, she shouted at Nani, 'What's so funny?'

'Your resplendent beauty!' Nani said mockingly.

'I'll show you!' Controlling her rage, Kalyani turned and walked back to the mango tree.

'I'll watch when you show me! Now go away!' Nani shouted back.

At the base of the mango tree, the mother hen was sitting still, with the rest of her brood under her wings.

Kalyani looked up. 'Keeya....keeya...keeya...' The kite was still flying up and away with the chick.

Kalyani was so dejected that she was unable to eat anything the entire day.

∽

Soon the chicks grew into four strong roosters and five beautiful hens.

The mother hen began to lay eggs once more. Kalyani sold all those eggs and put away the money under the hearthstone, and it had grown to a decent amount. Every day she had to put up with Gopalan's ire for not giving him money to spend in the tea shop.

One day, he secretly watched Kalyani putting away the money underneath the hearthstone. The following day, when she loosened the hearthstone to put away the day's earnings, there was no money there.

'Ayyo! This demon has stolen my money!' She screamed. She uprooted the hearthstone and threw it away. She threw Gopalan's trunk outside. She tore up his old jacket. Her rage didn't abate with all that. She hit Kuttappan several times. The child began to bawl.

When Gopalan came home, Kalyani rushed at him like a lioness. Gopalan stopped her. Pandemonium broke out.

She did not cook that day. Everyone starved.

The next day, Kalyani called Madhavi and asked her, 'Matavi, will you tell anyone if I told you something?'

'What is it? Tell me. I will not tell anyone.'

'That is...I will hand over to you the money I earn selling eggs. Can you keep it for me?'

'Oh, yes! If I keep it in my tin box, no one will take it, and I won't tell a soul about it.'

'If I keep it in my house, it won't remain here for long. Even after I hid it beneath the hearthstone, he took it away.'

'Give it to me. I'll keep it safe, and will give it to you when you need it.'

Thus, Kalyani found a way to keep her money safe.

The five hens soon began to lay eggs. With that, Kalyani's income increased as well. Sometimes, she got as much as one and a half to two chakrams selling eggs.

The weight of Madhavi's tin box kept increasing.

Meanwhile, Gopalan rummaged through every nook and corner of the house looking for the money he believed Kalyani had stashed away. He could not find even a single chakram anywhere.

One day Gopalan asked her, 'Where's all the money you make from selling eggs?'

Kalyani's ire grew. 'Did you buy the hen for me to ask about the money I make selling eggs?'

'Do you want to watch me catching all your hens and roosters and selling them?'

'Hmmm! You'll sell! For that, you'll have to get into your mother's womb and be born again!'

Since threats did not work, Gopalan mollified her. 'Hey! Are you giving someone the chakrams for safekeeping? They'll hoodwink you, mind you!'

'Let them hoodwink me. You are not losing anything, are you?'

Days, weeks, and months passed thus; the summer month of Edavam (mid-May to mid-June) had arrived. One day, Kalyani asked Madhavi.

'How much money is there now, Matavi?'

'I haven't counted it.'

'Let's count it. Bring me the box.'

Madhavi brought a small tin box, struggling to carry to it. The box was full of chakrams—Kalyani's earnings for a full year!

Kalyani brought the torn rug that belonged to Kuttappan. Madhavi lifted the box and poured the chakrams on the rug. Kalyani was thrilled to hear the jingle-jangle of the coins.

Kalyani and Madhavi started counting the chakrams—five rupees and eleven and three-quarter chakrams. Kuttappan, who was playing, rose to his feet with effort and tottered towards them. Holding Kuttappan off with one hand, Kalyani said, 'There's a surplus of eleven and three quarter chakrams.

'What's this five rupees for, then?'

'That? I'll tell you that later. Now, take the box back to your house and keep it safe. If the man of the house comes to know about it, I will not get even a paisa.'

Kuttappan crept and crawled towards the rug on which the chakrams were stacked up. He snatched a handful of chakrams.

'Off with you!' Kalyani knocked away Kuttappan's tiny hands and the chakrams were strewn all around on the floor. Kuttappan started to wail.

'Take the box back to your house and keep it safe, Matavi,' Kalyani said after picking up all the chakrams and putting them back in the box.

'I'll buy you a blouse.'

Hearing the humming of a tune from the alley, Kalyani turned her head around. 'Ayyo! here he comes. Take the box and scoot!'

Madhavi picked up the box and left in a flash. Gopalan entered still humming the tune. Kalyani resumed spinning the coir.

∫

The tenth of Edavam had passed. One day, after dusk, Kalyani was lighting the hearth in the kitchen. Kuttappan was playing near the hearth.

She heard a noise from the outside: 'Hoo...hoo...hoo...hoo...' Kalyani went out and looked around. She saw Gopalan was standing in the courtyard, shivering.

'What happened?' Kalyani asked him anxiously.

'Hoo...hoo...hoo..hoo...I have a fever. Spread the mat. Let me lie down.'

Moving into the house, Kalyani spread the mat for Gopalan to lie down. He lay down and covered himself with a sheet. Kalyani placed her palm on his brow.

'His fever is raging like fire! If paddy is placed on his brow, it will turn into puffed rice! My Ochchira Bhagavane!'

That night, Gopalan did not eat anything. Kalyani too did not have her supper.

Madhavi came in the morning.

'He's down with fever, Matavi!' Kalyani said.

'When did the fever begin?'

'Last evening. He came home shivering.'

'Did he drink any water?'

'No and he has not eaten anything either. I have also not eaten anything. The rice I cooked is still in the pot. After feeding Kuttappan a little rice, I stayed up till dawn, with the lamp lit. What will I do now?'

Madhavi said, 'Go and get that lame kaniyaan. He has a particular kashaayam and a pill. When my younger brother was stricken by fever, we gave him that kashaayam. The fever stopped like a horse is halted by pulling the bridle.'

'In that case, will you please stay here until I return with the kaniyaan?' Saying that, Kalyani put on the mundu and blouse she had kept aside to wear when she would go to the market. She turned her face towards the rising sun and paying it obeisance, walked out quickly.

Within an hour, Kalyani came back with the lame kaniyaan. She pulled out the torn rug on the veranda for the kaniyaan to sit on. Putting his palm-leaf-woven umbrella in the courtyard, he climbed on to the veranda and enquired about the illness and its symptoms. Kalyani narrated to him everything as she had already told Madhavi without leaving out even the minutest detail.

The kaniyaan listened and said, 'Oh! It's just a cold and a fever. Nothing serious.'

He opened his bottle of pills, took some out and gave them to Kalyani.

'Boil dry ginger and cumin seeds in water, and give him three pills thrice a day, followed by ginger–cumin water.'

'Is there no need for the kashaayam?'

'The kashaayam can be given later on if need be. Give him the pills right now as I told you.'

Tying up the pills in a small bundle at the end of her mundu, Kalyani got out and beckoned to Madhavi. 'Shouldn't we pay him something, Matavi?'

'Yes. We must give him something.'

'I don't have any money on me.'

'Who said you don't have money? All that you have handed over to me—is it not money?'

'That's set apart for a specific purpose.'

'What greater purpose than this? What purpose will it serve if the concerned person doesn't exist any more?'

Kalyani hung her head. She recalled all that had happened between her and Nani. Her coming back from Ochchira with the uruli on her head. Nani's reply when she had asked its price. Her oath that she would buy an uruli come what may. She remembered Nani's derisive laughter when she had knocked against the fence and fell to the ground along with the fence, running after the kite that had swooped up the chick. She also reminisced how she reared the chickens with a single-minded purpose and entrusted Madhavi with the money she earned from selling the eggs to keep it safe from the thief Gopalan, her husband. By the grace of Ochchira Bhagavan, she had already saved enough money to buy an uruli. Ochchirakkali was also drawing near. Just when the dainty creeper of her desire was about to blossom....!

Kalyani said, 'No. I won't touch that money!'

'How can you say you won't take from that money? Shouldn't you pay the kaniyaan something? Shouldn't you buy the dry ginger and cumin and the herbs he prescribed for the kashaayam?'

Kalyani thought it over for some time. 'OK. Keep five rupees and bring me the remaining chakrams.'

Madhavi agreed and got up to get the money from the box. As Madhavi was walking towards her house, Kalyani ran after her and said in hushed tones, 'If you have betel nut and leaves at home, please bring some for the kaniyaan.'

'I'll surely bring some if there's any in the house,' Madhavi said and hurried on her way.

Kalyani counted the chakrams, took seven of them and tied up the remainder on the end of her mundu. Offering the seven chakrams to the kaniyaan, she said, 'Kaniyare, here's your dakshina!'

The kaniyaan smiled wanly. He stretched out his hand as if self-consciously. Kalyani dropped the chakrams into his hands.

'Don't worry. It's just a cold and fever! Give this pill right now. I will prescribe the kashaayam later on if necessary.'

Putting away the chakrams and the pill box in his waistband, the kaniyaan picked up his palm-leaf umbrella from the courtyard and left. Kalyani was now left with four and a quarter chakrams. She bought dry ginger and cumin seeds with a quarter chakram. She boiled these in water and gave Gopalan a pill with the herbal concoction.

That day, she did not spin any coir. She fed Kuttappan and herself the rice that was cooked the previous evening. Kuttappan began playing in the courtyard, scooping up the sand and crawling aimlessly. She went out to check on the chickens that she had let out of the coop in the morning. She then sat on the veranda and continued to daydream: 'Five rupees are left still,' she said to herself. 'That's enough to buy an uruli. Ochchirakkali will begin on the first. I must go and buy the uruli that day itself. Then I must watch how Nani comes before me as a male! There are eighteen days left for all this! I must sell all the eggs that the hens lay between now and that day. With the proceeds, I should buy a pot, an umbrella, and a mat. A blouse for Matavi and a dress for Kuttappan.'

It was midday.

'Hey you! I'll show you,' Gopalan was talking gibberish in his delirium. Kalyani quickly got up to check on Gopalan.

'What is it, chetta?'

'Hey, da, give me a bidi. The tea is not hot enough.... Where have you kept the chakrams, di?'

Kalyani was frightened now. She went to Madhavi's house and returned with her. 'He's talking gibberish, Matavi!'

'Did you give him the pill?'

'Hmm. His condition seems to have become worse after I gave him the pill.'

'It works that way. When you give him one pill, the symptoms will get worse. Then it will come down. Give him one more pill.'

Kalyani crushed a pill, made it into a paste and gave it with the ginger–cumin water. She vowed to light a neyvilakku for Ochchira Bhagavan.

Dusk was descending. Kalyani went to the market and bought some items for supper. She cooked the meal and ate a little with Kuttappan.

Gopalan did not even drink water. He was delirious. Kalyani stayed up the whole night. She was really frightened. The neighbours were all asleep. Even if she were to call someone, they would not wake up. Somehow, she waited until the day broke, then went over to the kaniyaan's place and told him all that had transpired.

'Don't worry. Now you can boil the kashaayam and give it to him!' He prescribed the herbs for the kashaayam and gave her the list. She took the three chakrams she got from the sale of the eggs of the last two days, bought the herbs and the molasses for the mempodi. She boiled the kashaayam quickly and gave it to him, with the mempodi.

That day passed like that. Gopalan did not show any sign of improvement. Kalyani did not cook any food that day. Madhavi took Kuttappan along and fed him kanji. Although she invited Kalyani too, she did not go.

The next day, a couple of women from the neighbourhood visited her, enquiring after Gopalan's health. 'This is a tough kind of illness. The lame kaniyaan won't be able to deal with it,' they opined in unison.

Kalyani's consternation grew. She and Madhavi discussed the matter in detail. Madhavi too said, 'It's true! The lame kaniyaan doesn't seem to be able to bring about a cure. The illness has got worse. We have to bring Vayalukaadan who is far superior to the kaniyaan.'

'Won't we have to pay him in rupees?'

'How can we do without paying him in rupees? His fee is two rupees.'

'Two rupees!' A flame leapt up, singeing the insides of Kalyani.

'Ayyo, di, if I take out two rupees, then there will be only three rupees left!'

'And the price of medicines, too.'

Kalyani said in a resolute tone. 'No, di, my dear! No! I won't take any more from that money!'

'If you don't take the money, you will lose your man! Do you want the money or your man?'

Kalyani did not say a word. She remembered how Gopalan had married her at the age of seventeen. When he had money in his hands, he had spent on her handsomely; he had fulfilled all her wishes. Then he ran out of money—frequenting the tea shop, smoking bidis, whiling his time away with his friends, he got into the habits of a wastrel. When her mother tried to persuade her to dump Gopalan, saying,

'What's done is done, leave him. I will look after you and the child,' Kalyani hadn't budged.

'Someone came along and settled down with me, and we have a child. I will not let my child call another man Achchan.'

Saying this, she had set out from her family home along with Gopalan and Kuttappan. Beating the fibre out of the coconut husks, and spinning coir from them, she fed him and looked after his needs. She did not have money to give him for his bidi and tea. Both of them would only quarrel over this issue. Sometimes, she would manage to set aside half a chakram or one chakram and give it to him for his tea shop expenses. Once he got the money for his bidi and tea, Gopalan was the best of fellows. In fact, she knew that he loved her very much, and he was sorry that he had not been able to provide for her adequately.

Sometimes, she would scold him. He would raise his hand threatening to beat her but he never beat her up. Sometimes, he would pretend that he was leaving, declaring, 'Hey, you! I don't need anything of yours!'

Once he left in such a manner, then Kalyani would soon be filled with sadness. She would cook rice and curry for him and wait for him. She would not eat until he returned. What she blurted out all of a sudden on occasions was because of the intensity of her own sufferings and the anger that welled up in her. She too loved him deeply.

Kalyani remembered all that and more. 'He put the wedding garland around my neck when I was seventeen,' she continued, sobbing. 'He gave me everything then…it is my fate that he has become insolvent. We'll be well off if our luck still holds.'

'Yes! Only if your luck holds will you be able to get him back,' Madhavi said.

Wiping off her tears, Kalyani continued, 'He is very loving, Matavi, really loving. Only that he doesn't have money. The taste of the foreign delicacies he brought me when he had money still lingers on the tip of my tongue. I will not forget any of that. But I quarrel with him when he fails in many ways. He doesn't even beat me when I quarrel. He just sits and weeps.' She wiped away her tears once again. 'Oh, my Ochchirapparadevare!'

She stood with joined palms, looking up to the heavens, she said, 'Even though he doesn't give me anything, let me die seeing his face!'

'Don't weep, Kalyani chechi,' Madhavi consoled her. 'Ochchira Bhagavan won't let anything bad happen to him. Go quickly, and bring Vayalukaadan. I will wait here.'

Wiping her face, Kalyani changed into a mundu and blouse. Stepping onto the courtyard, she meditated for a few seconds facing the east.

'Please keep watch on him, Matavi,' she said and walked away quickly.

Madhavi went to her house and picked up a finely woven metthappaaya mat and betel nuts and leaves for the vaidyan. Within the hour, they walked in—Vayalukaadan in front and Kalyani behind him. The vaidyan checked Gopalan's pulse. He asked Kalyani details of the ailment. Sitting on the metthappaaya, he chewed paan.

'Did someone attend to him?' Vayalukaadan asked.

'The lame kaniyaan. He gave some pills and kashaayam. The illness got worse when I gave him those medicines,' Kalyani replied.

'Hmmm. That has complicated the case. Never mind. I will cure him even though it is a bit complex. You must look after him well. Buy a powder and an arishtam from the vaidyasala. Give him only barley water. And make one kashaayam.' Thus the vaidyan prescribed the course of treatment.

'Bring me a paper and a pencil to write down the prescription!' he ordered.

Kalyani looked at Madhavi who ran to her house. Tearing off a page from her younger brother's notebook, picking up a pencil, and the tin box in which the money was kept, she returned instantly. She placed the paper and pencil before the vaidyan. Reciting a shlokam, the vaidyan began to write down the list of medicines on the piece of paper.

Meanwhile, Kalyani and Madhavi whispered amongst themselves. Kalyani counted the chakrams from the tin box, which amounted to two rupees. Another one rupee worth of chakrams she counted and kept them tied in the hem of her mundu. Then she handed the box back to Madhavi. 'Take this back, and keep it in your house. I will not take any more money from this.'

Kalyani's eyes brimmed over. The money she had accumulated over a year was thus being frittered away. The mansion of her expectations was crumbling down. The fire of her vengeance was dying down. She was being crushed between her revenge on Nani and her duty towards her husband.

'By my Ochchirappardevare....' Her sobs choked her words.

Wiping her tears, she scooped up fifty-seven chakrams in both her palms and humbly offered the money to the vaidyan.

He looked at the heap of coins and said with distaste, 'I can't carry this.'

'We are poor people,' Kalyani said in all humility.

'Bring this when you come to my dispensary to buy the medicines. Also, bring money for medicines.' Placing the prescription in front of Kalyani, he got up to leave.

'Don't be afraid. I'll cure his illness. Do everything that I say.'

Kalyani went to the dispensary and bought the powder and arishtam which cost one rupee and a quarter. She paid two rupees as the vaidyan's fee and one rupee for the medicine. She sought credit for the balance, a quarter rupee.

She gave the powder and the arishtam to Gopalan. She needed to buy the herbs for the kashaayam and barley, as well as meet her's and Kuttappan's expenses. But where was the money for all this? From what she earned over a year, only two rupees remained. What if she spent that as well? What if she did not? She wrestled with the question the whole day.

Her oath! Ochchirakkali! Uruli! Ayyo! The mansion of expectations she had built...having done so much hard work!

'No! I will not use that money!' she told herself.

Dusk was about to set in. She had to give Gopalan the kashaayam after dusk. The vaidyan had specified the timing for taking the medicine. Kuttappan started bawling, unable to bear his hunger. She too had not eaten anything that evening.

'Water...' Gopalan said. She was supposed to give him only barley water, but she had not bought the barley nor the ingredients for the kashaayam. Kalyani was deeply troubled. She forgot all about the oath, Ochchirakkali, the uruli—everything.

She called out to Madhavi and said, 'Bring me the rest of the money, Matavi!'

Madhavi brought the tin box and gave it to Kalyani. 'You can return the box later,' she said and left.

Kalyani took out twelve chakrams from the box and kept it in the fold of her mundu around her waist. She kept the box in a corner and covered it with a mat and then went to the marketplace. She bought the herbs for the kashaayam, barley, rice, salt, chillis, and kerosene—she returned with all these just after dusk. On one hearth, the kashaayam; on another was the barley; on yet another, the rice—she fired up all the hearths quickly.

Kuttappan was sitting in the kitchen and crying. Kalyani roasted the tapioca and gave it to him. He stopped crying.

'Water...water...' Gopalan was asking for water again and again.

Kalyani did not say anything. She did not have the energy to say anything. Tears fell down into the hearth and the pot. She continued blowing into the fire.

She boiled the barley water well. She cooled it and gave it to Gopalan. By that time, the rice was cooked. Then she fed Kuttappan. She too ate a few morsels, blowing to cool it down.

She boiled the kashaayam, filling up the pot with the prescribed amount of water; took it out and added the mempodi and gave it to Gopalan. Then she lay down beside Gopalan.

The next day, Kalyani got up and gave Gopalan medicine and barley water. Scooping out the rice from last night's kanji, she fed Kuttappan. She drank some of the rice water. Then she changed her mundu and blouse, scooped out the remainder of the money, tied them in the fold of her mundu and set out to meet the vaidyan.

She updated the vaidyan about Gopalan's condition and handed the quarter rupee she owed him. He then said that an aasavam was also needed for Gopalan. She bought that too.

When she returned, she had only two and a half chakrams left.

'Now what? What shall I do?' She thought as she walked away hurriedly. 'Even if everything goes bust, I will not rest till I have his illness completely cured,' she swore another firm oath.

Another day passed. Gopalan's illness had abated slightly. Kalyani was giving him medicines and barley water without a break. She reported Gopalan's status to the vaidyan daily.

'Now, we will change over to another kashaayam.'

He prescribed the ingredients for another elaborate kashaayam. She needed eight chakrams to buy the herbs for it. Every two days, she had to buy medicines from the dispensary. The vaidyan had told her to add milk and sugar along with the barley water while feeding Gopalan. So much for the patient. She and Kuttappan had to eat some food too!

Two oaths that were contradictory to each other! For both to be fulfilled, there was only one way left—six hens including the mother hen and four roosters.

She decided to sell the roosters first. She sold the four roosters at nine chakrams each and got thirty-six chakrams. She bought the medicines, barley, milk, and sugar and met the household expenses. Nothing was left after that.

What else was there to do?

'Even if I have to sell my child, I will have this illness cured.' She grew more resolute than ever. She decided to sell the hens as well.

Mathai Mappila offered to pay ten and a half chakrams for one hen. Kalyani agreed. She caught all the six hens, tied their legs, and placed them before Mathai Mappila. The sources of her one year's income. The offspring of her desire to buy an uruli. The hens who laid eggs for her daily. O God! All those hens were looking at her pitiably. Tears streamed down from her eyes.

'Why are you crying?'

'I tended to them like my own children, Mathai Mappile,' she sobbed. 'I wouldn't have sold any of them even if I were to die. Isn't he the one who gave me everything when he could? Shouldn't I look after him now that he is ill?'

'Of course! If not you, who will look after him?'

He counted sixty-five chakrams and gave them to Kalyani. He picked up the hens, put them in a basket, and walked away.

She stood, tears still trickling down her cheeks. The hens were still raising their heads and looking at her. Walking on, Mathai Mappila disappeared from her sight. The fountainhead of her expectations thus dried up.

'Oh, my Ochchira Bhagavaane...!' She felt dizzy. She sat down on the ground.

Gopalan's illness was cured. He could slowly move about on the veranda and later on in the courtyard.

Kalyani would say, 'This one had died and then came back alive! Although everything went bust, I got him back!'

♪

It was the first of Midhunam, the Malayalam month that runs from mid-July to mid-August. That was when Ochchirakkali began. People had begun to set off for Ochchira even before sunrise.

Kalyani rose early in the morning and got down to the courtyard. The old woman Nangeli, her daughter and the daughter's children were going to Ochchira. Nangeli asked her, 'Hey, Kalyani! Aren't you coming?'

Kalyani's eyes welled up. She did not say anything.

Madhavi and her elder sister, her husband and children, passed her courtyard on their way to Ochchira. Madhavi called out to her, 'We are going to Ochchira. Be back after some time!'

Kalyani nodded. The teardrops on her cheeks shone in the rays of the morning sun.

Next, it was Nani's turn. When she saw Kalyani, she drew herself up and gazed at her in utter contempt! Kalyani could not bear it. She turned her face away.

Walking up a little, Nani turned and looked back at her.

'I've seen you all right!' Gnashing her teeth, Kalyani muttered.

Nani looked back once again. Her derisive laughter!

Kalyani spat out in defiance, 'Hey, do you hear me? By Ochchira Bhagavan, I too will go next year!'

THE WORLD-RENOWNED NOSE

VAIKOM MUHAMMAD BASHEER

It's a stunning, staggering piece of news. A nose has become the subject of great debate among intellectuals and philosophers. A world-renowned nose!

This is the real story of the nose. The story begins as our hero turns twenty-four. Until now, no one has heard about him. I wonder what is so special about the age of twenty-four. One thing is for certain. If you turn the page of world history, you will find certain peculiarities regarding the twenty-fourth year of many great personalities. I don't need to point it out to the students of history, do I?

The hero of our story worked in a kitchen. A cook of sorts. He was no intellectual who needed any special mention. He didn't know how to read and write. The kitchen was his world. He paid no attention to anything outside it. Why should he pay attention to anything at all?

His daily routine was: eat well, inhale snuff to his heart's content, sleep, wake up, and begin cooking.

He didn't know the names of months. When it was payday, his mother would collect his wages and buy him snuff. And thus he lived an uneventful life until he turned twenty-four. And with that, the miracle was on!

Nothing special. Only that his nose grew longer. It reached past his mouth and down his chin!

Thus his nose began to grow. Could this development be hidden somehow? Within a month, his nose grew and grew and reached down to his navel. But was there any discomfort? No. He could breathe comfortably, inhale snuff, and smell. Practically, there was nothing wrong with the nose.

Such noses are also found in the pages of world history. Yes, a few were there, to be sure. Is this nose then that type of a good-for-nothing's nose? The poor cook was fired from his job because of his nose.

For what reason?

No trade unionists came forward clamouring that the terminated labourer should get his job back. All political parties turned a blind eye towards this grave injustice.

'Why was he fired?' None of those so-called humanists asked this question. Where did the intellectuals and philosophers go?

Poor labourer; the poor cook!

Nobody had to tell him why he was fired from his job. The reason was that the family who employed him lost their peace. An ocean of humanity day and night thronged to the house where he worked to see Mooken the man with an unusual nose. Photographers, reporters from the radio, cinema, and television, and journalists from all over the world came to see him.

A lot of things were stolen from the house. They even attempted to abduct the eighteen-year-old beauty of the house.

After Mooken lost his job and starved in his hovel, a thought occurred to him. That he and his nose had attained great renown!

People from distant places came to see him. They stood flabbergasted, looking at the elongated nose. Some even touched it. But none, I repeat, no one asked Mooken, 'Have you eaten? Why do you look so thin?'

He did not have even a nickel to buy a pinch of snuff. Was he a famished animal in a zoo? Wasn't he a human being?

He called his old mother and whispered, 'Get these louts out, and close the door!'

His mother managed to get all the visitors out and shut the door. From that day on, their luck began to show! Some started bribing the mother to take a look at her son's nose! Aren't people a bunch of fools? But some upright intellectuals and philosophers raised their voices against this bribery. But the government didn't take any action in this regard. It didn't even pay heed. Protesting this severe lassitude of the government, many of the complainants joined some anti-government terrorist party or the other!

To cut a long story short, the illiterate cook with the growing nose became a millionaire in just six years!

He acted in three films. *The Human Submarine*, a technicolour film attracted millions of people. Six great poets wrote epics on Mooken's exploits. Nine great writers wrote Mooken's biography and earned fame and wealth.

Mooken's mansion became a guest house of sorts. Anyone could have food there at any time and a pinch of snuff. At that time, he had two secretaries. Two beauties who were well-educated too.

Both loved Mooken fervently; both adored him. As a rule, there would always be beauties ready to love any fool, thug, or ripper.

When one turns the pages of world history, it is evident that troubles are afoot when two beauties loved the same man. It happened in Mooken's life too.

Like those two beauties, the entire population loved Mooken. Isn't that nose dangling down to the navel a beauty and a sign of greatness? Certainly, it was.

Mooken would air his opinion regarding all the important events that took place around the world. The press would faithfully publish all of them.

'An aeroplane that flies at 10,000 miles an hour has been made! Mooken opines thus about it....'

'Doctor Buntros Furasiburos brought a dead man back to life. Mooken opines thus about it....'

When it was heard that some men had scaled the tallest peak in the world, people asked: 'What does Mooken say about it?'

If Mooken said nothing about an event... 'Chhe...that event is so trivial'!

Thus, Mooken was called upon to opine on every matter like interplanetary voyages, the origin of the universe, painting, watch industry, mesmerism, photography, the soul, publishing houses, novel writing, life after death, journalism, hunting, and the like! And he would oblige. Was there anything that Mooken didn't know about in this great universe? Come on, tell me!

It was at about this time that great conspiracies were hatched to usurp Mooken. Usurpation is nothing new. A major portion of world history is the story of usurpations.

What is usurpation?

You plant some coconut seedlings on a piece of barren land. You water them, manure them, and fence them in. After years of anticipation, the young coconut trees begin to bear fruit. The trees put forth bunches and bunches of coconuts. Anyone would be tempted to usurp that coconut grove from you! So... usurp Mooken!

It was the government who made the first great revolutionary move to usurp Mooken. It was a ruse the government came up with. Besides conferring on him the title 'His Nosey Eminence', the government granted him a medal. It was the president himself who put the diamond-studded gold medal around Mooken's neck. After that, instead of shaking hands, the president held the tip of Mooken's nose and shook it. The news footage of the event was shown on television and in cinemas across the country.

By that time, all the political parties sprang into action and came forward. Comrade Mooken should lead the great struggle of the people! Comrade Mooken? Whose comrade? Oh my God! Poor Mooken...he should join the party!

Which party?

There were so many of them. Their goal was revolution. People's revolution. How could poor Mooken join all the people's revolutionary parties at the same time?

Mooken said, 'Why should I join any party? I can't.'

As things stood thus, one of the beauties, Mooken's secretary said, 'Comrade Mooken, join my party if you love me!'

Mooken didn't say a thing.

'Should I join some party?' Mooken asked the other beauty.

She understood. She said, 'Why should you?'

By that time, the partisans of a revolutionary party had already coined the slogan 'Our party is Mooken's party! Mooken's party is the Revolutionary Party of the People!'

Hearing this, partisans of the other revolutionary party were enraged. They got one of Mooken's beautiful secretaries to issue a statement against him.

'Mooken has cheated the people! Mooken is a reactionary bum. All this time, Mooken had been hoodwinking the people. He made me too a party to this great hoax of his. I apologize to the people. Now I tell the truth to the people: Mooken's long nose is a mere rubber appendage!'

This news made it to the headlines of all the newspapers around the world. That Mooken's nose is a rubber one! Such a bum, trickster, this Mooken! The thief, the swindler, the arch-reactionary! The nose is not real.

Wouldn't the millions of people be struck dumb hearing such news? Isn't the nose real? No! Telegrams, phone calls, and letters started pouring in from all corners of the world! The president was greatly disturbed.

'Down with the rubber-nosed man, who cheated the people! Down with the rubber-nosed man's reactionary party. Inquilab Zindabad!'

When the partisans opposing Mooken came out with this statement, the other revolutionary partisans made the other secretary beauty come out with another rousing statement.

'My dear countrymen and the people of the world! What she has stated is utter falsehood. Comrade Mooken didn't love her even a bit. She was jealous on account of that. What she tried to do was to usurp Comrade Mooken's money and fame. One of her brothers is a member of the other party. I take this opportunity to lay bare the true colours of that party of thieves. I am Comrade Mooken's faithful secretary. I personally know that Comrade Mooken's nose is not made of rubber. It is real like my heart. Zindabad to the People's Progressive Revolutionary Party, which has deployed its workers in support of Mooken at this hour of trial, without any intentions to reap future gains! Comrade Mooken Zindabad! Comrade Mooken's party is the People's Progressive Revolutionary Party! Inquilab Zindabad!'

What was to be done? The people were confused. By that time the revolutionary party that opposed Mooken's revolutionary party began berating the government, the president, and the prime minister.

'Such a foolish, craven government! It conferred upon that rubber-nosed cheater of people the title His Nosey Eminence and a diamond-studded gold medal too! The president and the prime minister are a party to swindling the people. There is clearly a caucus behind this conspiracy! The president and the prime minister must resign! The cabinet must resign! Kill the rubber-nosed man!'

The president was perturbed hearing this and the prime minister too. One morning the army and the tanks encircled Mooken's mansion. They arrested Mooken and took him away.

There was no news of Mooken for some time. The people simply forgot about him. All was quiet. Then came the real atomic, hydrogen, nuclear explosion! What was it, you may ask. When the people had forgotten all about Mooken, a brief communique from the president set it off!

'There will be a public trial of His Nosey Eminence to ascertain the authenticity of the nose. Skilled doctors from forty-eight countries will inspect Mooken. The representatives of all newspapers in the world would be present. And people from radio, film, TV, and the whole lot of such hordes. This trial can be seen by all on newsreel. I appeal to all the people to remain totally calm.'

Aren't people a bunch of fools?

Real nincompoops, these revolutionaries. They didn't remain totally calm. They flocked to the capital city. They raided hotels, wrecked newspaper offices, set fire to cinemas, took over liquor shops, and smashed up vehicles. They set fire to police stations. They damaged government buildings; communal riots erupted everywhere. A lot of people were martyred during this Mooken struggle.

All was well. Quiet.

On 9 March, at eleven o'clock in the morning, the front of the presidential palace had turned into a sea of humanity. Loudspeakers roared: 'The people are requested to be quiet. Shut your mouths. The check-up has begun.'

The doctors encircled the Right Honourable Mooken in the august presence of the president, prime minister, and several other ministers.... The anxious millions waited with bated breath.

A great physician shut Mooken's nose. Then Mooken opened his mouth. Another great physician pricked the tip of the nose with a pin. The miracle of miracles! A perfectly pure, red drop of blood oozed from the tip of the Right Honourable Mooken's nose!

'The nose is not a rubber one! No imitation! It is real.' The unanimous verdict of all the great physicians!

Mooken sahib's secretary, the beauty, kissed him deeply on the tip of his blessed nose.

'Comrade Mooken zindabad! His Nosey Eminence zindabad! The People's Progressive Party of Comrade Mooken zindabad! Janab Mooken's nose—it is original! original!! original!'

The roar reverberates like the universe collapsing... 'Original! Most original!'

As the din subsided, the rashtrapati, the great president, came out with another brand-new ruse. He nominated Comrade Mooken to the parliament after conferring on him the dashing title Mookashree.

Mookashree Mooken M. P.!

Two or three universities honoured Mookashree Mooken sahib with M. Litt. and D. Litt.

Mookashree Mooken—Master of Literature!

Mookashree Mooken—Doctor of Literature!

Still, the people are a bunch of idiots. Real nincompoops! And the government too, ruling over this bunch of idiots.

The activists—the beauty being one of them—who had failed to usurp Mooken, have now formed a united front, and were talking, writing, and making speeches. The president must resign! The prime minister must resign! The cabinet must resign. Cheating people...!

Mooken's rubber nose! It is not at all original!

The turns revolution takes!

The intellectuals, thinkers—what will they do?

Won't there be confusion afoot? It's the world-renowned nose!

Mangalam.

Shubham.

DHIRENDU MAJUMDAR'S MOTHER
LALITHAMBIKA ANTHARJANAM

Do you know who I am? My name is Shanti Majumdar. I am ninety years old. I was born and brought up in a village in East Bengal. I had nine children—seven sons and two daughters. Of them, five were sacrificed for India. And four for Pakistan. Then I adopted all the children of the new generations as my children and grandchildren. I yearned to live and die in the land I was born. All my ancestors had been born on the soil of East Bengal and had returned to that soil. If the soldiers of the Mukti Fauj had not by force hoisted me on their shoulders and ran, I, this Grandma Shanti, too, would have fallen in the battlefield and attained a dignified deliverance.

Are you asking me if I am afraid? Why should I be afraid? None of Shanti's children had been afraid. India is my own country. The bones of five of my children are disintegrating in the soil here. But Grandma Shanti does not like to be here as a refugee of another country. My children! You may not know it. But for us, Bharat was not merely a fistful of soil. She was the heavenly mother who was 'Suphala', 'Sujala', and 'Sasyashyaamala'. We brought up our children meditating upon the millions of flashing sabres in her hands. We sacrificed them for her deliverance. Have you heard the stories of those selfless, brave early soldiers of the struggle for Independence? Do they have a place in your history?

My memories are fermenting, and bubbling up to the top. Thrilling memories! Not of an individual, not of a family, the pitiable story of an entire nation! It will become clear to you from the story of Shanti Majumdar. Listen....

Our house was almost in the centre of what you call East Pakistan today. The zamindari was to the left of the river Padma that flowed towards the east into the ocean. Floods were very frequent. On such occasions, it was in the agrashala beyond the Durga temple that the villagers sought refuge. But the brides of the Majumdar family would only sit on the terrace of their tall mansion and watch the destructive dance of the waters of the Padma. They never got out of the zenana. Nor did they meet men who were outsiders. When the darling wife of my younger uncle Abani Majumdar was in extreme labour, he had insisted that a doctor from the town be brought in! But the elder Majumdar, who also bore the title raja saheb didn't allow it. If any woman of the Majumdar family were to be stricken by illness, the convention was that no man except Lord Yama would be allowed inside the zenana.

I was nine years old when I came to this family. I arrived in a covered palanquin, enveloped in red silk bridal attire with sindoor smeared in my hair's parting. Until I was fifty, I had never left the house. My eldest son was Dhirendu, Dhiren for short. When he was studying in college, he had brought one of his friends and had beseeched me to come at least to the threshold and meet him. When governor saheb visited with his wife, Dhiren insisted that I should go and receive them. Yet, I had not acquiesced to any of those requests. It was impossible for a woman born in the second half of the nineteenth century to do so. We were afraid to break rules. But what if one's own children were the ones to break all the rules?

Husband on one side; children on the other. What if a dharma yuddha of this kind happened? Where would the mother stand? Whom would she side with? You will not understand this intense battle of commitments, children! Never.

The Majumdar family was totally devoted to the king emperor. We had zamindaris, regional headships, and provincial governorships in many regions. Besides, my husband was a Rao bahadur, honorary justice, and a member of the Advisory Council of the Most Honourable English Government. The governor and the viceroy frequently enjoyed our hospitality. Besides, we had planned to send our eldest son Dhirendu into the ICS, as soon as he passed his BA. My husband used to say: 'Rao bahadur is a mere title. ICS will bring with it wealth and power.'

Dhiren used to come home from Calcutta and return, unaware of any of this. He was very good at his studies. Handsome, and of few words. Above all, everyone praised Dhirendu Majumdar's compassionate nature. He would always be surrounded by a group of destitute people. Some of them, he would arrange to accommodate in the outhouse, while others were housed in the dark room of the barn. He would arrange for food for them from the agrashala. The amount of money he used to take from me to spend on those people! The praise for Dhiren babu from so many mouths were sweet music to my ears.

One day, he came into the zenana with a purdah-clad woman. 'Mother! This is a yogini who belongs to the Bhairavas. She doesn't talk to anyone. She refuses to see anyone, as well. Put her in the small room next to the puja room! You must yourself serve her food!'

I was so happy! In those times, when most young men were going after strumpets, he had been serving sanyasins! The yogini did nothing but read and write while occupying the dark room. As soon as she had written a bundle of papers, Dhiren would come and take them away. They would talk to each other as if they were chanting mantras. But when I approached with food, the yogini would stand up covering her face and move over to the corner. She might have behaved that way because I was not her disciple.

One night, Dhiren called me to the dark room. The new moon was out. It was raining heavily. He said, 'The mother yogini is leaving tonight, Mother! As things have progressed so far, she intends to meet you and initiate you too into the Path. Come....'

Saying this, he removed the saffron cloth that covered the sanyasin's face. I was shocked. It was a man! A youth! He could be an older brother to Dhiren. Putting his palms together, he said: 'Please forgive me, Mother! I am Surya Sen. I am also known as Masterda. We worship the motherland in the form of Mahakali. Sabres in her hundred hands; the sacred disc in another hundred; her head daubed with the blood of the enemy! Entrails around her neck...! But today, for the first time, I have seen Devi in her Annapurneshvari form! Bless me so that this form would also be in my meditation.'

Bending down, Masterda touched the dust of my feet. Tears were streaming down his face. My eyes also welled up. Was this the famous revolutionary, Surya Sen? Terrorist! Traitor! Weren't the police hunting all around for his head? When I bent forward and placed my palm on the crown of his head, my heart too had travelled down to my hand. 'Surya Sen. No... Masterda? Is the mother who gave birth to you, my elder sister?'

Time was running out. A boat was waiting at the ghat on the river Padma. Masterda got into the boat with Dhiren. I stood rooted to the spot, watching as the boat sailed away on the tumultuous waves of the Padma and disappeared. At that moment Shanti Majumdar, the lady of the zenana, had died. Instead, a new woman, Banglamata, was born. I pretended not to have seen anything at all. Knowing everything, I lived as two persons simultaneously. When, after some time, I heard that the police had captured Surya Sen and he was sentenced to be hanged to death, Dhiren's father said, 'Look! This is what happens to traitors like him. The troubles that these hordes make! Just yesterday the governor said, "Majumdar saheb! How brave your eldest son is! I have decided to enrol him into the police service".'

Hearing this, I suppressed my sobs lest I burst out weeping. Was it because I remembered the death of Surya Sen? Or, the thought of my son becoming the future police commissioner? Oh, let it be. After the death of Masterda, Dhiren continued to bring home many types of people in different attires. I have had to give refuge to many of them. But, a bomb exploded all of a sudden. The day he learned from the police chief that Dhiren was a suspect, his father Rao Bahadur Niharendu Majumdar came to the zenana and roared, 'No! No! I do not have such a son! My eldest son is dead!' Saying this, he turned around and commanded me, 'If that traitor turns up here, do not even serve him water. We should catch him and hand him over to the police.'

Even after hearing this, and despite my being a dharma patni, this mother had given refuge to that son of mine, many a time. I had given him whatever he wanted. And I would tell him, weeping, 'My son! Please do not go around doing such things any more! Please tell me, son, that you won't get involved in such things!'

Before he got caught in the Chittagong Conspiracy Case, he said, 'Have you heard, Mother? Greek mothers used to sacrifice their eldest sons to the god of war. Attaining heaven is by dying for one's own country. My mother is the goddess herself. Please give up your eldest son for the motherland! You have eight other children!'

I burst out weeping. 'My son! A mother is greater than the country! She has a heart. It will burst. The country is mere soil and stones!'

Dhiren kissed the crown of my head. 'No, Mother, no! The country is made up of the hearts of millions and millions of mothers like you. They feel pain. They feel smothered. Their tears don't dry up. When I die for the freedom of this motherland, you must sing Vande Mataram and laugh! Tell, me, Mother, that you will laugh!'

Saying this, he touched the dust of my feet, and left. Later, when I heard that my son had died in a dynamite explosion during the assault on the armoury at Chittagong, within the earshot of his father, who was fatigued with grief and agitation, I sang Vande Mataram! Weeping, laughing, shouting like a madwoman, I sang louder and louder.... '*Koti, koti, karadhruta karaalakaravaale!*'

Oh! My children! I am thirsty! My throat is parched. Give me some water! Some cold water. Ah...enough! I should not have told you all this now. Shouldn't have recollected all this. Aren't I now a foreign woman, a refugee, who has come begging for your compassion? People have forgotten Dhirendu Majumdar long, long ago! How can they then remember his mother? Dhiren's ghost had possessed his younger brothers as well. Sharadindu who had gone to London to study to become a barrister shot an Englishman at the gate of India Office and then killed himself. Nityendu and Satyendu never even went to college. Their father had become bedridden with a paralytic stroke. Our property was attached. Yet, the fame of the house of Majumdar is very great even today, my children! It became the house of all the freedom fighters of the country. Tarakeshwar was arrested from the cellar of that house. Ganesh Ghosh, Savitri, Kalpana—so many of them were daily visitors to the family. Have you heard of Priti Vardhadar? She was the bosom friend of my daughter Minoti. The poor thing! She was not born to be a revolutionary. She would swoon if she saw blood. Would you believe that it was Priti who hurled a bomb into the European Club at Chahartali and killed herself consuming potassium cyanide before she was captured? It is the freedom that sprouted from their blood that you enjoy today. Nityendu, Satyendu, and Minoti did not live to see this day. Congress came; Gandhiji came. To Gandhiji, who argued that Gopinath Saha should not be pardoned, I said, 'It will be you whom history will not pardon, Bapuji! Bravery is not a crime! So many Bengali youths have already become immortal, killing and dying for the country!'

After all these events, when the country was divided based on castes and religions, Trilokya Chakravarti told Nehru: 'Who asked you to sever the head of Bengal? Who asked you to separate us? There is no Hindu or Muslim here. Only Bengali. Forever one Bengali. If the head and body exist in a separated state, the play of these Rahu and Ketu will be terrible! Eclipses will engulf the sun and the moon! Just wait and watch!'

Yes! That eclipse has come upon us! Only that this time, it engulfs everything. We too had thought of fleeing to India during Partition. Then we thought, come what may, we'll live here. Here or there, it's all the same. Wherever we are, we will prosper if we serve the country and live in unity. Thus, we once again engaged in the service of the new country. People once again flocked under the dilapidated roofs of the Majumdar mansion to meet me, whom they called Mataji. I walked with Gandhiji in Noakhali. Established Sevasram in Chittagong. Organized friendship committees in Dhaka. We did not break any rules. Yet the authorities suspected us. They dismissed Subhendu who was a professor in Dhaka. Samaredu was not given a licence to practise as a doctor. Yogendu died while engaged in relief operations during floods. This has always been the fate of us Bengalis, my children! Nature around us is always in commotion. The sea will constantly attack the shores and submerge them. There will be cyclones raging. The Padma will be in spate. Cholera and famine will spread. None of these is to be tackled, reckoning one's caste and creed. My youngest daughter Laila had married a Muslim. We were all living together. We once made my three-year-old grand-daughter sing 'Amar Sonar Bangla' by Tagore; we were thrilled to hear it. Oh! It's that child the soldiers snatched and threw on the road and killed.

Everything is over, my children! Everything is over. I was left with only one thing. My mother and daughter—the land. The land where I was born! My Bengal. The rivers, lakes, and the people of that land—always agitated. I have lost even that now.

Mujibur saheb used to say, 'Shanti Devi! You are the symbol of our Bengal. You are our mother! You are our grandmother! Through your blessing, let Bengal be independent once again!'

There was very little blood left in my body. Yet, I cut my index finger and marked a tilak on his forehead with it!

'Be victorious, son! Be lucky enough to make Bengal triumphant once again!'

This Grandma Shanti was carried bodily by her grandchildren, the soldiers of the Mukti Fauj, who fled from the scene. Finally, they reached India. Here she is a refugee! A beggar woman! A foreigner...!

Is it true, Indira? Tell me! Has Shanti Majumdar come here as a refugee?

Is the mother of Dhiren, Samaren, Satyen, and Nityen, a foreigner here?

I am asking the land of Tagore, Sarat Chandra, C. R. Das, and Netaji: is Shanti Majumdar a foreigner, or a citizen? If you tell me that this is not my land, I will not lie down here and die. Oh! Once again, tears spring in my eyes. I am feeling dizzy. No. I will not weep. Dhirendu Majumdar's mother will not weep. Come! Let us sing that song together, like old times:

> *Koti, koti, karadhruta karaalakaravaale!*
> *Suphalam...Sujalam...*
> *Sasyashyaamala...Mataram,*
> *Vande Mataram....*

THE SPEAKING PLOUGH
PONKUNNAM VARKEY

I

Avuseppu Chettan forgot about everything whenever he heard the word ox. The other farmers called him ox-crazy. They could not stop marvelling about his ox named Kannan. Kannan was Avuseppu Chettan's very life. The ox was ash coloured, had horns like budding mushrooms, and a good body length. From the middle of his back, a beautiful hump formed and the grand skinfolds from it met at his bellybutton. His eyes protruded outwards. Kannan's gait was graceful. When ploughing a furrow, Kannan instantly sensed what Avuseppu Chettan was thinking. In holding the levelling plank, in breaking the lumps of mud, Kannan anticipated whatever Avuseppu Chettan intended to do. He had never beaten Kannan, except raising his hand in a mock warning. He did not have to holler, 'ox, fox...' like the other farmers. He spoke to Kannan as if to a friend. Even if there were many more oxen, Kannan would be their natural leader. When the ploughing was done in one patch of the paddy field, Kannan did not need a reminder to move over to the next one. He knew when and how to do all of that. At the moment when Kannan would place his foreleg into the next paddy field, Avuseppu Chettan would request a concession from him, 'Hey, halt a little. Let me chew a paan. It's been so long since I chewed one.'

Hearing that, Kannan instantly stood still. Avuseppu Chettan hummed a tune once he finished chewing his paan made of betel leaves, lime, areca nut, and tobacco. Kannan would get into motion and proceed with the work. When he ended work in one field and moved on to next, he was very cautious and prudent. He made sure his hooves did not step on the freshly raised mud bunds between the paddy fields. He knew that those bunds, finely wrought and sharp like the blade of a machete, would break into smithereens if he so much as stepped on them.

There was no need to tether Kannan, who understood his master's wishes. He could be let loose on the ploughed-up fields without worrying. Avuseppu Chettan would issue the necessary warnings when he let him loose. 'Hey! Graze there and get some grub and fill your belly. But don't set your eyes on that banana tree!' He never touched banana trees or coconut saplings that farmers planted and nurtured with great care. He knew that to nip them would be worse than butting them with his budding horns.

Avuseppu Chettan washed and scrubbed Kannan free of all dirt right after ploughing. 'Raise your right leg, da. Why are you shaking your head? Listen, if your horn so much as touches my body, I will show you....! Da...stand still for a moment!' Kannan understood each word Avuseppu Chettan said. But for him, it was as good as speaking in tongues because he was protesting Avuseppu Chettan bathing him! He would bend his head in deference to the love this farmer had for him, nevertheless. Some farmers who do not know how to use a loving heart would say: 'Whatever godforsaken ox there is, if Avuseppu Chettan's hands feed it just once, its character will change wonderfully!' They thought he used some esoteric language with the ox.

For most of the day, Avuseppu Chettan would be wandering about organizing fodder for his ox. When someone began a discussion on 'maintaining' cattle, Avuseppu would be full of anger. He would ask, 'Everyone is speechifying that one should "maintain" cattle. Does the government give at least one field free in one kara for the cattle to graze? How else can they be maintained? By feeding them one's beard?'

His hunger was satiated only when his ox's belly was full. He believed that the prosperity of a house would cease if the cattle of the family go hungry. He was meticulous about what he fed the cattle. For example, let us assume that the ox is given the stem of the tapioca plant for want of anything better. Instead of throwing in the whole stem, Avuseppu Chettan would cut them into small pieces and give it to him. Or, suppose it is the leaves of the pineapple plant. He would cut away all the thorns from the edges of the leaves before he fed them to the ox.

Whenever Avuseppu Chettan returned home, he would call out as soon as he reached the courtyard, 'Hey Kanna!' The moment he heard that voice, the doting ox would begin his loving lowing. Till he reached near, Kannan would look at him with his raised head. Avuseppu Chettan would approach the ox with a treat—either a banana skin or a handful of sweet, tender grass. Kannan would eat the treat off his hand. He would begin to lick Avuseppu Chettan, who would gently stroke his body. He was very fond of the salt of the sweat that stuck to Avuseppu Chettan's skin.

Amid any din, Kannan would distinguish Avuseppu Chettan's voice. When he heard it, he would be full of exhilaration, like a peacock hearing the rumble of thunder. Kannan was insistent that Avuseppu Chettan should himself be present for any ploughing involving him. If someone else used him to pull the plough, he would start behaving mischievously. Avuseppu Chettan himself had to intervene to stop him. 'Hey, don't! Isn't this Kuttappan, our friend? Don't you know him?' He would start the conciliation talks thus.

There's a humming of a raga without word or line at the time of ploughing. Avuseppu Chettan would raise it beautifully. 'Ho…oh…oh…oh…!' For one or two minutes, that strain will reverberate in the air. It was a primitive version of the humming we hear in love songs and group songs. It would be correct to say that it is a cattle pranava mantra—the primordial mantra Om. When Avuseppu Chettan's humming rose, Kannan would be immersed in it, forgetting his physical strain, pain, and sweat. The bell on his neck and the incessant hoof falls in the field's slush would keep the timing of the humming.

Once there was a funny episode. It was Pachan, son of Thundathil Kelan, who was driving the plough. That day, Avuseppu Chettan was bedridden with measles. If that day one of his oxen were missing from action, the work in Kelan's paddy field would lie incomplete. Therefore, Avuseppu Chettan let Kannan and his oxen pair be handled by Pachan. Kannan got to the paddy field with the other oxen and the ox that formed his pair. When Pachan ploughed one furrow of a paddy field and began with another, he felt the need for humming. Pachan started on a raga right behind Kannan. Music had never even come anywhere near Pachan! When that pauperized music arose, revulsion gripped Kannan. He let his protest known, shaking his horns frequently. Pachan was going on without any let or hindrance. Pachan thought his singing was superb. One truth about singing is that the singer does not feel that he sings in an inferior manner! Kannan let his protest known for quite some time. Pachan was not paying any attention. For Pachan and the likes of him, all the ragas of the world were one. Kannan did not get justice from them. Kannan gave a tight kick to Pachan's right shin. The musician had to stay home and apply steam to his bruised leg for three days!

II

Kannan had been helping Avuseppu Chettan without a break for about twelve years. Kannikkoythu and Meenakkoythu, the paddy harvest seasons in September–October and March–April, respectively, came and went over these years. Autumn and winter caressed the trees and creepers many a time. The sceptre and the crown that the potentates of the princely states had wielded over their subjects fell. Many a wondrous thing had happened. Weighty arguments such as 'a new system in which man does not exploit man' were rising of late. But Avuseppu Chettan was now constrained to sell off his beloved oxen. The fertile land which formed his good fortune, the paddy fields which brought him his daily rice, had already been mortgaged. Not that he wanted it. Even if he did not want it, it had to be done. He was the loving father of a daughter who had reached marriageable age. The unjust system of demanding dowry while one seeks a girl's hand in marriage compelled him to do it. He mortgaged the paddy fields for a mere one thousand and five hundred rupees. That met the demand for dowry. For wedding expenses, he needed to make more money. For that, there was no other way than selling the oxen.

He had been toiling day and night for the last twenty years. He was an excellent farmer. But to what end? His hair had turned grey, eyesight dimmed, and skin wrinkled. Rheumatic troubles had become his constant companions. The callus on his toiling palms was so hard that a knife couldn't pierce it. He was struggling with farm implements in use since the last five millennia. The fertility of the soil had drained away. There was no fertilizer. Avuseppu Chettan continued the practice of the times of the Rig Vedic hymns—supplicating Varuna Bhagavan, the Lord of Waters, the raincloud, the mountain, and the wind for assistance in the greatest yajna of the world—agriculture! He had not risen from the helplessness of those epochs where the only prayer used to be work. In the meanwhile, markets and other means of exploitation had expanded exponentially.

At the time of changing Kannan's rope when the old coir around his neck which his old owner had put was being removed and replaced by the new owner, Avuseppu Chettan did not remain there to watch the scene. When the rope is changed, the old owner gets a rupee as kayattukaanam—ritual fee for the exchange of the new rope with which the new owner takes possession of the cattle. But he moved away, with tears that no money can buy. Kannan did not have the mind to move away from that courtyard. He raised his head and looked all around to see his protector, who meant to him more than his life itself. Sensing that something was amiss, he lowed once or twice. At that time, under the jackfruit tree in the southern side, a man was standing forlorn—a man who did not have anything to say to anyone.

Wordiness and demonstrativeness are never part of the soul of love. If love is the attraction between minds that can experience grief, there was no one else in this world closer to each other than Kannan and Avuseppu Chettan. They had never told each other about their hardships. Therefore, their hearts pained at parting.

When some farmers became humiliated and helpless, they migrated to the jungles of Wayanad. 'A land that people have neither known nor heard of. At such a distance that siblings or relatives cannot easily travel. A land which has been turned into a shambles owing to the depredation of malaria epidemics. How can we let you go, knowing all this, Avuseppu Mappile?' His neighbour Kittushaar said when he told him of his plan. 'What else can I do, Kittushaare! Give me some fertile virgin soil. My mind will burn up if I do not smell fresh soil,' said that farmer.

That farmer's painful life was like a wind roaming around. He indefinitely postponed his journey to Wayanad. Moreover, he had to sell the seven cents of land on which his house stood, at a reasonable price.

There was another problem, as well. Avuseppu Chettan's daughter Kathrikkutty was pregnant. Wasn't it her first pregnancy? He secretly planned to move away after having a glimpse of the tender face of his grandchild.

That day was Easter. Even in the houses of the poorest of Christians, it is a day of happiness. It is a day when the appetizing scent of meat curry wafts from the kitchen. The day when the velleppam—pancake made with the batter of rice flour leavened with toddy—being cooked in the cast iron pan accompanied by a hissing sound spreads its intoxicating aroma. Velleppam mixed with the gravy of hot meat curry with coconut kernel bits and curry leaves and two bowls of tempered toddy would make the day very special! On such a beautiful day, there would be no house without these offerings.

But Avuseppu Chettan was sitting alone, heaving deep sighs. Ploughing was going on somewhere near. A sweet cattle pranavam was rising. It scalded the poor farmer's mind. Seeing the cobweb-ridden plough tucked under the eaves of the cattle shed, he sighed deeply. 'Will my grief-filled life ever see an ox like Kannan, with another equally good one to pair him, four-five acres of wetland farm and this plough together, ever! Ha! Will there be a time when such luck holds!' That helpless man was thinking.

Along with her husband, Mariachchedatthy was also troubled, thinking such sombre thoughts. The very next day, she had to send her daughter and child back to her husband's house, after extending all the post-delivery courtesies. The infant was a boy. Lucky. There was a little leeway regarding gold ornaments to be given to a boy child. Yet, at least a silver aranjaanam has to be put around the waist of the child, and a baby cloth has to be bought too.

Because of the shortage of money, Kathrikkutty had not been given even a decent set of chatta and mundu. Her mother-in-law and sisters-in-law made fun of her about it. Come what may, three pieces of white, long-cloth and three chattas have to be given to her. Ordinary courtesies like the kaalppetti—a wooden box in which a bride brings her trousseau from her home to her married home—delicacies; milch-cow, etc., to be sent to her husband's house—could be avoided in the particular circumstances they were in. But could the bare essentials be missed? When she was deeply troubled thinking about these things, a bit of luck came to Mariachchedatthy. She had been subscribing to a Ponzi scheme. She had maintained it even by starving and tightening her waist. She won the lottery. Forty rupees. Avuseppu Chettan did not know about it. Seeing her husband downcast with sorrow, Mariachchedatthy said, 'How can you sit like a muni, my man? Shouldn't we send our daughter tomorrow? I had been subscribing to a chit fund and maintaining it. By the grace of God, we won this month's lottery. We got forty rupees. Go to Kottayam! Buy the necessary things!'

Avuseppu Chettan was relieved. 'You are so smart!' He thanked his wife from the bottom of his heart. He was supposed to raise that money and was not able to do it. Yet, his wife had found a solution to the complicated problem. Happily, he pulled out the brass box containing the items of his paan and said, 'Yes, I'll go.'

'Appa! The cloth for my chatta should be extra thick,' Kathrikkutty said.

'We haven't yet remitted the land tax. Make that payment, too,' Mariachchedatthy said.

'For all that, I have only so much money!' Avuseppu Chettan said.

'Whatever, I also need two chattas,' Mariachchedatthy added.

'Mundu and chatta for the girl; two chattas for you. I have to remit the land tax too. Do one thing. You go to Kottayam yourself. I can't go.' Avuseppu Chettan said.

'Women are supposed to cook and maintain homes; bringing money to the house is men's business. That's why I was handed over to a moustachioed one when I was young. Do one thing, now. Get into the kitchen, blow in the hearth and wash the pots and pans with your curly moustache.'

Listening to her mother go on, Kathrikkutty covered her mouth and suppressed her laughter.

Avuseppu Chettan set out with an umbrella under his armpit, a towel on his shoulder, and a bundle in his waistband.

✧

Even in Kottayam, the boisterousness of Easter was not any less. None of the shops run by Christians were open, but there were many dress and fabrics shops. He enquired about the different types of dress materials and their prices.

'Ayyayyo! What prices! They can burn one's pockets!' That old man's opinion was that clothes need not to be priced so high. 'Anyway. Let me enquire in two or three more shops. Let's see where I can these items for an anna less,' he thought. He moved in search of other shops.

He walked to the front of the municipal building. There, outside the compound wall, several oxen were tethered in a row. All of them were so skinny that one could count the segments of their vertebrae. Old ones in decrepitude; the ones whose tails were broken in various places; the ones with thick calluses on their neck and shoulders formed by the constant friction from a cart's yoke and the ones with aged and gnarled horns—all of them proclaiming the lack of compassion on the part of the humans who handled them.

On all of them, the municipality had struck its black stamp of death. Whatever flesh was left on them was what the public would eat during the Easter celebrations. The butcher who would kill a beast on whom the municipality had not stamped its approval would invariably be proceeded against by the law. The municipality which was ever vigilant about public health above everything else would not compromise on the examination of oxen going to be butchered for meat! If the municipality's 'examine-and-stamp approval' arrangement was not in place, the butchers would kill all kinds of unseemly cattle and compromise public health! Avuseppu Chettan was sensitized to the municipality's highest level of service through those stamps.

Most of those oxen could only feel consoled about one thing: at least that day there was going to be a decision about their lives. They toiled to their maximum when they were able to. When they grew weak, they were condemned to humiliation and cruelty. How better is death than a life full of shame and cruelty!

Avuseppu Chettan was rooted to the spot watching the spectacle. The compassion saturated in his heart pained him. There were about forty oxen. Some people kept bringing their oxen to get that black stamp of death. As if looking at his friends who were condemned to death, Avuseppu Chettan looked at each one of them.

He could not believe what he saw. To make doubly sure that his dimming eyes were not cheating him, he once again trained his eyes on a particular ox on whose body bones and skin were struggling with each other. The old man's heart was ablaze. His eyes were filled with darkness. His body shivered. Yes, it was Kannan!

'Kannaa....' That call rose from the bottom of his love-filled heart. He reached by the side of that beast in one spring. The advent of that voice which used to impart coolness and excitement to its ears thrilled the ox. He stood before the imposing building, with his head bent low. Life once again echoed in his ears. He raised his head and looked in all directions. 'Son! Don't you recognize me? I'm so sorry that I have to see you like this!' Clutching that beast's head to his breast resounding with the heartbeats of love, he stroked the ox's eyebrows and all over his brow. When his hands stroked him, the beast's tail was raised involuntarily. He lowed softly. Avuseppu Chettan looked all over Kannan's body to see whether the seal was stamped on him. Yes, it was there, clearly, on his foreleg. Blinded with love, Avuseppu Chettan rubbed hard on the stamp to erase it. But the black stamp of the municipality was not something that could be erased easily.

There was a big sore on Kannan's underbelly. Flies were buzzing in from all sides and alighting on it.

One of the butchers asked Avuseppu Chettan, 'Was this ox yours?' He asked the butcher back, 'Is it you who brought him here?'

'Yes,' the butcher answered.

Kannan began to lick the sweating breast of his loving master. He had toiled most of his life to cool his sweat; even at the evening of his life, he was trying to lick that sweat off. It was a sweat with a taste that was closest to his heart. That old farmer's warm tears began to fall on Kannan's face.

The butcher warned those interlocutors, 'Let go. I am late. I have to give the meat to the shops before noon.' The butcher who was setting off with some other cattle informed Avuseppu Chettan that it was time to let go of Kannan. Yes, within a few hours, Kannan would turn into meat for an Easter meal.

III

Evening was setting in. 'Di, before it's time for the evening lamp, sweep this veranda.' Mariachchedatthy who was waiting, her eyes trained on the homeward path for Avuseppu Chettan to return, told her daughter.

'Why is Appan so late, Amme?' Kathri said.

'He has gone somewhere, hasn't he? Let him return!'

'If he went to Kottayam he should have returned much earlier,' Kathri, who was anxious to take a look at her mundu and chatta cloth, said impatiently. Even her eyes were flitting towards the path. Mariachchedatthy too was looking in the same direction. Avuseppu Chettan was not to be seen.

They lit the evening lamp.

They saw a white flash in the dark.

'Appan has arrived. Yes, yes, it's Appan,' Kathri said with great joy. She was so proud that it was she who spotted him first. The mother and daughter stood watching him with utter concentration.

'Is that Avuseppu Chettan?' Matthu of the next house enquired. He was the one who stitched clothes. He had to finish stitching the three chattas through the night. Kathri had to leave early in the morning. For her to leave early according to plan, Matthu was entrusted with the task well in advance.

The man of the house approached his family waiting for the bundles of cloth with Kannan on a tether.

'Ayyo! Look! It's Kannan!' Kathri was beside herself with surprise.

'Where's the cloth?' Mariachchedatthy asked.

When he reached the old courtyard, Kannan lowed in exhilaration. A thousand tongues and fourteen thousand questions arose there.

Avuseppu Chettan was sitting silently, with a palm supporting his chin. Mariachchedatthy was on a war dance.

'Appa, I never thought you would do this to me!' said Kathri tears running down her cheeks.

'Mole,' the father, his voice faltering. 'For me, Kannan is also like you. The butcher….' the grief-stricken father wiped his tears with his towel; he could not complete the sentence.

The night was so cruel that they spent it without sleeping a wink.

Dawn broke in the east. Making a poultice with the soot scraped from the hearth, Avuseppu Chettan went into the cattle shed to administer it on Kannan's festering sore on the underbelly. That was an effective treatment. Avuseppu Chettan knew of some rare medicines for cattle diseases. He had prepared one of those for Kannan. He went into the cattle shed with the poultice.

Kannan was lying down, with his forelegs and hindlegs thrust straight, and with his throat turned upright.

'Kanna! Eda!' he called. Yes, that love dissolved in front of that heart that loved him. He would not awaken again. Maybe it was to avoid seeing that family in pain on account of him that he got away stealthily.

Above the corpse of Kannan and that farmer's heart in pain, sitting on a cobweb-ridden plough, a house lizard babbled something.

THE FARMER
THAKAZHI SIVASANKARA PILLAI

That fifty-para paddy field called the Fifty is owned by a landowner in Vaikom. Kesavan Nair has been cultivating it for the last forty years. Before him, Kesavan Nair's uncle was its cultivator.

The lease-rent was minimal in the early days. Now it has increased slightly. During the month of Meenam, from mid-March to mid-April every year, the paddy which is set aside as the lease-rent is dried, filled in gunny bags, and transported to Vaikom and handed over to the landlord. For the last many years, this has been the practice. The ownership and possession rights of the fields lying on the four sides of this fifty-para land have changed many hands during this period. But the landlord and the cultivator of the fifty-para remain the same two individuals. All the paddy that the landlord gets, is from this piece of land. The lessee is a traditional farmer. He too has only this piece of land in his possession.

About ten years ago, when paddy prices were as high as five to seven rupees a bushel, rich people from Changanassery and Tiruvalla had arrived there to cultivate paddy. They rented extensive clusters of paddy fields on lease. They used tractors for deep ploughing as well as new fertilizers to produce bumper yields. And they made huge profits. This is the style of paddy cultivation nowadays. Kesavan Nair's fifty paras are in the centre of a cluster of paddy fields cultivated by one of the rich men from Changanassery. Outhakkutty was the name of the big-time farmer.

One day Kesavan Nair met Outhakkutty on the mud bund of the field. The crop in the Fifty is poor in comparison with the crops around it. Outhakkutty broke in, by way of exchanging civilities, 'Why is the paddy not lush and robust enough? Haven't you used fertilizers?'

That question struck Kesavan Nair's heart.

The neighbouring farmer was insinuating that the paddy he cultivates is of inferior quality!

'After you big guys have come, can we drain out the water at the right time? No time is convenient enough for you. We can do farm work only at your convenience.'

Outhakkutty, a skilled diplomat, said 'Why do you say that, Uncle Kesavan? I had specifically arranged with my people to pay heed to your convenience.'

Kesavan Nair was cross. 'Oh! Great arrangements indeed! I could wet the land only after my paddy seedlings wilted in the sun. I begged your servant to release some water. He said he couldn't help because you had instructed him not to give water to me. It is a puncha-kandam and it being a perennially wet paddy field, excess water has to be pumped out in order to prepare the soil for cultivation.'

Outhakkutty countered the accusation. 'Will there be any such difficulty if you do the sowing at the same time as in the neighbouring fields?'

Kesavan Nair was piqued. 'Don't teach me how to farm my land. I did not start cultivating paddy yesterday.'

Kesavan Nair continued, increasingly irritated, 'No one becomes a farmer by pouring in money, dumping fertilizers, and raising a crop of paddy.'

Outhakkutty knew that Kesavan Nair aimed that dig at him. 'Why are you cross, Uncle Kesavan?'

'I am not being cross. I was just iterating some facts.'

After a few days, Kesavan Nair quarrelled with Outhakkutty's servant upon the mud-bund of the field. There was water on all sides. But the Fifty was parched dry and the tillers wilted. Kesavan Nair, heartbroken at this sight, cut a breach in the mud-bund. The servant sealed it up. They pushed and jostled each other. It could have culminated in murder. Luckily, that did not happen.

A few days later, the tillers in Kesavan Nair's Fifty were submerged up to their tips in water. That servant's doing! When it was the time to sun the paddy plants in Outhakkutty's fields, the water was diverted to Kesavan Nair's Fifty. How was he to drain that water away? Where would he take it to? Could he drink it all up? Kesavan Nair's tillers began to rot.

Everyone said that it was indeed a high-handed action. But what was the use? Kesavan Nair went looking for Outhakkutty for three or four days. He could not find him. Kesavan Nair didn't know what to do. That crop was doomed if the water remained like that for two more days. Kesavan Nair had almost become a mad man.

Kuttichovan, a friend of Kesavan Nair, asked in consternation, 'Why don't we cut open breaches on the bunds at night and divert the water back to the other fields?'

Kesavan Nair did not like that idea. He said, 'That should not be done in a puncha-kandam, the wet paddy field. Cut open bunds in the dead of night! Can a farmer do that, Kutty? Even if I perish I will not do what should not be done.'

Then another friend, Kutty Mappila, said, 'Are the things happening now, befitting for a puncha-kandam? Well, well! This is unheard of! Not only in these fields, but anywhere in the land: denying water to a field surrounded by other fields and flooding when not required.' Kesavan Nair said in irrepressible rage. 'Is he a farmer? Does he know the dharma of a farmer? He produces paddy crops, pumping in money. And makes money, selling it. Does it make him a farmer?'

'That's why I say, you should drain away the water from your field by cutting open the mud-bund at night,' Kuttichovan pressed. 'They don't care for any values. Why can't we follow suit?'

Kesavan Nair said he would never perpetrate such adharma. Kutty Mappila, who was listening to it all, said, half-soliloquizing, 'So it was well and good that I leased out my piece of land to Outhakkutty or else, my fate too would have been the same now.' Kuttichovan also said the same thing. Of a 500-acre-paddy-field-complex, only Kesavan Nair's five acres remained outside Outhakkutty's domain. The rest was in his possession. There was no one to help Kesavan Nair as a farmer. But everyone was sympathetic towards him. Listening to his friends' talk, Kesavan Nair said, 'I too would have entrusted mine to him. But what else is there for my livelihood? What work will I do? You, Kutty Mappila, get at least five hundred coconuts. Kuttichovan has four sons, working. I have only this field on lease. And I can eke out a living only by cultivating it.'

That was true. No one said anything. Kesavan Nair continued, 'From my ancestors' times we have been toiling on this piece of land.'

That night, the water in the Fifty somehow drained away. Someone had breached the mud-bunds at night. It was certainly not Kesavan Nair. Since the water spread evenly into the surrounding fields, no damage had been done to the crops in those fields. It was now clear that the farmer of the neighbouring fields had let in water to the Fifty on purpose.

Next morning, Kesavan Nair went out to the field and saw for himself. He was flabbergasted. It was not relief that he felt at the crop being saved by the draining away of the water. Who had perpetrated this adharma? The weight of that sin would fall on him only! He had not known anything about it. He wondered how he was going to prove his innocence if someone asked him about it. The infamy of opening a breach into a puncha-kandam would always trail him.

The poor man didn't look at the other fields to see if any damage had occurred to the crop in those fields. One the one hand, there was his fear of scandal. On the other hand, his relief at his crop having escaped destruction. So, he returned home. He was afraid that someone might turn up and ask him about it. So, he shut himself up in a room and hid there for two days. He instructed his family to tell anyone who asked for him that he was not there. Kutty Mappila and Kuttichovan came. He was too scared to meet even them.

At dawn on the third day, before anyone woke up, Kesavan Nair went to the field and looked around. The weak tillers which had been flattened to the ground had started rising up in the sun's warmth. His crop wouldn't perish. After three or four days of getting the sun, the tillers should be soaked a little by letting in water for one day, along with adding some manure. Then, the crop would be excellent, first rate. Everything pointed towards that possibility. Kesavan Nair's next thought was how to raise money to buy manure. He had to repay the debt of eight bushels of paddy and one hundred and twenty rupees including the seed paddy and labour charges incurred for the present crop. Besides, there were expenses for draining the water. It would have been enough if he could get a hundred rupees more. In order to boost the growth of the crop, he would need to provide the tillers at least a smattering of manure. Where could he raise the money from? Who would give him money? The household expenses were met by the proceeds from the four milch cows. Kesavan Nair toyed with the idea of selling one of them to raise funds. But his wife wouldn't agree to it. It was she who had raised the cows.

Kesavan Nair was standing lost in thought. His head was full of thoughts about the manure problem.

'The tillers are properly sunned, aren't they, Uncle Kesavan?'

Kesavan Nair turned around. It was Outhakkutty. Suddenly Kesavan Nair's obsession with the adharma upset him. The adharma of cutting a breach at night in the mud-bund of a puncha-kandam! Wasn't it that adharma that was pursuing him? Outhakkutty stood there as if he had caught the culprit. He, Kesavan Nair, should give him a proper explanation. He had to establish his innocence in the matter. With a troubled smile, Kesavan Nair said, 'Upon my grand-uncle, upon this puncha-kandam which is true to its tradition, it is not I who breached the bund, Outhakkutty! I am a true farmer. A farmer worth his name would never do such an adharma.'

Outhakkutty observed Kesavan Nair's anxiety. 'Why do you swear by your ancestors, Uncle Kesavan? It is not you who breached the bund. It is I who did it; I did it because I saw your paddy submerged when I was coming along this way.'

Kesavan Nair was relieved. His eyes shone. 'Is it true? Tell me the truth! Oh, this is such a relief! May you do well in life, my boy! I feared I would have to carry the weight of this infamy with me till my death.'

Outhakkutty once more said emphatically, 'Yes, Uncle Kesavan. It's I who did it. Although you hate me, how can I hate you? When I saw that sight, my heart nearly stopped. I opened the breach. Let my paddy perish, if it has to, I said to myself.'

Kesavan Nair was not sorry about the crop being lost. The infamy!

Outhakuty said, glancing all over the Fifty, 'If you could sprinkle a little manure, the crop would be excellent, Uncle Kesavan.'

'I was thinking of that just now.'

'Then you have to do it.'

'One should have money for that. Money! I don't have money.'

'If you want a good crop, you should spend money.'

'The times are such.'

Outhakkutty said as if it was because of his fondness for Kesavan Nair: 'Uncle Kesavan, may I say something?'

Kesavan Nair raised his head and looked at Outhakkutty's face.

'Why are you taking all this trouble, Uncle Kesavan? I'll give you the lease-rent for the landlord at Vaikom and fifty bushels of paddy extra. Hand over the field to me. Why toil so much in your old age?'

Kesavan Nair suddenly became another person altogether. He was furious. Yet, controlling his anger, he said: 'No, no. Keep that thought to yourself, Outhakkutty. We have cultivated this field right from the times of our ancestors. No one else shall cultivate it.'

'That's all right. You are the lessee of the Vaikom landlord. And I am your lessee.'

'No. That won't do. I was born a farmer. Farming is my occupation.

And I have five heads of cattle besides. They need hay. No. It won't work, Outhakkutty....'

Kesavan Nair walked away without saying anything more. He was afraid that he might quarrel with Outhakkutty if he stayed on and talked. Or, he would have to agree to what Outhakkutty proposed.

Outhakkutty couldn't help laughing, looking at the old man hurrying away.

No manure was put in the Fifty. The crop was bad. It was dismal. During the harvest season, Kesavan Nair could not get hold of reapers. All around, he saw Outhakkutty's first-rate crop; if the labourers reaped it, they would get two bushels of paddy as percentage wage. Would they reap that for Kesavan Nair's poor crop for which they wouldn't get even one-fourth of that? For four or five days Kesavan Nair went around requesting reapers to harvest his crop. The paddy was getting overripe. At last, the members of Kutty Mappila's and Kuttichovan's families, the servant Pulayan and his Pulayi and Kesavan Nair's family members together reaped the field. They couldn't even cut the hay. For that matter, there was not much hay there in the field.

The crop was woeful. It was doubtful if there would be sufficient paddy to pay the lease-rent. Kutty Mappila, Kuttichovan, and Kesavan Nair conferred together. Kutty Mappila's opinion was that the lease-rent should be proportionate to the crop output. Till that moment, there wasn't even a grain of paddy for outstanding payment of rent. 'You can give more if next year's crop is better.'

Kesavan Nair couldn't agree to that.

'This is the only piece of land the landlord has. And he will get paddy only from this field. We have harvested the crop. We should give the whole rent. The land will turn barren if the landlord's tears fall on it.'

Kuttichovan asked, 'What if the entire crop is not sufficient to pay the rent?'

Kesavan Nair came up with a quick answer: 'The deficit will be made good by buying some paddy.'

That evening, a boat was ready to carry the paddy to Vaikom. The whole of the paddy was kept on the threshing floor, after winnowing. The paddy set apart for lease-rent was measured, filled in gunny bags, and carried to the waiting boat.

The entire crop was just about sufficient for the payment of the lease-rent. What remained for Kesavan Nair was just ten and a half bushels of paddy which was the spillage on the threshing floor and the chaff! He couldn't make good even the seed paddy and the labour charges!

The lease rent paddy was carried to the landlord's house. The landlord was Thirumulpad. Kesavan Nair had sensed that there was a slight change of expression on Thirumulpad's face. What was unusual was that he asked whether the entire lease-rent paddy had been brought. And he made this comment, 'My information was that this year I would not get the entire lease-rent paddy.'

Kesavan Nair replied boldly, 'Isn't it at least a hundred years, since we took this Fifty for cultivation, Thirumeni? Has there been even a grain of paddy outstanding as lease-rent payment till now?

Thirumulpad didn't say a word.

The lease-rent paddy was measured out without leaving even a grain as deficit. Still, Thirumulpad's face didn't exhibit any trace of satisfaction.

He gave lunch to Kesavan Nair and the boatmen as usual. After they had eaten, as Kesavan Nair got up to leave, Thirumulpad said he had something to say to him.

'What is it?' asked Kesavan Nair.

The reply was abrupt.

'Someone has approached me with an offer to take the land on an increased rate of rent. He is a very smart person too. Kesavashaar, you must relinquish the land.'

Kesavan Nair stood there, thunderstruck. He couldn't utter a word.

A few moments passed. Thirumulpad continued: 'A first-rate paddy field. You are enjoying it for low rent. That's not possible any more. Leave the land free.'

Kesavan Nair came out of his daze: 'The land is yours. But, there are certain things we all should remember.'

'There is nothing to remember.'

An idea dawned upon Kesavan Nair. 'What increase in rent is proposed now?'

'A hundred bushels of paddy. And the party is very sound. How will I recover any arrears that you may accumulate?'

No answer.

Kesavan Nair finally said: 'I'll tell you one thing, Thirumeni. I know who has approached you. It's Outhakkutty. But he is not a true farmer, Thirumeni. The likes of him don't love the soil. They'll put a lot of fertilizers, prodigally extract the fertility of the soil and raise good crops.

After four or five years, your land will turn into useless, bran-like soil. Not even grass will sprout there.'

Thirumulpad was walking back and forth the length of the veranda. He didn't speak a word. Kesavan Nair continued to speak. The words choked his throat. His eyes brimmed with tears. 'It's that field that I saw when I was born. The sweat of my ancestors has also added to its fertility. I have loved only that field in my entire life.'

Kesavan Nair broke down. 'N-no! You shouldn't evict me from there, Thirumeni.'

Even Thirumulpad's heart seemed to melt a little. He said, 'I must get my rent.'

Kesavan Nair returned, having taken the same field for an increased rate of rent.

Usually, the field would be ploughed two to three times, while the soil was still dry, just after the harvest. The wages for it would be given as paddy right from the threshing floor. This year, there wasn't even a grain of paddy left after the harvest. The money borrowed for carrying out the preparatory work of the last crop too had not been repaid. There was no one to borrow from either.

The next day after his return, Kesavan Nair called the ploughman and had the field ploughed once. He didn't even think of how he was going to pay them wages. From that day, the ploughmen pestered him for payment of wages. How could he have the land ploughed again, without paying the wages for the first ploughing?

Thus the field fell fallow. The neighbouring fields were regularly ploughed every month. The Fifty was overgrown with weeds.

Outhakkutty approached him again. He said he would give the increased rates of rent Kesavan Nair agreed to pay to the Vaikom landlord, plus fifty bushels of paddy. Kesavan Nair was enraged. 'No! Don't ever imagine that'll happen! I won't hand over this field to you.'

It was time for the sowing of the next crop. The work of putting up the mud-bunds was over. The water was being drained. The Fifty lay vacant—without being ploughed, being weeded, or the soil being prepared. Poor Kesavan Nair didn't even have the necessary seed paddy.

His fight then turned toward his wife. One cow must be sold. She didn't like the idea though.

She said, 'We are pulling on just on account of the cows. I won't agree.'

Kesavan Nair was incensed. 'How'll we sow the paddy, then?'

'Don't sow.'
'I am a farmer. I must sow.'
'Ah! A farmer, indeed!'

Kesavan Nair sold a cow without the consent of his wife. As the person who bought the cow went away tugging it along, she cursed: 'Damn, this crop.'

The money the cow's sale brought in was sufficient only for ten bushels of seed paddy and ten rupees for the labour charges.

Kesavan Nair tied up the seed paddy and put it in water. He took out the seed the following day. Not even half of it had germinated. And he was supposed to sow that day itself. Kutty Mappila advised him to sow it as it was. It will germinate in the soil! That was the only way out, besides. He did just that.

Paddy was growing robustly in the neighbouring fields. In the Fifty, weeds had grown thickly. Not even a single tiller was to be seen. Kesavan Nair bore the infamy of having spoiled the field.

The harvest that year was over. There was no need to reap the Fifty. The date of handing over the lease-rent paddy had expired. Thirumulpad reached the spot. Kesavan Nair was in hiding. For three days, Thirumulpad went about looking for him. He was not to be found.

The next day, Outhakkutty's men got into the Fifty and ploughed the field. Thirumulpad stood on the mud-bund, looking on.

The sowing of the next crop was over. Early every morning, Kesavan Nair would go out to the fields, like a farmer who had a crop to look after. One watching him go would think that he really had a crop somewhere. He'd return only after the day had progressed. It had been his habit for forty-odd years.

The paddy in the Fifty was leaping as if challenging Kesavan Nair. He would go there every day. When once he spotted a slight yellowing of the plants, his heart burned. He sought out Outhakkutty and reported the matter. Not only that, he stood by and had the necessary remedial measures carried out.

ON THE RIVERBANK

S. K. POTTEKKATT

A small river snakes its way at the base of a rounded hill shaped like a sago palm flower-head. The riverbank is almost hidden by the low overhanging branches of old, gnarled trees, the thickets of stunted nux vomica trees and intertwining creepers. Horrid daytime darkness hugged the area.

Nearby, in the middle of the river, is a deep pool. There is a rock that lies partially submerged in the pool. Old-timers call it thalavettippaara—the beheading rock. It is believed criminals were beheaded on this rock. No one bathes there. The water has a different colour near the rock.

Close to where the hill begins, there stands a stunted sago palm raising its head over the ground. On the top of the plant, there is a flower-head like a blazing flame. The intoxicating fragrance from it wafts all around. Near the sago palm, there is a Barbados nut bush, half of it withered, and the other half distorted as if paralysed. On one of its branches hang five or six bundles wrapped in old screw-pine mats whose reflection can be seen on the sediment-covered river water's surface. These are the placentas of cows and goats that have been packed and hung on the branches of the nut tree. Next to the nut tree is the fat red taproot of some tree made bare by the eroding soil at its base. Around the slanting pulakkalli tree that is bereft of all its leaves, and looks like the ribcage of a dead horse, wild aloe vera plants stand like swaying snakes with their hoods open.

From somewhere inside that thicket, a gigantic wild jack tree stands straight reaching out to the sky. An almost dry brook joins the river below the pool. It is a tiny ford at this point.

It is midday. The sand on the riverbank scorches in the fire-like sun of Kanni, the months between mid-September to mid-October.

Madhavi Amma bathed her son, dried him off, brushed his hair with her fingers, polished his face, made him wear the silk loincloth and sent him off to the riverbank. That six-year-old boy, like an obedient child, sat on the rock in the shade of a tree, stretching his legs out.

Five minutes passed. All of his limbs began to move intermittently.

Childhood is like a drop of mercury. No one can keep it still. The boy's wide eyes flitted here and there, without resting anywhere. He began to count his fingers, to check if all ten digits were there. He measured the length of his brow, his chin, and his nose, using his index finger. Then he blocked one of his nostrils with a finger and started humming, letting his breath out through the other and tapping the opening lightly in rhythm. For some time, he played the fiddle in that fashion; then, he stopped it. He pressed his upper eyelids down with his pointing finger, looked all around at the trees and bushes and saw the distorted sight of them becoming double and felt exhilarated. Suddenly, an idea flashed in his mind.

'Mother! May I build a dam across the brook and play?'

'No, no! Don't play in the mud, Unni! Sit still there. See, don't lose that ring!'

Unni took the ring that he had placed on his thigh. A gold ring, studded with a red stone. His mother had entrusted him to take care of it until she bathed and returned from the river.

He tried the ring on all his fingers. Finally, he fixed it on the thumb of his right hand. Then he shut his eyes tight, crossed his hands on his chest, and sat wondering what else to do.

He opened his eyes and tried to touch his nose with the tip of his tongue. Then he filled his mouth with air and hissed like a snake. Thus, he was trying out several tricks.

'Now this place is in the sun. May I move over to the clump of bamboos, and sit in the shade, Mother?'

'Hmm,' Madhavi Amma said absentmindedly.

Imitating the walk of a lame person, the child walked over to the bamboo clump. Thus he escaped his mother's direct vision.

Next to the brook was the bamboo clump. In it, in a puddle, the image of the midday sun was blazing.

A dragonfly was frolicking there, rising suddenly in the air above the water's surface, diving quickly, touching the water and then rising again, hovering.

It attracted Unni's attention. Turning his neck, looking at it sideways, he rose gradually.

It was a pretty dragonfly, wearing a red loincloth like his. He knew a trick—catching the dragonfly and making it carry tiny stones tied to its legs.

As he advanced two steps, the dragonfly stopped its frolicking and flew across to alight on a coccinea shrub.

He stretched out his right hand, and forming his thumb and forefinger into the shape of a pair of pliers, crept stealthily to the coccinea shrub. Just as he reached the plant, the dragonfly flew away. Without halting, it flashed towards the east.

Unni didn't give up. Resolute, he went after the dragonfly.

He saw it rising from a lantana shrub. He crept inside the thicket. As he stretched his hands towards the dragonfly, it rose from the clerodendrum leaf where it was sitting and flitted across and perched on the Barbados nut bush. Presently it slipped away and descended on the aloe vera leaf and alighted tenuously as if it was prostrating.

Cursing the waywardness of the dragonfly, Unni, without lowering his raised hand, bit his lips, blinked his mischievous eyes, opened his mouth, and waited quietly for the dragonfly to come to a complete halt. But it rose and again settled on the Barbados nut bush with its wings flat.

The midday sun's rays penetrated through the porous foliage of the wild jack tree, drawing a chiaroscuro of circles of light on the ground. The sago flower, the skeletal ribcage of the pulakkalli tree and the mat-bundles on the Barbados nut bush showed themselves distinctly in the light.

There was a movement from a hole in the ground at the base of the wild jack tree. The dry leaves rustled. A king cobra came out, circled itself around the base of the rough, peeling skin of the tree trunk, and crawled over to the other side.

The dragonfly had settled down on the branch of the Barbados nut bush stretching towards the sago palm flower. Unni's tender hands were inching towards it. His entire being was stuck on that branch. The dragonfly's red tail was the only thing he could see in the whole world now.

The sunshine, like molten silver, fell on his fingers. Seeing the red stone studded on the ring on Unni's thumb, from behind the sago palm flower two tiny eyes like red glass hooks shone. The snake raised its head, drawing in the fragrance of the sago palm flower. The shining red stone on the ring attracted the attention of the snake. It raised its head further, flashed its eyes, drew air into its body, shook and inflated itself and stood with its hood spread.

The dragonfly did not flinch. Unni's hands had been lowered and moved forward almost imperceptibly.

Suddenly the dragonfly moved a little from its perch, beat its wings, and hovered up a little, making small circles and settling back in its previous spot. It seemed that it was reluctant to move away from that circle of the midday sunshine.

The king cobra was standing immobile staring at the shining stone on the ring. The tender fingers of Unni's hands formed like the head of pliers stood still as if stuck in the air.

Unni's fingers began to make the minutest movements. This time it was not directed towards the dragonfly, but in a childish shift of strategy, through a manoeuvre from the right. Unni's hands kept moving towards the right, towards the serpent's mouth. Following the tiniest movements of Unni's fingers and following the reflection of the stone on the ring, the serpent turned its hood around in its standing position. As the red light advanced further and further, the serpent withdrew its hood as if poised for a sudden strike.

The dragonfly was dozing off in the intoxicating sunshine. The fingers approaching the dragonfly reduced the space between them to that of the size of a mustard seed. A moment frozen. Unni closed in with his fingers like eyelids shutting. The dragonfly's tail was in his grip. The instant the dragonfly beat its wings and squirms, Unni twisted his body once like a lightning streak, let out a shout, and raced across the riverbank, disappearing from sight.

Perplexed, the king cobra turned around like a rubber doll. Then, as if having lost face, it slowly shrank its hood, turned its head, crawled on the ground, flipped its forked tongue, smelled the screw pine bundle on the Barbados nut bush branch, turned its head once again, moved forward, coiled around once on the bare root, then moving along the base of the pulakkalli tree and among the wild aloe vera plants, it slithered southwards.

THE FAIR CHILD

UROOB

It's midday. The horrible heat of the Meenam (from mid-March to mid-April) sun feels like flames leaping up from the earth. If someone set their bare soles on the sands, they would puff up like neyyappams in hot ghee. No one could walk along the sands at that time. Yet Kunjimon walked along that stretch. When reaching near children, the sun cools down a bit. But for how long can he remain cool like that? Kunjimon found a way out. A stream zigzagged through the middle of the paddy fields. He looked towards it. During the rainy season, tawny bull-calves would race through that channel. Their backs would be streaked with white blotches, like surf. They seemed to be rushing down the stream from some eastern jungles. It seemed they were crazed hearing the rolling of thunder. They would flash ahead without looking left or right. He had many times toyed with the idea of jumping on to the back of one of those calves and taking a tumultuous ride. But they would not stop even for an instant. Brushing their dewlaps against the thickets of wild honeysuckle on either bank, they would rush past. From the nearby thicket, a kingfisher would call out, presumably, 'Where are you headed, older brothers?' Hearing that, the calves would raise a gurgling sound that turned into a raucous noise and continue their race. Now, in this channel, there was not even a single bull calf. A couple of months ago, Kunjimon had spotted a bull calf there. It was prowling in the bottomless pit below Mannaatthippaara. He could not even take a proper look at it. His mother had scolded him by then. 'Dusk has fallen; come away, child!'

If only the calves had rushed down the channel right now! He would try something. There was no one to stop him.

He walked towards the bank of the stream, thinking on these lines. He felt sad. It looked like a fresh coconut flower spathe laid on its back. Kunjimon looked at the stream. A faint breeze rose from there, like Mother's sigh. He felt comforted. He could walk on the grassy patch along the bank that had not completely dried up. It is all right even if it is a slightly roundabout route. He remembered that the master would shout at him if he were late. He shuddered inward. Yet he did not feel like leaving that stream bank. As he walked on, he mused: why is the master shouting at me all the time? He would always shout while talking to me and the mistress of the household at Mother. Was it necessary? Kunjimon murmured, 'As if we are against them!'

His mother had done so much for that family! How many times a day would she fill up the copper water pot so tall that it would seem to touch the sky and carry it on her hips to the house, towards the kitchen and the bath house! He used to watch his mother gasping after pouring each pot of water into the big vessel.

On certain occasions, he had even blurted out, 'That's enough, Mother!'

'Hasn't the master got to take his bath?' his mother would ask. Even when it rained, Mother would draw water and carry it. If he needed so much water, why did the master not get out in the rain and have his fill! But he would not do that. How much of firewood to split, how many clothes to wash! She had to sweep the courtyard and smear cow dung paste on the floor. His mother had to do everything! Yet, why does the master quarrel so much with Mother? When all the chores were over, Mother would stand hovering like a kite, panting. Seeing her leaning against the wall of the kitchen, her hands akimbo, he would feel sorry for her. When she panted, her breasts, like dried banana peels dangling, would heave and rise. On such occasions, he would feel an urge to throw his hands around her waist and exclaim, 'My mother!'

Yet, Kunjimon never did so. If the mistress saw them holding each other, she would rage, 'No such cuddling here!' Next, the news would reach the master. They would talk as if him holding his mother was some kind of crime, and a trial would follow. Therefore, Kunjimon merely stood watching his mother pant and gasp. As he was watching his mother pant today, the command came, 'Run. Go to the washerman, and ask him to bring all the clothes. Now!' He ran till he moved away from the mistress's line of gaze. Now, he could not run any more.

Kunjimon walked along the stream bank in a leisurely manner. Blazing, singeing sunlight; even the air was hot. Yet, he walked slowly. He was really irritated. He was hungry too. Just when he had reached the kitchen to ask for some kanji, the order had come to run to the washerman. Even as he thought about kanji, his hunger doubled. Yet, he could not but walk on.

There were appakkaadus along the stream bank. But the leaves of the green flowering shrubs were drooping. They stood as if they were saying, 'I can't pull on any more.' Kunjimon caught hold of the neck of a tiny plant, straightened it and stood looking at it for some time. Then he began to sing softly:

> The appa had an appan.
> An appan who was curved like bitter gourd.
> An appan who came wearing Onam's flowers.
> As he reached without a palm-leaf umbrella,
> the blazing goddess caught him and held him
> and he died of the smallpox that rose on his body.

Hearing the song, the appakkaadus turned bashful and lowered their heads. Kunjimon laughed and ran along.

The stream negotiated three bends. At the third bend, there was a peepul tree. It always stood in a frenzy. Its possession by Kali never abates. Kunjimon remembered something suddenly. The temple in front of the peepul tree was closed after the recent vela festival. For seven days, the temple would not be opened. Today was the third day. This seven-day period is when the goddess lets her demons loose. The thought frightened him. He looked all around. There was no one in sight. Do demons move about in the midday sun? What times of the day do the demons move around? He did not know. What if it was a time when they ran about?

He did not feel like moving ahead. What if he returned? All hell would break loose. The mistress would beat him black and blue. If someone had come this way, he could go along with them back to the master's house. He looked around as far as his eyes could reach. Not a living being in sight. Should he go on? Should he turn back? He decided not to pursue either course of action. He would sit at the base of the peepul tree and wait until someone turned up.

He climbed on to the dilapidated platform built around the base of the peepul tree. There was a blue spread spangled with golden blotches. Kunjimon reflected that even the mistress's bed chamber did not have such a fine spread. He was not sure whether he deserved to sit on it, yet he sat on the spread. What a luxurious feeling! He felt as if someone was caressing him all over his body. Like his mother's caress!

He leaned against the bole of the tree. His eyes were closing automatically. The golden blotches on the blue sheet spread on the ground had begun to rise and walk about, or rather swim about. Golden boats were moving along in rows in front of his eyes. The boats kept coming and going. A procession without end! Were these flying boats? They were rising higher and merging with the swirling clouds and disappearing. Kunjimon kept watching.

Suddenly he realized that the bole of the peepul tree against which he was leaning had a very soft and yielding bark. He pressed and leaned further back into the bark. He felt as if he had leaned against a fleshy body. He leaned his head as well. How comforting!

He heard the tunes of a reed pipe from somewhere above. He listened keenly. Oh, it is the wind singing. The notes went into a high pitch and then low, undulating. He felt as if they were passing through his nerves. Those special notes were travelling like silvery wires. Nnim... nnim...nnim...it went. So engrossing!

Suddenly there was a roar from above. Kunjimon started and shuddered. He lifted his head to have a look! It was horrendous! Two canine teeth were gleaming white like ivory and curved like sickles! Their thickness had pulled back the corners of his mouth. Thick moustaches like thick paddy bunches, hung from either side of his upper lip. Blazing eyes like torches! In place of hair, flames leapt up. Kunjimon looked at him just once, and then he shut his eyes. It was a demon! Kunjimon realized that he was leaning against the leg of a demon. Neither was he able to pull his body away nor was he able to press against it. He was frozen on the spot. He just sat there like a corpse.

Loud laughter rose repeatedly. That noise was enveloping Kunjimon's body. He felt it like the pricking of a million pins. Each peal of laughter was pushing a sheath lined with thorns down his body.

Suddenly the demon withdrew his leg. Kunjimon should have fallen on his back; instead, he was rising. The demon kicked him like a football. Kunjimon rose high. He felt heat and cold intermittently. The raindrops in the clouds fell on his body. In the same instant, the hard rays of the sun dried them up. The wings of silvery birds flying past brushed on his nose. But he kept rising without a halt. Again, a great roar! Kunjimon plummeted to the ground instantly. That dark child was falling down like a raw mango. He felt as if a flame was rising from his chest.

He imagined he had died. But he did not fall to the ground. Instead, he landed on something soft. Panting, he looked around. He was sitting in the open palm of the demon. He felt as if he was a smouldering chirag upon a stone lampstand. The demon's torch-like eyes were turned towards him. The flames leaping out from them were touching Kunjimon's face. The demon shouted once more. Then he asked, 'Who are you?'

'I....' Kunjimon was at a loss for words. He showed some sign with his hand. Seeing that, the demon asked him again, in a voice as calm as he could muster, 'Who are you, child?'

'I am Kunjimon.'

'Why did you come here, Kunjimon?'

'I was on my way to the washerman's.'

'Don't you know that this is our demesne?'

'I know.'

'All right. I will accept that you have come here knowingly.' Placing Kunjimon down on the ground like a black plaything, the demon continued, 'You can come along with me.'

'Ayyo! I can't.'

'Why?'

'I....'

'What's it about you? Tell me everything.'

'I.... I am afraid,' Kunjimon said, in a feeble voice.

'Are you frightened of my appearance? I will not harm you. I will let you live with me. I will give you everything you need.'

'I don't want anything.'

'Fool! Listen carefully to what I am saying. I will collect for you the nectar from all the flowers of the world. I will clothe you in garments studded with jewels. I will collect from the netherworld diamonds like stars, guarded by serpents over endless time, and give them to you to play with. What do you say?'

'I don't want any of these things. I want to go to my mother. She will be waiting for me.'

'People forget more than they remember. After ten days, your mother will forget you.'

'No. My mother lives just because of me.'

'All that's what people merely say. Do you have a father?'

'No.'

'Didn't your mother love your father very much?'

'Yes.'

'Yet, your mother lives on, although your father is dead.'

'Mother says that I am my father's spitting image. Her sorrow about my father's absence is compensated when she sees me, she says.'

'Then, your mother will adopt another child and see you in him and be happy.'

'That cannot be.'

'Why?'

'It's me who grew up drinking my mother's milk.'

'There's nothing special about it. Look there.'

Kunjimon looked towards the direction the demon had pointed. There, at the base of a tree in the jungle, a lioness suckling her cubs.

The demon asked him, 'Will this cat-eyed one live forever with her cubs. Once the cubs grow up, they will go on their way. I know the mother of this lioness. But she doesn't know where her mother is. This lioness has forgotten about her. Your mother too will forget you.'

'My mother is not like the lioness. She will never forget me.'

'It is this kind of belief that makes men powerless.'

'I grow powerful when I think of Mother.'

The demon laughed. It reverberated as if from the interiors of a cavern.

'Please let me go!' Kunjimon begged.

'You are powerful, aren't you? Think about your mother. Then you will get more power. Then you can defeat me and go.'

'Why do you detain me so?' Kunjimon asked the demon.

'Because I like you. I like Kunjimon very much. Please come along with me.'

'Please don't take me with you. Is it right to do so, merely because I am less powerful than you?'

The demon thought over it for a while. He looked keenly at the child's face. The flames that leapt out of those torches did not have the heat they had a little while ago.

'I don't plan to defeat you using my might. I will make you as powerful as I am. You can defeat me then. If you can do that, you can leave.'

'Will I be able to defeat a demon?'

'Try and see. If you defeat me, I will be your slave. If I win, you don't have to become my slave. You need only to live with me. What do you think?'

'Please don't!'

'I have done all that I could do for you. Now, do as you like.' The demon caressed the thechchi thicket next to him. It turned into a black rock with red blotches on it. Sitting on it, the demon said, 'You decide.'

The demon raised his hands upward and roared, 'Come.'

He did not know from where the sweet fruits had fallen to the ground. Then, the skinned thighs of a bison also fell. The demon pushed the sweet fruits towards Kunjimon and said, 'Eat!' Then he tore at the bison's thighs between his enormous canines.

Kunjimon did not touch the fruits. His head was bent, he was deep in thought. The demon hurled the leftover bones to the marsh beyond. They got stuck in the mud. A moment later, those bones turned into tree branches and bloomed. Flowers like blood drops! When his repast was over, the demon asked Kunjimon, 'Why don't you eat anything?'

'I will eat only after I am back with my mother,' Kunjimon said with finality. The demon laughed. On that tummy like a rocky slope, there was an undulation.

'Then, defeat me and go to your mother. I will teach you everything, to begin with. Do you agree?'

Kunjimon was convinced now that there was no other way. He looked at the corners of the demon's mouth, which were extended because of his giant canines. Then he said, 'All right. Make me powerful.'

'Now you are talking sense,' The demon rose from the rock. It turned back into a thechchi thicket and swayed in the wind.

The demon drew Kunjimon close and instructed him on everything. He attained the ability to move about anywhere on earth or in the sky. He could shape-shift as he wished. It came to pass that space and time were no more obstacles to him. When he had learned everything, the demon said, 'Now we are equally powerful. Let us engage in a contest. You can try to escape, and I will try to block you.'

'All right.'

Kunjimon suddenly turned into smoke and rose up high. Reaching the sky, he began to swim, turning into a cloudlet. The demon laughed. Then he blew. The storm that rose from it drove the cloudlet back to the earth. When it touched the ground, Kunjimon acquired his own shape. Suddenly Kunjimon turned into a blazing ember and fell on the tawny moustache of the demon. The demon wept. His tears rained torrentially. The ember was put out. Kunjimon rushed away like a storm. The demon blocked him by turning into a big mountain. Kunjimon assumed many shapes and tried to escape and hide. But the demon raised blockades in each case. Finally, what happened was a battle. Both of them fought to turn into big mountains. Kunjimon was defeated. From his head, streams of blood flowed down and spread even as far as the plains. In the end, Kunjimon told the demon, 'I shall come along with you.'

The demon hurrahed in great joy. Then he picked up the child, placed him on his shoulder and flew through the sky. The demon told him lovingly, 'You are a good boy. You are intelligent and, now, all-powerful. Whatever victories you wish to win, you may win them now. I will help you.'

'Hmm....' Kunjimon hummed holding fast on to the round ear of the demon.

'Whenever you manage to defeat me, it is at that moment you can return to your mother.'

'Do you swear?'

'Yes, I do.'

After that, Kunjimon did not speak. He was sitting on the demon's shoulder, holding on to his round ear. Below, hills, plains, and mountains came into view and rushed past. Past great rivers in which hippopotamuses frolicked; mighty oceans in which whales roamed like sentries; towers with domes adorned with intricate carving; ancient snake nests that turned blue because of the poisonous air—he flew, and they flew back past him. He could not say that the journey was not pleasant. Yet, he sighed when he thought about his mother. The figure of his mother, with her hand resting on her eyebrow, training her eyes at the paddy fields in the distance, waiting for her son's arrival, rose in his mind. Suddenly he felt like jumping down. But where to? Will the demon let him go? It was impossible. He sat quietly. Suddenly they dived into a cloud of mist.

'Demon!' Kunjimon called out.

'What is it, Kunjimon?'

'Where are we going?'

'To the centre of the universe.'

'Why are we going there, O demon?'

'That's where I live.'

'Why such a mist?'

'It is this mist that makes everything exist.' Saying that, the demon swung his arm once. The mist at that spot parted, and they proceeded through a reed pipe made of mist.

'Do you know what this mist is for, Kunjimon?'
'How would I know?'
'Don't you wish to become a king?'
'My wish is to go back to my mother.'
'If you were to become a king while you are with your mother?'
'Then I'd wish to be a king.'
'That wish is made of this mist. The virgins of heaven would be called here and made to weep standing over this. Their tears will fall in showers. A wish is made of this mist mixed thoroughly with those tears. If it's not there, then none of the beings will have any wishes.'

'Wow!' Kunjimon sat, his mouth wide open in wonder. He shut his mouth only when the speed of the flight made the wind rush against his open mouth.

He was sitting, looking afar. Suddenly he spotted a golden ring in the sky ahead. It gained in size as he approached it. The ring was now as big as the mouth of a copper cauldron; presently as big as the dome of a tower and then as big as a pond. It looked like a silk band around the earth.

'What's that, demon?'
'It's a ring of fire.'
'Are we going to fly through it?'
'Yes.'
'Ayyo! Won't we get singed?'
'Don't be afraid. Do you know what it is used for? It's with this that the eyes of tigers and the fangs of wolves are made. The single horn of the rhinoceros is also made of this.'

As the demon finished, they had already been through the ring of fire and emerged outside. Kunjimon looked back once. It was blazing. After that, he saw ahead a mountain that had spread its wings and was dancing. There were several streams flowing down the mountain slopes.

'Look! Elephants get into musth when the waters from those streams fall on their heads.'

'Oh! Is that so?'

They then passed through an arch formed by the combined beaks of two gigantic roosters standing on either side. With their fighting toes touching the earth, small wells were being formed. Kunjimon and the demon flew past their necks.

'Those cocks will always peck at each other.'

Before Kunjimon could listen fully to the demon, they had already left the cocks far behind. Darkness spread everywhere.

'O demon, I can't see anything.'

'Remain patient for a while.'

He remained patient. They were descending. When they passed through the darkness for a while, they landed in a garden full of light.

'You can get down now.'

Kunjimon got down from the demon's shoulder. He looked around. It was a beautiful garden.

'You can roam around anywhere here. This is my place.'

Kunjimon moved towards a tree which was in full bloom. Suddenly there was laughter. That tree was walking towards him! It was now a skeleton. It had a jewel-studded crown on its head.

'Ayyo!' Kunjimon turned and fled.

The demon stopped him and calmed him down.

'Isn't he the emperor? He was my friend for long. I subjugated an entire continent for him. Finally, he came along with me. Turning towards the skeleton he asked, 'What's it, Your Highness?' The skeleton burst out laughing once again and went back to his place and turned again into the tree.

The demon walked on, and Kunjimon followed him. There was a huge hill on the way. They had to walk along its slope.

'Do you know what that is?'

'No.'

The demon extended his hand towards the hill. It was a heap of human skulls. Then the demon said, 'These are the heads of the heroes of so many battles.'

Kunjimon stood without batting an eyelid.

'Come along.'

As he was walking, the demon placed his hand on a jasmine creeper bower. There, Kunjimon saw a skeleton wearing flowers on its head!

'She was a royal dancer. She succeeded in deposing nine kings.'

Seeing such sights thus, they neared a big rock formation. Suddenly a door opened on it. The demon and Kunjimon stepped in. Eating, drinking, and dancing were going on there. Everyone around was naked.

'This is my home.'

In that well-lit place, an intoxicating scent was wafting in the air. Kunjimon felt like opening his nostrils wider.

'Whatever you want, just extend your hand. You'll get it.'

Saying this, the demon fell on his back on to a flower-bedecked rock. He lay with his eyes closed. The fangs extending from the corners of his mouth glittered. Kunjimon sat watching.

He felt exhausted. He was about to lie down on the floor when suddenly a flowery bed rose up towards him from the ground. Kunjimon reclined on it. The light dimmed gradually. Darkness filled all around.

Kunjimon lay down, his eyes blinking. But sleep evaded him. Thoughts were racing into his heart. What would Mother be doing now? Would she be going around in the paddy fields in search of him? From those solitary tranquil fields, a call would be rising to the skies from the darkness, 'Kunjimon.... O Kunjimon!'

He felt as if his mother's call was echoing in his ears. He sat up and pricked up his ears. No. He lay down once again. The house, its surroundings, the master and the mistress kept coming and going in his mind. His heart was in revolt.

He opened his eyes and thought hard. Throughout the night, he thought about the best way to escape. He could not find a way.

The rays of the early morning sun were peeping into the cavern. Kunjimon raised his head and looked around. That light was entering through a flight of stairs towards the east—a corridor of light. Kunjimon roused himself up and walked along that corridor. He began to ascend those stairs. A soft breeze bearing the fragrance of lotus flowers was blowing in through the vent. He felt exhilarated, excited. He climbed the stairs quickly.

That staircase led to a wide courtyard. At its centre, there was a lotus pond. It was full of lotus flowers in half bloom. That courtyard did not have a roof. It was an open place. From there, he could see the gigantic hills in the distance, kissed by the rays of the rising sun.

Light was on its forward march, moving the curtain of darkness aside. Kunjimon stood watching beside the lotus pond. He had not seen such a beautiful morning ever. He felt as if his heart was boiling. The universe was smiling at him.

Suddenly he felt as if some light had entered his head as well. Kunjimon sprang up and burst out laughing. He inadvertently said out loud, 'I will pass this off!'

'What?'

Suddenly a question came from behind him. Kunjimon turned his head back and looked. He saw those fangs—white as ivory, curved like a sickle—glinting in the morning sun.

'O demon! Will you go back on the word you gave me?' Kunjimon asked.

'Never. Do you want to conduct another trial of strength?'

'Yes.'

The demon chuckled, his tummy rippling.

'Okay. Let's start.'

'Look here!' The demon looked.

'I will smile once. If you can smile like that, O demon, I will concede defeat. If not...you know what that'd mean?'

Saying this, Kunjimon smiled sweetly.

The eyes like torches stood emitting flames.

'Now, please smile like that, O demon!'

The demon tried once. But it turned into a roar.

'Do you call it a smile?' Kunjimon mocked him.

The demon tried again. But failed. He tried repeatedly and watched his reflection in the lotus pond. No. It was not turning into a smile.

His thick canines that almost filled his mouth did not let him smile. Even after trying repeatedly for a long time, the demon was unable to accomplish that feat. The sense of failure raised a gasp in his heart. He felt like pulling out those fangs. But that meant certain death. The demon was in a quandary. He paced up and down, perspiring.

'What now, O demon? Have you conceded defeat?' asked Kunjimon.

In a melancholy tone, the demon admitted, 'I am your slave now.'

'If so, take me on your shoulder and carry me to my mother.'

Kunjimon sat on the demon's shoulder, holding his round ear. The door of the rock tower opened. Passing the garden, the cocks' necks' arch, the ring of fire and the mist, they were flowing through the sky.

'O demon!' called out Kunjimon.

'Hmm?'

'Are you sorry?'

'No.'

In an instant, they reached the base of the peepul tree on the bank of the stream.

'O demon, let no one else but my mother and I see you.'

'All right.'

They walked on. When they reached home, his mother was lying down, weeping. Kunjimon embraced his mother.

'Where did you go, my son?'

'I have brought something for you, Mother!'

He pointed towards the demon. The mother was startled.

'Don't be afraid, Mother. He is my slave. Aren't you, O demon?'

'Yes.'

From that day on, the burden of looking after the mother and son fell on the demon. He had to scour around for their food, then cook the food, wash their clothes, make their beds—the demon carried out all these tasks instantly without any trouble. But guarding them at night was the toughest. Kunjimon commanded that the demon should turn into a dog and bark. The demon turned into a dog and barked. Hearing that, the other demons raised a din of shouted derision. They called him to his face, 'Dog of humans!'

The demon's head was lowered in shame. He went to a corner and wept bitterly, sobs shaking his huge body.

Kunjumon's mother, who was returning from the temple, was bewildered seeing that. She came near him and asked, 'Why are you crying?'

'Nothing.'

'My dear demon son! Why are you crying?'

Telling her about how the other demons were laughing at him, he burst out crying again. Stroking the demon's giant back, the mother consoled him. 'Don't be sad. I will tell Kunjimon.'

The mother raised the issue with her son. The son said only one thing in reply,

'If he can succeed in smiling, he is free to go.'

Days passed like this. Looking at the demon sitting in a melancholy mood, the mother asked, 'O demon, my son, why are you unable to smile?'

'I have these protruding canines.'

'Can't you pluck them out?'

'That'll be the end of me.'

'Suppose they drop off by themselves?'

'How?'

Thinking for a brief while, the mother said, 'If you have no objection, there's a way.'

'What is it?'

'You must assume the form of a human child. Then drink milk from my breasts for some time. Do you have any objection?'

The demon sprang up and said, 'I'll happily do it.'

The demon changed into a tender child. A handsome child, chubby and fair. The mother leaned against the pillar on the veranda, picked him up, and placed him on her lap. She thrust a breast into his mouth. The demon suckled on it.

On the first day, the breast did not let out milk easily. The second day, the milk flowed smoothly. As four days passed, the canines began to become somewhat loose. On the fifth day, one of the canines fell off. On the seventh day, the other fang also came off. That fair child rose from her lap and smiled.

Kunjimon looked at him and said, 'Now you are free.'

'You can go now, son!' The mother also said. 'Go along the right path. Don't be afraid of anything. I will watch you go, standing on the base of that peepul tree.'

The fair child stood looking at the mother. A tear rolled down from his eyes. He said sobbing, 'Mother, please don't send me away. I will live with this older brother of mine. Please give me a new name.'

The mother looked at the faces of both the children, from one to the other. Her breasts were oozing milk. She drew the fair child and the dark child to her bosom and cuddled them close. Both the children were smiling. Shedding tears of joy, the mother called out, 'O my fair son!'

THE SHADE TREES
K. SARASWATHI AMMA

Passing through the imposing gates of the convent, a saffron-clad man entered the compound. The walkway was broad and long. The buildings were far inside, so they could be seen only upon reaching halfway. It was comforting to walk in the cool shades of the trees.

How aptly have the trees on either side of the pathway been selected for planting! Near the gate, only shade trees with dense foliage have been grown. Even the passers-by along the road could get in and take rest under the shade before proceeding on their way. A little further along the walkway, wild jack trees were grown on either side. The inmates of the convent wouldn't know if marauding and gluttonous children prowled about and gathered the wild jack seeds spread on the ground like specks of quartz. Good fruit-bearing trees that would be of use to the owners could be spotted as one came very close to the buildings. Walking there one would get the impression that charity narrows down gradually to selfishness as an end in itself when pragmatism sets in.

From the courtyard, he slowly climbed on to the veranda. There was no one to be seen outside. The rooms were all shut. From the reception lounge, the notes of a piano were rising. It seemed someone was singing softly too—a hymn in English. He loved music in a general way. In his ashram too, there was regular bhajan singing. But the works of Jayadeva and Tulasi Ramayana were not in English! Besides, he didn't know how to enjoy Western music which gave one the impression that howling and hurrahing were going on.

Yet, this hymn was melodious. Its tune not only stirred the heart but also touched the soul and resonated. As if a tiny teardrop of melancholy oozing out, growing larger and larger. As if one was sitting in a tiny boat in boundless waters and flowing on towards the horizon.

He felt as if that stream of the song was touching now and then the wilted memories in his mind and creating movements there. It was not clear what it reminded him of. His intellect was not functioning properly to force a recall. Not only that; there was an inherent paradox—as if one was reminded of a hibiscus flower when one saw only a lily—in his mind being moved by that song.

The song stopped. A nun opened one of the rooms and came out to the veranda. She ushered the visitor into the reception lounge, sat him down, and said: 'I'll send the Mother just now.'

She left through one of the doors at the back of the room. Sitting on a chair, he looked around the room. It resembled an exhibition gallery. The artistry of the nuns seemed to be like the skills used in a cottage industry in which museum building came naturally to their hands. Trash such as eggshells and bus tickets had been converted into interesting artefacts, using a little painting or related craft! Even the colourful birds which fell dead in the compound had not been left unused. Sitting on painted tree branches, stuffed tree pies, kingfishers, red-whiskered bulbuls adorned the room. He couldn't believe that in the barren life inside a convent, such artistic hearts were at work. Is it that those fingers were not only fit for counting the beads of a rosary and earning punya, but also to make props that could be used in demonstration while teaching science and geography?

He reflected that he had not seen any of those things during his previous visit. Only then did he remember the circumstances of that visit. His heart didn't have the time then to look at beautiful objects and enjoy them or even to think about anything else. His entire attention was then centred around the pain of the people of that locality. When the horror of the epidemic reached alarming proportions by the passing minute, and the heart-rending lamentations of the people grew more strident and engulfed the bhajan singing of the ashram, the inmates who realized that it was the humans who needed them more than God at that moment, had set out ready for anything. But their numbers weren't enough to defeat and rout the enemy. He had sought help from all quarters.

It was thus that he had set foot in the convent one day. The women of the convent would have been stunned seeing a shirtless saffron-clad man as a visitor. But he had not paid any attention to that. As soon as he broached the purpose of his visit there, the Mother had understood; and promised to help him right away. She took responsibility for half of the epidemic-affected area. She promised that she would do whatever she could in her area.

It did not take much time to understand how great her abilities and compassion were. The families living close to the convent had already received some aid from the nuns. After his visit, the extent of their reach was expanded to match her promise, and the scale of the aid was increased accordingly. He didn't check on anything more on that score then, as he was fully engrossed in the relief work in the other half that he had taken responsibility of the inmates of the ashram. But without even enquiring, many things—in fact, a lot—reverberated in his ears. There were people who even claimed that the untiring hands of the Mother Superior had forthwith arrested the march of the epidemic. She might be such a lady of uncommon abilities. Would the imprint of her expert hands have left their stamp on the exhibits in the reception room as well?

It was at the same moment he rose to have a closer look at the exhibits that the Mother entered the room. In an apologetic voice, she said: 'Pardon me! I was a little held up because of my busy schedule. Please sit down.'

He said: 'I am leaving this locality. I haven't come to bid farewell, but I felt it wouldn't be proper to leave without thanking you for accepting my supplication that day.'

'Why thank me?' is what she felt like asking him, but didn't anyway. Her heart also had pained so much, seeing the pathetic situation of the community. Though she knew the need of the hour was organized relief work, she was not in a position to go outside the convent as she wished and work among the people, circumventing the rules and regulations of her organization, and was grief-stricken about her inability. It was at that juncture that he came to her with a prayer for help. The ashram of the Hindus and the convent of the Christians worked together without showing the differences of their respective religions and worked at tandem to alleviate the sufferings of the stricken people. By that time, the government's aid too had arrived, breaching red tape. Because of the pooling of all efforts, wellness and peace were restored in the community. And, also, into her heart, and that of the head of that ashram. In the place of the agitation that she saw on his face then, wasn't she witnessing tranquillity now?

Seeing her immersed in thought, he said: 'I troubled you because there was no other way. And, I believe that service to humanity is greater than worshipping God.'

She smiled.

He continued: 'It's not devotion to God that I have. It's plain love for humanity. I haven't until this moment acquired the Vedantic attitude that sees sorrows of the material world as irrelevant.'

'The majority of the people are the ones without that Vedantic attitude,' she said. 'Since it is not easy to change their mindset, it is our responsibility to understand the sorrows of the material world and to find solutions.'

'I am someone who has suffered the pain of losing someone I loved. I haven't experienced it from the third position, without actually experiencing it and merely imagining it,' he said. 'Therefore, I am unable to be impervious while it is happening to someone else.'

'That inability is called empathy,' she said in a compassionate voice. 'In essence, even that is selfishness. It won't be wrong if we call it lofty selfishness. Anyway, it is a blessing—for others and also for oneself—to be able to forget one's own grief while steeped in others' sorrows.'

Both of them sat silent like two introverts. He thought about the personal loss he suffered and grieved over it. She analysed herself and concluded that she was experiencing others' grief, not through her heart, but through her imagination.

The sound of the piano was heard from the reception room. The song was the old one. From being immersed in thought, his mind turned towards it.

Listening to it for some time, he asked her: 'That song is very familiar. But I am not able to place it. Will it be too much trouble if I ask you to tell me its words?'

'Oh, not at all! It is a very famous hymn,' she said in a sing-song voice. It begins, "Lead kindly light." For us, especially for me, it is the most favourite hymn.'

He closed his eyes and leaned back in the chair. Suddenly he realized where in his past memories had that song created an echo. The picture of a young woman sitting in front of a picture of Jesus Christ, singing the song with pain in her heart, came rushing. Many other scenes followed.

In the countryside, two magnificent mansions stood on either side of the road. Above the front veranda of one house, on the wall, a picture of Sri Krishna playing on his flute; in the other house, at the same place, a picture of the crucified Christ. In both houses, there was no dearth of money; and also of offspring. The firstborn of one family was a male; of the other family, it was a female. Lillikutty was the smartest when it came to the making of the atthappookkalam for Onam; Madhusoodanan was the foremost to adorn the Christmas tree.

Lillikutty would place on the nilavilakku in the puja room the candles to be lit before the image of the Sacred Heart. Madhu would light joss sticks and place them before the picture of the Virgin Mary. Onam and Christmas were joint festivals for both the families. During the Onam festival, there would be a feast every day for the family members of Lillikutty at Madhu's house. And vice versa, for Christmas. Madhu's younger sisters always complained that their achchan loved Lillikutty of the other house more than he loved them. But Madhu was afraid to think how deeply achchan would love—or hate—Lillikutty in the form of his son's bride. Lillikutty too was fearful as to what Madhu's position would be in her own house if they were to marry. By themselves, they couldn't seek a way out of this situation; to consult others—even to hint at it—they didn't dare. She prayed to God fervently for guidance.

He was listening to that song Lillikutty would always sing in a voice damp with tears, after so many years!

His eyes closed, he said as if to himself: 'I have heard it sung plenty of times. Not only this—another one with the meaning that life is but a dream. It was a very long time ago.'

'Those days when you went about in a tweed suit, right?'

There was a faint tone of mockery in that voice. Oh! Where did this question come from? This mocking voice was more familiar to him than the song. Calling out 'Lillikutty!' he opened his eyes and gaped at her in amazement.

She said: 'My name is Philomena Benedicta Beatrice. There is no one within these walls who has a name such as Lillikutty.'

He sat gazing at her for long and said slowly: 'I never expected to meet you again. Haven't I said earlier too that it is a past-life connection? It is indeed that.'

'But,' she said, suppressing a smile, 'Christians don't believe in past life or rebirth.'

'Lillikutty made me lose faith in humans too, me who never had faith in God much earlier on.'

'How did Lillikutty who gave up the handsome Paulose, cause that to happen to you? Leaving the rich Paulose behind, she eloped with the impoverished Jesus!'

'Which Jesus?'

'Good question! Has Madhu forgotten the Jesus he had worshipped with lit candles in Lillikutty's house?'

'Paulose?'

'Don't you know Paulose?'

'I haven't gone in search of the handsome and the rich.'

'The complete truth is that he had not come over to my home, either. Paulose was a friend of Georgekutty. He had insisted on marrying Lillikutty. Don't you remember Lilli's younger brother Georgekutty?'

He looked at her intensely, meaning, 'How can I forget him?' For some time, he remained silent. Then he said: 'I hope at least by now you have realized what a tempestuous course of action you had undertaken. Couldn't you have waited patiently for some more time, before plunging into this?'

'Is it the same person who knew Lillikutty so closely from her time in the cradle, asking such a question?' She threw a counter-question. 'Didn't you know that being patient has never been part of Lillikutty's nature? Madhu said he could not live without Lillikutty. It was quite certain that their marriage would never materialize without the consent of the respective families. Then what else was left but to elope? She was ready for that. Then what happened?'

'How would we survive without anyone's help in a strange land?'

'Working.' She said passionately. 'Weren't the two of them educated? Wouldn't they get teachers' jobs in colleges or schools? If that didn't happen, they could have earned a livelihood by giving tuitions. For that, one needs courage and confidence. It's not enough that one rolls one's head about chanting "love, love". One should be ready to sacrifice some comforts and to struggle. Not just tweed suits without creases....'

'And silk saris....'

'Yes,' she said in a mocking tone. 'Lillikutty's body should be touched only by silk.'

'Isn't it silk sari that a nun wears!'

He looked at her dress. That soft body used only to soft, filigree dresses, was covered in black, coarse cloth.

His face carried the expression, 'How this sight pains me!'

'That worthless man didn't have the guts to do anything. That chicken-hearted fellow always loved to wail.'

'It's such a long time since I listened to this kind of special name calling!'

'Oh! Aren't they badges of honour!' She smiled. 'That face gives me the impression that it gives pleasure to you.'

'Will I remain here so, if it is not pleasurable to hear? It is such a great good fortune to hear it from the mouth of the smart one!'

'Yes, it is because she is a smart one that you chanced to come over here to express gratitude.'

'Leave aside today's happening,' he said in a pleading tone. 'I am talking about things of that long ago time. Didn't he go to that godforsaken foreign land, just because he was unable to take a clearly thought-out decision? Hadn't he given her word that he would come back after finding a solution? What an atrocity was done, without even speaking a word about it to him?'

'What a joke! Is it atrocious to join a convent?'

'Is it not? Destroying two lives?'

'Keep your heart in check and use your intellect, and then tell me!' She said in a serious tone. 'Two lives destroyed, you say? How many hundreds of lives were saved because of those two lives during the space of the last two months? Just take it that Lillikutty died young.'

'I cannot do that,' his face turned more pathetic. 'I couldn't even imagine that. I will take it that I lost her.'

'That's fine. But there was only one Madhu to suffer deep grief over that loss.'

'Chicken-hearted and worthless, he is used to wailing earlier on!'

'Yes! Because of that, even that is not to be taken into account. Then, for parents who have many more children, what if they lost a daughter? In the case of Lillikutty, there was another speciality. If she had married, it would have brought not only grief but loss of face for the family too. It's for the best that things ended this way. Isn't it because love is wrong that it has to be concealed so?'

'If everything that is to be concealed is wrong, then our very body is a big wrong.'

'Yes! Have you understood at least now why we cover it up with more and more cloth?' she said with a playful smile. 'The Hindu sanyasis who believe that the body is not wrong is going gradually to nudity! Someone who went about in a suit might have given up wearing a shirt in the same way. Or, is it that the suit is worn inside, and the saffron cloth is draped outside? What I wonder is how this saffron-clad man can bear the sight of shop-windows displaying tweed dresses.'

'One has to grin and bear it. Hasn't one chosen this habit? I too have a doubt. During Onam, when Onam songs are heard from the neighbouring houses, do you feel like making an atthappookalam in the courtyard of the convent?'

'Hearing this question, one would think one can see a Christmas tree in the ashram during Christmas season.'

'Oh!' Looking at her head, he said in a pain-filled voice, 'how could you bring yourself to cut off that thick, curly, beautiful hair?'

'Suppose I ask you that question?'

'I have an answer,' he said, running his hand over his shaven head. 'The most beauteous thing I had, left from my life. I decided there shouldn't be anything beautiful left any more in my life. I felt as if I had taken revenge on Lillikutty.'

'It is not on Lillikutty that the revenge was taken.'

'On whom then?'

'On baldness!'

He couldn't help a smile. The taunt about his impending baldness was one of Lillikutty's stock items in mocking him. She had not forgotten any of that even now!

He said: 'It's because the inside of the head was empty that God adorned the outside so, according to Lillikutty! I gave up even that adornment.'

'Good that it was avoided well in advance. It is a good tactic to pre-empt an offensive by striking first. For, Lillikutty, who grew up in the lap of Madhu's achchan, has an excellent grasp of the origin and development of baldness. Wouldn't the apple of the eye of achchan inherit that baldness?'

'Hasn't Lillikutty escaped the ignominy of being the wife of a baldie?'

'Not only that! Lillikutty escaped being the mother of a baldie son when she grows old.'

Both of them remained silent for some time. Her words lifted the mind within the saffron robes from that visitor's chair and flew it into an atmosphere of a sweet and loving wedded life. As if its wings got caught in its further flight, he suddenly said: 'Just one son, and five daughters younger to him for his parents. If he did something unthinkingly, his younger sisters wouldn't get good husbands. His happiness would invite sorrow into the lives of all others.'

'What about her?' Realizing where he was getting, she said. 'What would happen if a girl with younger sisters, in the same way, went after her own happiness alone?'

'It would be worse than the first case,' he agreed. 'In the case of a male, people will show a little more accommodation. A girl can get out only after shaking loose her entire family. Even though you knew it, how did you then propose that we should elope?'

'She said it seeing the pathetic condition Madhu was in. Although she proposed it once, she never followed up on that. Lillikutty has always rejoiced that Madhu didn't agree to it. There is another thing. Both the families had left them free together, only because of their trust in them. She was not able to face the parents of both the families for such a long time after she had spoken endearments secretly to Madhu. The thought that she was committing breach of trust had always plagued her. It was because of that feeling of guilt that she didn't send a letter on that occasion.'

'My complaint is not that she didn't keep sending me love letters,' he explained. 'But before she decided to join the convent, shouldn't she have written two lines to me at least to consult me?'

'What for?' Her voice acquired lightness and pleasantness once again. 'Lillikutty put up a proposal. That was rejected. And he left for an unknown destination, without offering any alternative. Paulose entered the scene sometime later. For how long can one hold off one's parents? Knowing that at the other end was someone who went on cogitating endlessly, how long can one wait without doing anything and waste one's life?'

'I was ready to wait until the next birth.'

'For those who believe in many births, that kind of patience may come naturally,' she said with a mocking smile. 'In their view, time may not be of any value. That's why such people turn worthless! But, I, who has only one birth, felt that I shouldn't waste what little time was left for me.'

'Isn't life being wasted now?'

'Certainly not! I am not spending my time dressing up and gossiping like the women of big families. I do not have even a single minute to waste. Seeing the epidemic spreading, all well-to-do families escaped with their children. There were women like me whom no one wants, to look after poor people who didn't have anyone.'

'What loss was there on account of that?' He said, mixing jest and seriousness. 'People have started describing her as an incarnation!'

'Incarnations are found only in Madhu's religion. I need sainthood only.'

'Is it as compensation for not being able to become a bride?'

'Who said she didn't become a bride? Don't you know that nuns are brides of Christ?' she continued, 'I didn't say how Lillikutty passed her time waiting. She made some preparations to go and live together with Madhu if he were to come with a firm determination to elope. With the intention of not letting the glutton go hungry, she took many lessons in cooking. Whatever she learned at that time didn't go waste. Instead of one family, now it has become of use to several families. Bread, biscuits....'

'I've heard about it. When we could only pour some kanji for the poor, you gave them delicacies as well, as I learned. In sum, is it that she does not at all repent whatever she did in seeming haste?'

'Whatever is there to regret about handing delicacies to the poor?'

'Why is this pretence of not understanding what I am saying? What I asked is whether there is no sense of regret in the running away from home as the bride of Christ?'

'What I believe is that I escaped from an act which I would have regretted later on. Who should feel regret, but the ones who have done things that should not be done, causing grief to others in the pursuit of one's pleasure?'

'Is it because of that you undid a life of your own and chose to have an existence where there is no place for pleasure or pain? And caused the life of another person also to become likewise?'

'Is it because you existed without pleasure or pain that you rushed in here last time agitated to near death? Where had your pleasant face gone at that time? Ask the people if I have done anything to regret about.'

'Let those songs of praise alone. I want to know whether you are sorry for making me the way I am today.'

'I am really glad, on the contrary. I would have been sorry if you had become one who hates the world and hated everyone else. Or if you had become an envious person who wants all others to grieve like you. But if it is Lillikutty who brought you to your current level, then she is very happy. When people say that the person I loved is so full of virtues, my happiness knows no bounds.'

'Oh, oh! Has the opinion that I am utterly worthless changed now?'

'If the public says otherwise, what is the value of just a single person's opinion? The praise I heard was capable of even resurrecting the dead Lillikutty. She felt proud that without confining himself to the binding responsibilities of one small family he was able to make use of those abilities on a grand scale.'

'But didn't I earlier say the reason why I struggled even risking my own life for those who were not related to me in any way?' He reminded her.

'Yet, the greatness of man consists in being able to love—serve— without being related in any way. Over the last fifteen years, I learned perfectly well how to love immaculately. If not, within the last two months, Lillikutty would have resurrected, and burst out of these black dresses, got out and rushed to Madhu's side!'

'I was not able to accomplish anything like that. If I could, I would have pretended not to have recognized you at all.'

Smiling at that accusation, she said: 'Truth be told, that would have been the best way. How much time have we wasted on old stories? The inmates of this convent would be amazed by now that I have spent so much time with a single visitor alone. Only that no one will dare oppose me.'

'Why is that? Is everyone else as chicken-hearted as Madhu?'

'Wouldn't the husband's family bestow more respect on the wife who brought the most amount of dowry? I sent considerable wealth by way of money and vessels to the convent, ahead of my joining. Besides that, upon emergencies, even now help reaches from my family. By now, how much has been spent by way of medicines, clothes, and food! Money is from my family, and the good name goes to the convent. Therefore, they are quite afraid of my displeasure.'

'In short, it is like in every other family....'

'Not in every aspect. There are increased levels of virtues as well as bad habits. Like charity, gossip-mongering, jealousy, and spying are on the increase. It's just like that if there are so many co-wives living together, right?' Though she laughed, her voice carried the gravity of thought. 'We cannot blame them. Many of them are their parents' objects of vow-fulfilment. The parents will send them to a convent; the natural dispositions of the daughters will pull them in the opposite direction. I often feel that if they were brave enough to rebel, they would have landed in a communist camp than in a convent.'

He said with a sigh: 'Can a woman block out her motherly instincts?'

'Don't you feel sorry for me on that account,' she laughed. 'Those outside are hell-bent on keeping that instinct of the inmates nourished. Our orphanage here hasn't been able to satisfy all applicants. Then, isn't it the common dictum that even if the fruit is the bitter nux vomica, a fruit tree is levels above a shade tree?'

'I do not want to trouble you further, keeping you here sitting and talking to me,' saying so, he rose. 'Let me ask you one last thing before I leave. Did you really recognize me when you saw me last time?'

'Having known from Georgekutty that you had taken sanyas, I had my doubts. Not a mere doubt, but almost a certainty.' She too rose to bid him farewell. 'I didn't really wish to ascertain its factual status completely.'

'It was Georgekutty who wrote to me about Lillikutty joining the convent. Immediately I resigned from my job in that college and returned home. I yearned to see Lillikutty, visiting her in the convent. But wasn't it the wish of a worthless fellow? It didn't happen.'

'That was really fortunate. For, Lillikutty could not have been able to bear the sight of Madhu's pain. After joining the convent, she could return for good within three years. What if that had come to pass?'

'What if you had done so? Again the thought of getting good husbands for your younger sisters would assail you; your mind would have been troubled; you would be singing "Lead kindly light"....'

'Do you know what a consolation it was to sing that song? It also gave me the strength of mind to be resolute. Only good has happened to all because of that resolution, and nothing bad....'

'Let us not start arguing again about good things happening to all,' he said. 'There is no time for that now.'

For some time, they sat silently watching each other's face. A naughty young girl with thick black curls of hair frolicked in his mind. Oh! That beauty and sweetness are lying dead on the head covered with coarse, black cloth. Because of him, religious observances had killed her. It is not possible for anyone to resurrect her.

Suddenly turning towards the veranda, he said, 'As the representative of the ashram, I request that my gratitude maybe let known to all the inmates of the convent. I am leaving.'

CHANKRAANTI ADA
T. K. C. VADUTHALA

Thim thimi-Thim thimi-Thim thimitthaara—thai—thaara—
Thim thimi-Thim thimi-Thim thimitthaara—thai—thaara—(thim)

Hear O hear my Chengannooramme!
I have to go on a journey, Chengannooramme!
Where to, where to, O my darling son?
I have to go to Kunnumam Desam, my mother dear!
Isn't the girl at Kunnumam my wedded wife, my mother?
I had left her in the wedding pavilion and come away.
I need to see the girl at Kunnumam once again,
Please give me some kanji, as soon as you can.

The notes of the song rise like waves from the bosom of the paddy fields that stretch far and wide beyond what the eyes can see, and beyond the reach of a beckoning call. The song that is sung during paddy-planting comes out of the sweet, beautiful throat of some wench close to nature and gets repeated by equally worthy throats simultaneously, in a lilting flow. O! What an otherworldly feeling! The labourers of the paddy fields are together immersing the entire universe in an ocean of bliss.

The plucking of paddy saplings from the nursery and planting them in the wet fields in the virippu way have begun. This is called Nirathu and this is the time of Nirathu.

Those women stand in a row in the paddy nursery where the saplings grow thickly together. The Pulaya women, young and old, are standing with their legs immersed in slush reaching to their knees. Theirs is a rather large number. They are advancing like an army column. Their struggle is but creative and not destructive. There are two or three men right in the front, leading the female army. Their job is to make the saplings in the nursery loose for those who pluck them for replanting. If the saplings are pulled upwards, they will be damaged. To avoid that happening, the base of the saplings with root and all has to be loosened along with the mud block they stand on. Men have to do this task. Using a hoe weighing 28 palams, they loosen the mud blocks by cutting below the root level in the mud on which the saplings stand; and they are quickly advancing. Won't they lose face if they fail to supply saplings to be planted, to those who move forward fast replanting the paddy saplings? That's the reason why they are in a hurry. Are they fools to be outdone by women? Indeed!

Thitthannam Thaithannam Thaaro-thimi
Thitthannam Thaithannam Thaaro
Thinthimi Thinnaayi Thaaro-thimi
Thinthimi Thinnaayi Thaaro

A spirited woman among the women labourers starts off the refrain, the intro of a new song. Following the speed and passion involved in the work, different sheels are being introduced. The others repeat the song.

The rains and showers are falling
The fields are all filled with water;
The fields have been ploughed, made ready
The sapling bunches are hurled towards the workers.
(Thitthannam....)

Following the waves rising in the universe of that song, those labourers are repeating the lines in the tone of a sob. They have completely forgotten that they are a people who have been immersed in mud reaching to their knees. They don't also think of the upper castes who climb on their shoulders and bite their ears. They have submitted themselves to the enchanting power of the goddess of music who pushes all their sorrows into oblivion.

However, Kochchukarumbi is not in that world. She is merely planting paddy and advancing like a machine. She is not aware of whatever is happening around here. Not even a trace of the sprightliness that is evident on the others' faces is on hers.

Last year also she had come to plant paddy saplings in this very field. It was Thevan who had loosened the saplings for her, advancing ahead. How exciting it was for her to plant the saplings he loosened and advance! That scene from last year hadn't faded from her eyes. She remembered even now the kutthupaattu—a light, ribaldrous song sung by farm labourers during planting or harvesting paddy. Other times, it is sung to control the tempo of the work—that the other women labourers sang in a chorus, linking her and Thevan. That song had begun thus:

> As the rain showers its showers
> As the thunder rolls its thunders
> Did you see the new bridegroom coming
> With a flowery mundu gracing his shoulder?

When she listened to it then, she was abashed. When she remembers it now, her grief's dam bursts.

Beautiful, curly hair. Large eyes, always with a reddish tint as if he was intoxicated. A broad chest covered with thick hair. Sculpted hands and legs, limbs that would even put Krishna to shame. There wasn't a Pulaya woman who hadn't yearned to become Thevan's life partner. But somehow it was Kochchukarumbi who became that lucky girl.

With a bouquet of expectations, she had entered Thevan's small hut. But nothing had lasted long. They couldn't even see a baby's feet. Couldn't even finish their honeymoon celebrations. The dark and bright days of conjugal life didn't last. The boat of life didn't move on, buffeting against the rocks of joys and sorrows. Before that, the helmsman fell off the boat. And sank deep into the ocean of life and disappeared, never to return.

Only Kochchukarumbi and her dead dreams remained. She was passing the days, swallowing the bitter pain.

It was during the span of a single night that the thirappurappaadu and the kalaashamkottal of Thevan's illness happened—like the curtain being raised and lowered alternately, in quick succession, revealing the stage, during a Kathakali performance. And finally, the last beats on the chenda drum signifying the end of the performance. It began with chest pain and shortness of breath. The neighbours remarked that a cheramallan— the demon that prowls in paddy fields—could have delivered him a blow while he was working in the paddy field. A blue line was said to have been seen diagonally across his chest! Exactly like the welt of the beating by a stick. Those who had bathed Thevan's body revealed this. She had not herself seen it. How could she have seen it? Wasn't she lying totally unconscious for two days and two nights following Thevan's death?

Around that time, many suggested that the ritual of Vettatthuvaruttal— where the soul of the dead person enters the body of a living person—

had to be conducted for Thevan. Kochchukarumbi had agreed. But how was she to conduct it? It was not an easy matter, as people think. It was an expensive ritual, one that could extend over one, two, or three days. On all those days, the ingredients of the puja should be ready. There should be toddy, the powders for the ritual, and the colours for drawing the sacred kalam diagram. The payment to be given to the sorcerer and the singers have to be kept aside in currency. From where would she have made all these preparations! All by herself, how could she conduct such a ritual?

> *Thathakkida thanthaare....*
> *Thanappam thakkida thanthaare....*
> *Thitthaka, theyyaka, theyyaka, thakkida*
> *Theyyaka thakkida thanthaare....*

The women labourers are singing the paddy-planting song, with panache. Kochchukarumbi isn't aware of any of that. Like a mere machine, she performs her work with her hands, and advances. The others have already proceeded further, hurriedly planting their saplings.

> *O Kothampel of Thekkaanthiri*
> *Why are you so late, hey you?*

Kochchukarumbi feels that the kutthupaattu that the chief woman labourer sings is aimed at her, who has not planted abreast of others and advanced. She quickly caught up with them planting the saplings all along.

The disposition of nature witnessed in the morning changed. The rain stopped. The wind subsided. The sun stretched his hot wings and began to whack on the heads of humans. Anyone who could climb their way up above their heads have all done the same way till now; what is being done today is the same; what's to come tomorrow too, will be the same.

The bare backs of the women labourers standing in knee-deep slush and hunched forward to the paddy saplings become parched like a desert.

Kochchukarumbi doesn't make much of any of this. Her thoughts and emotions are more intense than the heat of the sun that ravages her back.

As her mind drifts in different directions, immersed in the streams of thought, she isn't aware that the others have finished planting and have reached the other end of the field. Poor girl! She is heaving sigh after sigh!

She received the day's wages and walked back to her hut.

The universe was moving away from the world of din and bustle; initially towards darkness, then towards one-pointedness and then to contentment. Kochchukarumbi somehow reached her hut and entered. She had never been so fatigued as she felt that day. The hut was engulfed in darkness. She felt as if the fire and smoke that escaped from inside her had filled that space. In that darkness she felt suffocated. Her life was pressed and crushed. Her desires had collapsed on the ground; before they could spread their wings and rise high, the wings had fallen off, and the desires had crashed.

The stone erected in the southern yard of the hut marked Thevan's grave. A piece of granite lifted from somewhere. From that day, she would light an earthen lamp and place it on the stone. Nothing can interrupt this daily ritual.

Her belief is that Thevan's soul resides in that stone. It was not only her belief, but of all the Pulayas of that land followed that faith. In whichever Pulaya hut one looks, one can see blocks of stone in its southern yard where the dead of the family have been installed. None of the dead ones goes away from the family or the clan. Some of them enter the body of someone from the next generation and reveal their presence. If they are not propitiated with regular pujas, there will be recurring mishaps occurring in the family. Therefore, the living ones do not deviate from such duties. The ritual doesn't end with the lighting of an earthen lamp and placing it on the stone. Once a year, there would be kalamveppu, placing of the pot, and a blood sacrifice, kuruthi. Goat or chicken are the especially offered sacrificial animals. Generally, the expenses involved in these rituals are difficult for any one of them to bear.

Kochchukarumbi is not financially able to do the kalamveppu or kuruthi. Every day as dusk falls, she would light an earthen lamp and place it on the stone. Then, she would beat her chest and wail, saying to that stone thus: 'I am not able to do the kalamveppu or kuruthi for you. If ever I get some money, I will do that with the fullness of my heart. Please do not feel sad about it. I too am distressed that I am unable to do anything.'

That day too, after cleansing her body, she lit a wick lamp and placed it on the stone. The living should see the light only after the dead see it. Therefore, she lit a lamp inside the hut only after she lit the wick lamp outside and placed it on the stone.

She is feeling sorry about her life passing fruitlessly. Before the drinking of the elixir of honeymoon ended, the chalice had fallen to the ground and broken. Not that she doesn't have the desire to enjoy it repeatedly. But what can be done? Today, she is forbidden fruit. The two of them had sworn an oath that as long as the soul and body of either of them were together, they wouldn't even think of a third person. She will not attempt any breach of trust. She is keeping all her suppressed thoughts and desires under the white cloth of sincerity.

Kochchukarumbi is living alone. All around, there are the huts of other members of her caste. So, there is nothing to be afraid of. Yet, the loneliness of the night time is unbearable. There should be someone to keep her company during the night, just to talk at least. She doesn't have anyone like that. A life without the support of a male—pillarless!

Vallon is someone who has broken her solitude sometimes. Vallon had been in love with her from earlier on. Kochchukarumbi too was aware of it somewhat. Yet her mind was set on Thevan. Not that Vallon was in anyway inferior. People didn't like him much. The wealthy upper-caste people, and the poor people of his own caste feared and hated him. The reason was that some rays of the 'new light' had entered his brain. He opposed antiquated observances. He also challenged the beliefs and customs that had been deep-rooted since the times of the firangis. He asserted that all Pulayas should unite and oppose the ones who have made a practice of oppressing them and squeezing them dry. He worked hard towards this end day and night. Vallon, among the Pulayas of that region, was the first to study English, crop his hair in the new fashion and to keep it brushed neatly; he sported a moustache like the tail of a scorpion, had a silk shirt with collar and ironed it to get its natural sheen before wearing it; he wore a double dhoti starched and dipped in indigo and walked about making a rustling sound. Soon, all the youngsters had lined up behind him. They imitated and followed him. For the Tamil upper-caste masters who used to look at the Pulayas as cattle, he became the proverbial speck in their eyes. For two-legged cattle like Kandankoran, who happily submitted their necks under the yoke of the Tamil upper-caste masters, he became a kizhikutthi—someone who exerted extra pressure on their laidback attitude. This is the history behind the hatred and fear of Vallon. No wonder that Kochchukarumbi who was not knowledgeable about the new ways, liked the mild-mannered, traditionally-bent and hardworking Thevan more, than a rebel such as Vallon! She will sometimes say: 'Good things will never happen to those who do not respect the departed, the leaders of the land, and the elders.'

Vallon doesn't baulk at declaring his love for her, after Thevan's death. The idealist and the steadfast person that he is, he could not have loved another girl. He lived loving Kochchukarumbi and begging for her love in return. Kochchukarumbi spends her days remembering Thevan and holding on fast to their mutual pledge. It is impossible for two people travelling on parallel tracks, to meet!

Like on many other occasions, that night too there was Vallon's presence in that hut. It was past nine o'clock. Kochchukarumbi had not lain down to sleep. She had just finished her dinner. She was thinking about something, sitting before the burning kerosene lamp. That's when she heard someone clearing his throat outside the hut. She called out in a rough tone: 'Who's that?'

'It's me?'

'Which me?'

'Didn't you recognize me?'

'No.'

'Open the door!'

'What for?'

'I'll tell you once I'm inside.'

She had recognized who it was. She had wanted him to quit the place; that was why she had spoken that way. But he was not the type to quit that easily. Finally, she was compelled to open the door. He got inside. She asked in a slightly harsh tone: 'Why have you come?'

'Just like that.'

'To come just like that you chose this midnight hour?'

'I wasn't able to spare some time during the day.'

'Why is it so?'

'I have so much to do.'

'Then go away after telling me what you want to tell me.'

'Should I spell it out?'

'How do I know otherwise?'

'Kochchukarumbi, I love y....' The words got caught in his throat.

'Wasn't it long ago?' she interrupted him.

'No. I love you even now.'
'What use is that?'
'Why are we living like this?'
'Can one die instead?'
'This is my final supplication.'
'What is it?'
'Let us live together during the time now left to us.'

Kochchukarumbi turned her face away. Moments dense with deep sighs. For Vallon who waited for a long time, the reply from her was a heart-rending sobbing and weeping.

For the Pulayas, there isn't a more sacred day than Chankraanti day in the month of Karkkidakam. It is on that day that the thaakam—drink for the thirsty—is offered to the departed. Even if it is by letting the living starve, the affairs of the dead should be attended to. Chankraanti is the day when the souls of the ancestors, passing their time in deprivation and waiting for the devotional offerings of their descendants, would arrive to quench their thirst. Even the most destitute among the Pulayas would somehow find the means to offer a coconut-shell full of toddy, touchings, and other delicacies to the stones in the southern yard.

Kochchukarumbi had also not forgotten about this. She had saved a little money from the daily wages she had received. This was the first Chankraanti after Thevan's death. She wished to prepare something for quenching the thirst of his soul.

As dusk fell, the preparations were complete. When she had organized the delicacies and other things, there was money left just enough for a coconut shell full of toddy. She baked ada—stuffed savouries with fillings of molasses and scraped coconut kernel. She prepared beaten rice. Pounded the paddy grain and sifted the rice powder from it. She put all these together on a thooshan ila, plantain leaf. First of all, she lit a wick lamp on the stone in the southern yard. Then she placed the thooshan ila with all the items spread on it. She poured a shell full of toddy and placed that also on the thooshan ila as oblation, the well-formed end portion of a banana leaf. She bent forward, paid obeisance, and then retreated. She re-entered the hut. The daakam can be offered within the hut as well. If it is done within the house, there should be a stool placed on the southern end and a lit lamp placed on it. The toddy and the other items can be placed as offering in front of the stool. But Kochchukarumbi felt like offering daham to the stone outside.

It was there that Thevan was actually dwelling.

The writ is that the living should eat only the leftovers of the dead. A portion of whatever is cooked should be kept on the thooshan ila reserved for the dead. After a while, the same items can be eaten by the living. The essence of the offered items will be sucked away by the souls of the dead! Yet, the number of items offered on the thooshan ila or in the shell would remain the same.

After a few moments, Kochchukarumbi went to the southern yard. The earthen lamp which was lit there was still shining, somewhat weakly though. The thooshan ila and the shell were there just as she left them. It was when she bent forward to retrieve the items, that she realized it. The thooshan and the shell were empty and dry. Not a bit of the savoury or a drop of the toddy was left. Alas! Kochchukarumbi's heart was shattered. She beat her breast and wailed:

'Oh, my God! I never thought that you were so parched, waiting for the offering! If I had known, I would have somehow, brought you much more of these items, even if that meant taking a loan from somewhere....' She couldn't say anything more. With a broken heart, she returned to the hut.

She couldn't sleep after she lay down on the mat. She was tired, tossing and turning endlessly through the night. As soon as she shut her eyes, she would get the feeling that Thevan was sitting near her. She didn't have the strength to look at the face marked with extreme hunger and thirst. How could she look at his face? For this past year, he had been waiting parched and hungry for the offering today. And she alone was the person responsible for that. If she had given him something in between, he would not have been so famished! Poor Kochchukarumbi! Pressing her face into the inside of her palms, she sobbed and wept.

Kochchukarumbi rose from her mat in the morning, much later than her usual time. Her face and eyes were swollen. The incident of the previous night kept cropping up in her mind. Uncontrollable grief and a feeling of guilt filled her being. She was standing leaning against the doorpost. Vallon passed by at that time. He looked at her and smiled quietly. She didn't like it one bit. Incensed, she called out: 'What's there to laugh so much about?'

'Nothing,' he said.

'What's there if there's nothing?'
'The Chankraanti ada was very tasty.'
'Ngha. What of that?' Her lips quivered.
'Nothing,' he began to say slowly. 'But at least by now you must realize that it's no use waiting for the one who is dead and gone, and offering him the ada savoury.'

Without waiting for her reply, he walked away.

Her face turned ashen, then sallow. A change of expression as if she had made a blunder. Her body turned pale like tender coconut leaves, and she perspired. Without knowing what to say, she watched Vallon walking away and stood transfixed.

THE OMEN
KOVILAN

I am faced with a five hundred-rupee-headache. I have five hundred rupees in my pocket. Yet, the expenses to be met with the five hundred rupees I have in my pocket! I had the list of expenses even before I had the money. I must settle all dues. I had spent the whole night doing a mental calculation of rupees and paise. When I got up in the morning, Suja asked me: 'When will you return, Achcha?'

'When I feel it's time.'

She hasn't brought me my usual black coffee. I did not show my irritation when I replied. Instead, I asked, 'What do you need?'

Suja said, 'Bring me a ribbon.'

When the house was on fire, she laments that her hairband was singed! Typical of the fairer sex! Therefore, I said, 'Not today. Let Suran's surgery get over first.'

She cried, 'You only think of him, Achchan. A ribbon costs only forty paise.'

I had no control over the expenses that had to be met.

As I walked to the bus stand with the five hundred rupees in my pocket, I did not think about the ribbon. I must get into the bus that is about to leave. I have five hundred rupees in my pocket!

The footpath was swelling with people as never before. Who is it that's after me, among the multitude either flowing with me or coming opposite me? Who was that person who was observing me while I was counting the money at the cash counter of the chit fund office? As I left with hurried steps, I covered the pocket with my hand. I cursed the tailor who stitched pockets on the left breast of the shirt. The damned umbrella! I am accustomed to holding the umbrella with my right hand. In playing the role of a heart patient, my hand is not entirely covering the pocket. When I got into the bus and sat on the left row in the bus, I finally caught my breath.

The Mother Superior had said, 'Find the money. The rest is up to the Heavenly One!'

The doctor had said, 'This is the kidney stone.'

When we got out of the doctor's office, Suran had asked, 'What is that?'

His questions began the moment we passed the hospital gate. Is that a trident in St. Joseph's hand standing atop the terrestrial globe with a halo around his head? Where does the water in the fountain in the lotus pond come from?

The hospital buildings covered an entire valley. Suran was panting as we walked up the road of the hill.

'Slow down, Accha!'

I slowed down and told him old stories.

This road was a dirt track in those days....

This road was a mere path...man was a monkey!

What I meant to say was....

I would feel like saying something. By the time I started saying it, it would not be about what I thought of talking about in the first place.

In those days, the path leading from the market to Kanippaalam was a string of mere dirt tracks. There was something foreboding about this place. People would avoid this path at dawn, or midday, or dusk. Any wayfarer who ventured along that path would be so terrified that he could hardly breathe. As he reached the big pond that existed once here, he would call out in a trembling voice: 'O, Kali!'

For the wayfarer to put even a foot forward, he has to hear a reply. Hasn't Kali heard his call while he was passing along the valley? The wayfarer is not sure.

The wayfarer calls out a second time: 'Kalye!'

Where has Kali of the tank gone? As he waits, the reply is heard. The wayfarer, with a sense of fulfilment, calls out a third time and offers an oblation. When his call and its echoes commingle and reverberate in the valley, the wayfarer walks forward. He is perspiring. Is Kali of the tank following him?

Suran asked, 'Where did you stand when you called out to Kali?'

'I don't remember.'

The path of those times is now within the walls of the hospital and the convent that belongs to the nuns. It is no longer the valley of those times.

Suran said, 'I want to call out to Kali.'

Pretending that I hadn't heard him, I said, 'A Reverend Father came to this valley.'

'I want to call out to Kali,' Suran insisted.

'No, no! You'll perspire!'

He said as if in exasperation, 'Achchan, you are always scared.'

The fear in my mind was about his illness.

The doctor said, 'There's a ninety per cent chance of successfully removing the stone. Let's hope your son does not fall into the ten per cent of cases that we lose.'

Why did I then tell Suran the story of a Reverend Father who was resolute and upright? That man who created a hospital, a convent, and a church at the site of the Kali of the tank, was himself a boy once.

Me too.

Suran stopped near the wall by the pond in front of the hospital. 'Is this the tank?'

This is not a tank. It's merely concrete.

I, who grew up in brown mud, don't know how to deal with a child born in a concrete structure.

Along this path, there flowed a stream. A tree trunk was used as a bridge across the stream. The Kannippalam, the first bridge, became Kanippaalam, as time went by. Motor vehicles carrying patients moved along the public path of those times.

When we got out, Suran had asked, 'What's that?'

He stretched his hand from behind the curtain. In the doctor's room, in the corner.

Snatching the film forthwith, the doctor tucked it in the box on the wall. A yellow light shone in the box. In this light, in the fast-drying darkness, touching, yet not touching the white traces, the doctor said: 'There are stones.'

But Ramuvaidyar said: 'Suran is suffering from raktapittam. Four shallots should be soaked in sour buttermilk in an iron vessel, after dinnertime. After waking up in the morning and washing your feet and face, slice up the shallots, mix in the buttermilk, and drink it. For seven days. The bleeding will stop. The lore says that it should stop.'

His mother wept. She said, 'God gave us one son. Let humans do whatever they want to do.'

Suran asked, 'Is it a microscope?'

We were in front of the lab. The sister who wrote the test report came closer.

'Is this your son? There are RBCs found in the report. Red blood corpuscles.'

Suran said, 'I want to see it.'

The sister laughed: 'You can't see what all is in your body.'

Suran resisted like a calf being pulled away from the udder. 'That is....'

The sister who delves deep into the minerals and salts of the body laughed, getting inside his soul. Her voice resonated in the chest.

I said, 'Does he want to see the microscope? Let him see it. Perhaps....' Sister, why did you remove your habit?

Why should this virgin who is bearing the weight of the strictures of her spiritual life all alone, feel this anxiety about Suran's well-being?

The door of the X-ray room was closed.

Suran asked, 'Is it a single plank door?'

The sister in the X-ray room acted as if she was bored, as she answered the boy's persistent queries. 'You are a fool, boy. Rays come not only from the sun, the moon and the stars...or from the fireflies. Your eyes emit rays as well. From the sources of light—stop being rash! Here, it is electricity which is the source of light. You must strip your trousers. Wrap this mundu around yourself. Don't you know how to wear a mundu? You spoilt brat! The microlight rays that enter from the source of light...lie still.'

When the developed film was brought, the sister lamented, 'The talisman around his waist was not untied!'

I said, 'I didn't know. You should have told me!' Then I added, 'Sister, in our locality, when the coconut trees put out the first coconut or even the first bunch of flowers, we tie a waistband around the tree bole. There'll come a day when even you need a cord around your waist.'

When the doctor was searching for the stone on the illuminator, what I saw was...around the source of the cosmos.... No, it is not the cosmos! In the black darkness of the film on the screen, the silvery orbit loops around my son's naked image!

The doctor said, 'Admit him on a Monday or Thursday. Tuesday and Friday are surgery days.'

∽

I am thirsty.

Ten paise.... Iced water.... If there is anyone thirsty...ten paise. My five hundred rupees.

The rupees were in my pocket. If I sleep like this...my God! I sat, pressing hard on my shirt pocket.

Tomorrow is the draw.... Kerala Government Lottery. Just one rupee to win a lakh!

Suja had said, 'I need a ribbon.'

I am not thirsty.

Iced water...ten paise.

'Where to?' the conductor asked.

'Are you asking me?'

Kdikk...kdikk... (the bus conductor rings the bell.)

'Are you sleeping? Pay for the tickets and then sleep. No charges for sleeping. Where to? Give me the change....'

I had set out with small change at the ready. I shouldn't break the five hundred rupees at any cost.

I wasn't aware of the bus getting filled. If I sleep like this, no one's hand can be extended from the seat behind, over the hand bar, and reach my pocket.

As the bus rolled out, I saw the hawkers on the footpath flying lengths of loose ribbons. Don't provoke me! I won't spend anything from these five hundred rupees!

The bus was starting the nadathupandi rhythm. Loading people and goods, it stopped at the next junction. But my eyes were filled with the yellow light of the doctor's X-ray illuminator. In the dark X-ray film that quickly dries after developing, the white traces wax clear.

This is the stone.

Tomorrow is Thursday.

After Thursday, it's Friday (counting on the fingers). But I don't trust it much. Bending the finger, so as to not get Thursday wrong... straightening the bent finger. I sat pressing my fingertips.

Friday.

A surgeon's scalpel and a stone are going to fight it out. Sparks were flying from my eyes.

Are you there in the operation theatre, sister? Can I come in, and watch?

Yes, you can. Perhaps by then, you won't be seeing anything.

I sat in the bus, looking at the flow of humanity on the footpath. The hawkers and the crowds were competing with each other for six feet of earth, for air, for their very life. When one's feet touched the ground, one couldn't plant them firmly. I tried in vain to ascertain how many people crossed a point at a particular moment. One coulomb, one ampere... but these livings beings, people, are not electricity! I remember—as the dispersal of the charge of an atomic cluster that yearns to complete the electricity flow in the gigantic circuit called the universe—each living being, each human being, is a restless atom. Like electricity in the relentless circling of atomic clusters, living-being-clusters accomplish their life's journey. I orbit around in my own trajectory—in the hospital, in the chit fund office, in the ribbon, in Kanippaalam, in the operation theatre. The bus stops again. Right in front of me, on the footpath, a young couple. The young man is talking. He is of a good height. Her long neck...long round neck, isn't quite reaching his lips. She is not listening to what he says. This bus could have stopped a little ahead. They could have moved a bit this way. If so, I too could have heard what the man was saying. The words that were dripping from his thick lips, filling her eyes and throbbing in the blue veins in her throat.... Below her throat, inside the blouse she is wearing, like a piston moving in a cylinder bore, her chest and ribs moving up and down, making her laugh in the continuity of motion.

In the braid that creeps down the back of the red blouse, a red ribbon is fluttering.

'Let Suran's surgery get over.'

All dues have been settled today. Today is Wednesday. Last Thursday...when the finger joints were bent, I was once again caught in the rupee-paise mental math. I woke up when the bus moved. The couple was standing exactly where they were. Behind them, the flow of the crowd, uninterruptedly. The customers in the shops opening right on to the footpath jumped up and down at the cramped place where they stood. They alone were at peace. In front of them, a bus. The passengers of the bus who cursed the conductor who wasted their time. Yet, their world was blissful. The streets witnessed a medley of vehicles. In the maidan beyond the street, there is a flood of noise from the loudspeakers. Yet, the two of them exchange sweet nothings. The words which the young woman was sending upwards to him. The young man bent over, to absorb her words before they wilted on her lips or burst out owing to their air or heat. Her bosom and ribcage squirmed restlessly in the unfazed intensity of motion. I saw the sun rising in the young man's eyes which had expanded due to the energy dispersed from that continuous motion. But the bus moved on.

The energy, as blood and flesh, like specks of life in blood...in the journey of a living atom, a stone created an obstacle.

Let's hope your son will not get into the ten per cent of cases that we lose.... But, it is not just my son. The sights which are no longer destined for me to see but are for him alone...in the continuum of his journey, in the valley of Kali, in Kanippaalam, in the city.

The bus stopped again.

This ship that runs on land loads goods at the backwaters of the junctions.

A ribbon for me.

The red ribbon in the braided hair...I could not spot it no matter how hard I tried to look for it.

The bus began to move again. But it stopped abruptly at the next turn. Someone screamed from inside or outside the bus. When I woke up, the passengers were getting up. The crowd on the footpath and the hawkers were still...they stood sobbing. In the chance nudging of a moment, I looked up. But my five hundred rupees! The passengers got down. I sat down on the seat holding firmly on to my five hundred rupees. Now, there is no one else but me inside the bus. I too must get down!

When I got down and looked....

The young man. In his lap...in the braided hair filling with blood, the red of the ribbon can be discerned. But the red blouse is motionless now.

Her body laid out on the street, her head in his lap, the young man caresses her, strokes her, cuddles her. But, the sun has set on his face.

From the crowd that lost its flow, the reiteration of an accident stirred hot tears....

When they were crossing the road absorbed in their own blissful world....

That young man, through his eyes, through the rays that were burning out from his eyes, groped for her life all over her body.

I groped my pocket!

It's just fine!
Did anyone notice me laugh? No one can see the mind.
In my mind....
It's an auspicious omen!
A corpse!
Kalye!

FEAR

PAARAPPURATHU

A fragment of a dark cloud appeared from a canyon on the northeastern side. Its outline was like a cobra's with its hood open. As I stood watching, it grew larger and assumed the shape of an elephant raising its trunk. How quickly changes come about here! Perhaps by the time I reached my house, this beautiful sky would be covered entirely by layers of dark clouds. For an unknown reason, the thought of such a transformation filled me with fear. When I raised my head towards the sky, the countless tiny stars touching the peaks appeared to tremble. At the slope of the western horizon, a big lamp-like star was quivering—like a fawn that shivers before a hunter. How quickly had nature's arrogance that had once boasted of containing within itself all the light and beauty of the universe faded away. The army of darkness made a surprise advance through the back door.

Is it my awareness of the momentary nature of this light and the inevitability of assault that has filled me with fear? This lake that frolics as it lies on its back and reflects the sky on its bared bosom, these valleys adorned by holiday homes with red roofs, and the snow-capped mountains that radiate an eternal beauty—while all these would exist, the vitality in me would surely be extinguished. When I think of this, I am plunged into fear. To have to sever my relationship with nature one day is an inevitable fact of existence! Like a locust that has set out from a mysterious source and is on its course towards another mysterious location, had fallen somewhere on the way and is now decaying in the soil. Just ceasing to exist! I have flown some distance. When will my wings get tired and collapse? The pictures of those who had collapsed on the way remain etched in my mind. How many before me would have had sat on this stone plank and enjoyed the scenic beauty before dissolving in the unknown darkness of time! There is only a faint memory of the seeker of beauty who discovered this holiday resort a hundred-and-twenty years ago. Even the internationally acclaimed hunter who followed the pug marks of man-eating tigers in the forests surrounding the lake is no longer alive. I am the successor of countless humans who came here before me to prepare the path for me and add to the beauty of this holiday resort. So many who arrived to escape the heat of the plains and spend merry days in the coolness would not have been able to return the next summer.

Ram naam satya he
Satya bol sachch he!

Yes, there exists something that is nothing but the truth. It might be Ram's name. It might be something else. However, even now, I see before my very eyes a scene: ten or fifteen people carrying a bier, chanting and moving forward resolutely with long strides, proceeding along the town's main street called Mall Road. The funeral procession startled an entire crowd that had until moments been immersed in waves of immense happiness.

Ram naam satya he
Satya bol sachch he!

That bier had come behind a huge barat. The wedding party had gas lights, fireworks, band sets, cars, a decorated jeep for the bridegroom, etc. When they reached the crossroads, the musicians halted before proceeding to let out the finest stream of music that they were in command of. The men in charge of the fireworks displayed the best feats they had planned for this occasion. The crowd parted and lined both sides of the street to enjoy the barat's magnificence. There was a veritable flow of the river of humanity along Mall Road. From afar, it appeared like a multihued carpet had been spread out on which the seven colours of the spectrum blended harmoniously. High-value people in high-value attire. Their complexion like rosy apples. Laughter, cultivated to look beautiful. Their pretence that they had not taken the least care in maintaining their expensive attires or their own beauty. It was at dusk, when countless people jostled along Mall Road by the lake shore, that the colourful barat had passed followed by the bier. It could not be discerned whose body lay on the bed made of split bamboo. It was covered with a red cloth. Four people shouldered the bier. One of them also carried a dim petromax on his head. There were eight or ten people behind them. One man was leading the chant, 'Ram naam satya he.' The others chanted in refrain, 'Satya bol sachch he!' The detachment on the face of the man leading the chant was highly visible. His voice seemed to challenge the thousands who were crowding the street, as if reminding them that however fancy their attire was and however groomed they looked, each one had to embark on such a trip. As if reminding them that in the next hundred years, everyone—the groom, the bride, and down to the youngest child in this crowd—would have necessarily completed such a journey. Perhaps such a thought would have shaken the happy temperaments of those enjoying the barat. Yes, I saw that wan look on every face my eyes could search. Even newlyweds, who had been married for only a couple of days and had come to celebrate their honeymoon, were momentarily overcome by melancholy. Yet, the most fearful expression was seen only on the face of an old man leaning on his walking stick, as if death was close enough to be touched. His equally old wife stood beside him. Surprisingly there was no shadow of dread on her face. It was only helplessness; perhaps she had come to terms with the knowledge that this was the final path she would take.

As soon as they got off the bus, I was drawn to the old couple. I had looked at the man as if I had unexpectedly spotted in a distant land someone whom I knew intimately. Words were ready at the tip of my tongue, waiting to ask him questions like how he had arrived. I, who was standing below the old cannon installed in front of the military office and absorbed in the vibrant flow of humanity, quickly walked over. I had a hunch the old man was smiling at me. When I drew nearer, I realized my mistake. What foolishness! He was a Bengali from Calcutta or Patna. Though he was leaning on his stick, he turned around and addressed his wife who was struggling to catch up with him: 'Gote sener mote noye. E batsar Nainitaler hotelwalader besh bhalo sujog hoyechche (It's not like last year. This year, the hoteliers of Nainital have a bumper turn out of guests).'

The old woman simply grunted in assent. I went alongside them, trying to recall the familiar face I thought I saw in him. I was unable to remember. Perhaps it was a relative of a Bengali friend who worked with me and then parted ways. Roy Chowdhuri? Sengupta? Sachendralal Chakravarti? Perhaps this old man was the father or older brother of that friend whose name slips my mind. I felt an undefined connection. As I was walking behind the old man, the wedding procession had come abreast of us. The old man waited at the side of the road. A pleasant expression had appeared on his countenance. It was like he was telling himself, 'Ah, not bad. It's the barat of the son of an elite family.' The moment seemed to have reminded him of the times in his life when he had organized prestigious ceremonies in his family.

Before long, the funeral procession bearing the bier arrived. The scene changed—a burning lamp was extinguished; the pleasant expression on the old man's face faded for a fleeting second. He could not forget the truth that the day when the vitality on his face would irretrievably fade was near. After that day, that man who I distinctly felt resembled someone I knew very closely, would no longer be on the face of this earth. The unceasing motion of the world's machine goes on even after a person fades forever. Who is going to notice if one among the countless locusts in the cloud collapses and perishes? At the same time, while there exists this lake that frolics lying on its back and reflects the sky on its bare breast, these valleys adorned by holiday homes with roofs painted red and the yachts on the lake that appear from afar like paper boats children make and float on water....

In an instant, the light of life is snuffed. I don't know anything about the darkness behind it.... Nothing....

Oh...I can't say I don't know anything.... I know about the palace of Naini Devi at the bottom of this lake from the assertions the chowkidar, Pan Singh, makes. Only those on whom Naini Devi has showered her compassion can make that place their eternal home. It is a seven-storey palace built in white marble. Around it, there are seven tower gates. Seven thousand beautiful maids to serve you. Not many have been fortunate enough to stay in the palace as Naini Devi's guests. Last year, Devi took three people with her. One was a Sikh youth who was attempting to take a photograph of the valleys while balancing himself on the bow of a tiny sightseeing boat on the lake; he missed his step, toppled over into the water, and drowned. Devi returned his body only on the third day. The other two were a Bengali girl who was an epileptic; she fell off a jutting rock and into the water. Then there was a Kumaoni boy who unable to stand his wife's infidelity had sacrificed himself in the lake. All three of them may be resting in the seven-storeyed palace built in white marble. Pan Singh has absolutely no doubts about that. He has seen Naini Devi several times. Devi comes for her bath and water sports after midnight. At that moment, the entire lake would be in a state of commotion, as if in a storm. Only a true devotee could see Devi returning to her temple on the shore, her wet hair hanging down and touching the heels of her feet. Pan Singh is Devi's true disciple. Who else can protect Pan Singh when he is on sentry duty at night when ghosts and demons and wild animals come out hunting? Pan Singh also has no doubt that Devi will take him along to her palace when the time comes for him to leave his body behind. All these miracles are manifestations of Devi's maya. Devi owns this hilly track that stretches from Nilkantha mountains in the west to Panchkula in the east. This is the Devi who was born from the iris of the eye of Parvati who immolated herself in the sacrificial fire prepared by her father, Daksha. Pan Singh knows many stories that illustrate Devi's might. One such is the story of Dorothy Kellen's death, an English maiden in whose memory stands a beautiful monument atop Mount Ayarpatta. Pan Singh says Naini Devi took away Dorothy Kellen's life. No rational thought can break through the ramparts of the fort that is Pan Singh's faith. And I don't aspire to go in like that. Let whatever Pan Singh says be true. Let Pan Singh's beliefs never falter—all his beliefs, including what caused Dorothy Kellen's death.

At the time when Dorothy had accompanied her husband Kellen, Naini Devi's playground was not what it is today. One could not reach by a motor car from the point where the train stopped. The footpaths we used to climb to the top of the Ayarpatta peak were not there. No one could walk through the dense growth of ayar trees for the fear of prowling wild animals. Even the rocks lining the western slopes of the mountain were full of tiger dens. Yet Dorothy, who was a painter, could not sleep a wink without having climbed the peak and witnessing the grandeur of the great Himalayan ranges and their snow-capped peaks. The blue sky formed a parasol above her head and the blue lake could be seen far below like the grandchild of an ocean which had strayed in. Harmonious music streamed into the mansion of her soul. This uncommon beauty must be recreated on a canvas for the world to see! Perhaps Dorothy felt no one else was able to internalize such a generous bestowal of beauty and reproduce it on a canvas. She would have thought that although her own talent was limited, the secret of this wild beauty had been unravelled only to her. So Dorothy intended to reveal as much of it as possible to the world through her medium of expression: painting.

As the clock struck four in the afternoon, Dorothy sat in expectation of her husband's return. Dorothy could see the lane that juts out of the Government House from her courtyard. But Kellen would invariably be late. There was a lot of work that he had to attend to, needing him to spend more time in the office. Even then, he would rush back home before five. Barely finishing her coffee, she would set off for the top of the mountain, pulling his hand. Or they would both get into a dandy. The coolies would carry the accessories for her painting.

Kellen would have been aware that the worship of beauty was an integral part of his dear wife's life. That is why he gave Dorothy permission to climb the mountain alone even when he arrived late. The very reason why he had left a good post in Allahabad and come to this small town atop this hill range was for the sake of his beloved. It was during their honeymoon that she had first set her eyes on this haven of natural beauty, and she had then returned only after leaving a part of her soul in the Ayarpatta mountains.

It was a clear evening. The full moon stood above Sher ka Danda like a platter of gold. Dorothy was painting a resplendent picture of the valleys where darkness prowled and the mountains wore velvety, zaried coats. She had reached the spot at about five in the evening and had resolved to return home only after completing the painting. It was not that she had forgotten her husband was not home, and it was quite dangerous to sit alone on the mountaintop after dusk. Dorothy was simply immersed in an enticing intoxication, as if her painting was slowly assuming a live form. As if she had gained non-human energy and was flying off towards a distant empire nestled in the snow-capped mountains. It was when Dorothy was entirely engrossed in her painting, having forgotten everything else, that she noticed a strange woman standing right before her eyes. Her face blazed with unearthly beauty. Hair, thick and dark, reaching her feet. Clinging to her flowery body which was the complexion of the full moon that had risen above the mountain, was a wet raiment. In a strange, captivating voice she asked:

'Who are you, cheeky one?'

Her lips trembling, Dorothy said: 'I....'

'Who are you? Why did you poke at my eyes with this stick?'

'Me?'

'Look! Look into my eyes! Isn't blood oozing from there?'

Blood!

Dorothy gazed into those eyes. Indeed, there was a smudge, as if she had dipped her brush into deep red paint and dabbed it there. Dorothy was trembling. The beautiful backdrop she could see standing on Ayarpatta peak, she could now see reflected in those eyes. Not only China Peak and the lake, but even the distant Nanda Devi and Trishul could be seen floating in them as if in a mirror. As she watched, that female figure began to acquire a horrendous form. Her head touched sky. Her limbs grew like deodar trees. Then uttered thus, her voice booming like the roll of thunder:

'Come, Dorothy. I need you for something.'

'Where to?'

'Come along with me.'

'No. I cannot come, leaving my husband behind.'

Thunderous laughter once again.

'Can you help bidding farewell to your husband when the time comes? You can be my guest in my palace. You can go wherever you like and paint.'

That gigantic arm extended towards her. When found at dawn the next day, Dorothy Kellen's body lay rigid beside her unfinished painting.

The memorial her husband built at the spot where her body was found survives even today.

I don't want to hide the fact that my imagination has added a few creative details to Pan Singh's narration. Together, they form a captivating atmosphere woven around the central event—that Naini Devi took Dorothy Kellen away. If considered more rationally the truth may be that Dorothy Kellen died on top of that mountain. No. I am not prepared to stray that far. Let Pan Singh's belief remain intact. Dorothy lives in Naini Devi's palace as her permanent guest. Devi takes Dorothy in a golden palanquin to show her around the playground. Not only can those spots be seen from the Ayarpatta peak, but one can see from each summit and the lush Himalayan valley. I am trying to imagine that jolly trip of yours: through Ranikhet via Somasekharam, you are going to Nanda Devi and Pindari Glacier. In between, you may stop to rest at Bageswar. But that doesn't mean you will stay back in the rest houses of Loharkhet or Dhakuri for the night. You, who are journeying in Naini Devi's golden palanquin, will not suffer from thirst and fatigue. During the nights showered with moonbeams, you will journey through the valleys between snowy mountains. You will climb every peak in the ranges stretching from Nilkantha in the west till Panchkula in the east. When I think of the wondrous boons you have earned, I envy you, Dorothy. You have turned this arena into your immortal residence...an empire of beauty which will never be lost.

⁂

The clap of thunder disrupted my stream of thoughts. I am startled awake. Dark clouds had enveloped the entire sky. Not a single star could be seen. The street lamps and the lights that leaked out of the skylights of the mansions on the mountain slopes have all gone out. Not even the flicker of a diya remained. I rose when four or five heavy raindrops fell on my body. I walked away quickly. No, I did run. Can I reach my residence before the heavy rains catch me?

ALLOPANISHAD
PATTATHUVILA KARUNAKARAN

I recline on the canvas chair and read. She lies on a finely-woven mat spread on the floor and reads.

'Etta!' she calls out to me.

I pretend not to hear her.

'Etta!' she says once again.

'Hmm.'

'Listen to this!' and she reads: 'The lawgiver of the Hindus, Manu, has decreed just a single karma for the Shudra—to bow before the savarnas and perform menial tasks for them.'

'Yes,' I answer. 'Are you a Shudra, etta?'

'Yes, Your Highness.'

She is interested in the Vedas. Studies them. Chants mantras. But I am interested in something else.

'Listen to this, dear!'

I am reading about the revolution in Russia orchestrated by the Shudras: 'Exactly at 8.40 a.m., when a man in a dishevelled attire appeared on the scene, an applause that sounded like the roll of thunder welcomed him. A short, thickly set body. A balding head with a bulging forehead. Small eyes, snub nose, and a large mouth. On his face, shaven smooth, were the indications of a beard which was already famous and would be for years to come. The trousers he wore would fit much longer legs. There are only a few others in history, who were not colourful enough to become the object of adoration of the public, have earned love and respect as he did.'

'Who is this great man?' she asks.

'Lenin.'

'Etta!'

'Hmm.'

'Are you really forty-three years old?'

'Really.'

'May I pluck your white hairs?'

'No.'

'I saw Ajitha yesterday.'
'Where?'
'At the bus stand. She was selling the Red Book.'
'Alone?'
'No. There were several onlookers. What are you thinking about, etta?'
'Nothing. Listen to this: Those small eyes lazily travel over countless heads. He isn't even aware of the great and sustained roar of their cheer. Lenin said: "6 November is too early and 8 November is too late. 7 November is the right date. Congress is in session on that day. Let us tell them: Here's power! What are you going to do with it?"'

'Ajitha is too fatigued and thin,' she said. 'On whose side are you on, etta?'

'Before my hair turned grey and before you were born, I had undergone training in the gurukulam of Namboodiripad.'

'What was your role?'

'That of a servant. Isn't Namboodiripad a savarna?'

She has curly hair. She never restrains it by properly tying it down. She brought the end of a strand to her mouth and chews on it.

'Do you like me, etta?'
'No.'
'May I read the Vedas?'
'Mmm.'

She read: 'The soul is not gendered. But the body is. In the Vedas, Isvar is denoted by "it" and not "he". If "he" is used, it would seem that Isvar is male. But "it" which is "nirguna" or without qualities is used instead. This philosophy is called Advaitam.'

'Wonder?' I say.

She gets up and holds her hair together over her forehead.

'Look. Is it beautiful?'

'No, it is not. You look like a muni.' She likes to be thought of as a yakshi and not a muni.

'Shall I go and wear the sandal paste dot on my forehead?'
'Do whatever you want. Don't disturb me.'

She comes and sits on the chair next to mine.

'Edathy would not like me sitting so very close to you, ettan.'
'Then you must sit a little apart.'

'I won't.'

She spills her hair forward to cover her face.

'What did Namboodiripad train the Shudras to do?' she asks.

'Armed revolution.'

'How smart! What's this revolution for?'

'To give the paddy fields to farm labourers.'

'My father's fields too?'

'Even those.'

'The whole of it?'

'The whole of it.'

'How will we live, then?'

'We have to toil.'

'Me too?'

'You, and the one who marries you too.'

'O my mother!'

I read again. 'At this juncture, a man with long hair and sunken face—once a captain in the Czar's army and later exiled as a revolutionary, mathematician, and chess player—Antonov—was sitting alone in a room in the upper floor and crafting a detailed plan to overtake the capital.'

'Who do you truly love, etta?'

'Your edathy. My wife.'

'Look here! Didn't you quarrel with edathy exactly at 8.30 p.m. yesterday?'

'Hmm.'

'What for?'

'Just for fun.'

'No. Let me say it?'

'Hmm.'

'For placing your hand on my shoulder.'

I don't even pretend to hear what she said.

'Edathy had seen it.'

'You! Keep quiet.'

'Are you cross with everyone, ettan?'

'Yes.'

'It's because you went to study armed revolution? How old were you at that time?'

'Fourteen.'

'Then?'

'I went to join the revolution. At Vayalar.'
'What for?'
'For the Shudras to capture power.'
'Didn't you all get thoroughly defeated?'
'It's not like that. It paved the seeds for revolution in this land.'
'You are old enough to be my father, ettan.'
'Yes.'
'Why do you need revolutions now?'
'The revolution is not for me alone.'
She flips the hair away from her face and opens the book.
'Do you want to listen to what the Kathopanishad says, etta? Wake up, rise, and march until you reach your destination.'
She raises the book and stares at me.
'Isn't power now in the hands of Namboodiripad, the divine personality who taught you all about the revolution?'
'Yes. But Namboodiripad is not a Shudra. He is an Aaddhyan! Listen to this: Lenin read out the ruling of the revolutionary government. "All rights of the landlords at this moment are cancelled without any remuneration. Even if the land belongs to the feudal chief, or the church, or the landlord, its rights, including that of their produce, are now vested in the land distribution committees. This rule doesn't apply to the land of the farmer who himself tills his land."'
'Etta! The land belongs to God!'
'Yes! To Vishnu Namboodiripad. But the right to harvest the produce should be vested in the Shudras.'
'Ajitha and I are of the same age.'
'Yes. But she is strong enough to hold a gun.'
'They beat up very badly....'
'Who?'
'Ajitha's mother.'
'Hmm.'
'They kicked....'
'Whom?'
'Gopalan whose hand was severed in the explosion. The policemen....'
I read on: 'Exactly at 2 p.m., the proposed rule regarding land distribution was put to the vote. Only one hand was raised against it. Thus, knocking all obstacles aside, the Bolsheviks who captured power through armed revolution, moved forward with confidence.'

'Edathy didn't like marrying you, etta,' she says with a mysterious smile.

'How do you know?'

'I know.'

'Did she tell you?'

'She told Amma. Reason number one: you were much older than her. Number two: you were not as handsome as she expected.'

'How old were you, then?'

'Nine. Mother said ettan's family was very rich.'

She inched closer to him.

'Edathy did have other good marriage proposals.'

'What happened to them? Didn't they have enough money?'

'Oh, they too were all very rich. But edathy didn't like any of them. Achchan got mad. He kept shouting at her. Then edathy said: "Do what you like, achcha!"'

'Go and study the Vedas now.'

'Edathy wept the first time you came to see her.'

'You go to the next room and read, please.'

'I like you very much, etta.'

'Thanks.'

'Shall I go and take a bath?'

'Don't be late. And don't forget to smear the holy ash on your forehead.'

She goes, but returns quickly.

'Touch my forehead and see. I feel like I have temperature.'

I touch her forehead.

'Nothing. Your forehead is cool.'

'Your hand is very warm, etta.'

She leaves again.

Oh! What a relief! I began reading again: 'Two-thirty at night. Thick silence had settled in the hall. Kamanev was reading out the Executive Authority Act: "Until the Constituent Assembly is convened, the total administrative power will be vested in the government of the farmer–labourer–soldier. It will be called the Council of People's Commissars."'

The historian records passionately: 'It was for this moment that the martyrs of the March Revolution were lying expectantly in the chilly tombs of Mars Field. It was for this moment that several thousands of people sacrificed their lives in jails, in exiled foreign strands, and the mines of Siberia.'

The harsh noise of the shower rose from the bathroom, and in the background, you could hear her sing. She will come out right after her bath, saying she wants to dry her hair. Won't leave me in peace.

I continued reading: 'Leaning against the walls and corners of the Assembly Hall were rows of bayonets. All over the country, the Bolsheviks were taking up arms. Kerensky, who was in power, was preparing to launch a counter-revolution. The southwestern wind carries the clarion call of revolt. The preparation for that decisive battle in full swing. There was time left yet for dawn to arrive.'

The noise of the shower and the singing stop simultaneously. The bathroom was silent.

'Etta!'

'What is it?'

'Please get me the towel from the stand.'

A deep rumbling in the heart.

'Don't be afraid. Edathy is in the room upstairs.'

She takes the towel through the slightly opened door.

'Shall I chant a mantra for you?' she asks, and then continues, 'tamevaikam janetha atmanam anyavachopi munchana! It means know only the soul. Don't listen to anything else.'

'Edathy is sound asleep.'

I pick up the book again and purposely go back to the Russian autumn of 1917. Kerensky is preparing to retake Petrograd using armed Cossacks. The revolution was in jeopardy! People's Commissar Leon Trotsky exhorts the workers to save the People's Government born just the previous day.

'Move on to Petrograd! We have already captured power. Now preserve it! Extend a supporting arm to the Revolutionary Army and the Red Guards. Wherever there are arms and ammunition, commandeer them! For each revolutionary, kill at least five counter-revolutionaries.'

From the bathroom, she asks in a hushed voice: 'May I take one of your razor blades, etta?'

'Don't.'

'Miser.'

'What do you need a razor blade for?'

'I need it.'

'Ask your edathy.'

'I don't need it.'

The historian records: 'The giant cannons of three warships were trained on the entrance to Petrograd.'

She says aloud: 'Etta! The soul need not be a part of your life. That's why the soul doesn't age. The soul that gets liberated from life.'

The next day, Sunday, when Kerensky mounted on a white steed, entered Petrograd with the Cossacks bringing up the rear guard, the church bells began to toll.

'The city woke up to the sound of gunfire. When they got out to the dark, silent streets, the forbidding noise of factory sirens rose. Like masses of garbage drifting, thousands of workers—men, women, and children—were out and about. They move towards Moscowsky Gate with guns, spears, barbed wires, and whatever else they could get hold of. The unnamed, disorderly community flows along the slush-filled paths like the diluvial flow of a dam burst. The combatants were ready to salvage their revolution with their bare chests. This was their battle.'

She comes out of the bathroom, a big towel draped around her. Yet her expression suggests that she feels she is fully dressed.

'May I switch the fan on?'

'First go and wear your sari.'

'Don't rush, etta! Let my hair dry.'

'Don't let your edathy see you by my side, in this state of undress.'

'Oh! Aren't you an old man? If edathy comes now, she will say, "The virgin is offering an oblation to the revolutionary!"'

'Hey, you! Get you gone!'

Soft, white snowflakes were falling. Kerensky's counter-revolutionary Cossacks were ready for the battle. Their antagonists were the Red Guards of the Revolutionary Army and the crowds of bizarrely armed workers! When the poor revolutionary army of those poor people who didn't know war strategy was left with no other way in that decisive battle, they swelled forward en masse like a gigantic high tide. They pulled the Cossacks down from their horses and tore them apart. The Cossacks who broke from their battle formation turned around and took to their heels! An old worker, unable to contain his surging emotions, said: 'This is mine! This is mine entirely. My Petrograd!'

'Etta! Before Namboodiripad took over power, didn't he visit the comrades of Vayalar and thank them?'

'Yes. He thanked them and then took over power. But the first kick landed on Mandakini.'
'You are jealous, etta!'
'Yes. Of Mandakini.'
'Etta! Do you know about Allopanishad?'
'What Upanishad?'
'The Allopanishad that praises Allah and calls Muhammad Rajasulla?'
'I don't know about it.'
'The Allopanishad was composed during Akbar's reign.'

HUMANS AND ANIMALS
NANDANAR

Once the warm season starts, most of the soldiers go out after roll call. The barracks are located in a narrow place. It's about half a mile from the barracks to the main road. Once you get on to the main road, a cool breeze embraces you. At that time the green foliage of the neem trees that line both sides of the road dance enticingly. As one walks in the breeze for half a mile more, one reaches Sadar Bazar. The Sardarji, dark and stocky like a bear-cub, has his shop there. It is very interesting to see the Sardarji pottering about in the shop with his potbelly and broad smile. One gets into the shop. Drinks a meetha lassi or a namkeen lassi. Sardarji's lassi is famous. When the lassi is placed in front of you, poured into the crushed ice filling the tall glass tumbler, anyone would smack one's lips in anticipation. Each drop of the lassi descending the throat, gives the experience of the entire body cooling down. One feels like shouting, 'Sardarji, zindabad!'

After drinking the lassi, one moves outside and buys an expensive cigarette and smokes it. Or, one buys a meetha paan, chews it, and feels contented. As soon as one returns to the barracks, the first bugle to put out the lights is sounded. Then one sleeps, ordinarily.

But yesterday no one could go out. There was a command during the roll call. 'Tomorrow, the entire company should lay their kits out.'

'Damn!' everyone whispered in their mind. Because the process of laying the kits out is somewhat like what is meant by the expletive. Means, it is a vexing, boring, drudgery-filled task. There is a photo of the kit layout, framed in glass, displayed near the notice board. One becomes aware of the difficulty involved in laying out the kits only once one takes a glance at it. Not only that one should display the items issued to one, spread out as they are on the bed. Each item has its measurement, its dimensions. If one folds a mosquito netting, it should be so many inches. If one folds a vest, it should measure so many inches. The article called 'Brosess 26 inches' should be placed in such a place, in such a manner.... Many things like that.

Last week it rained continuously for two days. Thus the earth cooled down, and we had slept comfortably those two nights. Everything was fine. But when it rained, the raincoat, which was washed, ironed, numbered and kept safely away, had to be pulled out. Most of us had not folded the raincoat and put it away, despite the rain having stopped. To fold a raincoat properly and to stencil a number on it, at least half an hour is required. Which means a lot of work is involved. It was with this disquieting awareness that everyone had returned to the barracks after the roll call. The barracks were filled with noise. Stencilling in the numbers, folding the mosquito nets, putting a coat of Blanco on the web equipment—thus all were engaged in one or the other activity.

However, Charan Singh alone remained immobile. He was lying on his back on the bed as if he was aware of nothing around him. His eyes were on the tiny insects flying around the naked light bulb on the ceiling. Charan Singh had certain peculiarities. He wouldn't talk much. It was from Charan Singh that I had learned the truth that silence and words had their own value. His conversation had weight and depth of meaning. For that reason, I have deep respect for him, in the core of my being.

Charan Singh has no one in the wide world. He is utterly alone. But he was not at all alone till 1947. His mother, wife, and two children died during 1947. Not because they had contracted the plague or cholera, or any other contagious disease. Then how did they die? In lightning? Electrocuted?

Kuppuswamy, who was with him in Dera Ismail Khan says that Charan Singh stopped talking after his mother, wife, and children died. Maybe true, or maybe not.

I said that I have great respect for Charan Singh in the core of my being. That's what matters.

Charan Singh gets up early in the morning, takes a bath. Then he prays till the first whistle is blown for the parade. He has kept a copy of Guru Granth Sahib wrapped in a silk cloth. He opens it and recites sweetly, several quatrains from it. After the parade is over, he will remain in the barracks most of the time. He doesn't like watching movies, drinking or going out to the city. He deposits the entire salary he gets in the post office. Who was there for him to send money to? He had absolutely no one.

Charan Singh is a perfect soldier. He will work for sixteen annas. Now there is the stipulation that one should do naukri. It has to be done properly. One should be loyal to the food one eats and to the salary one takes.

Krishnan Nair said: 'I have intended for long, that I should fold the things necessary to lay out the kit, number them and keep them apart!'

Sunil Dutta said: 'Yes, it is good if you can accomplish that. Then you can rest easy like our Charan Singh, without any fear.'

'If I was rich enough, I would have had these buttons and the buckle of the belt made of gold, so that I could avoid polishing it with Brasso!' Krishnan Nair said, laughing.

Tilakraj came running into the barracks suddenly. He was the langar orderly for that month. Therefore, his dress was smeared with soot and ash. Tilakraj approached Krishnan Nair and said in a hurry: 'Nairji, please give me your mug.'

Nair was busy putting his kit in order. It was in the midst of such a thing that Tilakraj requested for the mug! Nair lost his temper.

'Get you gone! You won't get any mug-smug,' Nair said in his mother tongue, Malayalam.

Tilakraj said laughing: 'Aye, I'll hit you so hard that your teeth will come off! Abusing me in Malayalam!'

Nair and Tilakraj had completed basic training together. After the training, they had come together on transfer to the same regiment. And they were bosom friends.

'Why do you need the mug now?' asked Nair.

'To get some milk from the canteen and drink.'

'Would anyone drink milk today? Wasn't there be meat in the langar?'

'Meat was there. But I couldn't eat it.'

'Mmm? Why? Was it of an aged goat?'

'No no.... It was I who butchered the goat today. Don't you know that the day I butcher the goat I am unable to eat meat?'

'Here it is! Damn you!' Nair took out his mug from his box and gave it to him. Tilakraj ran to the canteen with the mug.

Om Prakash Sharma, who was polishing his boots, said in a surprised voice, as if to no one in particular: 'How does this Tilakraj muster the courage to slay the goat?'

'He is a Kshatriya. Not a pandit like you,' Kapoor, the humorous guy, said.

'I too have been thinking about it. This Tilakraj is really very young. Twenty, at the most. I can't believe it when I hear that this fair-complexioned, oval-faced, curly-haired handsome boy with pearly teeth kills a goat,' Abdul Aziz said while he was stencilling a number on to his raincoat.

'He is a handsome lad, I agree. But his guts is terrific!' said Sunil Dutta.

Lawrence said, spreading the fragrant smell of the smoke of Players cigarette. 'I have heard that an extremely beautiful girl had done something similar.'

'True?'

Abdul Aziz asked in great perplexity.

'Yes, true!' Saying that Lawrence put out the half-smoked cigarette, and put it in his pocket.

This gentleman Lawrence is no ordinary soldier. He has a lot of true stories to narrate from his real-life experiences. During World War II, he has seen the whole of Europe and the Asian continent. Lawrence doesn't see a place around as the other soldiers do. Wherever he is posted, Lawrence studies the geography, history, the social mores of the society, etc., of that region. Therefore, Lawrence has a lot to say about such places. He is an intellectual, artist, political thinker, etc., in our midst. Therefore, most of us listen to what Lawrence has got to say. Abdul Aziz stroked Lawrence's shoulder and prompted: 'Please tell us the story of that beauty who cut a goat! Quickly!'

'Che. Don't talk rot. It's not a goat that she cut. It was another animal which was cuter and harmless than the goat!'

Lawrence put back on his lips the half-burned cigarette he had put out earlier. Then he took out the box of matches from his pocket and continued: 'I was posted in Saigon for some time in 1946. You know that Saigon is in Vietnam. I had a girlfriend—a girl who was my friend—there. She was the most beautiful girl I have met to this day. A full, lanky figure. Narrow waistline. Blue eyes. Luxuriant, black hair. Long, beautiful limbs. Sweet voice. Musical, rhythmic gait—she was exceedingly beautiful on all counts. Her name was Tuyet Mai. I had made the acquaintance of her elder brother first. His name was Yu Tan. My closeness to Yu Tan grew stronger. Finally, I became their family friend. A mother, her son, and daughter—this was their family. The father of the children was a big businessman. He had amassed a lot of wealth. But he was not fortunate enough to enjoy any of it. He died just past middle age. Anyhow, that family lived in luxury as they had lots of money. They lived in a beautiful bungalow, in the corner of the least crowded locality of Rue Campagne. It was a French-style bungalow, with a garden around it. In the garden, date palms and casuarinas towered above the other plants.

'I used to reach their house around dusk every day. Tuyet Mai would be waiting at the gate, expecting me. Tuyet Mai means a tiny white flower. Whenever I saw her standing at the gate, I used to feel that she was more beautiful than the sky in the afterglow. Let me tell you in between. She was merely my friend, keep that in mind! We, Indians, do not understand the meaning of the term "a woman friend". Suppose someone walks with a girl here, people will be given to suspicion, complaints, gossip, scandal—all that!

'As I was saying, she would be waiting at the gate for me at dusk every day. As soon as she saw me, she would give me a flower: a smile flower!

'We would then proceed to the finely-furnished and adorned drawing room. Yu Tan and the mother would come in by that time. Then they would open champagne and pour it in the glasses. We all would sip the drink. Yu Tan and I would drink not only champagne but cognac too. Tuyet Mai and her mother would drink only champagne. Mai spoke French as fluently as she spoke Vietnamese. Yu Tan too. But he couldn't speak the English language as competently as Mai. She spoke English quite well. Then, she knew how to play the piano. When she was in the university, she had won championships and medals playing ping-pong. Till nine, we would spend drinking, playing on the piano and engaged in a game of ping-pong. At nine-fifteen, we would sit down to dinner. Daily there would be fish curry, pork, tomato soup, boiled potatoes, salad, etc., for dinner. After dinner, I would say good night to them and return to the camp.

'One day when I reached the gate, I did not see Mai.

'I entered the house and sat in the drawing room. After some time, the mother came. I asked her: "Where is Mai?"

"She is in the kitchen. She has bought a rabbit today. Don't you like rabbit meat?"

'By then, Mai approached me, cradling a white rabbit in her arms. I fondly caressed the rabbit. I then felt that a pathetic look was inundating in that poor creature's ruby eyes. Mai kissed that rabbit. Then returned to the kitchen with it. After five minutes, the hairs stood on my body hearing a pitiable wail of that rabbit from the kitchen. I sat there transfixed!

'When I sat transfixed thus, Mai was standing in front of me, with the rabbit, its head severed from its body. On her long and fulsome fingers, blooddrops were smeared. I shivered. I had never expected that Mai would cut the throat of such a harmless and meek creature. At that moment, I felt that her pretty figure was head to heel covered in that rabbit's blood. Distressed, I whispered in my heart: "You monster!"

"Mai, how could you gather so much courage?" I asked her, attempting a smile.

"What has courage got to do with it? It's just like tearing off a leaf from a letter pad."

'Saying that she returned to the kitchen.

'I did not eat the rabbit meat that day. Neither did I drink. I ate only a little salad. To think that such a beautiful girl killed a rabbit, as effortlessly as tearing off a letterhead from a letter pad!

'If it could be so, why can't Tilakraj butcher a goat?'

As Lawrence narrated his story up to this point and stopped, Charan Singh, who was lying on his back watching the tiny insects flying around the naked light bulb suddenly got up, sat bolt upright on the bed, and made as if to say something. But, he didn't say anything. As if he remembered something, he once again lay down on his back on the bed.

Abdul Aziz said: 'Terrible! Let alone a goat, I can't even cut a chicken! Hey Krishnan Nairji! Can you butcher a goat?'

'I can; but not in my right senses.'

'How then?'

'I'll tell you. Listen. I was born and brought up in a poor family. And we are poor still. I have many ideals that I zealously try to follow. For these attempts to fructify, I need money. At least fifty thousand rupees. If someone tells me that I will get fifty thousand rupees if I cut a goat, then I am ready. Still, I will not be able to do it in my right senses. To be rid of my senses, I would drink senseless. Johnny Walker, dry gin, or some such thing. Even at that stone drunk moment, I should be able to retain the awareness that I am butchering the goat to gain fifty thousand rupees. If you are ready to give me fifty thousand rupees, subject to the other conditions that entail it, I am ready to butcher a goat, or even a thousand, goats for that matter.'

Om Prakash Sharma said: 'Why should people eat flesh? How many vegetables are there which are rich in vitamins and taste! Tomato, spinach, drumstick, bitter gourd, cabbage—so many really good items!'

Abdul Aziz said: 'I am of the opinion that it is very bad to butcher and eat meek animals. But I like meat very much. Though I am fond of chicken curry, if a live chicken is given to me with the requirement that I should cut it, I can't still do it!'

Kapoor, the humorous one, said: 'I am very weak in this case. I too hold the opinion that it is not good to eat meat. Not only eating meat but smoking, using intoxicants, etc., are not good at all. Every New Year's day, and on some holy days I make the solemn pledge: "From today, I will not eat meat, I will not smoke, I will not even set my eyes on intoxicants of any sort." I may be able to live up to this pledge at the most for a week. Then I start indulging in all the old habits as before. How weak human beings are!'

Krishnan Nair said: 'Then, none of us can even cut a chicken! But how many were there in our land, who, like the beauty in Lawrence's story had remarked, could hack to death, with the ease of tearing off a leaf from a letter pad, so many human beings in Bengal and Punjab!'

'I can't even think about that! To plunge a knife into the breast of a human being, and as the knife is pulled out, warmblood spouting up, Allah!' Abdul Aziz, who hailed from Madhya Pradesh, said in a voice filled with revulsion and fear.

'The circumstances could have been such. The people were poised to avenge the deaths of their dear ones. The thought of revenge transformed them into animals,' Lawrence said, lighting another cigarette.

'Still, I dread to think of that scene,' Aziz said.

At that moment, Charan Singh sprang up on the bed and looked at the faces of everyone around him. All sensed that he was going to speak about something. His lips quivered, and along with that his eyes shone. He broke the silence with his heavy voice: 'Friends, what is your opinion about me?'

'A very good man!' Sunil Dutta piped up.

'Then, I am not a good man at all. I am someone who has hacked to death twenty people in a day. Like that Vietnamese beauty said, with the effortlessness of tearing off a sheet from a letter pad!'

Charan Singh had uttered the part in his statement, that he had 'hacked to death twenty human beings' in a loud tone of voice. Because of the force of words, and the hard way they were pronounced, the veins in his neck bulged out at that moment.

Charan Singh continued: 'Among those twenty human beings, there were old people as well as small children. These hands have chopped four infants like flowers. Would you believe it?'

Lawrence, the intellectual, artist, and political thinker sent an unsettled glance towards Charan Singh. No one talked for some time.

'Charan Singh, for what reason did you commit this heinous act?' Sunil Dutta asked him in consternation.

'For what reason?' Charan Singh sat for some time, his eyes staring sightlessly ahead. 'A month before the Hindu–Muslim riots had started in Punjab, I had gone home on leave. Our house was in the midst of Muslim homes. When I came back home one evening, the entire place was a huge expanse of blood. I never dreamt that my Muslim brothers would do such a thing. I had heard that cutting of throats had begun in our next village. We had been somehow confident that hacking people to death would not happen in our village. Therefore, in the morning, I had gone to my sister's house three miles away. When I returned in the evening, what I saw....' Charan Singh halted and swallowed hard. Everyone watched intently his Adam's apple moving up and down in his throat.

'My friends!' Charan Singh continued, in a slightly faltering voice. 'How can I describe what I saw? The head and the torso of my aged mother past sixty-five were separated and lying quite a distance apart. The necks of my children aged six and four were broken. The belly of my wife who was ten months' pregnant had been cut open with a knife. The head of the curled-up foetus was hanging out of her belly. Between the thighs of my wife lying on her back, a bayonet had been thrust. My friend, when I say "between her thighs" you may not understand it properly. I will say it in the barest way possible: That glittering bayonet was thrust into....'

Aziz's eyes brimmed over. He took out his kerchief from his pocket and dabbed at his eyes. Lawrence and the others watched Charan Singh's face, bewildered.

'Then?' Krishnan Nair asked.

Charan Singh continued: 'I had taken in this scene in a split second. Then I lost consciousness. I collapsed on the ground. When I opened my eyes again, there was a crowd of Hindus and Sikhs who stood around me. I looked at them intently. My eyes brimmed over. I burst out weeping.

'At that moment, a tall and hefty Sikh came forward from among the crowd and said in a hard voice: "This is not the occasion for you to lie unconscious and to burst out weeping. You lost everyone—your mother, wife, and children. None of them will come back, ever. For a slash, return a slash; take heads, in the place of chopped off heads. Hold this!" Then that man offered me a shining dagger that he held in his hand. I stood hesitant. Till that moment, I was someone who had not killed even a chicken. How could someone like me, then, hack people into pieces? I shuddered and shivered.

'Hold this! If we feel that you are a coward, we will cut you into pieces. Damned fellow! He isn't loyal even to his own blood!' Saying that he swished the dagger around.

'I was filled with a kind of wild courage instantly. I will admit it before you. My humanity had vanished. In an instant, I had turned into a brute! I took that dagger.

'Here, go along this road that heads south. Gather ten other people with you. You are the leader of this group of ten people. Like your mother, wife and children were hacked....'

'By the time that giant of a Sikh had said so much, everyone around raised a rousing cry. Slogans resounded: 'Head for a head; slash for slash....'

'My friend! I took up the leadership of that group of ten and marched in front. When we advanced about three miles, a horse cart covered with a purdah was moving towards us. Spotting us, the cart man shuddered.

'Halt!' I hollered. That old Muslim man who had dyed his white beard red, stopped the cart, alarmed. He fell at our feet and beseeched:

"We are poor people! Spare us!"

'But, within a second, that old man's head and torso were severed in two.

'It was someone from my group who had chopped off his head. With a kind of fiendish glee, I stood watching that old Muslim man writhing in death agony.

'My companion, who had cut the old man's neck told me: "Don't stand there hesitating. Instantly chop the heads of whoever you chance to find."

'I sprang up into the interior of the horse cart. I raised the purdah. There were two females and two males.

'Get down!'

All of them got down, shivering. I removed the purdahs of the two women and looked at their faces. Two beauties.... I plunged that glittering dagger into their hearts, one after the other. They fell on the ground and wriggled. Their last gasp! I was drunk with my sense of might. I learned that I could kill human beings with the ease of tearing off a leaf from a letter pad. I severed the heads of the two males, instantly, and their heads rolled on the ground. My mettle increased by the minute. Thus, my group hacked to death forty people that day. Of them, it was I who killed twenty. I.... This Charan Singh! Can you believe it?'

Charan Singh looked at everyone's face one after the other. No one made a sound. Everyone was highly emotional. Charan Singh sat like that for another moment. Then he stretched out on his back, looking at the tiny insects flying around the light bulb.

The bugle sounded from the guard room to put out the lights. Everyone rose silently and went to their respective beds.

CANDLE

N. P. MOHAMMED

A faint pain wriggles inside his head. Hamid pressed the back of the ballpoint pen with his thumb. Enough of writing addresses for the day. Tilting towards the side, he neatly arranged the envelopes on which he had finished writing the addresses. It was then that he noticed a card that had gotten under his foot. His dirty footprint on his own wedding invitation! As if a flame of fire had fallen on his heart and singed it! His head felt heavy. Hamid yearned for some light and fresh air. As he was about to get out, Umma asked: 'Where are you going?' He didn't have an answer. He wanted to just roam about. Merely that.

'Return quickly. There are hundreds of things to be finished.' Umma's voice had become a warning.

Hamid walked through the lane and got on to the street. He had intended to stroll along the main road, but the railway gate was closed. There was a black car, and from its inside drifted the spirited conversations of young women dressed in loud colours. There was a lorry next to the car, and beside the lorry there were tree trunks with peeling barks. They looked like they were about to tumble down. *Corpses of the forest*, Hamid thought. He continued lazily as the fading rays of the sun lent beauty to his surroundings.

He thought of going to the library. There, his friends would be sitting on the maidan wall, their legs dangling over it. At the crossroads, he noticed a large wall poster with his favourite star. *The Great Sinner.* How will it look when that celebrated actor plays the role of a great sinner? Should he watch it? Hamid checked the time. The film was about to start. He quickened his pace.

As he fumbled his way into the theatre drenched in darkness, the Metro-Goldwyn-Mayer lion was just beginning its roar.

When he found his seat, Hamid's enthusiasm waned. The house painters will come tonight. If he doesn't meet them and settle the deal, Umma would be sour-faced. He shouldn't have come away.

Why isn't he able to make a decision about anything? He was never able to keep his word. He didn't know what punctuality was. He would say something and do the opposite. He couldn't possibly live like this!

Hamid's heart shuddered. He was convinced that he was not competent enough to maintain a wife. What opinion can he offer about the designs of saris? He would lose his cool. The only way out would be to quarrel about anything and everything. But that would make her weep, and he didn't like to see anyone weeping. Why did he get himself into this tricky business? Again, Umma's serious face floated before his eyes.

He was only interested in reading novels. Their characters would laugh or cry, and they wouldn't come into one's lives. When you turned the pages, the day would fall dead. Then came the night. When he thought about the night, he trembled. His mind was disturbed.

The film had begun. He sat, blinking his eyes.

Umma stood at the threshold, pulling back the curtain. He raised his head from the canvas chair. Her eyes were brimming over. Tears streamed down her cheeks. His Umma was meek. She always acted according to his whim. The son whom she pampered and spoilt. That son used to say: I won't go to the godown; I won't take up a job either. Remembering that, he stood close to her. Has Umma heard the stories about him? Fear came into his mind like a lightning streak.

'Umma, is there a speck in your eye?' he asked.

She burst out crying. 'The speck has fallen not in my eyes, but in my heart.'

Oh my God! Umma has come to know about it! His only wish had been that at least his Umma shouldn't get to know about his clandestine relationship.

'How I yearn to see you marry before I shut my eyes forever!'

He surrendered. 'Umma, find a girl for me.'

As he uttered those words Umma wept. But those tears were laughing. It had been a blunder to tell her that, but he had realized only after he had spoken. Even his tongue had declared independence. Now he couldn't swallow his words. There were no opposing words coming out his mouth. Let what happens, happen.

He thought: my wife should be someone who knows her own mind, and be self-reliant. She should be able to do everything perfectly and in order, like my Umma. Let her rule over me completely. I will remain her doll. Then there won't be any problem.

His mind countered his heart: the problems will only increase. He and Umma will drift apart. The loud laughter from the bedroom will pierce Umma's ears. His wife and Umma quarrelling for possessing him. Marriage will be the beginning of a revolt. He couldn't help smiling. Even that smile didn't escape Umma's eyes.

'Why are you laughing like a madman?' she questioned. Her next words fell like drops of fire. 'Hamid, I know everything.'

Terrified and crushed by guilt, he faced Umma. Her blackened face. Her wrinkled and deformed face. Her eyes were as hard as glass beads. How did the softness disappear from her eyes so quickly?

'You should stop that game now.'

'What are you saying, Umma?'

'Hey, you! Should you make the mother who gave birth to you tell you that in bare details?'

Hamid had completely lost his face. He almost shrivelled up. Umma should never have known about the affair. When the sun dissolved in the sea like a drop of blood, when the waves raised a chorus, when he soaked the softness of her lower abdomen with his fingertips, when that softness spread all over his body like an intoxication, he had had no memory of anything else.... He never felt any emotion like love; she too didn't have any such feelings. Only bodily relations existed—they had a mutual understanding. He had never believed in love. She too didn't. But bodily needs were a necessity for both.

'At least try to become better now.'

He has no salvation. He was being punished so that he may live. The days of his freedom were over. Now, he should take over his father's shop from his maternal uncle, the manager. He must go to the godown in the morning with a bunch of keys. Must accompany his wife when she goes to cinema. Must take the child to the school. Daddy... bye...bye. Sitting in the shop for years on end, his hair will turn grey. He will develop a potbelly. One day he will find himself writhing in pain—a massive heart attack.

He will never hear that verdict. He should get his life extended to at least to hear those words. The stench of the corpse is a challenge to the nostrils of the living. When they lay the corpse down on the cot, when they carry that cot on their shoulders and take it to the khabar, opening the knot of the white shroud, breaking the cot down, and standing up, he should be able to shout: 'Friends, I am not dead!' How many from the funeral procession will collapse and die then?

Hamid opened his eyes There was a riot of colours on the screen. He blinked and saw Fatima. Some time ago, he had met her in person. He had gone to see the girl, succumbing to Umma's persuasion. He had sat alone in the spacious living room with its golden settees printed with groups of chenda players. His soon-to-be in-laws arrived. Hollow words and bursts of laughter.

On the teapoy stood an elephant made of black rosewood, with its elaborate caparison and ceremonial umbrella. Oh, elephant! How fortunate you are! You don't possess the madness called a mind. You are unattached like God.

'Let's have tea.' The brother-in-law invited him.

'No,' Hamid said.

Yet, when the young man caught his hand, he walked like a dullard towards the dining room. The horse shoe shaped dining table…it was trying to open its mouth and swallow him. He sat in the chair and waited. Finally, Fatima entered with a tray full of delicacies. He didn't wish to look at her. When she placed the plates next to him, he noticed her dainty golden bangles and the shape of her hands. She had the complexion of a faded orange peel. The uninvited fragrance of Intimate entered his nostrils. As she turned around, the ends of her flowing hair wriggled its way down her waist like the tail of a black snake. Hamid squirmed. Now he just had to look at her. Round eyes. A full, fair face marked by melancholy. The melancholy questioned why she had been born on this earth! It's a melancholy face! That's what he thought as he sipped the hot tea. He thought something else too… That she would burst out weeping any moment.

When he reached home, there was a crowd. Umma, uncle…so many others. That day, he became aware he had so many relatives. All throats roared towards him like guns: 'Is she okay for you?' Hamid had no straightforward answer. Nonetheless, they were happy. Then began the hustle and bustle. So many things to be done. The betrothal, the visit to the bride's house, the nikah, the wedding, the reception at Fatima's home, the reception upon return from the groom's house…. Words, like rubber balls, rose and fell.

Hamid wasn't aware of it when the lights came on in the theatre. Someone touched him from behind. Maybe one of his friends. He turned around. It was Madhuri. His insides burned. He tasted blood in his throat. Sweat beads rolled down his neck. Thirst. Horrible thirst.

He sat with his eyes closed. Slowly the lassitude passed. His brain began to clear. An unknown weight in his mind had made him immobile—he wasn't able to turn his head. Madhuri…. Great Sinner…. Hamid…. Great Sinner.

He had wished never to meet Madhuri again. He hadn't met her after his marriage was fixed. So many days, so many months. He didn't reply to her letters. He disconnected her calls. The word 'coward' was uttered from the other end—it drifted away

They had met accidentally. And they had drifted apart accidentally too. Hamid had not expected anything more than that. Neither did Madhuri. Whenever the need would arise for writing his autobiography, this secret relationship wouldn't be pried into. He thought: by that time, you would be a wife. You would be a good mother. We shouldn't break the integrity of the family.

Hamid reflected with wonder: how quickly was he turning into a conservative! He, who could imagine any cruelty in mind; he who used to consider humans a mere mechanism.

Why did she come to the theatre? To confuse him? The question was absurd. Events do not happen with one's consent. They would sit in the green cane chairs in the restaurant's terrace. They would discuss literature, life, art, philosophy, and politics. During those hours, they felt alive. They did not have jobs they liked. There were the jobless too. On holidays, they got together and read out poetry, short stories, and essays. They criticized each other's work. They enjoyed themselves, and then returned to their encampments.

He had met Madhuri in the college where she was a lecturer. He remembered her reading her first story. The flowery boughs on her tawny sari were yellow. When she slowly read out her story, he looked at her gold ring studded with red stones. The story was about a husband who immersed in the possessive love of his wife, had lost his personality and freedom, and in a rare moment, wanted to strangle her to death.

Madhuri portrayed each movement of that vacillating mind through radiant words. She wrote like a seasoned writer who had mastered her craft. The form was perfect; a good story, said Hamid. She raised her head. The borders of the red bindi on her forehead had begun to fade in the perspiration. When she raised her hands to push back the hair falling over her forehead, her breasts moved upwards. They smiled at each other. After the crowd dispersed, they walked together aimlessly. It was not along the way he had to go. He stood hesitantly at the entrance to the ladies' hostel.

'Is this the road you have to take?' she had asked.

'No.'

'Then why did you come this way?'

'Just like that.'

Hamid thought it over once again: was he in love with Madhuri? No. Was Madhuri in love with him? No. Their only intention was to build moments of light during those dull days. Gradually they had grown closer. They arrived early for discussions. Then they walked along the raw mud roads, their minds burdened with philosophical speculations. Things were like that in the beginning.

The shades of the casuarina trees had lent a tawny hue to the powdery sand on the beach. The sea and the sky met beyond the hospital, the beach, and the water. An unnatural coupling. They sat together. Did not speak about anything. The boats returned with dead fish. Dusk fell, but the calm sea was luminous even in the dark. When faint blue swords were raised by the sea's tired hands…it's hard for him to recall it.

They emerged from the darkness and into the light. The continuous tolling of bells pierced their ears. The fire engine rushed past with a roar. The hospital loomed ahead like a big mausoleum.

The gate of the ladies' hostel was shut.

'What is to be done?' Madhuri's eyes searched for an answer.

'Let's wake them up.'

'But tomorrow I'll have to face many questions from my friends.'

'Come then.'

Where did Hamid muster the courage to say that? She followed him silently. A hotel's neon sign blinked ahead of them. At the turn, bulbs burned overhead like a pearl necklace. When the receptionist at the counter passed him the key, his face was emotionless. The receptionist also gave them two candles. There was no power.

Hamid opened the door. Madhuri lighted the candles—a diffused, golden illumination.

Two cots, with clean smooth sheets without creases. A curtain beyond them. He sat on one end of the settee. He felt he should leave quickly. When she went into the bathroom, he sprang up and paced around the room. Let Madhuri come out. On the teapoy, there was cool water in a stainless pot. On the outside of the pot were droplets of condensation. He gently caressed its damp surface. He drew the shape of a beautiful woman with his fingertip. Hamid stood amazed, self-absorbed. That was when she came and stood behind him. The touch. He turned around. She was wearing only a skirt and a blouse. Like a butterfly sucking honey from the sari-flower, on the chair....

So many days like that....

Madhuri had never remembered the future. She hadn't even mentioned the word 'love'. There were no love letters either. Like him, she only believed in moments. He had decided to put an end to the affair several times. But the strength to say 'we'll stop it' had faded away.

But both should have realized that a day like this would come. If Madhuri had mentioned the need for it, they perhaps would have registered their marriage at the registrar's office. But his Umma's image bathed in tears... Or, were those flames of fire springing out of Umma's mouth?

He saw the audience dwindling as people kept rising from their seats and leaving. The film was over. He sat quietly. He turned once again. Madhuri was sitting with her head bent forward, with the small finger touching her mouth.

He rose.

Madhuri too rose.

He heard heartbeats which were not subdued. When he reached the door, she was already there. He entered the veranda. Like severed strings of kites, the rain fell in a slanting motion. A storm was raging outside.

They climbed down the stairs, shoulders brushing. Madhuri took out an umbrella from her vanity bag. She opened it and held it close to his head. His tongue had gone into hiding. He had felt a slight relief when they were trapped in the crowd outside. But it thinned quickly.

He followed the trail that turned towards his home. Here we part, looking for our own paths, Hamid thought. But she was still behind him.

'Have you sent out wedding invitations?'

'Hmm.'

'Have you sent me one?'

'Why are you troubled, Madhuri?' Words didn't bless Hamid. He didn't know what to do.

'I am on leave for a month.'

Why does she rake these things up now? In that moment, he hated her even though his mind opposed it. Hamid, why should you behave like a thief? Say it openly. Go now, Madhuri. We will not meet again. But he didn't have the strength to voice his thoughts. Around the street lamps, there were spheres of light. Beyond that, the broad expanse of darkness. The victory was for darkness.

They walked along the patches of illumination and darkness. On the iron fencing around the tank in the middle of the city, perpendicular tube lights stood as fence poles. Their wiggling reflections resembled snakes…mating and disentangling snakes. Mating and disentangling.

When they crossed the street, the trees in the park shed tears.

Hamid momentarily reflected on the cement cross atop the church. It stood helplessly. So much was flashing through his mind. His lips were dry. He yearned to smoke a cigarette. He did take out one and put it to his lips. He struck the match, but his hands quivered. The drop of light became stillborn even before it was born.

'I'll light it for you,' Madhuri said.

'Aren't you leaving, Madhuri?' he suddenly asked.

'Yes, I am going.'

He was stuck once again. She held his hand firmly. He hated her bitterly. Yet he was unable to push her away. He swore he would go home.

'Madhuri….'

He took long steps, but she didn't let go of his hand. He saw every detail of her face. Her face, shining like an unsheathed knife, was wet in the rain. Were they raindrops or tears?

He shivered. The empty city with its voice caught in the throat. Rows of taxis lay still. Solitary wayfarers here and there. Beggars sleeping soundly on shop verandas.

'Madhuri, may I leave?'

'You can leave…after leaving me at the hotel, you can leave.'

The fountains in the hotel's courtyard had stopped spouting.

She opened her vanity bag and took out the key. What was the colour of the flower on the plant in front of the cottage?

She opened the door. He switched on the light. The room was filled with milk foam. She put out the light. Hamid felt suffocated in the darkness. Then came the sound of her striking the match. She lit two half-burned candles and placed them on the teapoy near the cot.

Flames like a snake's gluttonous forked tongue.

Madhuri let out a suppressed laughter. The room was full of saris. Skirts scattered everywhere. The suitcase was open. For how many days had she been holed up here?

Sitting on the settee, she began removing hairpins from her hair methodically. Hamid got up.

'Sit down.'

'Let me go, Madhuri.'

'Let me watch you for some more time. I will go tomorrow. We will not meet again. Please sit down.'

Harmless words. Yet, why these candles? Lit candles. She was ever fond of lighting candles during the night. Suddenly, like an arrow of fire, a thought pierced his mind. Had Madhuri been loving him deeply, sincerely?

She was untying her sari without any hesitation, gently placing her palm on the creases and folding the garment in a precise manner. She didn't pay any attention to time slipping away. She didn't value time at all. She placed the folded sari on the teapoy. Then she laughed silently. Like a melancholy song soaked in silence.... He was curious. Did he ever love her? No. Never.

'Do you hate me?'

Madhuri's sharp question felt like she could read his mind.

'Yes.'

'Then I too hate you. Hamid, I must be liberated from this hatred towards you.'

Step by step, she came towards him. He was rooted to the spot. A white flower that blossomed before him. A large white flower on a single twig was moving towards his face.

Hamid was not certain what happened. Her blood red nails sank deep into his waistline and lapped up the blood from the cuts; his bodily aches had disappeared. He was being subjected to a rare kind of intoxication.

Her red lips flew down to his lips like dragonflies. Red lips, charged lips...the entire body was charged with a rare energy. He forgot himself. Madhuri too. His legs grew powerless, and they fell onto the teapoy. Then there were no tears. No more saliva in his mouth. The mild warmth of their bodies travelled up and down like waves. They lay, without any letting off. They weren't aware about anything at all.

He opened his eyes, feeling the heat. Madhuri wouldn't let him go from her grip. He didn't wish to extricate himself from her hold. The flames were spreading, its burning tongues licking everything around them—the many saris spread all around, the curtains, the bed linen. Flames everywhere.

They lay like snakes who couldn't wriggle away.

LUNCH
V. K. N.

When it was one o'clock in the afternoon, hunger caught hold of Payyan with the exactitude of an alarm clock. When it was five minutes past one Indian Standard Time, it became unbearable for Payyan. He feared he would fall into a lamentation mode. Payyan counted the money in his pocket. There was one rupee and eighty paise. Setting aside the cost of two packets of Charminar cigarettes which where indispensable to sharpening his intellect for the rest of the day, there was one rupee and forty paise left. In the Madras Hotel, a meal would cost one rupee and twenty-five paise. This was the recently increased rate. Before that, for a very long time, it was the golden age of 'one meal, one rupee'. Thus, after a 'lunch that filled you till it touched your throat' and buying two packets of cigarettes, fifteen paise would be left. To return home in the evening, the roosting time, the bus fare is thirty paise. What was to be done to fill the deficit? Payyan reflected. Let alone giving up the cigarette, there was no question of even cutting down on smoking. Cigarettes were an essential item of his daily needs. Payyan believed the manufacturers of the brand of cigarettes he smoked were filling them with pepper powder and salt. That he could experience the pungency and saltiness when he smoked the cigarettes. If one smoked a cigarette after drinking buttermilk to the full, one would get intoxicated too! And to leave off something that brought about so much of good effects? Say something else, if any, Payyan told himself, knitting his brow.

Payyan thought: Why not go to Menon's office? Menon gets packed lunch daily from the canteen of the party that organizes revolutions. A variety of food items that reminds one of the sadyas of feudal times. First-rate gravy made from curried buttermilk. Original avial in pale yellow colour. The green of curry leaves, raw bananas, drumsticks, green chillis. Number one mezhukku puratti. Mango pickle made the same day with cubed pieces of raw mango, rubbing them with chilli powder, salt, and asafoetida. Crispy pappadam. Fresh buttermilk. Two persons can have their fill with just one meal. But, what Menon's colleague Beard Govindan says is that Menon himself, in one go, as if he is two persons, polishes off the entire meal! Even for dinner at his house, he gets the same packed meal. Three-fourths of this meal too, he finishes off in the night. The rest of the rice, he pours water into and eats in the morning, calling it watery rice. What Beard says is that he sees Menon in his house in the position of 'Enter Menon, dining....'

The Fierce One says that like an army, a revolution too marches on its stomach.

Yet, as a last resort, he would not be averse to let Menon starve for a day, Payyan mused. The only trap is that he might have to risk being lectured to in accented Oxford English. But, Menon's office is far away. And he wanted to avoid the heat. Will go to the Madras Hotel, and finish off that Pattar, he thought. Eat devastatingly. Get rice served three or four times; the gravy, buttermilk, pappadam and pickle, too, the same number of times. If he ate for ten days continuously thus, the Pattar would have to pack up and travel ticketless in the train to escape from the scene. His scent too would not be let into any of the nearby provinces! Here I come, hey! Payyan rose, got out of the room, took the lift to the ground floor and began walking along the corridors of Connaught Place—destination Pattar!

Payyan stopped in front of a shop window where readymade dresses were displayed behind glass panes. A light-ash coloured coarse silk bush shirt caught Payyan's attention. The one who stitched the stuff has got taste! Payyan said to himself. See how neatly the collar is cut! Mouthwatering. It would be so classy to wear it! Middle-aged dames will swoon and collapse in rows and rows! The price—thirty-seven rupees and fifty paise—was printed on a square white piece of paper of two inches on its breast. Looking at the bush shirt, Payyan declared: If I am still alive, I will start wearing you before three months are out!

Walking across the corridor, Payyan got out into the sun, crossed over to Janpath and walked on. A sunshine that held in it the cruelty of revenge. Only some crows were out and about. One should treat to tea party, the one who made this city the capital of the country. A city! Like this?

Payyan reached in front of the most upmarket hotel in the city, The Laughing Lord. Opposite, the roadside was filled with parked cars. The nouveau riche had arrived for lunch. Payyan remembered the existence of a committee the government set up to enquire into where the total of all the surplus wealth created through three Five Year Plans had gone. If the committee visited such hotels, they were sure to get at the statistics of a fraction of such undiscovered wealth. Food and drinks that cost like gold, band music, dance, slum-clearance scheme, universal adult franchise, socialism, too. Thinking where he could spot any gap to let out a ceremonious guffaw, Payyan looked left and right.

Suddenly, that familiar number caught Payyan's eyes. Anandavalli's Volkswagen, with the number 3463, was parked slantways in the middle of the cars in the car park.

Standing with his arms akimbo, he looked at the car and said: 'You little girl thief! You never told me you eat your lunch in this heaven! Is this your level of wifely fidelity?'

Maybe it was decided at short notice, Payyan reasoned to himself. Or, some other smart guys would have invited her. If it were prearranged, she would surely have told him!

Let's go and do a recce, Payyan said to himself. Would it cause her loss of face? No loss of face, ever, Payyan said to himself. She doesn't have any such airs. Whoever it is, she will introduce them to him. Sometimes, it will be soldiers. If so, introducing, she will say: 'Meet Colonel Vasishta', or 'Brigadier Shukramuni', or, 'General Vishwamitra'. Then Payyan thought he would introduce himself as Field Marshal Payyan!

Payyan walked over to the entrance of the hotel. The legend 'Laughing Lord' in English in large, brass letters were hung on hooks stuck on the background of a black marble wall. The front door which was an epitome of classic engraving was created in the architectural style of the Pallavas. A giant of a Sardarji in khaki uniform, with a cross belt made of leather worn diagonally across his torso, was standing guard at the door. Before he got into this downswing of fortunes, he would have been in the army, thought Payyan. He reminded one of a tired lion.

As Payyan climbed on to the threshold, the lion bent forward, straightened again, and pulled on the brass wire of the door. The door opened halfway. Payyan entered. Strains of band music emanated from behind the thick, maroon curtain.

Payyan parted the curtain. The spacious hall. Couldn't see the other end. Nothing could be seen clearly. In the light half radiating from the bulbs on wall brackets here and there, it was a faint glow that was emerging, showing the figures at the tables as deep, dark forms. The band players wearing full suits, were hard at labour on a platform at the far end. In front of the mic, a foreign female figure resembling a perpendicular, straight line, shuddered occasionally and emitted certain foreign noises. She must have been singing, Payyan mused. Let her sing, Payyan said. Music is no one's monopoly. In the distance, at the north-eastern corner, two people were sitting on opposite seats at a table. Women. Of them, is the one sitting with her back towards him, the colonel? He hesitated. Payyan walked on through the coolness provided by the invisible air-conditioning system. When he walked on the thick carpet, he felt his feet getting bogged down, and as if his feet refused to move forward. When he traversed half the distance towards the table, he could gather that it was the colonel herself. Then who was the other woman? He thought. Payyan walked on, or rather, rushed forward. As he felt he had already passed 'one miles', he reached right behind her. Payyan piped up: 'Good afternoon, colonel!'

The colonel turned around. 'Hey, Payyan! You?'

Payyan stood near the table. The other chick was younger to the colonel. She was slim. Hair cropped at the level of her ears. As if she had undergone a ritual of some sort. Strictly, no ornaments on her body. No lipstick either. She had worn pure white. Which group she can be assigned to, Payyan thought. Picture, literature, social work, money collection, cooperation? Payyan couldn't place her quickly.

'Bearer!' The colonel called out. 'Bring a chair!'

Then she introduced Payyan to the other one: 'Journalist, an intellectual in the developing stage, my neighbour (I won't say my good neighbour.)'

Then, she introduced the other one to Payyan: 'Miss Neelima. My friend since childhood, from my Calcutta days. Daughter of the central minister, Sarkar. The Indian representative in the youth organization of the United Nations. She is abroad always. Just back from Rome last week.'

Payyan paid obeisance to the Roman lady. And she returned the greetings. Then said: 'Renu had mentioned you just now!'

Payyan laughed, then said to himself: 'Look! She has talked to one of her friends about you, even though you were not around. It was because there was no one around to hammer you hard that you suspected her fidelity a little while ago while standing on the roadside. You are such a lowborn, even otherwise!'

Payyan told Renu: 'Thanks for remembering me at such a beautiful place!'

'But I never forget you at the time of a meal!'

The UNO woman laughed.

'Ya don't have to laugh, madame, ya don't have to....' Payyan remembered the Hajiyar telling Umma.

The bearer came with a chair. Payyan sat down.

'How did you get here?' Renu asked.

'I was going to Madras Hotel for lunch,' Payyan said. 'On my way, I noticed your car parked outside so I decided to come in.'

Payyan espied a lightning flashing and fading in the eyes of the one who returned from Rome. Maybe she is congratulating me for blurting out the truth, Payyan thought.

'I had telephoned you,' Renu told Payyan. 'The exchange said that you were not in the room.'

'At what time did you call?'

'At twelve.'

'I would have been in the library.'

Suddenly applause rose from all around. Payyan turned around and looked. The straight perpendicular line beauty had ended her singing.

'Have you been here for a long time?' Payyan asked.

'Barely five minutes,' Renu said. 'Waiting for the menu. That's when you gatecrashed.'

'So you haven't had your meal yet?'

'No.'

'What's your opinion about me too joining in the ceremony?' Payyan asked, looking at the faces of the women, from one to the other.

'You both are my guests,' Neelima said.

'You can't do otherwise since I've gatecrashed, right?' asked Payyan.

'C'mon, Payyan!' Neelima said.

What? Payyan thought to himself. Are you so familiar with me, to dare call me Payyan? Aren't you rather fast, you Roman coquette?

Payyan looked at Renu. She sat as if she hadn't heard the dialogue. Payyan said:

'When I saw your car outside, I thought it would be one of your boyfriends.'

'I am sorry that I have disappointed you now,' Renu said. 'Will try my best next time.'

When the bearer approached with the imposing tome called the menu card, taking it over and handing it to the Roman lady, Renu said: 'Place the orders, Neelima.'

'Let Payyan place the orders,' Neelima said. 'Let's see what his taste is like.'

Payyan thought to himself: My taste has been tested and approved by smarter ones than you long ago.

Taking the menu card, Payyan said: 'You won't tire of my taste.' Then smartly placed orders: Spanish soup, tandoori roti, chicken Kashmiri, roast lamb, salad, two types of payasam, coffee.

'First rate,' said Neelima.

So, you too are very fond of food, like me—Payyan thought to himself. Good!

Renu was laughing.

'What's the matter?' Payyan asked.

'Your nonchalance!' Renu said.

Right, you laugh. Payyan thought. In between, let's conduct a cross-examination of the Roman lady.

'So, what were you doing in Rome?' Payyan asked.

She leaned forward, and planting her elbows on the table, said: 'I was taking part in the executive committee meeting of the United Nations Youth Organization.'

'Was Monsieur Pellevon from France, there too?'

'He was there! Do you know him?'

'Old friend,' Payyan drawled.

Payyan had only met him once, two years ago. That too, in a press party. Payyan does not in the least bit believe that the performing oracle was going to remember him, ever. Yet, why yield her space?

Neelima's eyes gleamed. She said: 'This year, he is the president.'

'Oh, then I should send him a congratulatory cable.'

'He may come over to Delhi this winter.'

'Please let me know when he arrives.'

'Certainly.'

So, I have cut you down to size, Payyan reflected.

'Weren't you there in this organization, Payyan?' Renu asked.

'Till about two years ago,' Payyan said.

'Then, why did you leave it?'

'Where's the time for all this?' Payyan said. 'If one can't work actively, what's the use of continuing as the member of an organization?'

'That won't do. You must become a member once again,' Neelima said.

'I insist!' Renu asserted.

Your sarcasm won't stale, honey, Payyan thought.

'Especially, the Indian friend of our president. You must certainly become a member like us.'

'Let me see,' Payyan said, laughing enticingly. 'Won't we meet again? We can talk about it then.'

'Thank you.'

In that moment, Payyan felt a pressure on his right shoe. Renu is applying the brake, he thought. He looked at her. Anandavalli was sitting as if unaware of anything, looking at the perpendicular line beauty, who had begun crooning once again.

Payyan looked at the Roman lady again. She was looking at him, 'keenly', as would any of those educated unemployed types who write items like novels, short stories, etc., would have described her expression.

At that moment the soup arrived. Preparing to do justice to the soup, Payyan continued the cross: 'How's Italy?'

'Beautiful country!' she said.

Scoop! Payyan reminded himself. If you had not been to Rome and seen things for yourself, nobody would have believed you.

'Can't you write three or four articles about the country and its people?' Payyan asked.

'Can they be published?'

'I will try in my paper.'

'That'll be great!'

What's the big deal about it, my red-lotus-stalk, Payyan mused. When I tell the editor that you are the daughter of the central minister, the illiterate former Hundi dealer will walk on his nose to approach you.

'But there's one thing,' Payyan said.

'What is it?'

'You may have to do me too, little favours,' Payyan said, eating the soup.

Suddenly Renu looked at Payyan with severity in her eyes. Disregarding that, Payyan said: 'You must collect details of what's happening in the top echelons of the government and leak them to me in advance. Scoop. Do you understand?'

'Please, Neelima,' Renu said, 'you are perfectly able to do that. Please help Payyan.'

The essence of her severe look was that I shouldn't blurt out some idiocy, Payyan realized. That's why she felt relieved when what I said turned out to be astutely intelligent stuff. Are beautiful fatties so dumb?

'I will do whatever is possible in my power,' Neelima said. 'I'll introduce my sweet father to you. He'll like you very much.'

Now what remains to happen in my life is the love of a blockhead minister, Payyan thought.

When the singing of the perpendicular line girl ended, applause rose once again. This time, it was intermittent and thin. Payyan looked around for the reason, which was that the majority of music aficionados had suddenly turned cuisine aficionados!

Payyan: (Aside) Now we'll create some fun! (Direct) 'The applause sounds like the wingbeats of a scared pigeon that was trapped inside a room.'

'It's poetry,' raising her head from the soup plate, the Roman lady asked, 'do you write poetry?'

'No,' Payyan said.

'I have always thought that if Payyan wrote poetry, it would come out really well.'

'Poet you are!' declared the other.

If you laugh now, I'll banish you, Payyan told himself.

'Let the trust of both of you save me,' Payyan said.

Rounding a bend afar, the bearers, dressed in headgear and plumage, followed the bugle call and marched towards them with dishes of roti–chicken–lamb.

Payyan said: 'The Kashmiri fowl and roast baby of the sheep should be eaten in rapt attention and silence. Therefore, when these items are consumed, there won't be much of a conversation. Renu knows this fact. Neelima, you must forgive me.'

'Even otherwise, if generally some conversation crops up, I know that we need not expect even a word by way of your contribution.'

'That's a good one!' said Neelima.

Those who knew Payyan intimately, people like Renu, say that it's a joy to watch Payyan eat. He will perform the act to perfection, they say. The saying goes that the stomachs of those who watch would be filled!

Now Payyan was attacking the roast lamb. Using the fingers of both his hands, he silently gnawed at the parts of the deceased quickly. Licking the bones white, he stacked them neatly at one side of the plate. He drank pure water in between in instalments. When the lamb was over, he drew the plates of Kashmiri chicken and tandoori roti close to him. He tore the roti into fine shreds and wiped the gravy off the edges of the plate, dipped in the gravy, and chewed it with relish. Two rounds of roti–chicken, one round of salad, again, two rounds of roti–chicken, one round of salad—that was the plan of action. Not a drop was spilled or made to splash. It's not when people look at the dishes, but when they see Payyan eat them, that their mouths water. So beautiful!

Like every good thing ends when the limit arrives, eating and eating, Payyan's yajna too ended finally. Wiping his mouth and fingers with the cloth that he had spread in his lap, he leaned back on the chair and said: 'What a fine lunch!'

The female subjects were trying their level best to come abreast of Payyan.

'Can we resume the conversation now?' asked the Roman lady.

'Let the pudding be over too,' Renu said.

'Never mind,' Payyan said. 'Two women have so far remained without uttering a word, haven't they? As you have broken the record, a concession is allowed. Now you can talk.'

'If I write an article,' the minister's daughter asked. 'Would you take a look at the draft?'

So, this is what has propelled you, thought Payyan.

'What does that mean?' Payyan asked.

'You must correct it for me,' she said. 'Because I haven't written prose, so far.'

Ayyo, Payyan was alarmed. So, is it verse that's your constant enemy?

'We can make it okay,' Payyan said. 'But you must commit yourself about the scoop!'

'I'll do whatever is in my power,' she said.

Payyan once again felt the pressure on his shoe.

'Now that you have told me that you haven't written prose,' Payyan probed ignoring the continuing pressure on the shoe, 'do you write verse?'

'Now and then,' she said.

You are in a quandary, Payyan admonished himself. The tragedy of correcting verse is also going to befall you. For your brashness, you deserve this, too.

'What was your last creation?' Payyan asked.

'Natural sceneries inspire me,' she said in a frenzy like that of a female oracle. 'There's a distant vista of the Alps that you see when you fly from Rome to Paris. With snow, streams, and wooden cottages.'

'You dashed of one on that scene, didn't you?'

'I am in the process of writing one,' she said. 'I don't think such poems are found in our vernacular literature.'

'So, in which language do you write?'

'In English.'

Payyan felt as if someone had whacked him one across the shoulder blades. Her direction is not right, Payyan thought. This tendency has to be nipped in the bud. If she writes a poem in English about the Alps, then that mountain can never hold its head high in pride. It will be a scandal that will resound until the end of time. This news item has to be buried before it is mentioned within anyone else's earshot.

'It is not entirely right to say that such vistas are not there in our literatures,' Payyan said.

'In the hoary past, when there was no aeroplane, there is an aerial view of the Ganga from high up in the heavens, described by Kalidasa.

Tatsyotsange parinata iva
Shrasna Gangaadukulam
Natvam drustva napunaralakam
Jnaashyase kaamacharin

Ganga that slips off like a waistband
coming undone from the waist of Himavan.

'Howzat?'

'Oh my!'

Swallowing a mouthful of pudding unwittingly, the beauty said, 'What a picture! What a picture! Do you know Sanskrit as well?'

'By the time I was sixteen,' Payyan said. 'I had polished off all the classics both in Sanskrit and English. I have only that knowledge as my capital.'

You have done such a good job of jackhammering her Payyan, Renu pressed hard on Payyan's shoe.

'What a pity someone so talented like you, ruining yourself stagnating in a newspaper like this,' Neelima said with feeling.

I will mind that, thank you, Payyan said in his mind. That's not the issue. Now you go and versify, excelling Kalidasa. Let's see how the ditty goes.

The Roman lady said after some time. 'If I have some doubts regarding the article, where can I contact you?'

So you have let poetry alone, Payyan thought. Great escape for the Alps!

'You can call the office.'

'Come home one day,' she said. 'For dinner. Will you come tomorrow?'

Before Payyan could say anything, Renu said, 'We will certainly come, Neelima. Let this heat be a little down.'

The pressure that he felt now hurt Payyan.

'33124 is my telephone number,' said Neelima.

'I will remember it,' Payyan said.

'You may not recall it, perhaps. Note it down in your diary, please!'

'Won't it be in the directory?' Renu asked with severity.

'It won't be,' Neelima said. 'Mine is a special phone. It's only three days since I got it. It's something my father arranged for me.'

'Never mind,' Payyan said, stroking his forehead. 'It has been scribbled here. 33124 belongs to the class of 182.'

'Oh, my!' She hooted, half rising from her chair. 'You are a mathematician too?'

Payyan laughed indulgently. It was the character of Ravana in Kathakali that he remembered. Who am I, pooooheyyyyy!

'That's great,' she said.

The stage is completely and entirely yours, Payyan told himself. Haven't you seen the adoration for you in her eyes, striking a match on the Peacock brand matchbox.

When there was pressure again on his foot, Payyan looked at Renu's face. She said, 'Do you want a cigarette, Payyan! The boy's passing by.'

Payyan looked. Someone dressed strangely like the crew member of a circus was going around with a tray suspended from his neck, filled with smoking accessories. Deciding that he'd try a cigar, Payyan beckoned the character over to his side.

'Do you have a Havana, hey?'

'Yes, sir!'

'Let's have one!'

Opening their purses, both the ladies vied with each other to pay for it.

'I'll pay, Neelima,' Renu said.

'No, no! I'll pay!' Neelima said.

By the time Neelima entered the scene brandishing a rupee note, Renu had long ago put the money on the tray and banished the boy from the precincts.

Hey you! Payyan told himself in his mind. Is there any reckoning for your appreciation by the ladies? You are a minor Fierce One!

When the bearer entered with coffee, Renu said, 'Bring the bill, too.'

'Why are you in such a hurry?' Neelima asked her.

Glancing at her watch, Renu said, 'There's a medical conference at two-thirty. I haven't even gone through the agenda papers.'

'Let's tarry awhile, for fifteen minutes more, please!' Neelima said.

'Sorry, my dear!' Renu said, 'another time.'

The Roman lady looked helplessly at Payyan.

'The lunch is mine, mind you,' she reminded Renu.

'What's the big deal?' Renu said. 'What does it matter who pays it?'

'That won't do,' Neelima said. 'You are my guests.'

'Right.'

'No. I'll pay the bill,' I said, blowing the cigar's smoke with an enticing fragrance. 'There's a lot of small change in my hand!'

Neelima laughed.

'Of whatever you said so far, only this is humour!'

'What we needed was a dash of good French brandy along with this coffee,' Payyan said.

'A little Chartreuse is sitting at home!' Neelima said.

'We'll fix it one day,' Payyan said. Instantly he pulled his foot away from under the table.

'You are welcome,' she said.

When the bill came, Neelima opened her bag, took out a hundred rupee note and put it in the platter. A crisp, new note! Payyan felt as if the minister, her father, had applied his mind to have that note printed especially for his beloved daughter.

'When I see this hundred-rupee note, I remember the first occasion I came here,' Payyan said. 'Just following a fancy, I walked in here. It was my payday. After drinking coffee, I asked the bearer: "Won't there be change for a hundred-rupee note?" The derisive smile that spread on his face! I should have been dead and gone! And a counter-question: 'Did you say it was a thousand rupee note, sir?'

'Then, then?' The Roman lady was all ears.

'I don't remember what happened after that. "He was carried hence!" This was what the newspapers said in their evening specials.'

'That's cute!' The Roman lady shook all over, suppressing the waves of laughter. 'Is this the first time you are coming here after that?'

'Yes.'

'You are sure, aren't you?' Renu asked, her eyes flaming.

It was a line from the Mahabharata that came to Payyan's mind: 'Panchali teekshnanayana....'

'Sorry,' Payyan said. 'Last month I had come for Renu's birthday lunch.'

'What a convenient memory!' Renu said.

'Sorry, baby!' Payyan apologized.

'Never mind. You can forget it,' Renu said, putting up the show of a smile.

The Roman lady sat with the expression, 'I am helpless' as if lending moral support to both parties.

When the bearer came with the change, Renu rose: 'Let's go.'

Payyan took special note of how generously Neelima had tipped the bearer. Your disdain towards money is not tiresome at all, he chuckled.

They got out following the traditional dictum, ladies first. Pointing to the shop opposite, Renu said to Neelima: 'Didn't you say you have to go to the watchmaker?'

'Yes. I need to go there.'

'Can you finish that business and wait there? I will drop Payyan and come back for you.'

'I'll walk. Isn't it close by?' Payyan said.

'No,' Renu said. 'I will drop you.'

That's right, Payyan thought. You may have something to tell me. I'll come along.

'So, that's it,' Neelima told Payyan. 'We must meet again.'

'Won't be a problem,' Payyan said. 'Thanks for the lunch.'

'Don't mention that,' she said with her eyes. Also implied that winding up this meeting so early was truly a tragedy. She smiled a smile which she had produced then and there especially for Payyan.

As he was getting into the car, Payyan looked at the Sardarji who was standing at the door. The lion was fatigued and was exhibiting a hangdog expression.

As the vehicle moved, Renu said: 'How's Neelima?'

'She's your friend. Can she be any less?'
'You are such a strange type, Payyan!'
'What happened?'
'Your entire attention was on her. You did not find time to look at me or even say a word to me even once.'
'C'mon baby,' Payyan said.
'Amidst all that, you even forgot the birthday lunch I gave you.'
'Sorry, fatty,' Payyan said. 'That's my mistake. Please forgive me.'
'Look here, Payyan,' she said. 'If you phone her or meet her without first informing me....'
'What will happen?'
'I will kill you!' Crushing the steering wheel under her fingers, staring fixedly ahead of her on the street, she said.
Payyan touched his neck and said, 'You are mad!'
'I will get treated for my madness,' she said. 'But from today, you are under my observation.'
The car stopped in front of the entrance to the office. As Payyan got out, she asked, 'At what time will you get back this evening?'
'At seven. And you?'
'Before that time.'
'Bye.'
'Look, Payyan! Let's have some cognac this evening. Okay?'
'Say that aloud!' Payyan hurrahed. 'You are verily a lioness, hey!'
'Bye.'
Payyan stood, watching the car turn and speed away. As the small vehicle, the shape of a hut in cream colour, was rounding the bend of Janpath, Payyan put his hands on his head and lamented internally, 'Kill me, you sluts, kill me.'

THE HANGING
O. V. VIJAYAN

Vellaayiappan set out for Kannur. As he began his journey, a wailing rose from the family members gathered in his hut, and from Ammini's hut. The fifty or so families in the village of Paazhuthara listened to the mournful sounds, and grieved along with the mourners. If they had had the funds to accompany Vellaayiappan, Ammini and the rest of the villagers would have gone with him to Kannur. But the villagers were so poverty stricken that Vellaayiappan made the journey alone.

He left the last of the huts of the village behind and took the earthen bund that led across the paddy fields. Behind him, the lament of the villagers grew faint as he walked on. The bund he was walking on led to a footpath that meandered through pasture land.

'My gods, my lords,' Vellaayiappan wept within himself.

The footpath was lined by palmyra palms on both sides. A strong wind rattled the fronds of the palms. Today, the familiar sound seemed strange, it was as if the gods and ancestors were communing with him. As he walked on, he felt the dampness of the cooked rice his wife had wrapped for him in a piece of cloth begin to soak into his arm. The tears of his wife, Kodachi, as she cooked the rice, must have seeped into the sour curd that it was mixed with, he thought; it was the wetness of tears that was dripping on his arm.

The railway station was four miles away. As he walked towards it, he saw Kuttihassan approaching. Kuttihassan reverentially stepped aside as he came up to him.

'Vellaayi,' said Kuttihassan.

'Kuttihassan,' said Vellaayiappan.

Just two words. Nothing more. Yet both the travellers could sense the strings of sentiments and unspoken sentences that lay beneath the surface.

An unvoiced conversation passed between them:

'Kuttihassan, I have yet to pay you back the fifteen rupees I borrowed from you.'
'Vellaayi, you shouldn't be thinking about this matter today.'

'Kuttihassan, it's just that I might never be able to repay you.'
'Unpaid debts are for the Creator to keep. Let it remain that way.'
'I am burning up inside. I feel my life force is being drained away.'
'May God keep you, may His beloved Prophet comfort you, may your gods and mine help you.'

Vellaayiappan continued his journey. The wind in the palmyra fronds turned dense with intense intimations of the deities. Soon, he encountered another acquaintance, Neeli, the washerwoman, carrying her bundles of freshly washed clothes. She, too, stepped aside from the path.

'Vellaayiappan.'

'Neeli.'

Just two words once again. But, as before, they contained a torrent of unsaid things.

Vellaayiappan walked on. The path widened into a dirt road that eventually came to a river. On the other side of the river was an embankment, and beyond it, the road that led to the railway station. Vellaayiappan waded into the shallows of the river. Schools of fish nibbled at his calves. He walked deeper into the waters. Memories arose within him—bathing his father's corpse, teaching his young son how to swim. The memories overwhelmed him, and once he'd crossed the river, Vellaayiappan sank down to the riverbank and wept.

Presently, he picked himself up and continued towards the station, although tears continued to trickle down his face. When he got to the station, Vellaayiappan stood in line to buy a ticket. The train fare was knotted up in a corner of his mundu. When his turn came, he said, 'Kannur' to the ticket clerk. The clerk gave him his ticket, and as he did so, Vellaayiappan thought: The first stage of my journey is over.

Carefully tying the ticket into a knot in his mundu, Vellaayiappan made his way to the platform, and sat down on a bench to wait for his train. Over the darkening palmyra trees in the distance, birds were returning to their nests. Vellaayiappan remembered how, as a little boy, his son would look in wonderment at the birds returning to their nests at dusk, as they walked through the paddy fields. Then he thought of walking with his own father in the gathering dark through the paddy fields, holding on to his hand with his little finger just as his son had done. Two pictures in his memory, and between them an ocean of unexpressed things.

An old man came to sit beside him on the bench.

'Going to Coimbatore?'
'To Kannur,' Vellaayiappan replied.
'I'm off to Coimbatore,' the other said.
'I see,' Vellaayiappan said.
'The Kannur train will arrive at ten o'clock.'
'I see,' Vellaayiappan said.
'What are going to Kannur for?'
'Nothing in particular.'
'Oh, just for fun, then.'

The stranger's conversation began to grate, his words began to wind themselves around his neck like a noose. He thought, once you leave the paddy fields of Paazhuthara behind, you enter a world of strangers, and their uncaring, impersonal conversations form countless nooses around your neck.

The Coimbatore train arrived and the old man got up and left, leaving Vellaayiappan on his own once again. He did not feel like eating the rice his wife had packed. He could feel its wetness through the cloth in which it was packed. He dozed off, and dreamed unquiet dreams. He called out in his sleep, 'O, my son, Kandunni.'

The hissing of steam and the rumbling of the tracks woke him from his sleep. His train had arrived. Vellaayiappan got up from the bench, checked that his ticket was still securely knotted into his mundu, picked up his packed rice, and walked down the platform looking for a compartment he could get into. He was turned away from the first one he tried.

'This is the first-class compartment, O elder.'
'Oh? Is that so?' He walked further down the train.
'This is a reserved compartment.'
'Oh, really.'
'Try elsewhere, O venerable one.'
The voices of strangers.

Vellaayiappan finally managed to climb into a crowded carriage. There was no space to sit but he mused to himself: 'I'll stand, I don't need to sleep. My son is certainly not going to sleep tonight.'

The train's rhythm changed from moment to moment with changes in the terrain; he noted the trackside lamps flashing past, the dim contours of the riverbank, trees, other objects vaguely glimpsed. He had travelled by train just once before, many years ago. That journey had taken place in daylight, this was a night train. They were passing through a long tunnel, on the walls of which there was fading graffiti.

It was not yet daybreak when they reached Kannur. He still hadn't opened the parcel of curd rice his wife had packed for him. Getting off the train, Vellaayiappan made his way out of the station; he handed over his ticket to the ticket collector at the gate. In the far reaches of the darkness above him, there were signs of the coming dawn. The tonga drivers clustered around the station did not pester him.

He asked one of them: 'Which way is the jail?'

Another driver laughed: 'Look at this old man enquiring about the way to the jail so early in the morning.'

A driver standing nearby sniggered and said: 'Eh, old man, just steal something. Best way to land in jail.'

The voices of these strangers wrapped themselves around his throat, and began strangling him. Vellaayiappan felt asphyxiated.

Finally, someone took pity on him and pointed him in the direction of the jail. Vellaayiappan began to walk towards it. The skies above him slowly began to lighten; the cawing of crows filled the air.

At the gates of the jail, Vellaayiappan was stopped by a sentry.

'What are you doing here so early in the morning?'

Vellaayiappan felt so helpless, he was on the point of breaking down. Then he slowly unknotted a portion of the mundu tied around his waist, and took out a crumpled, yellowing piece of paper.

'What's this?'

Vellaayiappan handed over the piece of paper to the sentry, who cast a cursory glance at it.

Vellaayiappan then said, 'My child is here.'

The sentry said gruffly: 'Who asked you to come so early? Let the office open.' The man then looked down again at the piece of paper he held in his hand, and registered what was written on it. All at once, his face softened, grew compassionate.

'It's taking place tomorrow, isn't it?'

'I don't really know,' Vellaayiappan replied. 'What's written on the paper?'

The guard looked closely at the document in his hand and then said, 'Yes, at five in the morning.'

Vellaayiappan's face filled with sorrow.

'Please sit down, sir,' the guard said, pointing to the steps leading up to the gates of the jail. Wearily, Vellaayiappan slumped on to a step looking like someone waiting for the sanctum of a temple to open and admit him.

'May I get you some tea, O elder?' the guard asked him.

'No.'

Vellaayiappan thought: 'My son would have remained sleepless all night. If he hasn't slept, how is he going to awaken, break his fast?' His hand reached down to the bundle of rice he had brought with him. 'Son, your mother packed this rice for me. I haven't eaten it. This is all I have to give you.' In the heat the rice had turned rancid.

The sky began to brighten, the day grew hotter.

The jail office opened, employees took their places behind desks. The guards took part in the morning parade. Everywhere, there was activity. Officers shouted out orders, sentries checked papers. All these voices twined together to form impersonal nooses that wound themselves around Vellaayiappan, suffocating him. The day grew even hotter. Still, he waited.

Eventually, the guard led him into the prison. Down cool corridors that had never known the heat of the sun.

'Here.'

Kandunni stood before him, behinds the bars of a locked cell. His son looked at him without emotion as if he were a stranger, his mind seemed incapable of giving or receiving consolation. The guard unlocked the door and let Vellaayiappan into the cell. For some moments, father and son faced each other, motionless, without a sound. Then Vellaayiappan embraced his son. Kandunni wailed in terror and pain, a sound almost beyond the range of hearing. Weeping, Vellaayiappan said brokenly, 'My son.'

Kandunni said, 'Appa.'

Just those words. But what lay between them was the enormity of sorrow, and unexpressed words:

> 'Son, what did you do?'
> 'I don't remember, Appa.'
> 'Son, did you murder anyone?'
> 'I don't remember.'
> 'It's all right, son. You don't have to remember anything any more.'
> 'Will the guards remember?'
> 'No, my son.'
> 'Will you remember my pain, Appa?'

Again an intense keening issued from Kandunni, a wail so high-pitched and shrill, it was on the edge of auditory perception.

'*Appa, don't let them hang me.*'

'Time's up, sir. Please come out.'

Vellaayiappan walked out of the cell and the door clanged shut. When he looked back, he saw his son looking at him from behind the bars as a stranger might from behind the barred window of a train hurtling past.

Vellaayiappan kept walking. Just before he turned the bend in the corridor, he looked back one last time, to bid his son farewell.

For the rest of the day, he wandered listlessly around the jail compound, keeping a sort of vigil for his son. The sun rose higher and then the day began to ebb away. When night fell, Vellaayiappan wondered whether his son would sleep that night. When dawn broke, Kandunni was still alive within the walls of the jail.

Vellaayiappan heard the sound of bugles at dawn. He wasn't aware that they signalled the start of the execution. The sentry had told him that the hanging would take place at five in the morning. Vellaayiappan had no wrist watch but his peasant's instincts told him what time it was.

✧

When the guards delivered his son's body to him, Vellaayiappan received it as a midwife would a baby.

'O, elder, what funeral ceremony did you have in mind for your son?'

'I don't know.'

'Don't you want the body?'

'Masters, I have no money.'

The prison officials handed the body over to the scavengers who took care of such things and instructed them to transport the body to the public burial ground. The scavengers put the body on a trolley and began pushing it towards the cemetery. Vellaayiappan walked along with them. On the outskirts of town, a place of desolate marshes; vultures wheeled in the sky above them.

When they got to the burial ground, the scavengers dug a pit and laid the body in it. Just before they closed the grave Vellaayiappan looked at his son's face one last time. He placed his hand on his cold forehead in a final blessing.

After the scavengers had filled in the grave, Vellaayiappan walked aimlessly away from the burial ground in the intense heat of the day. Eventually, his wanderings brought him to the seashore. He was seeing the sea for the first time. He became aware of something cold and wet in his hands, and realized he was still carrying the rice his wife had prepared for his journey. Vellaayiappan opened the bundle, and scattered the rice on the ground in remembrance of his dead son. From the gleaming sunlit dome of the sky, crows descended on the sacrificial rice—like embodied spirits of the dead come to receive the offering.

THE APOLOGY
RAJALAKSHMI

'So, the most disgusting of pronouns is...' she paused. 'She.'

The answer came from the back bench.

The class fell silent.

A class of twenty students, and only one girl among them. But that day she wasn't present. Besides nineteen boys, the only woman in that small room was the young teacher.

The most revolting sound: 'She!'

That voice was very familiar.

She knew she could make him stand up and berate him. Yet, she stood before those boys, her face as white as paper. Then she walked out, without even picking up her book that was lying on the table.

When she returned to the staffroom midway through the class hour, the other teachers were all there.

'Ah, stopping the class and returning to the room as and when you like, right? Great, indeed! Lucky the principal didn't spot you!' Karthaavu master remarked half-jokingly.

She could not bear it. She put her head down on the table and began to sob. Sobs that would not stop despite her best efforts.

'Ayyo, what happened?'

All of them stood up. Their chivalry was roused into action.

'What did Karthaavu master say to the poor thing?'

This was such a demeaning moment. It was so shameful to cry in front of these men. Though they were good-natured, they were not her friends. But in spite of everything, she could not control her sobbing.

Someone rushed to the next department to fetch a lady teacher. All the male teachers left the room.

That good woman, the mother of three children, did not ask her questions. She pulled a chair and sat down, stroking her hair. Slowly, her weeping stopped.

The teacher brought her a glass of water. 'Wash your face.'

She went over to the window and splashed water on her face, and wiped it with the soft handkerchief the teacher had given her.

'May I leave for the day, teacher? I cannot return to that class today.'

'Rema, you can leave. I'll take care of the permission. Go home, lie down, and rest. Then come tomorrow. I will make them adjust the class.'

She accompanied her to the steps. Those who were on the veranda and the courtyard noticed her leaving, her face hidden behind her umbrella.

What had happened?

The entire college was drowned in commotion. Karthaavu master spoke to one of the boys in the class and found out what had transpired.

The news spread like wildfire. Something like this was happening for the first time in the history of the college.

A lady teacher walked out of the classroom, weeping! That too the meek Rema teacher! As yet there had not been any complaints about her teaching.

As the incident was discussed over and over again, its dramatic intensity seemed to grow.

That the teacher had come out of the class weeping.

A boy had stood up in class and said something obscene, and she came out of the class…crying!

That poor Rema teacher, who would not harm a soul. And who uttered those words? It was Paul Varghese, the president of the college union. And then complaints about Paul Varghese, which were not heard as yet, began to come out one by one.

He was a bit of a rowdy, and after recently becoming the president, was full of himself.

Someone discovered he was always loitering around the girls' waiting room.

There were people who had noticed him entering the liquor shop through the back door.

Within twenty-four hours, Paul Varghese became a hoodlum. What had really happened in the classroom? Was that all? Were the other boys lying to save him? How was it possible for the lady teacher to be so hurt? Why would someone come back to the staffroom and break down for nothing?

What had happened that touched her inner being so much? Rema too pondered over the same question.

What was the reason for her sitting there and weeping? Was it because of what that boy said? Was she so good-for-nothing to feel like that? If she could not manage to control a student.... Was it because Karthaavu master had mocked her? No, she was not such a touch-me-not.

She was fond of Paul Varghese. Yes, that was right. He was a bright and active boy. When she heard what she heard, in his voice.... But how did she feel so much...?

Was it because she had suddenly remembered what she had lost... something that had been irretrievably taken out of her hand? In that moment, did she see before her naked eyes, in the merciless glare of light, the hollowness of something that she called 'life'? The pain of the past, the futility of the present, the meaninglessness of the future—did she see all of it out in the open?

Is that why she burst out sobbing?

The next day, she entered her department with her head bent low.

Everyone was very affectionate towards her. The professor came up to her and told her not to take classes for the Final Main students any more.

So she did not need to go to that class any more.

She should have felt happy. It was there that the impudence was revealed to her. She did not need to see those boys any more. Shouldn't that make her glad?

Paul Varghese.

That boy would never have imagined his utterance would blow up to become such a serious case.

What would he be thinking about her now? Would it be something like, 'Isn't it because she went about snivelling that all my troubles shot up?'

Why did that boy say that word? Was it intended to insult her?

In Strachey's essay, the description, of the 'the most disgusting pronoun' was reserved for the first person singular.

The love for the word 'I'.

The most disgusting pronoun.

Was it not her biggest problem that she projected a big 'I'?

'Let me not feel the sentiment of "I".'

She had gone to the class thinking how this Western concept stood close to the Vedanta tradition of the Hindus. And just after she had introduced the topic and started on the central theme with complete earnestness....

Paul Varghese.

The lanky, handsome boy. What was he to gain by insulting her?

The case was becoming bigger and bigger.

She heard that it had reached the principal, and he had taken it very seriously.

He asked the boy to bring his guardian.

Oh, it would end with that. The guardian would come, say something, and return. The case would be closed, and peace would return! If only this would somehow reach a conclusion.

However, the matter did not conclude as expected. Paul Varghese did not bring his guardian.

The principal became angrier. He barred the boy from attending classes as well.

That very bright student, not being able to attend any class, just because of her....

But why could he not bring his father along for once?

No one in the department mentioned the case within her earshot.

Now they would all be thinking: that woman will start moaning... chche....

But in every other department, this was the hot topic. There were female teachers there as well, but nobody brought up the incident around her.

Rema too began to receive fresh updates regularly.

It was not Paul's fault alone that he had not brought his father over. His parents were not on the best of terms. It was the father who bore the expenses of his studies. But apart from that, he was not involved in any of his son's affairs. It was unlikely that he would come over to find a solution to Paul's case. If he found out that the boy was embroiled in a quarrel, he would simply tell him to stop his studies forthwith. That was what was going to happen.

He had no other relatives except his father. Thus, he was unable to bring a guardian.

The principal had turned malicious towards the boy.

It was heard that one could hire any number of parents at a nominal cost of two or three rupees. It seemed students frequently resorted to such tactics when they were required to bring their guardians. Could he not do something like that? Did he not have any uncles?

He did none of that. The president of the college union had

remained outside classrooms for more than a week by then.

That boy was supposed to write his final exams that year.

Because of her, a student....

Rema could only set the wheel rolling. Couldn't she bring it to a halt if she set her mind to it?

The boy may have blurted out that word while a passing mischief crossed his mind.

For that?

Because of her....

What if she met the principal and told him that she had cried not because of what Paul had said.... But what if he asked her the true reason behind her outburst?

She would not have anything to say.

She mulled it over in her mind. Finally, she decided, come what may, she must approach the principal.

Seeing her, he smiled broadly. She remembered how the students had nicknamed that middle-aged man Tiger.

Pleasantries were exchanged. Now she had to broach the real topic....

'Sir, Paul Varghese...'

'What is it? Did he make more trouble?'

'No. He has not been able to attend classes.'

'It's because I have forbidden him to attend classes.'

'He is a bright student.'

'But that alone is not enough.'

'Sir, now that so much has transpired, can't you conclude this case here and permit him to resume classes?'

He laughed. One or two other teachers in the room laughed as well.

Did they believe she was such a damned fool? First, she burst into tears because a student had said something. Then she approached the principal to request him to let the same boy off.

'Rema, you don't need to feel any compunction about it. What's wrong with their generation is the lack of discipline. That too, when he is the union president. As the elected representative of the students, Paul Varghese should be a role model for others. I intend to mete out severe punishment to him. It should be a lesson for all.'

'Ayyo, sir! Just because of me, a student....'

'I'll do one thing. As you have taken the trouble to approach me with this request, I will give him a choice. Let him apologize before the entire college. Or else, he must collect his transfer certificate and leave.'

'In front of everybody?'

'It won't be embarrassing for you, Rema. All of us will be there. You just need to come along.'

'But that boy, in front of all the other students....'

She felt the principal regarding her in a peculiar way.... My God!

'I have a class in the next hour. Shall I leave?'

The entire college found out about this too.

It was heard that Paul Varghese had agreed to apologize. In front of more than two thousand students who had voted for him as their leader.

The apology was scheduled for Monday. Sharp at 4 p.m., as soon as college was dismissed for the day, all were to assemble in the main hall. A notice was circulated.

How could she avoid being present?

The principal arrived at 4.10 p.m. On the platform stood more than seventy teachers. An ocean of students below. Were those two thousand pairs of eyes riveted on her? The principal waited impatiently till 4.15. Paul Varghese did not turn up.

That day itself, a notice was put up on every board: Paul Varghese, No. 3572 of IIIrd D.C., was dismissed from the college.

The next day, against the advice of her colleagues, Rema availed a week's leave to visit her native place.

She returned with a fairly calm mind. As she entered her room, the watchman Raman Nair, approached her with a packet.

'A day after you left, a boy came to meet you. When I said you were not here, he handed me this packet. He insisted I should deliver it to you personally. It was a book. He wrapped it in paper and gave it to me when I said you had left.'

Inside was a collection of Pushkin's poems. A low-priced Moscow edition. On the first page, written in clear, bold letters:

> *When I approached to kneel down,*
> *thou shut the door.*
> —Paul.

CHIDAMBARAM
C. V. SREERAMAN

When he entered the temple compound through the gopuram, he remembered Appayya Dikshitar's lines: 'Chidambaramidam prathamitameva punyasthalam.' (This spot is Chidambaram placed first among holy sites.) He looked around. The sheer magnitude of the mighty shapes and forms of the temple complex birthed a mind-boggling terror within him. Four colossal gate towers that kissed the sky. Although at first glance they looked similar, each of the hundreds of stone sculptures was different in all of them. The countless passages, walkways, and cells connecting them gave one the impression of a fortress rather than a temple. He walked along the path around the inner temple, paved with granite sheets. The sunshine remained harsh, only mildly fading. He ambled along the adjoining lawn. When the thorns from the punctured vine pierced the soles of his feet, he remembered the sandals he had untied and kept outside…and another thought followed. Although Chidambaram Temple had four gopurams, why did he choose to enter through the southern gate? Had it been through any of other entrances, would his mind have been assailed by such deviations?

The beginning of the deviations was not from the southern gopuram, was it? It began as soon as he had passed Manaloor on his journey from Cuddalore. Upon sighting the 'Manaloor Village' signboard, he had unwittingly said: Sarppannan Senkodan Konaar Chunnaampukaar Theru Post Manaloor. Via Chidambaram.

Those days, he would write this address on the inland letter that Akhilaandammaal would bring. They were filled with her writing.

Immersed in thought, he reached the tank—a large reservoir within the temple's walls lined with stones, and built-in stairs all around the sloping sides. He sat on a step, just behind two sanyasins. Picking up the bag of sacred ash that fell from the matsyakkaavadi, one of them picked it up and hung it from the kavadi again and continued the conversation. He watched them with interest. Such sound health! And the full-bloodedness of contentment on their faces. What would have prompted them to become sanyasins? The sight of those ascetics and their blooming health made him ponder about his present situation.

'You can live for some more time if you can obey my instructions.'
It was not a Vedantin who said it. But the doctor who was treating him.

When the doctor met him after a short stretch of time, he said: 'You haven't stopped, I am sure. Do you know the condition of your liver? It is very alarming... I am a heart patient and had certain vices, though not so acute. Do you know how I stopped? I became more and more religious. Whenever temptations came my way, I would read the Bible. I suggest that you too—become religious. Read religious books....'

While returning from the trip to the doctor, he passed by advertisements that desperately enticed him. He went inside a bookstore where he had hitherto never stepped in. He browsed through the titles arranged on the racks, seldom coming across familiar names. When he bought books by Tilak and Romain Rolland, he felt melancholier. He couldn't find anything in them that he didn't already knew. Yet he envied their rhetoric. He went on to read more books. At that time, the inflammation had set in in his legs. Then he visited the doctor, who once again advised: 'If you really want to stop, you must move away from this environment. Travel to some other part of the country. Preferably religious places.'

Thus had begun this journey.

Today when he observed the muscular, powerful body of the sanyasi who leaned the matsyakkaavadi on the pillar, sitting in the lotus pose, and imparting Vedantic knowledge to a listener, he began to ask himself:

Is physical mortification the beginning of sanyas?

Is sanyas the refuge of the infirm?

Or is it the reckless adventure to sustain a mighty desire to live on?

His mind didn't dwell for long on any of these questions. Yet the thoughts plaguing him as he walked in through the southern gopuram did not leave.

The more he tried to forget, the onslaught of thoughts advanced from all fronts.

In his bruised mind, the building of Durgaprasad at Haddo waxed clear.

Port Blair wanes until it ends at a place called Haddo. Haddo's hill slopes play hide-and-seek with the sea. The days and nights he had spent gazing at the sea. The sea's cheeks turned ruddy in the swell of the spring tide and they lengthened during the neap tide; and rocks...oh the protruding cheekbones of the sea....Vaachchaapuri and his wife came to live in another part of that house. Her name was Akhilaandammaal. A face that showed the faint wilting of a freshly transplanted plant. Except for the gigantic burden of a hair bun, there was nothing attractive about her. Calling her a grown-up girl would be better than describing her as a young woman. Like him, she too would sit gazing at the sea. Once, she asked him: 'Why is the sea here so black?'

He had answered: 'That's why this land is called Kalapani in Hindi. That word also meant exile.'

The solitude of that place brought them closer, as if constantly engulfed by the flames of melancholy. Throughout the day, Akhilaandammaal would be alone. Sometimes she would be seen crying, immersed in the memories of a village nestled somewhere in the interiors of the land beyond the big sea. Other times she would go on writing letters to her father. He would write the address for her in English.

For them to be close, breaking all moral boundaries, didn't take much longer. Initially, he called her Akhilaandammaal. Then, slowly it became Akhila. Finally, when she insisted on it, he called her Paappa, little one. When her lips ran all over his cheeks, he called out unwittingly, 'My Paappa.'

But following a development, it had become apparent that their relationship had to come an end. Vaachchaapuri was allotted quarters in the nearby labour barracks, and they shifted. But once, as a surprise, she had visited him at midnight. Seeing him standing, his face pale, she said, 'Vaachchaapuri is on night duty.' He wanted to ask her why she had come to him at midnight. She answered that unasked question: 'I felt like meeting you. And I came.'

Then on, whenever Vaachchaapuri had night duty, she came to his room without any prior information.

Now he cannot recollect the first time he had gone over to the labour barracks at night. But how could he ever forget how he had left the barracks for the last time? Looking through the chinks in the wooden walls, one could see the lights in the government sawmills on Chittham Island. From time to time, he used to peep out. That night, the lights went off. He came out of the room instantly. He waited in the yard waiting for them to come back on. The odour of sawdust and sweat spread in the courtyard. He shuddered. A shadow loomed before him. It was Vaachchaapuri. He quickly began to walk away. Vaachchaapuri was chasing him. By the time he climbed onto the road through the bushes, he had broken into a run. Then he heard the hooves of death in the sounds of pursuit. He wasted no time; as soon as he spotted a light in the attic of the Malayali hotel, he rushed inside. They had lit a candle and were sitting around it, playing a card game. Even when he joined them and sat brushing against their bodies, the fear didn't leave him. He kept raising his head and looking outside. All that time Vaachchaapuri was waiting. When the workers from the powerhouse arrived at daybreak, they found out the reason for the power failure. There was an explosion in the powerhouse. The engineer Swami and two employees had died of electric shock. And when the day dawned, another alarming update surpassed the earlier news. Vaachchaapuri had slashed his wife all over her body. Then he ran off to an area near Corbyn's Cove Beach. By midday, Vaachchaapuri had hung himself from the branch of a mangrove tree. From that day, he felt only one thing...a pale, cool, omnipresent fear. Two days later, when he went to his office for an attachment warrant to recover a Taccaavi loan, the officer looked at him with great sympathy; he didn't say a word about the rumours circulating in the area. But his face said it all. He said: 'I will transfer you to a place as far from here as possible. Colonization is going on in Atlanta Bay. A group is going there tomorrow. You can leave along with them....'

That kind officer who often used to bail him out of tricky situations had once again come to his rescue. The next day, when he was going around bidding farewell, he suddenly asked the truck driver to stop near the hospital. In the female ward, a group of Tamil women were standing around a cot in total silence. The body on the cot was bound in bandages. She resembled a bundle of cotton. In her case, death was playing shy. Yama's rope was hesitant to tighten its grip around that bundle of cotton. After several months, this much was learnt. Even the most serious slash on Paappa's neck had healed. Two fingers were entirely chopped off. The Tamil Paattaalar Sangam funded her passage to the mainland on a ship. Paappa had returned to her land.

Today, sitting on the stairs of the Chidambaram Temple, he remembered those moments. The sanyasins were still engrossed in the enchanting milieu of a puranic story.

He walked on. The dwarf granite pillars were inscribed with Tamil quotes. He felt sorry he couldn't read the language. He only knew how to write his name, and Paappa. She had taught him. He had reached a dark passage where a foreigner with the ritual markings of a Vashnavite Vaidik and a tuft of hair at the back of his shaven head was haggling with a temple servant. Perhaps it was about paying an advance for robbing a temple idol or a bribe to open the sanctum before the appointed time and enjoy an illegal darshan.

He continued along the alley, stopping in front the sanctum's thick doors which were shut.

Imagining the form of Lord Shambhu as Nataraja, he stood quietly.

He remonstrated with himself: what does he have to beg of the Lord when the door is opened, and the Nataraja idol right before him fills his eyes? That his liver ailment is cured, or peace of mind is accorded to him, or to bless him with moksha?

Suddenly, he felt like laughing. Liver ailment, he scoffed. The very liver ailment he had accrued by intentionally and systematically neglecting his body for so many years!

Peace of mind? Had he ever thought of the mind when he chose to distort it over and over again to fulfil his own desires?

And then, moksha? Has he ever prayed for the moksha of anyone who had sinned along with him?

He quickly exited the corridors of temple. Instead of shame, his attire repulsed him: a saffron shirt and a pyjama. He chanted:

Kamyaanaam karmaanaam nyaasami
Samnyaasam kavayo vidu

Walking along, he repeated those lines with difficulty. He took out the token for the sandals he had deposited outside the temple for safekeeping. He thought he would retrieve them and pay ten paise. He looked for the woman who had spoken to him while accepting his sandals. It was her voice that had triggered Paappa's memories. The woman was sitting on the remains of the parapet of a sunken well. She had a black muffler wrapped around her neck. He watched her keenly. Is she hiding his Paappa within her grey hair and swollen cheeks ridden with folds?

As he slipped on his sandals, he asked her: 'Amma! Is your home somewhere near here?'

'No. My native village is quite a distance from here.'

He asked her name, but not that of her village.

'Hey, swaamiyaar! What will you get by knowing my name? You, who are going around clad in a saffron dress in search of moksha? Get going!'

He put on his sandals and walked on without looking back.

THE DEATH OF MAKHAN SINGH
T. PADMANABHAN

Night had fallen by the time the bus reached Banihal. As usual, Makhan Singh stopped the bus in front of Panditji's restaurant. As the passengers hastily got out, he leaned his face on the steering wheel and shut his eyes. He was overcome by indescribable fatigue and discomfort.

In fact, there was no special reason for him to be late. Usually, several military trucks would be on the way, and he would slow down, letting them pass. But that day, there were no trucks. Yet he was late.

He had been late before too. But nothing of this sort had ever happened.

When he remembered the reasons, he thought his head would split. He had resolved not to think about anything, ever. But could he keep that resolution even once? Makhan Singh said to himself: death is better than this. Why didn't I die that day?

So much had happened. Weren't they uprooted from the land of their birth? Still, he was alive. Not because he wished to. But it was destined that way. He calmed down by telling himself: never mind; the roots may sprout again in fresh soil.

He had been searching. Where was that fresh soil?

He wasn't certain. Sometimes he felt it was in Delhi. In any case, he was sure it would be in India. For now, it was enough if he could somehow go on living.

He must forget the past if he were to live. However tired he was he could not prevent himself from brooding over the past.

When he recently met Bachchan Singh, he had said: 'I am going to the Andamans; there are fifteen acres of land for me.'

Fifteen acres! I can't believe it! Why should one have so much land? Bachchan Singh cannot cultivate it by himself. He needs someone to help him. So....

Will wheat grow there? Maybe. They say the soil is very fertile.

If only he could get one acre!

Yet, he would never go to the Andamans, even if he died here! Even death holds forth solace! Man holds his pride in the greatest regard. To leave this soil where his father and grandfather are laid to rest....

In Makhan Singh's choking heart, the smoke of memories billowed.

As if coming from a great distance, he heard the muffled sounds of the tarpaulin being removed and luggage being unloaded from the top of the bus. He thought to himself: it is very late. Everyone must have had their supper. Only I am late. The very thought of eating made Makhan Singh nauseous. He decided to skip the meal.

Getting off the bus, he walked to the restaurant. He dragged his legs, as if a heavy chain was weighing him down with every step he took. When he reached the front of the veranda, he stopped in his tracks. The two of them stood there. The old woman and the young lady. Their hollow eyes seemed to be searching for him, like a blade of grass in the grasp of someone drowning.

Those fragile forms of misery moved over from the darkness to a lighted patch.

Makhan Singh was unable to confront them. He turned around. He was aching all over.

His lips trembled; eyes shut by themselves.

If only the earth would open and swallow me!

I am a disgrace even to my father!

Coward!

'Sardarji!' Someone tapped on his shoulders.

It was Panditji.

'Panditji!'

'What happened?'

He couldn't answer.

Panditji put his palm on Makhan Singh's brow.

'You have a fever.'

'Let it be.'

'Come. Let us go inside.'

He didn't budge.

Why go inside? To avoid seeing them?

'It is snowing.'

'Let it snow.'

Makhan Singh wanted to lie on the bare earth and weep. He wished to stand before them, his head erect. But he recollected painful images. In his mind's eye, he saw his parents and his wife. He pressed his chest hard. Memories were flooding out of his heart in the form of blood. He said to himself: I will help them; certainly, I will.

He went in with Panditji.

Moonlight spread across the Banihal Pass. A cold wind began to blow.

He sat still in front of an empty fireplace. Instead, the fire was in his mind. It was not blazing, and so no one saw it. Yet, he was aware of its all-consuming heat.

All this while, he was brooding. Panditji served food to everyone.

(They did not have any money on them. I had guessed it all along. If only I had some money with me! They didn't ask for anything. They simply stood in the far corner. Like me, they also must have a lot to ponder over.)

Can't human beings keep away from thinking about anything?

Then I said to Panditji: 'Give them something.'

He asked for money. I am not angry; I am only amazed. Does one keep an account of feeding one's own mother and sisters and demand money from them? To think that he is a Brahmin. He is a dog!

Everyone retired for the night, and they too lay down. Makhan Singh alone sat up.

When the midnight cock crowed, he got up and walked out. Ramlal was snoring away inside the bus. He thought: 'He must be sleeping all wrapped up in blankets. It is really cold. Let him sleep! Isn't he young! But I cannot sleep tonight!'

In that cold, he recalled his childhood when he would keep vigil in the fields.

Wheat lay ripe in the fields.

It was before the harvest. Who would be there now?

Makhan Singh sighed. He strolled along the streets of Banihal. There was silence everywhere. The road that crept into the pass shone like a black snake in the moonlight. He took that road every day. And would take it tomorrow too. But....

The moonlight seemed to have a peculiar sheen. The colour of blood!

The smell of burning human flesh.

He thrust his hands into the pockets of his old corduroy trousers and walked on.

The moonlight, road, and hillsides faded from Makhan Singh's vision. He was only aware of the comforting touch of the old corduroy.

Makhan Singh felt the cloth again.

He couldn't bear the thought.
He had bought it in Lahore.
She was also with him that day.
My first....
Lahore!
Lahore is now in Delhi!
How contented life was then!
He sighed. If only the past were a mere dream!
But how could it be? Lahore is gone. Rawalpindi is gone. Punjab.... Where were they coming from? He should have asked. The next morning, he would ask them everything. He went back to the restaurant. He was exhausted. but couldn't sleep. The sight of that mother and daughter would not fade from his mind. They seemed to be asking for something from far away, weeping. It was for help. Makhan Singh felt infinitely sad.

He should help them. It was his duty.

If he didn't help them out in this condition, what was the use of being alive?

To think that he didn't have any money at all with him.

He would ask Panditji. If he received some, well and good.

God would find a way.

He comforted himself.

Towards morning he dozed off a little. Even in that reverie, a vague memory of them filled his mind like a mist.

Where did he spot them first? Must be at Pathankot. But his attention turned towards them only at Madhopur for a special reason. It took almost an hour for the search on the bus to finish. Even bedding and boxes were not spared. Standing under the tree before the tea bunk, Makhan Singh had enjoyed watching the fun.

The proceedings of that day were very strict. It was not just a usual, cursory affair: each person was individually subjected to the search. People were impatient to have it over and done with. Maybe a high-ranking official is visiting the area.

Munshiji took the register from Ramlal's hands and went through it.

'There are two extra people,' he said, raising his still damp pen towards the sky.

Munshiji is always impatient.

'Where are they?'

They were there.

Munshiji lost his temper. Once he was angry, he wouldn't talk.
'Don't you have ears? Where are your things?' he roared.
It was Ramlal who said: 'Munshiji, they do not have any baggage.'
'Is that so?'
Advancing two steps, he asked: 'Where are you going?'
'Srinagar,' the old woman answered.
Makhan Singh thought that her voice faltered.

He got up from under the tree. Something was wrong. Why did the women weep, standing by that roadside in Madhopur, in front of all the soldiers, passengers, and shopkeepers?

He saw the old woman producing the tickets from the bundle in her hands.

'Aren't these to Jammu?'

No one spoke....

Munshiji drew something in the air with his pen.

At last, a soldier said, 'Never mind, Munshiji, this is not your headache! Let them go anywhere. Why do you bother?'

Munshiji flared up. 'Oh, is that so?'

As he was leaving, he said: 'It is also you who did away with Punjab.'

Hearing those words, Makhan Singh turned pale. He had not forgotten the fate of Punjab. He hailed from Punjab and had never wished to go anywhere else. His father and grandfather were farmers. At home, they kept old swords that were not rusty. But he had never seen anyone use them to strike another.

Makhan Singh could not contain himself. Who did that scarecrow-thin Munshiji have in mind when he said that? Was it aimed at him? If it was so...he was never vengeful. But whether he could have retaliated was another question. He could have if he wished. But he didn't. It was why Munshiji spoke thus.

Why didn't he retaliate?

Makhan Singh gnashed his teeth. He should have struck back. Later, Bachchan Singh had said, 'They hacked your father to pieces.' He had not witnessed the scene. Then, who did?

It is a son's sacred duty to avenge his father's death. But upon whom should he take revenge?

Thank God! Mother was long dead by then. Otherwise, what would they have done to her....

When I went away that day, my Preetham was with Father.

Nothing was heard of her.

I searched for her everywhere!

Who knows what has become of her.

She might not be dead.

Makhan Singh felt his heart shudder.

Her name must have been changed. She must be thinking about me and sighing this very minute as I sit here, wondering what might have happened to her. We will never meet again.

Oh, my Preetham!

Where are you?

In Karachi?

⏳

The bus was waiting for him.

Ramlal said, 'Let's go, Sardarji.'

With a sigh, Makhan Singh started the bus.

As the bus hurtled towards Jammu, leaving behind a wild expanse of bare land strewn with gigantic rocks and corn fields irrigated by camel-drawn Persian wheels, he thought: whatever the provocation, I am incapable of harming anyone. Why should I rack my brains thinking about revenge? What is past is past.

Makhan Singh thought about other things. It was a few days since he had received a letter from his aunt in Delhi. Her son was going to school. He should send them something. Next week was Roop Chand's daughter's wedding. Shouldn't he give some gift? The old man was short of money. He smiled wryly. He felt a sense of contentment. What a paltry sum he spends for himself! And the rest gets spent this way and that....

As he passed the military camp, he called out goodnaturedly to an old taxiwallah who had taken the wrong side, 'Mind your precious life, uncle.'

Stopping the bus near the rest house, Makhan Singh went into the restaurant he usually ate at. He had forgotten the mother and daughter by then. When he returned, the passengers were discussing them. He heard a young man say: 'They were in our compartment till Pathankot.'

There was still time for the bus to start.

Someone asked, 'Are they going to Srinagar?'
'That's what they said.'
'Looks like they are in dire straits.'
'Aren't they refugees?'
'Why are they going there then?'
'Her son in the army is sick.'
'He must be dead by now.'
'Don't say that, brother.'
'Oh.'
'Isn't she that soldier's mother?'
'The other must be his wife.'
'God, help them.'

Makhan Singh was hurt. They were not to be found anywhere, even if he wished to help them.

He said to no one in particular. 'It seems they are gone.'
'Where can they go?'
'They are gone for sure.'
'What? Walk up two hundred miles?'
'They might.'
'They had to have at least two new pairs of shoes to do that.'
'What about clothes?'
'Still, they left.'
'No wonder.'
'They were weeping.'
'They will freeze to death tonight. That's why.'
'Or…'
'The young one is pretty. If someone takes a fancy to her…'
'Things like that happen in Calcutta and Delhi.'

As Makhan Singh headed for Banihal, those words echoed in his ears. A picture of his aunt swam into his mind.

His aunt in Delhi.

The refugee women of Delhi…. The thought was revolting.

He was leaving behind Jammu's crowded, colourful streets. The bus was merely crawling. When he rounded the bend in front of the palace, he suddenly stopped the bus.

The woman and daughter were walking along the road, which looked like it had been created only for them.

They halted in confusion.

He didn't look at their faces, but asked, 'Coming along?'

The daughter looked away.

The mother's eyes filled with tears. 'We do not have money, son!'

Makhan Singh recalled his dead mother. Only she had called him son with such love.

He said: 'Come along!'

They still hesitated.

'Get in.'

Ramlal opened the rear door.

'God will reward you.' The old woman's voice quivered.

The bus moved. Makhan Singh was melancholic. Alas! Punjab's offspring are orphaned. Families are broken, and relationships are wrecked.

But a mother has set off, without a second thought, to meet her sick son hundreds of miles away. She has only love in her heart.

That young woman must be craving to meet her husband. He must be longing to see her. When their eyes meet....

That relationship will never be severed.

Like the mother and wife of that sick young man in Srinagar, had his father and wife survived....

He was sad and angry at the same time.

Makhan Singh loved to see life planting fresh buds in that fertile soil. The beauty and freshness of the hillsides sporting lofty pines and hillocks dotted by fruit-bearing pomegranates had never been lost on him. Occasionally, he used to glance around as he passed them. But not that day.

The storm of memories kept up a swell in his heart.

He had met refugees from Punjab on earlier occasions. But he had never felt anything like this before. What is past is past. One can never return to old times. So he convinced himself to somehow survive in the new circumstances.... He had decided not to hurt himself thinking about the past. But today, witnessing such love and self-sacrifice, he was pulled back to his own relationships. He knew he couldn't, yet he yearned: if only he could return to the past!

Familiar faces paraded before the windscreen.

The wind carried voices from times gone by. His father was calling him. He stepped on the brakes—the bus was heading for a chasm! The vehicle shook violently.

Makhan Singh perspired. How many lives were in his hands!

He remembered his old resolution—he wouldn't think about anything.

The bus was moving very slowly.

They failed to reach Banihal before nightfall.

※

Makhan Singh rose as the first rays of dawn fell on the hills.

People were preparing to leave.

Panditji was making tea.

Makhan Singh said, 'Panditji, I am in trouble.'

Putting down the teapot, Panditji studied the face of the tall Punjabi driver. He had never heard him say anything in that tone. What had happened? Is it the beginning of some contagious illness? Then he should not be allowed to stay in the restaurant.

'Panditji, I need some money. As soon as I get my wages, I shall pay it back.'

For the first time in his life, he was asking for a loan.

Opening his empty palms, Panditji said, 'Money, Sardarji? I don't have! And look at the time you thought fit to ask for money. It is hardly dawn yet.'

Makhan Singh's face fell. He shouldn't have asked. The humiliation was for nothing. He stood in front of the restaurant, immersed in thought.

After the lethargy of the night, Banihal's noisy life began pulsating once again. Shops opened. Ruddy-faced shepherds came out of liquor shops although it was still early morning. What a commotion! The trucks began to leave one by one. The racket of the porter-urchins. People went down to the stream with neem twigs in their mouths and sleepy eyes. Gurgling springs.

Makhan Singh was in low spirits, but it was time to start. With a heavy heart, he got into his seat and started the engine. The bus laboured to reach the road, heaving and swaying along the way. As he proceeded a few yards beyond the toll gate, his legs froze. Cold sweat ran down his face.

The inspector!

Till then, Makhan Singh did not have a blot on his career. But now...

What accursed moment let this devil in!

Was he lying in wait?

Damn him!

The inspector took the register from Ramlal's hands and counted the passengers.

'There are two extra people.'

Ramlal looked at Makhan Singh, and Makhan Singh studied the inspector's face.

'Who are they?'

The mother and daughter were in the back seat. The passengers' eyes turned towards them. They hung their heads.

The inspector asked: 'Where are your tickets?'

There were no tickets.

'Get down.'

The inspector noted down the driver's number.

I will lose my job, thought Makhan Singh

What if....

Let it go!

He remembered that young man in a sick bed in Srinagar. He must be waiting for them. The bus was scheduled to reach by midday.

First Panditji and now this inspector halting them. Makhan Singh was enraged.

None of them understood human misery.

He went to the inspector and said: 'They have to reach Srinagar by noon today. That old woman's son is ill.'

The inspector said contemptuously, 'So what?'

Sparks flew from Makhan Singh's eyes: 'So what? So, you should permit them to travel on this bus. They are poor. Let alone how they became poor! If I had some money, I would have helped them. But I don't.'

Makhan Singh stopped. The passengers were taken aback. His voice was still booming....

Again he said: 'I shall get the tickets right in front of you. I will arrange for the money when we reach Srinagar.'

The inspector turned and walked away without a word. Upon hearing the commotion, another policeman arrived from the toll gate. The inspector told him, 'These Punjabis can't be trusted.'

The blood boiled in Makhan Singh's veins.

'Can't be trusted, eh? I will show you.' His emotions broke loose like the deluge when a dam burst. Pain, sorrow, anger, and hatred blinded him.

Makhan Singh lunged forward with raised fists.

The inspector stepped sideways. A few others rushed to stop Makhan Singh. Ramlal caught him around his waist and begged: 'Sardarji, Sardarji....' Ramlal was seeing the good man in such an inflamed state for the first time.

As if delirious, Makhan Singh blurted out: 'Leave me! Let me slash open his entrails! I will die after that.'

The policeman intervened: 'Leave it, Sardarji. What he said is absolute rot. I apologize on his behalf. Enough...'.

Makhan Singh did not hear him. He said, 'I don't want this job. Let another person drive the bus.'

'Sardarji, don't say so. You....'

Makhan Singh didn't let him complete his sentence. Raising his palms, he asked him: 'Do you see these calluses? It is not by hitting people that I got them. Nor by holding the steering wheel. It's by tilling the soil that I got them. My father and grandfather were farmers. We have not cheated anyone. Now this fellow says, we Punjabis can't be trusted.'

He was infuriated. The policeman appealed: 'Leave it, Sardarji. It is all over; forget it....'

'Forget? I used to forget. But now? No!'

The policeman was worried.

'How many persons must be waiting for these people? Just imagine.'

'How many? There is a sick young man. But he will not be able to meet his mother and wife. Why should I then?'

There might be other similar cases.... Many such persons would be waiting for their beloved.

'Go, Sardarji.'

Makhan Singh thought for a moment. Without uttering a word, he started the bus. Droning on, the bus began to climb the pass. Its wail, as it climbed along the belly of the mountains where the mellow morning sun played hide-and-seek, was painful. Hills towered, one behind the other. No end to them. The wind whistled and howled.

∫

A shadow fell over a small hill, darkening it. Another hill in the distance seemed to move in the sun.

Are the hills alive? Do the hills die?

Hot springs of memories boiled in Makhan Singh's heart. People were killed in Punjab. Bachchan Singh said they had hacked his father into pieces. Shall I, too, kill everyone on this bus? Oh, my chest hurts. I feel suffocated. Is the bus going to overturn?

If it overturns, jackals will carry off everyone from Madhopur at night. The bus won't fall. It will suspend from the sky. Then I will ask: aren't the Punjabis trustworthy?

Oh, such pain. I think I will die....

I will go to Lahore. I had gone to Lahore taking Preetham along. But...oh, what pain....

The bus reaches at noon. But I won't reach. I won't find any of those early migrants in Delhi. If I die declaring I have calluses on my palms, wheat would be ripening in Lahore.

I feel cold; terribly cold. This corduroy from Lahore...

⁂

As the bus approached the tunnel, the rush of memories stopped. Makhan Singh felt great exhaustion. He was being carried off in a current. The bus entered the underpass without waiting for the sentry's signal.

Makhan Singh was choking. The dim lights in the tunnel twinkled like the stars from another world.

As soon as the bus reached the other end, it slowly came to a halt. Opening the driver's door, Makhan Singh fell out.

Waves of sunlight had engulfed the beautiful Kashmir valley.

When Ramlal and the sentries came running, Makhan Singh was lying on the raw earth. Tears rolled down and soaked the cloth that held his beard tight.

Someone among the passengers said: 'God saved us. Otherwise, we would now be there, fifteen thousand feet below!'

'Sardarji, Sardarji....' Ramlal cried like a child.

Ramlal's Sardarji did not hear the call. He was dreaming of the ripe wheat fields of Punjab.

YOUR STORY (MINE TOO)

N. MOHANAN

There was a police firing. O Poulose, you died.

I don't have details about this incident as I was not present on the spot. There are only newspaper reports before me, and they describe the incident in two different ways, in the news reports originating from two opposing sides.

One of them described you as a freedom fighter, the object of the nation's pride; you were a brave revolutionary. That you belonged to the exalted tradition of the nationalist movement, and the police shot you dead because you were leading a peaceful procession.

In another version, the notorious goon Poulose, as he led a gang of about two thousand rowdies and attempted to attack the police station, was shot dead in the ensuing melee.

I have only these news reports before me. I was not an eyewitness to what had happened.

Yet—O Poulose, who is dead and gone!

I knew you. You were my cook and domestic help.

Let me ask you with an incredulous tinge: 'When did you become a brave revolutionary? A freedom fighter? When did you become a goon, a rowdy, and a troublemaker?'

One rainy morning in June, Raman Nair, the college peon, had brought Poulose to my house and introduced him: 'Mashe! Here's a hapless boy. He has no bad habits and is very obedient. If you agree, let him be your domestic help!'

To be honest, I had not liked him at first sight. I was not ready to engage his services as my cook and domestic help. His attire and expression were untidy.

Poulose's hair was thick and unkempt; his clothes were torn and dirty. On his skinny, protruding chest was a scapular on a cord encrusted with dirt.

But his face exhibited helplessness and innocence. His eyes were doorways of pain that had opened as they searched my face.

At that moment, I could perceive the naked agony of an orphaned soul. I didn't feel like sending him away as he had approached the threshold of my house on that rainy morning. I only told him to bathe and come back when he was scrubbed and clean. Once he returned from his bath, I gave him a white mundu and an old shirt of mine.

After that, we lived in the same house for two years. It's not a very long period. It may not even be as big as a moment in human life. Yet, even a little moment can trigger great changes in the human heart.

⁂

O Poulose! I had begun to feel affection towards you without being aware of it. Today, I feel that I was wrong to feel that way towards you. I never had any claim on your affections.

(Who has any claim on anyone's affections?)

You were a Catholic, and I was a Namboodiri.

A Catholic and a Namboodiri!

What was my claim to be affectionate towards you? What authority did I have?

But I am this way, O Poulose! I was like this from my early childhood. All around my illam, people of different castes and communities lived— those who were untouchables and the ones who could not approach us. I had no playmates who belonged to my caste.

I was a mere child.

I yearned to make friends, quarrel and frolic about with them, shouting and clamouring to my heart's content.

Do you know how often I was subjected to severe beatings at home for befriending lower caste children? How many times they performed the punyaham, the ritual purification, for me! ('Will you put your hand around Govindan's shoulder? Will you go to Jacob's house again? Will you...will you...will you eat with the Chovans and Christians?')

I would sit on the veranda of the western wing of the house, leaning against the pillar, looking at the welts the beatings had left on my thighs. At that time, I would also notice ruddy welts on the thighs of the western sky! The evening sky with its dark clouds shed tears along with me.

How many leaves had fallen! How much water had flown away!

Even today, as I sit in the centre of the noise and bustle of this city, with ruddy welts in my heart, sobbing and thinking about you, the sky too is weeping.

My soul has been assaulted. Someone has severely tortured it.

Or, didn't I get the severest beating for undeserved love?

Yes, there's no doubt.

But, O Poulose! Why do you stand like a dark shadow in the empire of my grief? Wearing a large shirt that doesn't fit you at all (yes, isn't that my old shirt?) and your thick, unkempt hair. Slithering like a black shadow, why do you come into my empty land and stand here?

You were an inadmissible guest in the world of unpermitted affection.

The two years I lived in that small house on the bank of the river were the most cheerful ones in my life.

At that time, I was being loved. And I loved too.

You didn't know any of those things, Poulose. You were a small boy.

Yet, in my letters you used to put in the mailbox every alternate day, the story of my life wriggled. In those letters, my desires weighed heavy, beating their wings and ready to soar.

(You are my life!
Without you, I have no life, dear!
We are made for each other.
I yearn to see you. Please come....)

That was the story of forbidden love, destined to crumble. You didn't know anything about that, Poulose! You were a mere child then. And there's no need for you to know.

When I got a job in this city and prepared to leave that small house, O Poulose, you were ready to accompany me. I told you: 'Let my marriage happen. Then I will get a house ready and inform you. You need to come over only then, okay?'

But Poulose! That marriage didn't happen. And that will never take place, ever. I will never have a house, ever. That was why, my boy, I couldn't call you over. I realized if that marriage had taken place and I could keep a house, perhaps you wouldn't be dead today. (Would I have called you over even if that marriage had taken place? Perhaps, my wife would have said, 'We shouldn't keep a Christian boy in our house.' Because she was a Hindu, though not from my caste and I would perhaps have acceded to her request, as coming from my wife.)

There was something else too. I had owed some money to Poulose, on account of unpaid wages. He had told me in the beginning: 'Mashe, you keep the money together and give it all to me when I can finally start a paan shop with it.'

When he said that, I felt his eyes gazing at the pleasant horizons of the future. His greatest wish was to run a paan shop of his own. Whenever he said this, he would also mention Varkey, the powerful textile merchant who had his shop at the junction. In front of that beautiful shop adorned with different varieties of beautiful silks—white, red, blue saris with borders of rainbow colours—hung a grand sign surrounded by neon bulbs: Varkey Scaria & Sons, Textile Merchants. Varkey too had built his fortunes from a paan shop!

When Poulose expressed his dreams about the future, I too would enter his fantasy world momentarily. With a slight tone of derision, I would say: 'After some time, I too will come to your big textile shop, mind you! I'll come to buy dresses for my daughter's wedding. Please give me the saris on credit....'

He would walk away with a smile, his head bent bashfully.

But when I came to the city, I was unable to pay his accumulated wages. (I was a simple teacher in a private college at that time.) I told him I would send him the amount as soon as possible. That discussion happened when I was about to leave my old house. My friends waited by the roadside, putting my things in a car to go to the railway station three kilometres away. Despite my best efforts, I could not find Poulose. Just a moment ago, he had carried my box and bedding and put them in the car.

Where was Poulose?

When I got inside the house and looked for him, I found him standing leaning against the soot-covered kitchen wall, his eyes brimming with tears. I thought: 'He's crying because I didn't pay him the wages.'

Pressing a five-rupee note into his palm, I had said: 'Poulose! Don't cry! I will send you the whole amount as soon as I reach there.'

He burst out weeping. Between sobs, he said: 'Mashe, you can pay me my wages whenever you want! I feel so sorry that you thought about me that way. Please take me with you. I am also coming along with you. I don't have anyone....'

He didn't accept that five-rupee note.

I got into the car, promising I would call him over once I got married and set up a house. At that time, it didn't occur to me that he would be interested in accompanying me in the car till the railway station. But, when I saw that little boy who ran three miles to the railway station to reach before the train started, a severe pang of remorseful pain rose inside my heart.

It was night. There was a drizzle. I was chatting with my friends on the nearly empty railway station.

Suddenly, I spotted him. A short distance away, he stood like a dark shadow that had fallen from the lamp post. I was wonderstruck!

Poulose!

It was him.

'Why did you come, Poulose! At night! In this rain?'

To see you off, mashe!'

When I went closer, I saw his face was flushed, and his eyes were full of tears. Pushing a small paper packet into my palm, he said: 'This is for you, mashe! My gift....'

He could not finish what he was saying. Poulose covered his face with his palms. Turning towards the lamp post, he sobbed.

There was a chocolate toffee inside the packet. A piece of cheap chocolate!

⁂

O Poulose, you can't imagine the pain I felt at that moment. You should never come to know about that. I felt like holding you close and weeping with you. I had wanted to caress you and say, 'You are my younger brother. I can never, ever forget you.'

But I had stood silent, merely gaping at that child who had turned his face towards that lamp post and stood weeping, covering his face with his palms.

(I was a Namboodiri, and you were a Catholic....
I was the master, and you were the servant.
I was a grown-up man, and you were a child.)

Within me roared an ocean of grief. When its waves were expelled through my eyes, I turned and walked away, unable to reveal my weakness before him.

My dear child!

The uncommon sweetness of love and the innocence of cheap chocolate still ooze inside me....

⁂

When the train pulled out, I turned my head and looked at the almost empty small platform. Bundles of reed mats set out in a row. The old railway station office building, its walls smeared with coal tar, and the gulmohar tree close by spreading its foliage. And, at the base of the streetlamp near to the gulmohar tree, like a dark shadow cast by the lamp post.

'I don't have anyone, mashe! Take me too along with you, mashe!'

Those words resonate within me. That was true. There was no one to love him. His mother had died many years ago. His father, Mathai Mappila, was a drunkard. He had another wife and children. They didn't like Poulose. He had told me his father would come home drunk, tie him to a post, and beat him black and blue. On the other side of the hill across the river, I had seen a small cottage with walls of reed mat and the roof thatched with hay. It was to that impoverished, loveless situation that he had to return.

After my departure, he would have smouldered away in a world full of negativity. Each day, he would have waited for news from me to join me in the city. He would have readied himself and waited to come to my house after I got married, to become my domestic help.

༄

But that marriage didn't take place, O Poulose! That wouldn't take place, either. My desires have all died down. My dreams have all collapsed and writhed to death. I was broken and destroyed. I did not get the opportunity to enquire about you.

But I could never have forgotten you. You were an impermissible guest in the world of my impossible love. When rain fell incessantly during June mornings, you would come before me like a wet kid. I see a small boy wearing a shirt too big for him, with a head full of thick, bushy hair, carrying a letter in your hand, at a time when dusk walked along the slopes of the horizon flourishing the rim of her red skirt. The letter in your hand would be the last one that girl who was lost to me forever had written—a long, long letter. That letter would never reach me, my boy! Death, the devilish truth, has already fallen between you and me. You are lying by the side of the tarred road, bathed in blood....

Who did this? Who destroyed your paan shop? Who set fire to your textile shop?

Some say it was the policemen in khaki who did it. Some others say it were priests in black cassocks.

I don't believe any of this. I know who did this! I know who fired the shot into your soaring dream aeroplane—who dashed your cup of joy.

It's we who did this. We, including me.

When I include myself, you can't believe it, can you? Then, listen to me. For us, this is mere jest. We have white shirts. Degrees that go along with our names. We have the means for subsistence and a surplus.

We reach the maidans in the evenings and deliver speeches rich in eloquence and rhetoric. And when we enter hotels to ease our fatigue while innocent people like you rush away in excitement.... And while you rush away, death, the cruel truth, befalls you.

O Poulose! It is we who murdered you too. (This is not the first incident; neither is it the last.) It's been thousands of years since we began this game.

The only difference is in different eras, we kill differently. Long ago, we shut you away in a dark dungeon in Athens and murdered you, making you drink hemlock. While still alive, we burnt you to death in the streets of Rome. We thrust a crown of thorns on your head and made you carry a heavy wooden cross on your shoulder along the tortuous path of Golgotha. We crucified you at the crest of Mount Calvary, on the same cross you carried. We hurled stones as you fled from Mecca to Medina. Finally, on 30 January, we murdered you, shooting you three times in your chest in front of Delhi's Birla House.

Now, once again....

You lie bathed in blood by the side of the tarred road.

O Poulose! It is not by the side of the tarred road in that distant small town that you lie fallen. It is on the untarred street of my weak conscience where you lie covered in blood. Shedding the worthless blood of orphaned humanity, here you lie pathetically.

As I prepare to write your story with your blood, I hear the leader speaking about you from the nearby maidan: 'Although that body has fallen, there has been no death. He is the unvanquished man. He has no death. He is born again and again!'

What a spirit!

How grand! That leader needs you to shoot and kill you tomorrow. O! You must not die!

'He has no death. He's born again.'

Is this correct, my child? Is there no death for you who lies in the street of my conscience, covered in blood, with your eyes half-open and mouth gaping?

Will you be born again?

If so... if you were born again....

I have one request. Please do not return to this earth. If you are born here, we will kill you all over again. Please do not come here again.

You were the love-filled vitality of innocence. You were the smile of purity. Therefore, I wish you blossom as a white lotus. Even that is unnecessary. O! Man's hand will reach for the stem of that lotus flower. Please don't be born again here, even as a flower to be plucked.

Please blossom like a flower that never fades away in the far distances of the skies, in the invisible infinities, beyond the world of stars. Illuminate the fearsome, terror-stricken nights with your smile of silvery light.

In the wet June dawns, during the bright noon, at ruddy dusks, and dark nights, I will discover you from this soil millions of miles away. And then pray silently: 'Our Father who art in Heaven! Hallowed be Thy Name! Thy Kingdom come! Thy Will be done, as it is in Heaven!'

The white, red, and sky-blue silks are now spread out in heaven; saris with rainbow borders will be sent to me from the textile shop you have built there. I can even read the signboard written with the neon bulbs of stars: 'Poulose Mathai, Textile Merchant'.

When I come to buy dresses for the wedding of that daughter who was never born, O Poulose, please give me those items on credit...!

VISION

M. T. VASUDEVAN NAIR

From time to time, Sudha would go home from Madras to her village to visit her mother. But she shouldn't have assumed that the news of her marital woes wouldn't have reached the village. She had eaten her breakfast, and was relaxing on the veranda of the house, when Amma came over and said abruptly: 'Is what we have been hearing true, Sudhakutty?'

'What have you heard?'

'That you and Prabhakaran have separated.'

Amma was blinking hard, a nervous tic that came over her whenever she was trying to talk about difficult matters. Sudha looked at her mother severely. She decided to go on the offensive rather than try to explain herself.

'How did you hear all this? Over the radio?'

Amma said: 'Sreedevi from Narayanankutty's house had come over the day before yesterday. Her Devu's husband also lives in Madras.'

Sudha's older sister was also responsible for spreading the news. 'Vishaalam wrote. Her letter got here yesterday.' She had no doubt her other sister Chandri too would hear about this from her older sister and write to Amma as well.

Wanting some respite from the interrogation, Sudha walked into the yard. Although it was still quite early in the day, it was already very hot. She went for a walk in the shade of the compound wall. She could hear the sound of her rubber slippers echoing off the yard as she walked.

Amma lived alone in this old house. Sudha kept visiting not only to see her mother but also for the calm these visits brought her. No telephone ringing. No parties to dress up for. No need to wear a fixed smile when she hosted parties. No need to listen to the creepy jokes of colleagues. Her visits would have been more frequent but she didn't always get permission to go on leave. And even when they were approved, they were rarely for more than three or four days. After a brief walk, as Sudha returned to the veranda, Amma said: 'People are saying all sorts of things. What actually happened?'

She did not reply.

'From what I heard....'

Amma stopped midway.

'That's right, Amma. It was better for both of us to part ways....'

Amma looked away into the yard.

When the girl who helped in the kitchen came out to ask about something, Amma rose and went inside.

Sudha had taken fifteen days' leave from the bank to make this trip home. She needed to escape the gossip and tension at work. Her colleagues had begun alluding to her troubled marriage even though she had only really opened up to the cashier, Nirmala Sreenivasan. It was Nirmala who had arranged a room for her in the YWCA.

Amma liked to live alone. She did not encourage relatives and others to visit. She had no complaints if her children did not visit. Every month, she would write an inland letter card to all three of her offspring, whether she received replies or not. She always had a girl from the neighbourhood to help out in the kitchen. On Sudha's last visit, Amma had told her about the impending wedding of the girl who had been working in the house. She was planning to give her a gold chain worth a sovereign.

'The three of you must help out as much as you can. Send a money order in the name of Kuttiraman. It's all right even if you send it in my name.'

Her older sister, Vishaalam, and Chandri, the younger one, were to give three hundred rupees each. Sudha was to give four hundred, because she and her husband were working, and they did not have children.

When the girl who worked for her got married, her younger sister replaced her.

Not all her children were comfortable with Amma living alone. Vishaalam who lived in a huge house in Thiruvananthapuram with a number of servants was the most vocal about her concern. At one family gathering, she had said: 'There isn't even a doctor nearby if she were to fall ill suddenly.'

'I won't fall ill,' was Amma's response.

A clump of banana trees grew near the compound wall, which had crumbled here and there. Through one of these gaps, a black hen and her brood entered the courtyard, hesitantly. They cautiously began foraging for food.

'It's a junglefowl and her chicks. They come around at the same time every day,' she heard Amma say.

Sudha looked at them amusedly. The mother hen kept looking around warily, clearly nervous at being so close to human habitation. Trying not to startle her, Sudha cautiously moved a little closer to get a better look at the junglefowl. But her actions spooked the hen and she scurried away with her brood.

Amma did not bring up her marriage at lunch. That evening, Sreedharan ettan arrived. The older brother of her younger sister's husband, he was a high school headmaster and a local leader.

Mentally bracing herself for questions about her marriage, outwardly Sudha remained calm. She asked after his wife and children. She spoke about the weather, how hot it was.

'How many days' leave do you have, Sudhakutty?'

'A week.'

Amma butted in, 'There isn't a drop of milk to make tea for you, Sreedharan.'

'No need.'

Sreedharan then began chatting generally about things in Madras, the blazing sun of Madras, Jayalalithaa's assets, Karunanidhi's rule, etc. Sudha sat listening. There was nothing to add. She had heard that at the time when marriage proposals were coming her way, his horoscope was also under consideration by the family. Sreedharan left after a while.

In the evening, a host of dragonflies hovered in the wind. She had heard it said in her childhood that if dragonflies flew low, it indicated the onset of rains. She wished it would rain at least once. The scorching heat of the month of Meenam here was no less than the Vaikasi sun of Madras. There were no fans inside the house, and none of them had been able to agree on who would pay to have fans installed.

'You can sleep in the room in the southern wing. You'll get some breeze there,' Amma said, as she ladled out supper.

'I'm fine anywhere.'

In Amma's room, there was an old, rusty table fan which Father had bought a long time ago. Sudha hadn't brought along anything to read, nor had she bought anything on the way. On the round table in Amma's room, Father's old books remained as they were years ago. Amma used to read at night. But there were no new books. She looked at the book that Amma had placed above *A Concise History of the World*. It was *Himagiriviharam*, a book by a guru.

Amma had made up a bed for her in a room on the south side of the house. Sudha changed into a nightie. She looked at her watch. Eight forty-five. This was when Prabhakaran would return home after playing rummy and finishing two beers.

Amma came in.

'You can bring that table fan and put it here. Though it makes a sound, it still works.'

'No need.'

Wishing that Amma would go away, she made as if to go to sleep.

'And yet....'

Amma wanted to say something.

'Go on, Amma!'

'To part ways after living together for five years....'

She didn't say anything.

'What will people think?'

She turned away. Now she could avoid seeing Amma's face.

She changed the subject.

'What does one do to make a phone call here, should the necessity arise?'

'There is a booth in the room next to the medical store. You can make a call to any place.'

Sudha couldn't think of anything else to say.

'What have you decided?' Amma asked.

'I am thinking about it.'

'Should I come to Madras? Have a talk with Prabhakaran?'

'No. No.' She said quickly.

Amma looked at her with pity. Sudha said, trying not to lose her temper, 'There is no need for any mediation in this matter, Amma.'

༄

Without a word, Amma left the room. Sudha knew that Amma wouldn't raise this issue any more. It was in Amma's nature to suffer silently. Father had died after one and a half years of being bedridden, having suffered a paralytic stroke. Amma never complained in all that time. She refused to say anything even when people were whispering about his kept woman who had swindled them of all his savings.

In the morning, Amma said, 'Valyamma of Cholayil said she wants to meet you. Janu told Valyamma that you were expected. She met her when she went to buy milk from her neighbour.'

'I will go and meet her.'

'You said you would visit her during your last visit, too, but you didn't.'

'Right.'

'She is going on eighty-four. We don't know how long she'll live. Her eyesight is almost gone. But, she doesn't fuss about anything.'

Valyamma of Cholayil was the older sister of their grandmother. They had called her Valyamma hearing Amma call her that. Valyamma had lived in the house as her younger sister's guest long ago. In the mornings, she would often braid and tie up Vishaaledathi's hair. In the evening, she would gather the girls together to recite the evening prayer.

Grandma would sleep on the floor and leave the cot for her big sister, Valyamma. She was fond of telling stories at bedtime. Night after night, Sudhakutty was her only avid listener. Vishaalam would avoid getting caught in that situation and Chandri would be dozing off. Grandma listened, half-nodding, she recollected. The story of Unniyamma who shielded Palat Koman behind her thick, long hair, and the legend of Kannaki and Kovalan were imprinted on her mind. When they had visited Madurai for the first time, they recalled how Valyamma told the story of Kannaki. She would narrate it as if she had been an eyewitness to Kannaki plucking out her breast and burning the city with it.

Sudha had met Valyamma last when she had gone to get her blessings before her wedding. That was more than five years ago. Even when their grandma was alive, they were fonder of Valyamma for some reason. In the last five years, she had visited Amma seven times. Yes, seven times. Prabhakaran was with her on two of those visits. Valyamma had asked after her on all those occasions. Her house was not even three furlongs away, yet she hadn't gone to see her even once, something or the other had always cropped up. The last time around she had planned to get her something. But on the day fixed for shopping, she and Prabhakaran had quarrelled. She had ended up spending the day lying down quietly in the hotel room until it was time to catch the train.

The junglefowl family came out to the front yard again the next day. They did not seem as afraid this time. Sudha slowly walked up to the hen and her brood; their black feathers were shining in the sun.

Just then she heard someone calling out: 'Guests have arrived.' The hen and her chicks scurried away in alarm.

She turned to see Sreedevi Amma and her younger sister standing in the courtyard.

Amma invited them to sit down as was customary and asked Janu to make tea. Then, after giving Sudha a disapproving look, she went inside.

The look conveyed something like, 'Listen to a mouthful from her!'

Sreedevi Amma said: 'Sit down, Sudha. Let me talk. Don't be annoyed.'

Sudha did not sit down. She tried to smile, but failed.

'Go on,' she said.

'Why beat around the bush? I can't help but talk. If what I heard is correct, it is in bad taste.'

Sudha made as if to smile. And then, as if it were a simple matter, she replied, 'Yes, it's bad. But there's no other way.'

Sreedevi Amma's face turned dark. She glanced at her younger sister as if to prompt her to speak. The younger sister picked up from there, 'If there's something to what Narayanankutty was saying, it'll be a matter of shame for our family.'

Sudha didn't respond.

'To say that you want to separate after living together for five years....' She looked at Sreedevi Amma, 'Why don't you tell her what you were thinking.'

'Certainly, things go wrong sometimes; there may be problems but one must put up with them. That's what marriage is all about. Your Amma put up with so much, don't you know?'

Sudha tried to stay calm. The first thing she felt like blurting out was, 'O Sreedevi Amma! The fault is not Prabhakaran's, but mine!' Then she decided against speaking her mind.

They went on talking.

♪

She had, from early childhood, developed a miraculous ability to tune out unwanted conversations. She would start to think of other things—the names she had forgotten, the characters in novels, the topography of the places she had seen in childhood, the faces of her classmates from elementary school—and the voices would go away at once.

As she was leaving, Sreedevi Amma said, 'Do you think shouting myself hoarse has been utterly useless?'

'No,' she said.

'Don't you think there's at least some sense in what I said?'

'Yes.'

Sreedevi Amma heaved a sigh of relief. 'What's your decision, then?'

'Let me think about it,' she said, laughing.

With the satisfaction of having succeeded in their mission, Sreedevi Amma and her younger sister left in good spirits.

Amma asked, 'When are you going to see Valyamma of Cholayil?'

'I'll go soon.'

Valyamma too would be waiting for her, wanting to give her advice.

At midday, Sumathi, who was her classmate in high school, visited with her three-year-old daughter. She used to wait for her at the boundary wall of her compound, around the carpenter family's homestead, every day when they went to school together. The wart below her nose looked as if it had grown bigger. She had married before she had completed Class X.

Sumathi did not sit down, although Sudha urged her to take a seat.

'How are you, Sumathi? Happy?'

'Just going on.'

She wore a shiny sari on which blue, violet, and red stood out loudly. Her husband, who worked in the Gulf, must have bought it for her. Every two years, he would visit on two months' leave. A pungent perfume encased her. Her neck and her hands were covered in gold ornaments leaving not an inch uncovered.

'I heard that you had come. Are you going to be here for a few more days?'

'Yes. For a few more days.'

Next Monday would be the housewarming of Sumathi's new house.

'Sudhakutty, you must certainly come!'

'I will, if I am around.'

Tousling the hair of the girl who stood tracing the flowers on Amma's sari, Sudha said, 'I'm sorry, I've forgotten her name.'

'Karthika.'

She tried to get hold of Karthika's hands and draw her near. The child snivelled and stood by her mother, winding her tiny hands around her body.

Sumathi whispered: 'I heard something is amiss....'

'O, did you hear it too?'

'When the wife of Sankara ettan who does the mosaic work told me, I didn't believe it.'

Sudha hummed under her breath.

'Is it true, Sudhakutty?'

Sudha laughed, 'Somewhat....'

Widening her eyes in alarm, Sumathi leaned forward and said softly: 'Please don't think that I am advising someone who has more education and wisdom than me but it's better to live together whichever way you look at it.'

Sudha stroked her hand.

'Hmm. Let me think about it.'

'Your first mistake was to decide to not have children immediately. If there are children, there wouldn't be any unwelcome thoughts in the man or woman.'

Sudha looked at Sumathi wonderingly. A local phrase she should inscribe on her mind was 'unwelcome thoughts'.

Sumathi left. Later, Janu who had gone out to buy milk, said upon her return that Valyamma of Cholayil had once again enquired after her. Amma said, 'Go and meet her once, please!'

'Hmmm. I will go tomorrow.'

'She does not need any money. Nevertheless, give her something. When Vishaalam went to see her, she gave her fifty rupees and the old lady wouldn't stop talking about it.'

Amma laughed. This was the first time that Sudha saw Amma's face brighten up ever since she had arrived.

Sudha thought of countering, 'I am not going to compete with Vishaaledathi.'

She decided that she would return to Madras on Monday. There was no way she was going to spend all the two weeks of her vacation in the village. There has already been so much commotion within three days of her arrival.

Should she call the one in Hyderabad, she wondered. She had jotted down his mobile number in her diary. His direct number in the office, she had inscribed in her mind.

There's no one who could book a ticket for her. Never mind. She could get into the ladies' compartment. It's just a matter of a night.

He had told her to call him when she got to her ancestral home. 'If possible,' he had added.

The next day, after breakfast, she said, 'I'll go meet Valyamma now.'

'Take Janu along with you.'

'No need.'

First, she went to the newly built house of the Aashaaripparambil family. Sumathi was beside herself with wonder and joy. She belonged to a lower sub-caste and had not expected Sudha to visit her at home. She was at a loss as to how to entertain her guest. Two workers were varnishing the window shutters, under the supervision of the carpenter Narayanan.

She was taken on a tour of the house.

'Both rooms have attached baths,' Sumathi said with pride.

She struggled to sidestep Sumathi's request to drink something before she left.

'My husband has written that he'll come on leave in July.'

'Ask him to take you along the next time he returns to Dubai. That way you too can see the city.'

'That's not possible. Only those with high salaries can manage that, he says.'

Yet, Sumathi was very happy.

'I'm off, Sumathi. I have to visit Valyamma of Cholayil.'

'You remember what I said, don't you?'

'Yes.'

She laughed.

On the way to Valyamma's house she passed a clump of bamboo by a dried-up stream. Earlier, there were thickets on either side of the stream. In those days, it used to be full of water in all seasons. During the monsoons, it would brim over the banks. Farther down, it would become broader and become a small tributary of the river downstream.

Valyamma's house had been built in her father's elder brother's time. There was a bamboo stile in place of the old gatehouse now. When she climbed the steps and reached the courtyard, there was no one around. Black pepper had been spread out to dry on the bamboo mat in the yard.

She stood there hesitantly. It was Thankedatthi, the cousin who lived with Valyamma, who came out on the veranda.

'What a surprise to see you here! Grandma had mentioned you just this morning. She was worried that you'd go away without meeting her.'

Thankedatthi sat her down on a chair placed next to the woodwork railing.

She began to talk about her family. Both her boys were studying. They had returned to the hostel the previous week because they had to prepare for their practical exams. Her daughter, the youngest, was in Class IX. Thankedatthi's younger sisters had divided the property when their mother died. They had sold their shares and built houses on their husbands' land and were living there.

'This tottering, mouldering old house fell to my lot. There was no one to take my side....'

She choked on her words as she remembered the passing of her husband, as a kind of ritual she was expected to perform. She went through the motions of wiping her eyes.

'Where's Valyamma?'

'In the vadakkini, the northern wing of the house. Her eyesight is almost gone but she resents anyone holding her hand to help her. Who knows when she's going to stumble and fall...!'

Just then she heard Valyamma saying: 'No one will have to face any trouble on account of me.'

When Valyamma held out her hands to feel the frame of the door opening on to the veranda, and carefully stepped on the threshold to the veranda, Sudha hurried over to her. Even at eighty-four, she stood ramrod straight. The rauka, traditional blouse, and the upper cloth she wore over it were dazzling white. The mundu with a decorative border that she had draped around her waist was stiffly starched. Her luminous face that Sudha had seen in her childhood had not dimmed even a bit. She took special note of the thickness of her snow-white hair, done up in the classical style. When she had heard the tale about Komappan of the *Northern Ballads*, she would imagine it was Valyamma herself who had hidden him behind her hair, while bathing in the pond.

When Thankedatthi tried to bring a chair for her, Valyamma said, 'No, I'll sit here. Sit down, Sudhakutty!'

She extended her hand towards Sudha's.

Sudha sat next to Valyamma and leaned against the parapet of the veranda.

'Haven't you put on weight, Sudhakutty?'

She looked at her own hands. Yes, Valyamma was right. She had indeed put on weight.

'You were gasping when you walked four steps towards me? I could make out that you had put on weight just by listening to your breathing, without actually seeing your body.'

Valyamma laughed.

There were lifeless spots in her ashen eyes, but her face was smooth. Only a few folds on her neck were indicative of ageing.

'Thankam! Make some tea. Fry some jackfruit kernels too.'

'No! I don't want anything. Just half a glass of tea will do,' Sudha said.

Valyamma waited for Thankedatthi to go inside the house and then said: 'What did you decide, my child?' Valyamma's abrupt question made her flinch.

'Don't be afraid. I didn't call you here to shout at you or admonish you. Hasn't it been four or five years since I saw you last?'

She felt relieved.

'The ones around here merely grin when I speak my mind about anything. They think, "What does this old one, with both her eyes blinded with cataract, see?" But are they able to see what I see?'

She guessed that it was for the benefit of Thankedatthi in the kitchen that Valyamma raised her voice as she said this.

Valyamma lowered her voice again, 'What have you decided?'

Her breathing quickened. She continued:

'If you feel that you are through with him, get rid of him. This arrangement called marriage is for our convenience. There's no point in engaging in an act for the benefit of others.'

Valyamma sighed deeply, crossed her legs, and leaned forward.

'None of you met my first husband.'

'Amma has seen him. He was a Bhagavathar, a vocalist, wasn't he?'

'That's how the trouble started. Music classes were held at the Shaarathu (the household of the Pisharoty, a higher sect Sannyasi Brahmin) he would eat at our house. His singing was excellent. He wore gold earrings in which red gemstones were embedded, sandal paste on his forehead, and looked so striking. I was infatuated with him.'

Valyamma laughed quietly, running her fingers through her hair.

'He went away before the year was out.'

'Amma said so.'

Valyamma whispered, 'He didn't go away on his own. I asked him to leave.'

Valyamma kept smiling, her sightless gaze fixed on nothing in particular.

'He wasn't able to provide for me. I let that be. But he had a kind of lisping affectation in his speech and coquettish gestures! Mannerisms of women. Shouldn't men be at least a bit manly and smart? I told him bluntly that he would have to leave, that our marriage was over. What else was there to do?'

Although she had heard about Valyamma's first marriage with the Bhagavathar, she didn't know much about it. She had then married Valyachchan. He was a peon in the government salt depot. The couple had three children. Valyachchan died. Then the children died too. Valyamma was left alone.

'Hadn't you seen him? Valyachchan was not that handsome or anything. Was he?'

'I saw him when I was a child. He was on his deathbed at that time.'

'There wasn't anyone like him in this entire land. He'd always be there right in front of the temple festival procession.'

Thankedatthi brought tea.

When Thankedatthi was standing nearby, Valyamma sat with a serious mien without saying anything. When she went back into the house, Valyamma began to smile, as she remembered Valyachchan.

'Those who saw only his exterior would say he was a boor. He would shout and create a ruckus most of the time. But only I knew how gentle a soul he was. Even if I so much as caught a cold, he would fuss about it.'

Valyamma suddenly laughed out aloud.

Sudha forgot about her troubles. She sat waiting with the same eagerness she'd had as a child for whatever Valyamma was going to say next.

'Everything was going smoothly, suddenly some trouble arose. It was just after I had given birth to Kuttinarayanan.'

'What?'

'Imagine… I was attracted to another man. I told myself, "You wretch; control yourself, forget about this." So, things didn't go out of hand. Still….'

Without completing the sentence, Valyamma laughed out loud, open-mouthed. She saw that Valyamma had lost only her wisdom teeth.

'I was exactly your age, then,' Valyamma heaved a sigh.

'Is he still around, Valyamma?'

Valyamma's face clouded over.

'Gone. Everyone's gone. I am the only one left. Till I'm called, when the time comes, I'll just lie here. I can't kill myself!'

She shook her head.

'Who is the other one, Sudhakutty?'

She was startled, 'Eh?'

'You met someone. You like him. And you decided that you are going to be with him. Isn't this what has happened?'

'Who told you?'

Valyamma pulled up her legs.

'There's no need for anyone to tell me. Who is it, my dear girl?'

She tried to control her agitation.

'Is it someone who you work with?'

'No.'

She could not explain it to Valyamma. She had met him at a farewell dinner hosted for the manager of the branch when he'd been transferred. Late in the evening the chief guest, the organizers of the party, other guests were all quite drunk. It was then that she had spotted him, standing by himself at one end of the hall. She had not heard him earlier. He held a glass of orange juice. He stood looking at her now and again and then finally moved towards her. As he walked towards her, she thought to herself in a frenzy of excitement: 'My Lord! He is coming towards me. Please God, what am I going to say?'

She was so happy when he told her that he would be in Madras for ten days every month. Watching other people move towards them, he said, 'Can I call you at the bank?'

She nodded quietly.

Valyamma said, 'Does he have a wife?'

'No.'

'Does Prabhakaran know?'

Her reply was a bit delayed, 'I think he suspects.'

'Then, you must separate immediately. Prabhakaran will also get another girl. Don't bother too much about such things. Get rid of him.'

Sudha was amused. 'It's not that easy to get rid of him like in the old days, Valyamma.'

'If you don't want him, you don't want him. Doesn't it end there?'

'No, it doesn't end there. First, there needs to be a joint petition. The judge will then summon both of us after six months and ask us whether we are still bent on parting. Even if we say yes, we have to wait another six months.'

She watched agitation spreading over Valyamma's face.

'Does it need the judge's consent if two people meet, like each other, and decide to live together?'

'That's the law, Valyamma.'

Valyamma was not at all satisfied.

'If there are children, their expenses and other things have to be settled, yes. That's the proper way. But what has the judge got to do with two people who like each other living together?'

'That's the law.'

'What law...?'

Thankedatthi came over to pick up the empty glass. Valyamma mumbled something to herself.

Thankedatthi said, 'Till last year, Grandma could still see things faintly. Now she's completely blind.'

Sudha said, 'She can regain her eyesight with surgery, even at such an advanced age. I can take her to Madras.'

Valyamma laughed bitterly.

'No, no. Why should I have eyesight at this stage? I'm done with all that I've seen so far!'

Sudha prepared to leave.

Thankedatthi said, 'You can leave after lunch.'

'Oh no! Amma would've prepared lunch for me.'

'The rice is cooking. When you come next, visit us, please, Sudhakutty.'

Thankedatthi went inside. Her fourteen-year-old daughter arrived at the gate just then. Valyamma looked over to the gate. Removing her chappals and leaving them below the veranda, the girl looked at Sudha and smiled. Lowering her head, she walked inside without making any noise. When she reached the door, Valyamma asked, 'Hey! Where have you been?'

The girl was startled.

'To the Shaarath. To get a book from Shaarada.'
'Why should you wear a silk skirt to the Shaarath, like a vamp?'
The girl went pale and quickly escaped inside.
Valyamma turned her face towards Sudha.
'There was no book in her hands, was there?'
'Aye, no.'
'I knew that it was silk by the rustling of the skirt.'
'She is a child, Valyamma.'
'Hmm.... The girl is flirtatious beyond her age. I can see everything.'
'May I get going?'
Valyamma stood up.

Remembering what Amma had said, she opened the purse in her hand.

Valyamma said, 'No need. It seems you are going to give me some money. Don't. What need does this Valyamma have for money?'

She closed the purse in amazement.

'When you come...next time....'

Valyamma's voice faltered.

'...if I am around, just come and meet me. I need only that....'

She saw Valyamma's lightless eyes tear up. Her eyes, too, were brimming. She bent down, touched Valyamma's feet, paying obeisance. She remembered having done exactly the same thing five years ago.

Valyamma placed her hand softly on Sudha's head.

'Let the best happen to you, at least this time around.'

She walked out. When she reached the market, she saw the signboard of the STD booth from a distance.

She turned the two phone numbers she had memorized over in her mind. She reminded herself that she should look up her diary and confirm the mobile number. If, after making the call, she was able to reach home quickly, she would not miss the junglefowl and its brood entering the courtyard.

She quickened her steps.

SCENT OF A BIRD

MADHAVIKKUTTY

A week after her arrival in Calcutta, she saw an advertisement in the morning paper. 'Wanted: An able-looking, intelligent young woman to be in charge of our wholesale business. Must possess working knowledge of new designs and colour schemes of fabrics. Send hand-written application directly to our office.'

The office building was in a busy street where milling crowds jostled. It was eleven o'clock in the morning. She reached the building dressed in a pale-yellow silk sari. She carried a white handbag. The building was huge—it had seven storeys, more than two hundred rooms, and an equal number of balconies. There were four lifts. Crowds had formed in front of the lifts. Fat merchants and office workers carrying leather bags. She didn't see a single woman. Much of her courage had ebbed away by that time. She began to wonder if she had made the right decision disregarding her husband's advice and applying for the job. She spotted a peon in front of the lift and asked him, 'On which floor is...Textile Industries?'

'I think it is on the first floor,' he said.

She felt all the eyes of the men waiting for the lift on her face. *Chhe, I needn't have come. Putting myself amidst these perspiring males? Even if I were to get a thousand rupees as salary, I would not work here....* But she couldn't turn back.

She now had to get into the lift. Struggling not to touch others' bodies, she pushed herself to one corner of the lift.

She got off at the first floor and looked around. The lobby was spacious and there were big doors in front of her leading to different rooms. There were nameplates outside each of the doors.

'Export, Import.'

'Wine Business.'

She saw many such nameplates and passed through many doors, but she could not find Textile Business. By then, her palms were clammy with perspiration. She asked someone who had got out of one of the rooms: 'Where is the...textile company?'

He looked at her from head to toe with his reddened, narrow eyes and said: 'I don't know. But if you come along with me, I will ask the peon and tell you about the office you are looking for.'

He was a short man. Middle-aged. His fingernails had dirt under them. Perhaps having noticed that, she didn't feel like going along with him. She said, 'Thanks. I will make enquiries and find out by myself.'

She walked away quickly towards the other side of the lobby. She saw big doors there too. 'Dying' a nameplate read. She laughed at the typo. Anyhow, she pushed the door open to make enquiries. The room was big and empty except for a couple of chairs and a glass-topped table. She called out, 'Is anybody here?'

A fan was whirring overheard as the curtains rustled lightly. Gathering courage, she sat in one of the chairs. She felt she couldn't move any further without catching her breath for a few moments. What kind of an office is this, she wondered. Where have the workers gone, leaving the door open, and the fan on?

Since these people were connected with dyeing fabric, they would certainly know where the textile department is. She opened her handbag, took out a small mirror, and examined her face. She decided she had passed the requisite 'able-looking' aspect described in the ad. *Shall I ask for eight hundred rupees as salary? It would be lucky for them to get a candidate like me*, she thought. She was well-educated; had good social status and was well-travelled.

She started awake, hearing the cork of a bottle being opened. *Chhe, what a fool I am, sitting in a strange place!* A tall, young man, sitting opposite her, was pouring whisky into a glass of soda. His bush shirt was made of white terylene. Thick hair was growing on the back of his fingers. Watching those powerful fingers, she panicked suddenly. Why did I enter this devil's residence?

He looked at her, raising his head. His face was long, like a horse's. He asked her, 'Did you sleep comfortably?'

Then, without waiting for her reply, he raised his glass and drank the whisky in one long draught.

'Are you thirsty?' he asked. She nodded.

'Do you know where the textile department is? I thought you people will know. Aren't you the ones who deal in fabric dyes,' she said and smiled.

He didn't smile. He poured himself another drink of whisky and soda. The expression on his face seemed to say, 'There's so much time for conversation and all that.'

'So, you don't know?' she asked. She was growing impatient and wanted to get out of this place and go home.

He smiled suddenly. His lips were very thin, adding a grotesqueness to his smile.

'What's the hurry?' he asked. 'It's only 11.45.'

She walked towards the door.

'I thought you knew where that office is,' she said. 'You are also connected to the textile business.'

'What connection? We are not into dyeing fabrics. Didn't you read the signboard? It's Dying.'

'So...?'

'It means what is. Haven't you heard about dying? We are the ones who arrange comfortable deaths.'

Leaning against the chair, he blinked and smiled looking at her. Her legs quivered. Her palms were sweaty, and her eyes were brimming with tears.

She ran towards the door and tried to open it.

'Please open the door!' she said, 'I have to go home. My children are waiting for me.'

She hoped that her plea for help would somehow make the man help her. But he continued to sip his whisky. He looked at her and laughed grotesquely.

She pounded on the door. 'Ayyo! Are you trapping me?' she said aloud. 'What crime have I committed?'

Her sobbing stopped a few minutes later as she collapsed on the floor.

She could hear the man saying something in a soft, kind voice. She could only make sense of a few words:

'Long ago, during a winter, a bird was trapped in my bedroom. It was tawny, with a mix of yellow. The same colour as your sari. It tried to break the window glass with its beak. It flapped its wings on the glass trying to break it! What happened finally? It dropped to the ground. I stamped on it and crushed it under my shoe.'

Then, after a prolonged silence, he asked: 'Do you know what the scent of death is?'

She looked at him slowly opening her eyes but couldn't move her tongue to say anything.

It was not that she did not have an answer for him. Death has more than one scent. Who else but she, would know the various scents of death? The odour of suppurating sores, the sweet fragrance of orchards, the heady scent of sandalwood.... In a dark, narrow room, lying on a mattress spread on the bare floor, her Amma had said in a voice that didn't even have any trace of dignity, 'I am not well, my dear.... Not that it's painful...yet, am not well.'

In the sores on Amma's feet, white, fat maggots squirmed. Yet, Amma had said, 'It's not painful....'

Then her father. When her diabetic father suffered a stroke, she felt as if a breeze from the orchards had arrived in the room he lay. Thus, the scent which spread in that room was sweet.... That too was death....

She felt like saying all those things to him. But the power of her tongue had drained away.

'You don't know, do you? Let me tell you. Death has the scent of bird feathers. You will come to experience it. Soon enough. Do you want it now? What is your favourite time? At a moment when this world lies naked without shame beneath the sun looking down from overhead? Or at dusk? What kind of a woman are you? Courageous? A coward?'

He got up from the chair and came over to where she was.

She said, 'Please let me go. I had not planned to come here.'

'You are lying. So many times, you have planned to come here. So many times, you have yearned for a very comforting death! Aren't you like a river rushing to the sea? Tell me, dear! Don't you desire to experience that unending caress?'

'Who are you?'

She got up. She thought his fingers had a macabre attraction.

'Haven't you seen me?'

'No.'

'I have come near you many times. Once, when you were an eleven-year-old child. A time when you were lying in bed suffering from jaundice, unable to even lift your head. At that time, one day, when your mother opened the window, you said, "Amma! I am seeing yellow flowers. I am seeing yellow oleander leaves. Yellow flowers everywhere...." Do you remember that?'

She nodded.

'I was standing among those yellow flowers which only you could see. To hold your hand and to take you to the place you were supposed to reach.... But at that time you did not come along. Then you had not known about my love. You had not yet known that I am your guide and of everyone for that matter....'

'Love? Is this love?' She asked him.

'Yes. Only I can show you the perfection of love. You will offer me as oblation everything you have, one after another.... Your red lips, your dancing eyes...your body with beautiful limbs and parts...all. You will surrender each and every follicle of your hair. Everything will be devoid of your ownership. But will become everything: you will be there in the roar of the sea; you will be there in the ancient trees on which new buds shoot up after winter. When seeds in labour sob underneath you, your weeping will also rise along with those sobs. You will turn into wind; you will turn into raindrops. You will become grains of mud. You will become the beauty of this world....'

She rose and stood steady. She felt that fatigue had completely left her. She said with a newfound courage: 'All this may be correct. But you have got the wrong person. It's not yet time for my death. I am twenty-seven years old. I am a married woman. I am a mother. My time has not yet come. I came here in search of a job. It will be around twelve thirty or so now. Let me return home.'

The man didn't utter a word. He opened the door and gave her permission to leave. She hurriedly walked out of the door in search of a lift. She felt that her footsteps were reverberating all over the lobby.

She stopped when she reached the lift. The peon who operated it was not there. Yet she got into the lift, closed the door, and pressed the button. It suddenly rose up, with the initial notes of a crash. She felt that she was in the sky and that thunder was rolling. That's when she saw the board hung inside the lift.

'The lift has broken down. Danger!'

Suddenly, it was dark everywhere. A resounding, roaring darkness. She could never get out of it.

THE WAR ENDS
KAKKANADAN

Three yakshis—Shaarada, Kartayani, and Bhavani—lived atop Vettikkuttiyaal, the giant peepul tree.

Half a dozen serpents also dwelled in the hollows of Vettikkuttiyaal. Their names only Oolanthara knew. Many times, Oolanthara was heard yelling, 'Vasuki!' after invoking thirty-three crore deities, cutting the throat of a cock (one for each god), offering them cock blood, drinking it followed by a draught of arrack and then shaking his big, blood-smeared whiskers and brandishing Kali's bloody sword in his right hand.

Hearing that voice, the new moon of Karkkidakam, the mid-monsoon month, would tremble. A beggarly drizzle, the hallmark of the month of poverty, would quiver.

But Unnoonni would not.

Unnoonni's god is Kalladamooppan, his departed great-grandfather. Unnoonni's young son Mathaikutty believes the ancestor sports a tail.

Unnoonni would offer bali to Kalladamooppan on the night of the new moon. He would put rice in a silver dish and place it atop the main beam of the house. When Mathaikutty, with bulging eyes and a cage-like chest, wearing a dirty loincloth, stood on his rickety legs and stared into the silver dish, his mouth watering, his mother would say: 'My son! That's the bali for your great-great-grandfather.'

Yet Mathaikutty would look on, craving the food. That's when he discovered the ancestor's tail.

Kaleekkal Aashaan's son Vettupothu, the butting buffalo, set fire to the tail of Mathaikutty's konakam, the thong-like cloth piece. One day at dusk, Vettupothu was squatting atop Anappara, the elephant rock, smoking a bidi, intent on ogling at the girls returning home from work in the cashew sheds. When he spotted Mathaikutty, he wanted to have fun at his expense. That's how the fire incident came about. Like Hanuman descending on Lanka, Mathaikutty jumped down from Anappara. Then he ran eastwards through the paddy fields, with the blazing tail behind him.

It is Kalladamooppan who took revenge on Vettupothu. It took

Unnoonni just two cocks. He vowed an offering. A burnt sacrifice. A puja.

Smallpox pustules sprouted all over Vettupothu's body.

When Vettupothu was down with the deadly pox, his mother burst out laughing. She is said to have called Oolanthara over and said: 'O Master! Finish off this Kaarkodakan somehow.'

People say that on the day he turned twenty, Vettupothu had come home drunk, threw his mother to the ground, and kicked her.

Vettupothu, after getting drunk every day, hurled obscenities at the passers-by. Hiding in the Pezhumvila Paramuchar's coconut grove by the stream, he caught and violated women returning from the market; he played 'flash' with the Muslim goons from Tamilians Street.

People were scared of him.

Oolanthara dispatched the pox-weakened Vettupothu easily. (As was the practice in those times, Oolanthara, a smallpox survivor, was in charge of looking after pox victims who were quarantined in a very rudimentary manner.)

The bribe his mother paid for getting her son killed—twenty-five rupees!

Oolanthara put up a shed in a small patch of land by the paddy fields in front of Kaleekkal's house. He spread green banana leaves on the floor and laid Vettupothu down on them. Oolanthara built a bonfire in front of the shed. He cut chicken and drank arrack. Chanted spells. The parayas, Oolanthara's acolytes, stood vigil.

In the midnight darkness, lying before the raging fire, Vettupothu breathed his last.

The mother roared with laughter when she got news of her son's death.

⁓

Of the three yakshis residing atop Vettikkuttiyaal, two are Eazhavas and one belongs to the goldsmith caste. Rumour has it that Vettupothu had turned Bhavani, the goldsmith girl, into a yakshi.

When Bhavani began working in the cashew shed, she turned somewhat fashionable. She applied scented oil to her hair, bathed using perfumed soap, dusted her body with talcum powder, wore a bindi on her forehead, and collyrium in her eyelids. She kept her curly hair loose and walked about, swaying her wide hips lasciviously.

Vettupothu slyly approached her. Slowly, Bhavani became close to him.

The day she started to vomit, Bhavani realized she had become a little too close to Vettupothu. By then, it was too late. Vettupothu told her to leave.

The goldsmith girl told her closest friends: 'I won't let him go scot-free. I'll stage a dharna in front of his house with red flags and all.'

Her friends said: 'Bhavani won't really mind going that far.'

But no one saw Bhavani after that. She was found drowned in the flooded stream by Vettikkuttiyaal. People said she had drowned herself, but some whispered Vettupothu had done her to death. The panchayat kept quiet about it.

Anyway, Bhavani died and turned into a yakshi. Then she went about looking for a palmyra tree to inhabit. Finding none, she sought refuge atop Vettikkuttiyaal.

She began to live with the two other yakshis—Shaarada and Kartyayani—who like her had failed to find palmyra trees for themselves.

Unnoonni, who was scared of Vettupothu, said when he died, 'He killed the goldsmith girl. And Oolanthara killed him. Now, at whose hands will Oolanthara....'

Unnoonni stopped short of pronouncing the word. He kept quiet, looking all around him.

Pezhumvila Paramuchar, lustily tipping the toddy bowl into his mouth, slurred, 'At whose hands will Oolanthara...?'

'Now someone will kill Oolanthara too,' Unnoonni blurted out as if committing a blunder.

'And who is this someone?' asked Neelaantan, Oolanthara's chief disciple and protégé.

'God!'

'Oh, come off it, Unnoonni Mappila,' Neelaantan said. 'No one can kill Oolanthara.'

As he got out of the toddy shop and walked through the paddy fields, Unnoonni told the moon, the grand uncle, secretly: 'I, Unnoonni, will kill Oolanthara.'

Unnoonni was walking along the mud-dykes, continuing his tete-a-tete with grand uncle moon. And there, by the dyke was Vasuki with his hood spread. Ready to strike!

Unnoonni froze, standing where he was like a solid block. His limbs didn't move. His tongue didn't move. Vasuki mistook him for someone standing dead! The self-respecting serpent lowered its hood and slithered away.

After a while, Unnoonni came to his senses. No sooner had he come around, he yelled, 'O my Kalladamooppan!' and fled like a flashing harpoon.

Finding his father collapsed on the veranda, drowned in sweat and lying on his belly, Mathaikutty raised a hue and cry: 'Mother, Father's lying dead like a mountain.'

Sosamma, Unnoonni's wife, the monster that she was, rushed out from the kitchen, covered in soot and a ladle in hand. Her voice was full of expectant anticipation: 'Is he finished?'

Putting her finger on the nostrils and chest of her husband, she said dejectedly, 'No, he isn't dead yet, son. He is stone drunk, that's all.'

Mathaikutty sat gaping as his mother sprinkled water on his father's face. Slowly, he was revived.

As soon as he was up, Unnoonni cried, 'It's he, for sure.'

'Who's he? Are you crazy?'

'It's your paramour who's crazy, not I,' Unnoonni shouted. 'It's he, no doubt. I'll show him.'

'Who is this he?'

Unnoonni continued his tirade: 'Oh, my ancestor, protect me from the clutches of that terrible one and finish him off!'

Unnoonni's eyes were brimming. 'He sent a cobra to kill me! A king cobra!'

'Cobra? How?' his wife said.

'Huh-huh. Don't I recognize him by his raised hood? The original king cobra! He was swaying to the snake charmer's pipe! And a plume above his head. O, my great ancestor! Your grace!'

'Tell me what happened. Where did it happen?' his wife egged him on.

'I was coming home. As I reached Unnithan's paddy fields, he lay across the path. He raised his head as he saw me and opening his hood swayed back and forth and to the sides.'

'O my God! You must have nearly lost your life out of fright.'

'That's where you are mistaken. You don't know your husband properly, dosa.'

Sosamma didn't say anything.

Unnoonni continued: 'With my mind fixed firmly on Kalladamooppan, I kept staring at the serpent. And he virtually turned into ashes before my fierce gaze and then fled. Will I let him get away so easily? As he flashed past, I chased him. He hissed. I hissed back. Finally, he escaped into the bamboo clumps in Kuzhikkala house and I lost trace of him there. I'll get him. All this running left me exhausted. No wonder I passed out.'

'O my Lord! I was afraid you had died. And yet, you have escaped,' lamented his wife.

'That's Kalladamooppan's power. He is my protector. I'll not let that fellow off now. He is the one who sent the cobra.'

'Did someone really send the serpent?'

'What did you think?' said Unnoonni. 'It's he who sent the cobra. Don't I know that he sent the snake to kill me? But he is mistaken. Unnoonni can't die of a snake bite.'

'Who is this he you keep talking about?'

'Oolanthara. Who else?'

⁕

Unnoonni began preparations for a puja as an offering to Kalladamooppan.

About that time, Oolanthara Aashaan, the master sorcerer, was stricken by scabies. The skin behind his knee joint cracked. He didn't take it seriously. When it itched, Aashaan asked Neelaantan and the other hangers-on to scratch it. Neelaantan and the parayas took turns scratching. But the itch only intensified.

Soon, the itch turned into immense pain. The pain spread to the nerves and became a terrible, throbbing ache. He was unable to bend his right knee.

Neelaantan got Mukkoottu, the medicinal oil, from Kesavan Vaidyar of Thekkedam. After rubbing in the mixture, a warm poultice made of bran was applied.

But to what avail?

The itch and pain only increased. Scabies turned into an abscess that grew bigger every day.

It was Neelaantan who first raised a serious misgiving: 'Is it someone trying to get at you, Aashaan?'

Aashaan was lost in thought. The stragglers on his head stood on end. His face, pockmarked by the black welts of smallpox, blazed. His intense eyes, deep set in well-like hollows, glinted. Aashaan grunted to the accompanying twang of arrack in his mouth. Then he asked his hangers-on: 'Is there anyone in this locality who'll dare to do that?'

Neelaantan whispered the name of the one he suspected.

Aashaan sprang to his feet and fell back into the easy chair owing to the pain in his leg. Aashaan roared: 'Him! I'll....'

It was not only to remove his ailment that Aashaan chanted mantras now.

Unnoonni saw the smoke rising from Aashaan's sacrificial fire pit. That night itself, his brother-in-law, Thomaskutty, died of a snakebite.

'He is bent on destroying our family,' said Unnoonni. 'I'll finish him off.'

Cocks died.

Pots of arrack were emptied.

Thechchi flowers used for magical rites stopped blooming.

Yajna.

Counter-yajna.

Homa.

Counter-homa.

Mantra

Counter-mantra.

Hreem, Hroom, Hram.

Pustules appeared on Aashaan's buttocks and armpits. They burst.

Serpents wriggled about in Unnoonni's kitchen and backyard.

The serpents in Vettikkuttiyaal's hollow were not to be found any more. Only the yakshis stayed on, looking for prey. They were afraid of sorcerers.

Smallpox spread like wildfire during the winter, a highly unlikely occurrence. Oolanthara Aashaan began to do brisk business. He could perform all sorts of black rituals against Unnoonni, financed by others, so to say.

The pox caught Unnoonni's son, but Kalladamooppan saved him.

Battles raged on earth and in the sky between Kalladamooppan and the demons under Oolanthara's command

Screaming, flying serpents; wailing, roaming, pestilences.

Vipers took up permanent residence in Unnoonni's courtyard.

Oolanthara developed leukoderma.

Arrack and cock blood flowed in the Elayi paddy fields.

The battle progressed.

But Oolanthara had an edge during the monsoon. Unnoonni never ventured out for fear of snakes.

The trend changed when the first intense stretch of rains had passed and the month of Karkkidakam commenced. Nearing the new moon, Unnoonni's strength grew a thousandfold.

At midnight, after the usual offering of bali to Mooppan, Unnoonni clad in tattered clothes splattered with cock's blood and arrack, screamed as he raced through the Elayi paddy fields with a flaming torch in his right hand. He was headed west, towards his ancestral home.

Hearing him yell, darkness stood petrified. The serpents slithered away and hid in the burrows and the hollows of Vettikkuttiyaal. The yakshis shuddered.

As Unnoonni entered Oolanthara's gate, a sleeping Aashaan woke up startled. He began howling. Neelaantan too awoke. As he rubbed his eyes into wakefulness, he saw that a big pustule on Aashaan's chest had burst. Blood and pus were oozing out. Aashaan died in Neelaantan's lap.

As dawn brightened the next day, Kalladamooppan's great-grandson was found dead in Unnitthaan's paddy field, lying on a piece of rock. There were marks of a snake's fangs on his calf.

DIMENSIONS

ANAND

Whoever knocked on the door at night
didn't knock a second time.
By the time I reached the door
I heard footsteps.
Climbing down the wooden stairs,
opening the door, I looked down below.
Into the street devoid of sound and movement
empty like a cremation ground.
I couldn't make out,
who walked along, without looking back?
Man or woman?
Had he or she come to give, get,
tell, or hear something?
How different are the one or two travellers at night
from the innumerable people who walk along this street
raising a din during the day.
When he/she walked away and disappeared....

Why did I give this the form of a poem without taking the lines to the right-hand margin of the paper and reversing the order of words here and there? Is it to give you the impression that I was writing a poem and not describing an event? It won't be right either if I surmised that a reader would think this is real if it was written in prose. Because it could be a story. But who knows where the story ends and where the essay begins? I don't think we will reach anywhere if we attempt to ascertain in what all states how much different forms of writing like a poem, a story, or an essay can be real and how much fiction. Those who write know this is not a problem that affects readers alone but writers too—perhaps even more than what the readers ever experience. Anyhow, let all this be for the time being....

    Closing the door of my room, I hurriedly climbed down the wooden stairs as I had to find the person who had walked away after knocking at my door. But the stairs were not the kind that would cooperate. Old wooden stairs of an old building. One which had put up with a lot of rain and sun as it was not covered. They had been worn out and seasoned with the ascent and descent of two generations. The banister would rattle when one touched it. I was always anxious that there was a higher probability of the stairs caving in than that of the climber slipping to his fall.

The stairs took me straight to the street. By the side of the road, on the four-feet wide space which may be called a footpath, hawkers would spread out their wares during the day. Pedestrians could only walk on the street, braving the vehicles. Now, there were only a few sleeping dogs and cows. The person I was looking for hadn't disappeared from sight. Maybe because of the cold, the figure had covered himself/herself from head to foot with a cloth. By the manner of walking, it appeared to be a woman racing ahead (as could be made out from such a distance). For the sake of convenience, let me call the person a female. I walked faster. Since it was night-time, I didn't call out to her by raising my voice.

The night was cold, but I didn't mind it. I walked past the shut doors of merchants and businessmen. Apart from street lamps, only a few buildings had lights on. From an illuminated room on the second floor, I heard a man and a woman quarrelling. Something fell down and broke. With that, their conversation came to an end. I stood hesitantly for a moment. Then I decided to follow her, my visitor. But by that time, she had disappeared.

I was not put off. Picking up my pace, I reached the spot where I had last seen her. It was a level crossing. To the left and the right, the roads were empty. Taking a fifty per cent chance, I decided to follow the road to the left.

Along this route, it was mostly houses. They were quiet...sound asleep. There were lights in the veranda or at the gate, here and there. After I had walked for quite a distance, an elderly person came into view. He was standing at a door that opened straight on to the road. Yellow light flowed from inside his home, elongating his shadow that fell on the street.

He was clad in a kurta–pyjama. The expression on his face was poised somewhere between vacancy and anxiety. I looked at him again. I was wonderstruck. It was the same man who had come to meet me two days ago. He had come around noon to speak to me about the problems people face in the city's overcrowded hospitals. He had introduced himself as someone who was working alone without the help of any organization. He had spoken with a lot of passion and anger about the hardships faced by the patients from far-off villages and their relatives—how people stood in long queues and searched for counters and rooms endlessly with patients who were unable to even move and who died on the way without being able to see the doctor or receive treatment in our government hospitals where the systems were so complex that they confused even the most educated people. He was determined to find volunteers who could guide and help such patients. I had then thought: how could one fix such hospitals where the doctors, nurses, and even the safai karamcharis were likely to go on strike any moment without notice.

However, the man at the doorway didn't feign recognition. To make sure that I hadn't made a mistake, I went closer and peered at his face. No, I hadn't made a mistake. The protuberance on his forehead that had distracted me during our last conversation was still there. His figure: lean and bowing a little. Lips with drawn-down corners. Everything was the same. What more? He was wearing the same kurta which had a black stain on the chest.

There was only one difference. The vacant look on his face had turned into grief. Grief and anxiety had made an appearance. Although he did not talk or betray any trace of recognizing me, he moved away from the doorway just enough to invite me in. I entered the house.

A bulb was burning on a holder stuck to the wall, casting its yellow glow on the sparse, old, and damaged furniture in the room. I sat in a chair and he, in another. Even then, he did not say a word. Although I had so many things to ask him, I too did not say anything. I looked at the wooden table he was staring at.

From the next room, I could hear footsteps and the sound of things being moved around. Sometime later, a short, fat woman appeared at the door. Paying little attention to my presence, she approached him. She walked while swaying slightly to one side, her hands held slightly away from her body. She spoke to him about something. I didn't understand a thing. It was not a language I had ever heard. My host didn't utter a word in reply. When she went inside, he stood up, thought about something for two minutes, and sat down again. Again, his gaze was fixed on the table.

Why were these two elderly people sitting up so late at night and foregoing sleep when almost no one else was awake? Something was troubling them. They obviously thought it was their own business. I was clearly left out of the scheme of things. I didn't understand why he had let me inside in the first place.

The noise of things being knocked about was again heard from the next room. The woman was talking. But no one responded. Perhaps, she must have been talking to herself. Whenever her voice was heard, my host lifted his head and listened intently.

All my efforts to make out something out of the whole affair was proving futile. Moreover, I was not clear about what I should be looking for. Was it the woman who knocked at my door at midnight or was it for an answer to the riddle of these two people who were awake at this time of the night? Is there someone lying indisposed in this house? Or dead?

The short woman reappeared at the door. Standing there, she again spoke to him in a language unknown to me. He got up. But this time, I caught two words from her conversation: railway track and suicide. When she turned and walked away, he followed her holding a lit wick-lamp. They disappeared beyond the door.

Their voices could be heard for a little longer. Then that too stopped. No one returned to the room. I was left alone. As time passed, the silence and solitude seemed unbearable to me. Disturbed at the turn of events, I got up without any more deliberation and walked out

The railway tracks were not far from that road. As I continued, the fencing with black iron anglers that separated the railroad from the residential quarters came into view. I crossed over to the other side through a gap in the fence. My pace quickened.

A deserted place. In the light of a searchlight set up high above somewhere in the distance, the top half of the rails, smoothened by constant friction, gleamed in the night. I could clearly see five rail carriages but the spaces between and outside them lay steeped in the darkness. These areas were covered with slush and the excreta. I did not know which railway track and what suicide the man with the protuberance on the brow and the dark, short woman were talking about—I did not even think about them. I had already left the regions of the specific and the defined. My surroundings had become eyes affected by the cataract of the night. I walked along, scanning the five tracks one by one. After a short distance, the fifth rail merged with the fourth. This made my work a little easier.

My efforts were not in vain. Although it was what I was looking for, what I saw in front of me took me by surprise, as if I had hoped not to see it at all. It was maybe because of this ambivalence that my scream got arrested in my throat. The body was across the third rail. With revulsion and fear, I moved near it.

Only when I came closer did I realize that what I had seen was not what I had expected to see. It was neither a suicide nor an attempt at it. A woman, somehow bound to the rail, was struggling to break free. Her voice was muffled as she had been gagged. Even in that darkness, I could see her eyes looking at me, craving for compassion.

Before I could do anything, some people pounced upon me. Three or four of them. Instantly they sealed my mouth with tape. They hoisted me, hand and foot bound, and carried me away walking over the tracks. In the meantime, a train that came hurtling down ran over the woman. My strength to fight back drained away. Limp as I was, they could have laid me on another track. But they didn't. Instead, they carried me to a jeep that was waiting on the road beyond the tracks. They deposited me on the back floor, beneath the seats. Then they climbed in, and in a few moments, the jeep was on its way.

What bewildered me during the difficult hours of the night was the lack of a common language between me and the people I met. The person who knocked on the door of my room didn't wait to talk to me. The woman who was ground to her death on the tracks didn't get an opportunity to speak. The language spoken by that the man and woman in the house was unknown to me. It appeared as if language didn't help them to face the problems that they encountered. But the blows that fell on me as I lay on the floor among the seats suddenly rendered the necessity of any language between human beings ethereal. Whatever that happens may not be what we want, expect, or fear about. Neither need it be extraneous to us, for that matter. There may not be any relation between any of these people I had met. At the same time, any of them could have been any other. The blows that fell on me at lightning speed made me realize that there existed some membranes, ligaments, tendons among all of them—the ones who slept on through this night and those who didn't. I didn't know how to describe this bond—fear, suffering, shock, or even strength? Whoever could imagine that naked blows had so many possibilities?

They tore away the tape they had stuck to my mouth. They had made sure the first set of blows they delivered on my body would ensure that I couldn't scream even if they twisted my elbow or pulled out my hair. They interrogated me: who was I, why had I come to the railway tracks, who had sent me, and things like that. My answers didn't satisfy them. And they didn't want to be satisfied, either. There was something else on their mind. I realized this by and by.

The jeep must have traversed a good distance. The interrogation and beatings had stopped somewhere in between. I lay waiting for the next scene, the pain and the darkness as my witnesses.

The jeep stopped at the gate of a compound full of light and people. The person who had been questioning me lifted me by my collar and sat me down. 'We are letting you off here,' he said. 'You must sit here and pray for your life. For the rest of your life. Your life is to be lived here. There is no escape for you from here.'

This was the hardest of all the blows I received so far. The prison where I was to spend the rest of my life! I didn't know what that place was. Since they said so, it would be so.

They pushed me off the jeep with a kick, and I fell on the ground. The man pulled me up by my collar once again and said, 'Remember. You haven't come to the railway tracks. Seen nothing. You don't recognize us. All through the night, you were here. Here!'

They were in a hurry to leave. They jumped into the vehicle that had already started moving. I stood by the road. Taking out the kerchief from my pocket, I wiped off the blood from my face. It had also stained my clothes. Within such a short time, several spots on my body had swollen.

It didn't seem that the people who had left me there had any connection with the place. They had not handed me over to anyone before they fled. Still, I was afraid to go away without entering the compound. Such a move wouldn't have been in keeping with the command I had received.

It was a large complex with a lot of space between the front gate and the building inside. People were moving over the place, as if the night didn't make any difference. It resembled a marriage procession. But what was heard over the loudspeakers was not film music. It was a hymn repeated by all the participants. It fed fear in me. I had been deposited in the midst of an esoteric band. I fled from the scene.

My flight, as I feared, did not succeed. Two people clad in a strange attire caught hold of me. Their hands, as powerful as steel, effortlessly dragged me in past the gate. Passing through the courtyard and the corridors beyond, they threw me onto the floor of a vast pandal.

The prayer was going on in the pandal, the arena full of men and women wearing long gowns and necklaces. Bright lights that turned night into day. Everyone was singing with raised hands, swaying and swinging, their eyes half or fully closed like in a state of intoxication or stupor. At one end of the pandal, standing on a dais three men with long, flowing beards, wearing long gowns in strange colours and woollen caps, were singing. They were praying with their hands extended to the sides and looking up. But there was no dancing. These were the men who led the people. Their followers sang what they intoned.

I could not dance along with them. Nor could I repeat the song after them. If I was to pray, it was solely for my life, as the ones who had brought me there had said. But to whom should I pray?

The bright lights in the pandal and the din and the heat radiating from the human bodies around threw me off balance. The night was entering its last phase. A night in which I had not slept at all. The end of this night, filled with events without cause or effect, people who had shed logic or intelligence, miracles, anxieties, tragedies, and finally threats and blows, had proved to be harder to endure than what I experienced till then. The only thing to be done for the one who had been sucked into its vortex-like midst was just to surrender to it. Those who had been inside didn't go out of the pandal either. But my desire to get away enabled me to act against all inhibiting forces.

My efforts were certainly disturbing the dancers. If I knocked against them, they didn't hesitate to kick me or push me with their hands or feet. They were doing so while their eyes were closed. Although I was being kicked, I slowly made my way outside. Once, when my anger was aroused, I too kicked a man. When I lost my balance, lurched, and fell, I steadied myself by grabbing a man's beard. Suddenly the atmosphere changed completely. The ones who had kept their eyes shut opened them. All of them pounced upon me.

They realized I was not praying. Besides, my clothes were different. I wasn't wearing a necklace around my neck. I had not kept my head covered. They tore away my clothes. Some frisked me to see whether

I was hiding any weapons on my person. They took away my pen and wallet from my pocket.

That moment, a miracle happened again. A tall and broad-chested man crept through the people and shielded me with his body. Then he dragged me outside. All along, he was arguing with my attackers and physically fighting them off. In the ensuing melee, his clothes were torn, like mine. Like me, he too received blows.

Passing through many corridors and doors, he finally brought me inside a small room. It was a long and confusing trip. He seemed to know the place very well. Finally, it felt we were wholly free from the crowd. Even the din of the prayer didn't reach that room. We shut the door and stood panting.

Perhaps it was his room. When he turned on the light, a cot, a chair, and some furniture came into view. He poured some water from the earthen pitcher in the corner and gave it to me. He asked me to rest in the cot for some time. I couldn't understand why this man had faced danger to rescue me from the midst of my enemies. Whatever the members of this group believed in, I was not one among them. But he was one of them. Around his neck was a necklace; on his head, the headgear they wore. He had a room of his own in the headquarters of this institution; therefore, he must be someone important. I didn't dare to ask him any of these things. To me the only truth then was that he took kindly to me and rescued me. I felt grateful for that. If he hadn't saved me, the crowd would have doubtlessly lynched me.

He put his hand on my shoulder. Sitting on the bed, leaning against the wall, I looked at him. The figure that stood putting his hand to my shoulder was extraordinarily big. Very tall, and robust, and muscular. Trimmed, black beard. Eyes sunk deep. He didn't smile.

'I don't know who you are,' he said. 'Whoever you are it is better that you get away from here. Somehow, I'll make that happen. But you should never tell, anyone, anywhere, that you had been to this place. You don't know the name of this place. Plant it firmly in your mind that you have never come here. And that you haven't seen me. Right? Not only for your own safety, but also for mine. It's absolutely necessary.'

'But why are you helping me?' Finally, I had come out with that question. 'You are one among them. Those who brought me here said...'

He put his other hand also on my shoulder. 'Don't ask anything.

Don't try to know anything. There is no time for us to waste talking. Get up.'

Time there certainly wasn't. Me—who had turned into a person with torn and blood-stained clothes, a bruised and swollen body, and a mind filled with fear and anxiety over the course of a night—I managed to hoist myself up. The man covered me from head to foot with a cloth that had been spread on the cot. I was barely able to walk. He supported my body, walking alongside me.

He put out the lights in the room, one after another. Plunging the world behind us into darkness, we walked on. There was no one present in that part of the building. Everyone was at prayer. As we came out of the room, the din reached my ears once again.

He asked me the name of the place I had to reach.

'Oh, the place is near Gandhi Market,' I said.

My answer made him enthusiastic. Stopping me in the corridor, the man asked, 'Can you do me a favour? A friend of mine lives in a house in Gandhi Market. The gate faces the street.'

'What should I do for you?'

'It is a small chore. Today is his birthday, and I have bought him a book as a present. But I am not able to go there. If it is not too much of a trouble, please take it to his house.'

'This is not difficult for me.' I gladly agreed to do it.

'Stay here.' Keeping me waiting in the corridor, he went back to his room and returned soon with a brown paper packet. On the way, he put it in a long polythene bag.

'The house number is G-12. It's a red house. The gate has black pillars, and there is a letterbox. The opening is fairly large. All you need to do is deposit this package in there. Don't wake up anyone in this unseemly hour.'

Unseemly hour! It was the first time after stepping out of my house many hours ago that I had thought about time. My watch had been taken away by the crowd. The man didn't have one. But the sky will begin to become pale very soon, and life would emerge on the streets. Before that, I have to climb back the stairs I had climbed down. I must get into my room somehow.... My eyes were wet with grief.

We walked fast. Only my saviour knew the twisted paths. Corridors, flights of steps, opening doors noiselessly, sneaking out of windows, taking cover behind rows of bushes. Finally, we reached the turnstile of a wicket gate. We heaved long sighs. He placed me in one of the turnstile's four segments, but himself stood on the other side. It turned and opened straight into a bus stop. The man didn't pass through the gate. It might be forbidden for the faithful to cross over. He told me I would get the late-night bus from there to Gandhi Market and stretching his hand over the turnstile, placed a five-rupee coin in my palm. The next moment, he was not there.

The bus came. Besides me, there were only the driver, the conductor, and a passenger who was an old man. Pretending to be cold, I wrapped myself, head and all, with the bedsheet to avoid their attention. The lonely street lay dazed by the mellow street lights and the dawn chill. None of the night's experiences remained in my mind; only the door of my house and the stairs. And the red house with a black pillared gate in Gandhi Market, G-12.

The bus took a long time to reach Gandhi Market. Entering the terminal, the driver reversed the vehicle. The driver, conductor, and the old man got out along with me. They moved to a wayside tea shop that remained open throughout night. The thought of hot tea lured me too. But I didn't wait there.

Though the market was sleeping, it wasn't lifeless. Those who slept in front of the shops and on the raised pyols of vegetable vendors, turned over again and again under the assault of mosquitoes. The fish had not yet been brought to the fish market. Behind the butcher's stalls waited the goats to be slaughtered for the day, rubbing against each other and bleating now and then. Dogs and cats went about, looking for yesterday's bones and bits. The house I was looking for was right in front of this line of stores.

A bulb was burning in the veranda, but the interior was dark. Absolutely no movements. Exactly like my saviour had described, there was a letter box with a big opening right outside the gate. I took the packet out of the bag, and put it in the box.

It was when the packet hit the bottom of the letterbox that a doubt arose in my mind. The sound it made did not resemble the one a book made when it fell. It seemed that there had been something metallic inside that package. But why didn't I feel it throughout the journey when that packet was with me? Why didn't I pay enough attention? Was it in my hurry to escape? I felt there was a kind of noise coming from it. This aspect too I had overlooked. Alarmed, I put my ear to the opening of the box. I held my breath as I tried to discern the sound. I clearly heard the tick-tick of a timepiece.

With my own hands, I had planted a bomb in front of a house where some good people live! Within a short time, the market will wake up. Vegetable, fish, and meat will be laid out on the stands. Shops selling all kinds of wares will open. The space between stores will be thronged by innocent people...those who sell and buy, cartmen, labourers, and beggars. The din that rises from Gandhi Market can be heard from afar. It would be then that....

And all because of me....

I began to run as if I was being chased by hounds. A lone man fleeing through deserted streets. I negotiated the roads leading to Gandhi Market quickly. Within no time, I was standing in front of the building that housed my apartment.

My legs began to slow down. Not only because I was exhausted and my breath was blocked and the frequency of my panting rose, but because something weighing down in my mind had begun to pull me back. I had run after planting a time bomb in a busy market. Though unknowingly...but that was the fact.

Many times during the night, the question as to what lies ahead and the anxiety as to what I should do had been vexing me. In none of those stages was it possible for me to turn back. Now there's a fire before me, a roaring fire. Each step forward singed me more and more. And although each of those steps were taking me nearer to my room—my refuge from this horrid night—all I would have desired when I was released from that prayer gathering was to say that I have put the night behind me. Now I can't say that. I am still trapped in the night. Not in the about-to-be-burnt-out night but in the still-burning night. Still, I can't now compare or translate the night to a problem, or the problem to the night. It doesn't matter whether it is night or day or whether one is awake or asleep...what matters is something else.

At an earlier hour, when I felt that the darkness was denser and therefore light shone more brightly, the matters that were in front of me appeared somewhat black and white. The person who knocked on my door and got me out of my room to the street, an old man and woman who kept vigil all night with a lamp, and the woman who lay bound on the railway track—they were all in some way victims of violence. Later, that violence was directed towards me at the railway track. But this moment, as I climb back up these stairs, I have turned into a violent person.... And yet, what matters is not even that.

I have already mentioned how in those terrible moments when I was being attacked, I became aware about the membranes, ligaments, and tendons that develop between night and day, between those who are asleep and those who are awake. I realized in a flash that none of them may be related to each other and yet anyone of them could have been anyone else and that the accident was connected somewhere with certainty and imagination with reality. And yet, those who had showered blows on me had hammered into my brain that I had never been there in those places and that I had never seen any of them. The command of the esoteric gang who inflicted on me another share of blows also was the same—that I was not there and I hadn't seen any of them. What matters is what is the ligament between being present at all these places and, at the same time, not being present at all these places? Is it fear, suffering, or strength?

As I climbed the old wooden stairs one by one, stomping down each of them with my fatigued, heavy feet, the bed sheet slid down from my body, revealing the bruises and blood stains. With that, House G-12 near Gandhi Market was also forgotten. I realized I had not seen the person who had handed the bomb to me. I had never been to the headquarters of the secret society of which he was a member. I do not know the people who took me there in a jeep. There was no woman lying bound on the railway tracks. Did anyone sit through the night sleepless, whispering of railway tracks? I haven't walked along the street in front of their house in that unearthly hour. The reality is that I haven't climbed down those stairs from my apartment.

When I stood on the topmost step, I felt free from everything. Even from the stairs that lay between me and the street. Somewhere in the far end of the street that now lies silent and deserted like a cremation ground, the woman/man who was my visitor had buried herself/himself. Whatever had taken form from the street, returned to the street. Suffering, cruelty, avarice, and extortion. I stood in front of my door with a calm mind—an epitaph for the street that rouses everything and then levels them by making them disappear. My curiosities turned lazy and meaningless. Like the knell tolling for the parting night, I began to weave the rest of the lines of the poem:

Dimensions

When he/she walked away and disappeared,
my clock struck three.
Hearing its boom that lingered on,
longer than during the day
I stood at the door looking at the street that was,
longer than it was during the day.
Do not measure night with day.
Night's dimensions are different,
colour is different.
The striking of the clock told me.

PEMPI

P. VATSALA

He could feel her standing in front of the black hut. He felt certain that his heart was frozen like the cold white leaves she would have worn on her hair, like the jungle around him, like the frosty stumps of paddy in the fields left fallow after harvest. In the faint light of the lamp placed in the veranda, flashing like a sword, appeared the yellow border of her dark chinta—a long cloth wrapped in a knot over one shoulder from where it hung loose down to the ankles. When she turned her face around, he was startled. Finally, the moment of farewell had arrived. He felt deep anguish; it was impossible to wrench her away from his mind.

'I am returning to my native place, Pempi.'

To the stubbles in the paddy fields and to the straw thatched on the roof last year, now lying burnt black in the sun, no one usually said farewell!

And there was no need to say farewell to her either. Rather, he had wished to believe so. She had lived with him for the past sixteen years! And yet he had not spent with Pempi, his consort of sorts, even one hundredths of the time he devoted to the cattle in the sheds of the nethyaaramma—the landlady, the zamindar's wife. That realization too startled him now.

The lamp in the veranda threw its light into the now empty paddy cellar. The cellar had been built and lined with clay by her own very hands, into which no cold or dampness could ever penetrate. From the time the paddy started to be accumulated in the cellar, she had not set eyes inside of it. He had himself measured and handed out into the winnow that she stretched before the cellar door, the paddy required for preparing rice for him and her for the day. He never looked at her face on those occasions. She took the paddy gratefully, husked it and extracted the rice, cooked it, and served it hot to him. On certain days he ate it. On certain other days, even though he was hungry, he lied to her: 'I don't want it. I have already eaten.'

'I am not the man of the house. Neither am I bound to reach home at regular times and partake of the meal she cooks. She is my kept woman. My servant maid. My cook. There is nothing called *tomorrow* between the two of us. Let her be aware of that and live accordingly,' he thought.

When he measured out all the paddy from the cellar and sold it to Mammath, the tobacco vendor, had asked: 'Why are you going back home to the plains so suddenly, Gopalan Nair? Am I going to be all alone here, then?'

Many more people from the valley were bound to arrive here. There would be honey in the jungle. The tribal people, the Kurumars and Kurichiyars who consider an eight-anna coin a treasure, would bring bottles of honey, in exchange for it. There were any number of tribal Adiyaathi women available here for a piece of tobacco. For a glass of tea and molasses, the tribal Adiyaar men would exchange a seer of green paddy. The land available here cheaply could be sold in the valley like gold.

'I am not a permanent settler here, for that matter,' he repeated his old refrain. Aloud. So that she, sitting inside, could hear. He has a family back home. Pempi who put up with him for sixteen long years is nobody to him. She is like the black, fertile soil, trapped within the deep forest. Meenakshi whom he had not even set eyes on during these sixteen years is his wife! Is she? 'Will her son recognize me today,' he mused. He tried not to think whether she would take him back again.

I must go back home, he told himself. He once again examined the lock on the iron trunk. He picked up the torch lying on top of the trunk. As he walked, his knees quivered. Was it that cold? He asked himself. He went and sat on the three-legged stool that had been placed close to the wall. When he touched the cool wall, which Pempi had polished with cow dung and charcoal mixture, he was startled once again. This was Pempi's touch. Whatever he touched, were Pempi's....

He had come to this place sixteen years ago, plucking away the leeches that crawled up his legs and sucked his blood. The frozen leaves of wild plants were shivering. In the paddy field covered with bushes, the chorus of crickets had risen. The land crabs hurriedly withdrew into their tiny burrows. The roar of the wild stream was frightening. The stream reminded him of the life of the Adiyaars that skidded over the boulders of hardships and rushed headlong frothing and foaming....

He felt that it was rank foolishness on his part to have come to this godforsaken jungle to cultivate paddy, listening to the words of the nethyaaramma.

The nethyaaramma had told him sternly not to look at the face of Valyammaavan, his older uncle, who had forbidden his daughter, Gopalan Nair's wife, to treat him as her husband. He had told her: 'Why should you have a husband who is unable to provide for you, give you clothes and oil for your body?'

Gopalan Nair had begun his new life as a full-fledged kaaryasthan—caretaker—of the nethyaaramma's land and entered the hovel which smelled of raw earth and cow dung.

'You will not lack anything here, Gopalan,' The nethyaaramma said. Her words had reflected the fullness of satisfaction and happiness she was experiencing, as if she had taken possession of a newly purchased, fattened and mighty ox.

'There's a lot of work here. Only that, till now there was no way to get it done.'

Upon her arrival in Wayanad she had realized that in the virgin soil she had acquired encroaching upon the forest land she could harvest gold, by way of the bountiful crops.

'Very good. Before being able to look squarely at Uncle's face once again, I should make a fortune, working this soil,' he had told himself.

'What would that work be?' He asked her with marked deference.

'There isn't very much...for the time being. Watching over the crops for a few days. Just that....'

He had only heard it said back home, 'The cold of Makaram, from mid-January to mid-February, that caused even a tree bark to get seizures....' about the customary cold during that season, and that too in the plains. But he had experienced worse, here. Cold that turned humans into rocks. The jungle that stood frozen all around. The watchmen's songs that he had heard from watch stations on all four sides of his location had gradually turned into resounding snores. It was so cosy, so warm and comfortable to rest awhile on the platforms raised over the bonfires lit at the separate watch stations built to scare away wild boars and elephants. The crop-watchmen, the Adiyaars, slept in the middle of the ripe, harvest-ready paddy fields where the wild boar roamed, grunting. They were habitual sleepers. Only he stayed awake, as real-time guardsman, vigilant, foregoing sleep. Heard the snapping of green bamboos in the forest where elephants rummaged. Holding his breath, he stealthily felt around for the torch, making sure it was in place. He held fast wound around the thumb, the launch rope of the slingshot, on which he had constantly practised stone launching. Kept dry logs ready to be fed to the fire. When he saw in the dark sky, the frozen moon crescent, he remembered the one-eyed monster. He squeezed his eyes shut. He wouldn't sleep with that kind of pressure on the eyelids. Yet, he pulled up the black, coarse woollen blanket above his knees. As a thousand arrows of acute cold struck his feet, he couldn't sleep. The nethyaaramma's paddy fields won't be laid waste by wild pigs. Not a single ear of paddy will be trampled underfoot by a wild elephant.

As he saw the crimson in the eastern horizon, his legs automatically snuck into the blanket. Sleep, which was prowling around hesitantly, sprang at him and overpowered him.

'Aye, is it Meenakshi? Has she come so early after her bath?' He woke up startled. Embarrassed, he rubbed his eyes. Pulling the blanket, he looked around. There was nothing to be seen. Just smoke...the mist rising like billowing smoke clouds.

'Aye...aye....' The voice that came shooting like an arrow, piercing through the mist and the cold. What creature is that, up and about in so biting a cold?

Right below the bamboo platform of the watch station, stood a girl swathed in a black chela. The crushed white leaves she had worn on her head shivered in the wind.

'What?' he asked her.

The girl pointed her finger towards the nethyaaramma's threshing yard and homestead.

The arrows of cold kept up the attack on her through her threadbare chela.

'You can go!' It seemed she understood. Holding the ends of her chela together, she disappeared into the mist-filled fields.

As he walked along the central dyke of the paddy fields, rubbing his palm together in the bitter cold, covered head to toe in the black, coarse blanket, he reflected: 'Would Meenakshi have come out after her bath?' The dewdrops that fell from the leaf tips reminded him of the water dripping from her damp hair. 'No! Though she is my wife, first and foremost Meenakshi is the daughter of Valyammaavan, the eldest uncle, the head of the family,' he thought. 'And here I am merely the nethyaaramma's servant.' He hastened on his way.

At the entrance to the threshing courtyard of the manor house, under the fig tree, lay crushed fruits and deer droppings.

Placing a jug of steaming black coffee, the nethyaaramma asked him, 'Last night's vigilance paid off, didn't it?' Her pale face carried a smile of contentment. 'I heard that last night the wild boars were running riot in the fields.'

'The watchmen in all the four fields surrounding ours were fast asleep.'

'All of them are losers! Getting one and half seers of paddy from me, making rice out of it, preparing rice gruel, drinking it, and sleeping soundly through the watch, and still they say they were on vigil!'

Even if one were to get a bushelful of paddy as wages, no one would willingly come up to this hill country from the plains to take up a watchman's job. But he couldn't say that any more. Hadn't he himself come?

'You are in it now. From now on, you are in for it,' he said to himself.

The girl in the black chela was sweeping the yard.

'Sweep it and clean it well! Today, too, the threshing yard is to be ritually cleansed,' the nethyaaramma said.

She raised her head once, put away the end of her chela securely and continued sweeping. Her expression resembled that of the cows in the cattle shed.

The nethyaaramma continued, laughing with an extra-brightness, in a diplomatic, yet decisive, gesture: 'This year we should sow the field at Pannikkaal.'

He shuddered at the thought. Sowing the field at Pannikkaal! Has the old hag's brain burned out because the price for paddy has shot up? As he thought it over again, coolly, realization dawned on him. Why she has left her home and countryside behind and come here to this forest where there is no man or vehicles, is not just to gaze at the scenic beauty. It was to make money! Couldn't he too act likewise? It's only four years since the kaaryasthan at Marar's homestead came and settled here. He has paddy cultivation in six acres of fields. And his job as the kaaryasthan, besides! All his expenses taken care of. He could cleanly save whatever he earned from his crops and his job!

When he thought of his Valyammaavan, he didn't express any discontent about sowing the field, which had not ever seen an ox and was leech-infested!

The nethyaaramma's face blossomed like the white rose that grew behind the cattle shed.

The coffee plantation lay overgrown with brushwood and undergrowth.

On one side was the paddy field where the leeches dived in the mire filled with land crabs. On all three sides, the reserve forest waited to swallow the coffee plantation and the paddy field. He was amazed at himself about taking on the impossible task of the kaaryasthan's job at Pannikkaal fields, which even the previous caretaker belonging to the tough, warrior-tribe Kurichiyars, had given up. What pluck, daredevilry!

He summoned the Adiyaars. Yoked the oxen to the plough, and thoroughly upturned the wet soil. It was so fertile that it wasn't necessary to add manure. He prepared the nursery of paddy seedlings, in time plucked them and replanted them in the prepared fields. Before the shadow of dusk fell each day, he escaped from the jaws of the all-devouring jungle, and reached his hut. And slept in the shed. When the paddy put forth shoots, grew mature and ears of corn appeared, the nethyaaramma commanded: 'You must yourself watch over this crop. Wild pigs and elephants won't let even a bit of this survive! All your toil and struggle till now will go waste, otherwise!'

Though it was an anticipated disaster, having to take on this responsibility, he was beaten to the ground when it did really materialize, so to say.

He ate the dosa and honey the nethyaaramma had personally served him, after sending away the helper. He made a bundle of the big, long torch, and the black, coarse blanket.

The nethyaaramma who accompanied him to the gate said: 'Come and meet me once in two days at least. I should know about everything that happens there.'

'I will,' he replied.

Below the paddy plants that grew extraordinarily lush, frightening even, he couldn't spot the dykes where the leeches hid themselves. The Adiyaathis who were bent over weeding, murmured in a low tone, looking at the bundle hung from his shoulder.

He spotted the gigantic ben teak tree that stood at the corner where the three jungles met, below the stream, at the bend. Under the tree, the skeleton of a new hovel was taking shape. Newly split and polished bamboo stems. Two or three Adiyaars were working in a hurry. Even at midday, the penetrating cold! He sat down in the courtyard, watching the big, broad paddy field in front, lying in expectation of the oncoming night. The noise of the Adiyaars rhythmically beating the clayey slushy soil to make a solid floor for the hovel, echoed from the surrounding jungles. Each resounding sound caused his mind to shudder.

Here, the whole thing was going to get finished. He waited for them to do that last beating of the floor. They finished their work by the time the shadow of the jungle began to spread its dragnet above them. He looked behind, at the hovel that had taken shape, and still behind, the thick, dark jungle that rose like a fort's walls. The Adiyaars who had finished their work came out. They fearfully looked at the darkening jungle and the paddy fields being engulfed by shadows. They desperately wanted to leave the jungle and save themselves from the darkness where wild boars and elephants lurked. They would have their breath back, only when they reached the several adjacent knolls on which their huts huddled. He gave them permission to leave. They turned their faces around, and kept looking back at their new thambraan, master. When they walked very fast, turned the bend, and reached the open fields after plucking away the clinging leeches from the calves of their feet, their songs without words reverberated from all sides.

He felt the cold encircling him. He had to pick up the bundle along with the long torch and the black blanket that he had kept on top of a rock in the morning as soon as he arrived. He had not yet opened the gunny bag the nethyaaramma had sent along.

As he was about to enter the hovel, he heard light footsteps behind him.

'Father, you may go now. I have no fear. Go home! Mother is waiting there to have a look at the chinta.'

He was startled and wheeled around. That girl in the courtyard! The servant maid at the manor house, Pempi! She who should have been collecting the wild jackfruit from the jungle, catch the land crab, roast it in the fire, and eat! Instead of that piece of chela he had seen her dressed in, in the morning, she had changed into a full-blown chinta. Setting down in the veranda of the hovel the big basket she carried on her head, she said: 'Pachchayan's wife has given this!' The fresh white leaves that she had worn on her hair put out a frozen smile and shivered in the cold.

'Did you come all alone?'

Instead of replying to his query, she pointed to the field which was down the courtyard. Her timid father was running away along the dyke, like an arrow in flight.

'So, you are here...' he bit his tongue. The nethyaaramma had all the intention to shackle him to this place! The figure of her father, who was constrained to leave his daughter alone with him here for company, struck his mind, piercing deeply.

The thought that he should take her back to her own hut, took firm root in his mind. Could he possibly return tonight itself, after returning her to her own home? He was trying to ascertain the situation in his mind.

The wild pigs were waiting at the edge of the jungle, for the humans to leave so that they could forage into the crop. There could be elephants too. Only that the nethyaaramma didn't mention them. The odour of the warm elephant droppings on the fields' dykes had not subsided. He could keep the torch, the catapult, and stones ready in his hand. He would do anything further, only after he dropped Pempi home at once. Without even breathing a word to him, sending off a young woman to the hut in the middle of nowhere, in the deep jungle, where he was to live alone.... He felt he could survive there as an exemplary watchman, even without female company. He needed to prove that to the nethyaaramma.

He wrapped the muffler around his head, shook the black blanket, and covered himself with it. He went inside the hut. On the floor freshly smeared with cow dung, a fire was burning in the newly raised fireplace, crackling and bursting.

'Don't you want to go back to your hut?'

She shook her head.

'Aren't you afraid to live here?'

'No.'

Seeing her sitting there firmly like a stone, he was convinced that she had no intention of returning.

Resentment rose inside him. Was the nethyaaramma planning to enslave him too, like she did with the Adiyaars? Let not the nethyaaramma pride herself over the belief that she has got a permanent kaaryasthan to watch over the crop to be raised annually in the impossible Pannikkaal fields where wild elephants could make a beeline for the crops. Let the harvest of the current crop be over. I must show the nethyaaramma, that I, Gopalan Nair, had not come coveting the women of Wayanad, he was resolved. Let morning arrive. He tried to sleep, thinking of Meenakshi, his wife. She was the daughter of that villainous character, his Valyammaavan. The one who insulted him and deeply wounded his pride. He tossed about on the mat. He got up and went over to the machan put up on the sprawling tamarind tree in front of the hut and sat there watching over the crop during the entire night. He had not slept a wink. Inside the hut that looked like a condensed mass of darkness, the kerosene lamp that kept burning, had gone out long ago. From the bonfire that was lit near the dyke of the field, smoke still spiralled upward. Descending from the machan, climbing down the pegs of the bamboo stem ladder, he walked, the blanket covering him.

He heard the iron bangles jingling from within the hut. Vessels clanging. There was fire in the fireplace.

In the big copper vessel, the water was warm.

It was for his bath! He told himself he didn't want it! What was wrong with cold water? He heard the water from the wild brook, carried up to the backyard through the aqueduct system built from halved bamboo poles, splashing down on the stone surface.

He took bath in the ice-cold water.

She brought steaming rice gruel in a hollow plate. Should he drink it? The rice that the Adiyaathi cooked? Should he surrender himself to the nethyaaramma? Yes, he should. Valyammaavan is an evil man. Meenakshi is the daughter of the man who insulted him and hurt his pride.

'More rice gruel, please!' he called out.

She smiled when she poured more rice gruel into his plate. White teeth glimmered. Lips turned red with murukkaan, the juice of the mix of betel-leaves, areca nut, lime paste, and the tobacco she chewed. He bought her tobacco, as a token of accepting her as his woman. And bought her a chela at the thira festival in the kaavu, the sacred grove-temple complex. And a one-rupee-coin-studded taali, too, the token of conjugality. Seeing that, her eyes shone much more than it usually did. The thambraan has finally wedded her publicly, her facial expression clearly stated.

A day before the reaping of the crop began, he went over to the manor house to meet the nethyaaramma.

'Pempi is a smart one, isn't she, Gopalan? Right after the harvest is over, we must change the hut for a proper cottage, built with laterite bricks cut from the quarry.'

'That's not necessary. I'm not going to be permanently settled here, anyway.'

'Why? Have you made up with your Valyammaavan?'

'No.'

'There's some revenue land around that bend in the river. Can't you get it tilled and sow it with paddy beginning your own cultivation, Gopalan?'

Was she planning to have him trapped with a woman and free seeds to grow his own paddy, he seethed within himself.

'No. All that is very cumbersome.'

'You could take the pairs of oxen, seeds, and the paddy required for valli—wages for the Adiyaars—from me.'

'No. I can't have my eyes trained on too many things at the same time.'

'Do as you like.'

The Adiyaathis looked on with envy in their eyes, as Pempi, wearing the one-rupee taali, and a clean chinta got down to the field and started reaping. She was the thambraan's Pempi! They had never anticipated that she would get down to the field to reap.

No. He shouldn't cherish her so much, he felt. She was someone he would have to discard sometime in the future. Like this black soil, like these jungles that surrounded him, like the cold wind that blew, doing the rounds, like the water in the brook, like this field filled with green swathes, then the paddy ears ripening, and then the hard mud covered with stubbles all over after reaping and cracked all over, he would have to leave behind her too one day.

Within the earshot of the Adiyaars who had gathered to collect the valli, he told Mammath: 'Why should one need to do agriculture of one's own here? I am not permanently settled here anyway! I will go back to my native place. I don't know when but sooner than later!'

'Really?'

'Don't you ever doubt it!'

Mammath smiled, shooting a sideways glance inside the hut. Then he looked at his face. Did he imply that one won't get such a nice woman back in his native place?

He had always kept her—the girl who gave him everything—beyond a particular line. He regularly paid her valli by measuring out green paddy as he did for all other Adiyaathis. He never handed her the key to the wooden granary that the nethyaaramma had gifted him. From that granary, he measured out the paddy that was required for daily use, into a winnow she held out every morning. His thought: was she my wife, to be entrusted with a supply of paddy for a week or two, which she would boil, dry, husk and turn into rice, and stock it according to her convenience?

The reaping was over. Mammath returned from the market in the valley with his cloth-bundle. There were chintas to be sold to the Adiyaathis during the festival in the kaavu.

'Buy a chinta!' When he spotted Gopalan Nair, Mammath urged him. He took out a pretty dress, with flowery designs, from a new bundle which he had kept apart from the chelas he had displayed, arranged in rows.

'For whom?'

'Take it, and don't crib around it!'

'For whom, I'm asking you?'

'For whom, indeed! It is for your wife, Nair!'

'My wife?'

'No, it's my fault! How can an Adiyaathi girl become your wife!'

Several Adiyaathis came and went, buying for fifteen rupees the coarse chelas with loud colours which were sold in the valley at eight and a half rupees. They stood a little farther away, waiting to watch Gopalan Nair buy a chela for Pempi. He bought one that everyone else had bought—a coarse one in a loud colour. The two fine pieces that Mammath had brought, remained unbought. Mammath's face fell. Who could he sell those two dresses to? Gopalan Nair thought. Let him sell it to whomsoever he wants to. He had not asked Mammath to bring them anyway.

She accepted the chela. She did not smile. She went inside with it, without even turning it over in her hand once....

Each time he set off with a new farming season, yoking the oxen and ploughing the soil, he resolved to go back to his native place, never to return, once the harvest of that season was over. But he could not go. Years passed thus. Not one or two. But sixteen.

'Leave behind those affairs in your native place, Gopalan! Why can't you settle down here with a bit of agriculture and other farming?'

Weren't the kaaryasthans of all the landlords here, doing that? No one can leave this place once you set eyes on it. It's like you have got into the tentacles of an invisible octopus.

All around, darkness gathered. Sleep did not visit him. He pricked up his ears. The unceasing tumult of the jungle. The chirping of the crickets. He yearned for sleep. He didn't hear any noise from within the hut. Was she asleep? For some days now, even her iron bangles were not clinking. Inside the silent hut, there was only the crackling of the burning firewood and the glow of the sparks that flew. What would she be thinking?

He had not even for a single moment reflected what would she be thinking—when he didn't eat the food she had served and waited for him to eat, when he took his bath in the ice-cold water spurning the warm water she had prepared for his bath, when he left the hut without uttering a word to her during the days when there was no work, when he whiled away days and nights at Mammath's shop, immersed in chit-chat with him. Wasn't she his, whom he had used for sixteen years? Wasn't his hut on the fringe of the jungle, this field where the leeches and crabs played hide-and-seek, the cattle in the nethyaaramma's shed, the paddy in the granary—weren't all those his? No. There was nothing of his here. He had nothing of his own here. If she thought that he would make her his own and cherish her, it was her foolishness.

He decided he would send Pempi back to the nethyaaramma's house the very next day. He recollected the fourteen-year-old who was sweeping the courtyard, whom the nethyaaramma had sent to his place to look after him. She could still be employed in courtyard sweeping, washing, and cleaning utensils there.... Or.... Or what? Wouldn't other kaaryasthans be employed at the nethyaaramma's place? Something tumbled down within himself and broke into smithereens. Pempi was not his own...no, no! Like this hut.... Who was the next kaaryasthan at the nethyaaramma's homestead? Was it the hunter Pothen? He must arrest his thoughts at this moment, he felt. Pothen whose eyes used to rove over Pempi's body behind his back! He couldn't bear the thought. He must take her back to the nethyaaramma's homestead first thing in the morning, he decided. Let her remain there as the servant maid.

Did he doze off for some time? What was that noise? Was a shot fired in the jungle? Was the hunter Pothen around? Wasn't it the trumpeting of the elephant that he heard? When he woke up, the birds were twittering. The tone of the crickets had changed. The chilly wind blew with unusual vehemence.

He rose, rubbing his eyes. He had to meet Mammath before he left. He must say goodbye to the nethyaaramma. Back at his native place, Valyammaavan died suddenly. There was no one in the family to look after the daily affairs. The nethyaaramma might raise objections. But let her. There was no other way. He rolled up the mat spread on the veranda where he had slept and placed it in a corner inside the hut. As he moved towards the iron trunk, to fold the blanket and place it over the lid, something on the floor struck against his feet. It jingled.

He bent over and peered at it. It was not yet light. He fumbled for it. He was startled. The kadakams and chooda, the bronze bangles and the light iron bangles he had bought for Pempi, the Adiyaathi consort.

His suspicion was not yet cleared. Where was she?

Light had begun to spread slowly. He went inside and looked for her.

'Pempi!' His words were caught in his throat. He entered, without uttering another word. Where was she? Did she rise so early? She might be outside, near the canal. She might be scouring the vessels, but he didn't hear any water splashing. Only the steady fall of water flowing from the end of the halved bamboo pole. Besides that, the din of the jungle. The croaking of frogs, the cackling of birds, the alternating shrill-and-shattered call of the Malabar giant squirrel. As he was moving towards the kitchen, he once again looked around. Her mat was rolled up and kept leaning against the wall in the corner.

In the light that was spreading, he noticed something else. Her new sari. The new sari which he had bought for her from the kaavu market for the Vishu festival. She had folded it neatly and left it wrapped in a clean newspaper. A small bundle of coins. The small change he had given her from time to time, to buy bangles and kumkum. In between, the one-rupee-studded-taali, like a small snake, was tangled on his fingers as he fumbled, and dangled from their trembling ends.

Stunned, he sat bolt upright on that cold, chilly floor! Pempi had left him, before he had left her! Through his brain, his heart, his veins, a cyclone went swirling. A cold wind swept around the hut, whistling. The dry straw bits flew up.

He heard the trumpeting of the wild elephant from within the jungle, once again. Even as the day grew bright, he was still sitting on the floor, with his hands on the lid of that locked iron trunk on the veranda of the now empty hut.

THE COURT OF KING GEORGE VI

M. P. NARAYANA PILLAI

A telegram arrived from Penang: 'Madathiraman sinking. Start immediately.' Such telegrams usually contain news of death.

'Sinking!' So Madathiraman's dead. Dead like a dog. Dead like a log. The wicked die; the righteous only return. That's the difference. Only very few return. Because the righteous are very rare.

This returning is also known as moksha.

White hair will turn black. Hair sprouts on baldness. Wrinkled skin smoothens out. The body waxes round; the hair on the hands, armpits, and chest fall off. Then the hair on the face. The voice fades. Teeth fall off. You study in standard seven. From seven to six and six to five. And get demoted to standard one. Then to the kindergarten; then the palmyra leaf-writing of the first alphabet learning; the days race backwards to the first writing of Hari Sree. The days of oblivion. A ritual degeneration into toddling; then down on hands and knees; then crawling; you turn into an infant, a suckler. Finally, one day, you return the way you arrived. Back to your mother's womb.

Then the counting is downward. Ten months, nine months, eight, seven, six. Then the pregnant mother's craving. Then the aversion to food, vomiting.

The unending journey of blood returning to the blood.

But...where is Mother for that?

Where is Mother? Father? The generations?

The generations are doors opening for the return journey. Doors with brass bolts shining like gold.

One has to return through the aeons. It is the first days of Chingam—the month from mid-July to mid-August—when one reaches Kollam. It is Christ crucified when one reaches Rome.

Then, the journey without touching any years.

All the incarnations of the past resurrected. The Boar retreats to the Tortoise, the Tortoise to the Fish, and the Fish to moksha.

From Dissolution to Creation, through Preservation. A state in which Creation and Dissolution become one and the same.

The wicked die. Jackals tear at their carcasses as if it was placenta.

The placenta is the only true relative of a human being. The brother whom dogs snatched away before one could even kiss him. He is dragged away through the garden.

The cow eats its placenta. It is nature's tonic for her recovery after delivery.

The mother cat, unable to contain her hunger, eats her own litter. Baby spiders devour their mother.

Man eats on the sly for he is intelligent.

Wicked ones who eat on the sly. Wicked ones like Madathiraman.

He stopped me at the sandy banks of the Periyar River. He snatched the two rupees tucked in the folds of my mundu. When I begged him to give me back at least two annas for a cup of tea, he twisted my arm. He was about to break my fingers.

He should be killed. All the wicked ones should be killed.

The good people live. When they are done with living, they return.

Gods come down from heaven to the earth. And mate with beasts. Good people are born out of such unions. Those who do not steal. Those who do not extort.

The sage Mrugaspaty was born thus. He curses and turns into a handful of ashes, Madathiraman, the asura, who polluted his sacred groves. From the spots where the ashes fell on the earth, cactus, thistle, bramble, oleander, and nux vomica trees sprout. Bitter leaves. Guava fruit on which the snake has spat its venom. Cactus milk that turns into a flame.

For cactus milk to turn into fire, the most potent black magic is needed; one that will send a roast chicken flying. The blackest sorcery. The fiercest ritual.

A black cat's skull is buried beneath Madathiraman's tulsi plant. Then he is nailed to a nux vomica plank.

Let us see whether Madathiraman moves then. He is pinned down.

Then he won't strip me of my mundu.

Let us see how he can throw stones at me. His hands are nailed to a plank.

It'll cause him great pain when he moves. Blue blood oozes.

The blood of the wicked is blue in colour. The blood that courses through their hearts and veins is polluted.

Heads of two dogs at the end of the staff.

The staff turns into a snake. And the dogs become rabid. A snake with the head of a mad dog. A mad snake bites him on his face.

That was a punishment for throwing on my face the water with which the chilli paste on the grinding stone had been washed.

The emperor Jahangir punishes him.

Whoever it may be, those who commit crimes deserve punishment. Be it Mehrunnisa begum, be it Madathiraman.

Deserves to be punished....

The case moves up from the magistrate's court to the sessions court. The verdict in the sessions court is death by hanging. The high court rejects the appeal.

The last meal. The executioner. The gallows. The noose.

Again, a telegram from Penang. The cremation is over. Do not start. Didn't I say, no need?

He should die abroad. A death which warrants no release for the soul.

The ancestors refuse to peck at the cooked rice offered at the shraadham. Only the kaakkaampeechi pecks at the sacrificial rice at last. Kaakkaampeechis are the ancestors of the asuras. The souls of the ancestors of humans are crows. Koels are the ancestors of gods.

The ancestors of Madathiraman are kaakkaampeechis. He is an asura.

The war between the devas and the asuras. A telegram from the abode of the gods. Madathiraman should start immediately. To fight in the war on the side of the asuras. Agreed. In the fierce battle that ensued, the asuras are all killed. Vishnu's sacred weapon, the Sudarshana, saves the gods. Parts of human bodies rain down from the sky. Headless carcasses. Whose head is this? The black mole and the thin moustache. Madathiraman. This hand. This chest with the welt of a stab wound. Whose is this syphilitic groin? Whose is this hairy ear?

O, Mother! Why do you weep? Your womb that bore the asura is accursed. Your teats sucked by the asura, your lips kissed by the asura, and the body that trembled in joy seeing the asura are accursed. Pray that you may be spared the curse. Pray for a boon to enable you to return.

Raman, you put me in the stock. You whipped me with ray's tail. You put the dust of the climbing nettle on my face. You rubbed devil-nettle on my thighs and back.

You starved me. When I was thirsty, you poured rock salt in my mouth.

The cure for insanity is eating rock salt when thirsty.

Rock salt is a medicine. What you put in my mouth was not rock salt. It was saltpetre.

Then you put sulphur in my mouth.

Saltpetre and sulphur. To explode in my mouth in the morning when I brushed my teeth with burned husk.

You, of course, knew that gunpowder was a mixture of saltpetre, sulphur, and charcoal. You scoundrel!

That day I stopped brushing my teeth.

The taste of saltpetre and sulphur still lingers in the mouth.

You came searching for me disguised as an inoculator, didn't you? It was not the dead germs of cowpox that you carried in the vial and needle. It was the live germs of smallpox that you carried.

The sage Narada appeared to me in the guise of a physician and told me this. That day I moved my residence to the sanctum of the temple. But the wicked Brahmins threw me out. And chained me to the base of a peepul tree. The very same spot where the elephant Padmanabhan of Ahor Mana was chained when he was in musth.

As rain and sunshine fell on me, moss slowly covered me. The soles of my feet were eaten by termites. The toes put forth buds. My hair turned into upward-growing roots. My hands became branches. New fingers. New branches put forth buds. Green leaves. When the butterflies settled on me with pollen, I was tickled. When the birds that flew all around perched on my branches, I was contented.

The Brahmins cut down the tree to build a shed for banquets on that spot.

You were the first one who wielded the axe.

The axe which is used in hacking up and burning a leper does not catch leprosy.

Who drowned the eight children of Queen Umayamma?

Madathiraman.

Who killed Maharaja Ayilyam Thirunal, mixing poison in the neypayasam of Sree Padmanabhan?

Madathiraman.

Who got from Vaazhappilly Kunjikkaavu, as a bequest, fields worth six hundred bushels of paddy as rent, and mortgaged it? I ask, who did it?

It was Kunjikkaavu who bequeathed the property. But it did not belong to her. It belonged to other worthies.

It was the Brahmin property of Ahor Mana.
It was the divine property of Aalangaad temple.
It was in the will and testament of Kallikshaarathu.
And the court of Kunjikkaavu.

Who is it that tempted Kunjikkaavu with marriage, got her six-hundred-bushel-rent-fields as a bequest and cleared out?

Madathiraman.

It is 'brahminicide' to cheat Brahmins, and 'deicide' to cheat gods. You won't attain any merit in this world or the next.

There are seventeen kuttichchaatthans—goblins—under the control of the kaniyaan—the astrologer of the Paalachchottil family. Seventeen of them. If he is nettled, the kaniyaan won't let anyone off. Didn't you pit him against me and make me mad? You sent me a magic potion, as prasadam from Sabarimala. When I was about to eat it, a lizard cackled thrice from the agnikon, the fire corner.

No! Poison! Don't eat!

I didn't eat.

Then came the kuttichchaatthans. Immediately, Perakkaappally Kunjan went to Chottanikkara and sat on a ritual penance in Devi's presence. And came back with the hibiscus flowers and crataeva leaves taken out of the garlands offered to the Devi. The kuttichaatthans went back. And told the kaniyaan that they were unable to do anything against Kunjan. Then the kaniyaan sent the yakshis.

The kuttichaatthans attack during the daytime. It is at night that the yakshis strike. Kaniyaan keeps the yakshis as his concubines. Under his strict control. Yakshis with hair as long as palm strands. They arrive at night, their anklets jingling. Not one or two. Several of them. They frolic in the temple pond. Their inviting looks lead men astray. The man follows the yakshi with a ceremonial piece of pudava. Where do they go? To a palace; to a harem. Whose harem? Is it the harem of Emperor Akbar? No. It is the harem of Paalachchottil Kaniyaan.

There, the Bhajagovindam is sung: The yakshi takes off your gold girdle, as you embrace her. As she kisses you, she licks your gold-filled teeth.

Then she sucks the blood. When only the husk of the man remains, she will let him loose in the harvested fields, under a spell. There, he will wander about like chicken let loose in a moonlit night, and then collapse, dead.

The day you won over Paalachchottil Kaniyaan, I stopped sleeping.

I haven't slept ever since. Shouldn't sleep at night. If I so much as shut my eyelid, my head will be mowed down. The night is a great cheat. Everything is deceitful. A total swindle.

Yakshis move around in disguise. Bloodthirsty ghouls. Elephant-shaped demons. Demons looking like children.

Policeman in the thief's guise and the thief dressed as a policeman! Who robs whom?

Pandavas head for the wilderness. Bhima in Keechaka's palace.

When is the House of Lac going to catch fire? The temple is also a house of lac.

Even if the temple burns, nothing will happen to the deity of the temple: Perakkaappally Kunjan.

The priest comes. The priest goes. The priests are dead and gone. The Vaarrier women who make garlands for the deity turn old overnight. The Maarars die. The temple treasurer is changed. The temple scribe is changed. A squabble over the property of the Bhattatiri. Who is the owner of Kuttikkaattu temple properties?

Is it in the son's name or the son-in-law's name? The case is in the high court. The verdict is given on Shivarati in the month of Kumbham from mid-February to mid-March—the temple properties are in no one's name, they are in the name of the deity.

The deity doesn't change.

Neither does Perakkaappally Kunjan. The Kuttikkaattu temple properties are Kunjan's own by virtue of his being a Shudra.

But one thing. He should not sleep a wink. He should not shut his eyelid.

Devils prowl among the tea bushes to drink the blood of cocks.

Devils and serpents need cock's blood.

The serpents should be worshipped without a break. On holidays, officials should venerate scorpions and centipedes, besides serpents. Serpent worship is to seek protection from yakshis and ghouls. Serpents should be fed with chicken blood. The blood of seven fowls such as the rooster, waterfowl, jungle fowl, death's harbinger-fowl, seagull, hen quail. All the serpents should be offered worship. Anantan, Thakshakan, Vasuki, the cobra, the king cobra, the rat snake, the water snake, the ear snake, the betel snake, the areca nut snake, the tobacco snake....

The god of the serpents is the old Namboodiri of Paampummekkattu Mana. Two serpents are brought in a bottle from Paampummekkattu Mana and installed in a burrow in the serpent groves of Vaarikattu. People worship them with offerings of milk—cow milk, buffalo milk, goat milk, hen milk, panther milk, cactus milk, rubber milk, breast milk, milk powder—milk is given until they are satiated. There is saying in the *Panchatantra*: 'If you feed the snake milk, it will turn on you and bite you.'

Bite whom?

Bite, Madathiraman!

The betel snakes that went crazy drinking cock blood; bite the yakshis.

O Krishna on the banyan leaf, deliver me from the betel snakes!

All because Madathiraman, the asura, has won over Paalachchottil Kaniyaan.

Eating flesh is nature's law. Cock eats termite. Jackal eats the cock. Man eats jackal. Man eats man. The lion eats man. The vulture eats the lion. Ants eat the vulture. An Australian creature eats ants. Termites eat that creature. Cock eats termites.

Man eats fish, fish eats man.

This is not good. One should be self-sufficient. One should not eat the flesh of another creature. One should eat only one's own flesh.

Snakes should eat their own tails when hungry. The elephant, its trunk. The manure for paddy is its own ear of corn.

Madathiraman, who is not self-sufficient, deserves punishment.

A telegram from England. A telegram from the West. Perakkaappally Kunjan should start immediately for England. He should reach the palace of King George VI. Perakkaappally Kunjan gets the job of doorkeeper at the harem. From today he is in England.

But Kunjan will not eat in the palace. Because George VI is a Christian. So, anything but eating in the palace.

One day Kunjan says to George VI: 'My emperor, my lord who feeds me, I am fed up with the onslaughts of Velupillai Raman Nair of Madathil House, of Kunnathunadu Taluk, Rayamangalam village, Pulluvazhy locality. Raman kills and eats human beings and animals. And collects taxes.'

George VI is beside himself with rage: 'Hey! I say is there another emperor in my own empire?'

Soon the command issues forth: 'Perakkaappally Kunjan must go immediately, bring in Madathiraman bound hand and foot, and present him before me.'

Kunjan comes with two constables and a bailiff and leads Raman away in fetters. And presents him in the court of King George VI.

At the court of King George VI are present the king himself with Queen Victoria, Chithira Thirunal Balaramavarma, the maharaja of Travancore, Vishnu Namboodiri, the young master of Ahor Mana, Dhanwantari Moosathu, the court physician, and Raman in the dock.

Kunjan starts reading the charge sheet.

King George VI says: 'Madathil Raman or Raman Nair of Madathil House?'

'Present.'

'Stand.... Sit.... Stand.... Sit....'

'What does "undulation" mean, Madathil Raman?'

No answer.

'What does geography mean?'

Silence, still.

'You don't know? Idiot. You haven't learned your lesson.'

'How do fleas come into being?'

'Big fleas give birth to small fleas.'

'Wrong. Kunjan, you tell him.'

'When the larva in cow dung develops wings, it turns into a flea.'

'Correct. How do flying termites come into being?'

'When they see the light.'

'Wrong. Kunjan, you say.'

'When termites develop wings, flying termites are born.'

'How is a glow-worm formed? Raman must answer this time.'

'When the ear snakes develop wings.'

'What are the creatures who thrive on parasitical plants?'

'Parasitical pigs.'

'How many British currency would twenty-seven native rupees make?'

'Twenty-eight.'

'Wrong. Twenty-eight native rupees make twenty-seven British currency.'

'All right. Adjourned.'

The verdict next day was to hang Madathiraman. To hang him publicly in the marketplace, as they did Velutthampi. That noon, Madathiraman had his last meal which was finished off with adapradhaman.

The executioner arrived bathed, wearing the holy marks.

Paalachchottil Kaniyaan was sent for, and the cowrie was cast to fix the time of execution. An auspicious time has to be fixed because the subject is a sorcerer. There is a chance of him turning into a ghoul. Isn't it going to be an unnatural death?

Who is that? Tell him Kunjan is not here. That he has gone to England.

The ghoul should be nailed down. Two measures of pine-gum powder on the nux vomica plant. 'Kayyittikkuruthy, three bushels full....'

Why do you go on asking? Didn't I say Kunjan is not here?

Eh? Who is that?

Ha! Is it you?

Don't play the fool with me, I say!

Oooh! Please don't bend my fingers! They'll snap. I shall give you the mundu. Don't bend my fingers, Raman. Here it is. The two rupees and four annas are in the folds of my mundu. Take the money. Don't take the mundu. I don't have another to drape around me. Raman, don't leave me like this... Please leave the mundu on me and go!

Ayyo! Raman!

Oh my....

King George VI, where is he?

THE SOCIETY
PUNATHIL KUNJABDULLA

It is the beginning of the humid nights of Karkkidakam, the month of the heaviest monsoon rains. As dusk fell, we shut our doors fearing robbers. The lamp in the front veranda was put out. Except for the single lamp that burned inside the house, the entire world was enveloped in darkness.

We lived in this house until now in utter isolation. We were oblivious of the world beyond our house. Yet, all around our house were other houses. Right in front was the house of the tehsildar. In front of that house, there would be crowds of people all the time. All those who visited him would have wads of papers tucked under their armpits. The tehsildar came out always like a monarch of yore. The waiting crowd would give way. After some time, the people would start leaving. Some of them would be smiling and those were very few. Some would be wiping their eyes and those would make the majority. We would pay attention to these others when we heard the cuss words they uttered. Many a times we thought of calling such people over to our house and advising them not to say such things and that even if a person commits some grievous offence, we should be patient. But we were not in the least interested in making the world a better place. Therefore, we did no such thing.

We never went over to the tehsildar's house. My ration card had come into force much earlier, so I didn't need his endorsement for that. I didn't have any land tax or other taxes to seek relaxation for, which would have been under his purview. I didn't have any surplus land to declare either. Therefore, I didn't bother to visit the tehsildar, though he was our neighbour.

But my wife told me once, 'Let's visit that house at least once.' I was mad at her. 'We don't need to go to any place where we don't really need to. Do we have any need to visit the tehsildar? We will live in this rented house all our lives. I will never be able to construct our own house with reinforced cement concrete during my lifetime. Why should then we need cement through the good offices of the tehsildar?

There is the special sugar permit that is also under the tehsildar's purview but I don't need any sugar at all—I who has to test my urine for sugar content thrice a week!'

My wife was mad at me in return. 'I am such an unfortunate wretch, to have been a wife for so long, to such an opportunistic, self-centred fellow like you,' she shouted. 'You don't even drop a single grain of rice on the floor when you eat for the ants. If God had given you wings there wouldn't have been a single bird flying in the sky!'

After lost in thought about something for a long time, she exclaimed: 'What a really good human being God is!'

But with none of this, did things improve in any way. One day, the tehsildar's father-in-law fell seriously ill. That day, the tehsildar, that low life, came to our house. For a long time, he told us about the various hardships he faced. Finally, he requested me to go and bring a doctor who was an acquaintance of mine.

Since I did not have the need of cement or sugar, I went inside the house without saying a word, and slammed the door shut.

Two days later, I saw a crowd had gathered in the tehsildar's courtyard. I heard the noise of a mango tree being cut, and as it came crashing down to the ground. The tree was obviously felled for the ritual mango wood to cremate the dead old man! I roared with laughter. My wife who was startled to hear the crashing sound, said: 'Truly a hard-hearted one!'

I then asked her: 'Me or the dead one?'

'One should feel a little sympathy at least when one hears the mango tree falling. Even the teardrop has dried up in your eye,' my wife said.

'For a patient afflicted with both diabetes and consumption, it is the biggest lottery win of his life, to die at the earliest.'

The pyre smouldered, the flames leapt up eventually, and the smell of the head exploding wafted.

With that, I forgot all about the tehsildar's house.

Then, it was the house to our left.

Though the tehsildar's house opposite ours is a big mansion with a broad courtyard, and aromatic smoke spreads out from its kitchen, the house to our left was a small one. When one looked at that house, the odour of cow dung stung one's nostrils. The coconut frond-thatched roof had come lower and lower, even covering the entire front veranda. That house was so pitiful. I used to look at that house with the mood of listening to some deep, melancholic song. A slim, tall figure, with shorn off hair, would come out to the courtyard. 'Why do you gape at women, you fellow?' The question would be shot at me. Only then would I become aware of the fact that, that figure was of a woman. Except for the sparse hair, everything else was smooth, plain. But the clothes too were that of a woman.

'Why do you look at her? She is a madwoman,' my wife said.

This woman was struck by madness three years ago. But, even two years before that, she had made her husband leave the house. He was a meek person, it seems. He would only worship God, and never other women. That was the only mistake of his life. Therefore, even before she was afflicted by madness, this beautiful woman chased her husband away.

Then, she and her three children remained in the house. Though she was a Thiyya woman, she never worked hard to earn a living. There were about sixty coconut trees in her grove. Coconut trees without bud rot in that locality were found only in her compound. The trees yielded plenty of coconuts. In the beginning, the expenses were very small compared to the income. Then, it was as if the balance was upset. She never did any improvement of the land. The grove and the trees grew weary and sparse. With this, her madness intensified.

Her madness was not so violent, as to make someone drill a hole in a plank and put her feet in the stockade. Her words and deeds were very matter of fact. That too I realized when I attempted to give the starving children some food.

She had three children. These children were ill-treated. Moved by the intensity of the weeping of one of the children, I stood gazing. The child would be suffering from severe stomach ache, I sensed with the kind of simple intuition that comes to a doctor. But I was disabused of my illusion when the child stopped crying and began repeating the words: 'I am hungry; I am hungry!'

I went down to the paddy field that lay between our houses and called the child over. He looked around. Then loped towards my house, apparently feeling a certain sense of security. I gave him a piece of Cadbury chocolate that my wife was eating and some boiled tapioca mixed in coconut chutney. He smelled the chocolate, then threw it away and glared at me. His expression seemed to imply that I was trying to poison him! Then he began to eat the tapioca mixture. When the plate was empty, he wiped his hands on his shorts, and ran away.

At that time, his mother was standing outside the house. I beckoned to her. She ran up to me as if attracted by some unknown force. I measured two seers of rice, put it in a winnow and gave it to her. When she accepted it from me and stood gazing at me, I felt like telling her that she didn't need to express so much of gratitude towards me. When she tarried still, I couldn't but blurt out, 'Make some rice gruel for you and your children!' That's when her eyes began to blaze. 'Hey, you! What do you think of me? That I don't have anything at home? The granary inside my house is filled with paddy. Only that I don't have the time to boil it, dry it, and husk it. Who needs your rotten rice!' She threw away the rice along with the winnow. Several crows descended on the scattered grains. All the crows of the village seemed to have arrived at that spot. For some time, the racket raised by the crows, and the obscenities she hurled reverberated.

The next time I was startled was when I heard one of the children wailing. She was beating the child with a big stick. 'Hey! Why did you go to that devil's house and eat his leftovers?' She said as she thrashed the child. As I stood there in despair and grief, my wife came and stood behind me. 'Don't you know that she is not mad? She is not mad or anything!'

I looked at my wife with a muted question on my lips: 'Then what do I see now here?'

She said flatly: 'Effrontery!'

My wife continued: 'The tehsildar is a mean fellow, indeed! I agree with you on that. But his wife! There isn't a more compassionate woman around! One day, when she saw this arrogant woman's second child going unclad and unkempt, she took it home, gave it water to wash its hands and feet. Will a woman of higher caste do such a thing? Then she ladled out in her own plate lots of choicest food. When its tummy was filled and bloated, she dressed it in good clothes. No sooner than the child reached home, this mad woman took off the child's clothes and rushed out. She reached the tehsildar's courtyard, where she came to a halt. She tore up the child's dress and set it ablaze. Then this mad woman said: "I have at home a boxful of clothes which are far better than this!" She then returned home, picked up a big stick and began to beat all the children. I felt like rushing out and restraining her. She began to stuff the wailing eldest child's mouth with a piece of old cloth. Thus, one of them was silenced. As I didn't want to be the eyewitness to a murder, I ran up to her house. She was holding on to the old cloth she had stuffed into the child's mouth. The child's eyes were bulging out like the glass marble in the neck of a soda bottle. As I attempted to catch her, she left the child and began to chase after me with the stick. After this incident, I have never set foot in that house. That was my first and last visit.' By the time my wife had narrated this much, she was exhausted.

Yet, none of that woman's children have died so far. Despite starving so much, and undergoing such torture regularly, they lived on, in tears and lament. It was when I began observing the life of the people in this house, that I realized that death can never snatch away life untimely. What all are lying hidden in our humble lives, about which we have never thought!

What we witnessed in the next house was such a hidden thing. There were only two—husband and wife. They had been married for seventeen years. Even now, there are only two people—the husband and wife. Neither of them was mad. But those who think about them will surely go mad!

In the tehsildar's house, even as the day dawned there would be crowds of men. Even when the rush of the men outside subsided, the number of people inside the house was indeed pressing. The tehsildar had no interest in family planning, but he would take good care of his children. He had seven children. They were placed under a kind of military discipline. The children would wake up early. Because there were men on business jostling in front of the house, the children were dealt with at the back of the house. Those of school-going age would go to school. They would be at their naughty best when they returned from school in the evening. The tehsildar would be at the club at that time. They would raise a din at home and in the entire compound.

The madwoman's house too was equally noisy. There, it was all about pain, hunger and beating with the big stick. And in the tehsildar's house, it was a tale of plenitude and discipline in equal measure.

But how about the third house?

We had heard it said, 'flowers that slept for seventeen years'. But could there be any house that slept continuously for seventeen years? If someone asked us this question, we would say, 'Yes!' If someone asked which house is this, we would say, 'The house next door.'

The inhabitants of that house, the husband and wife, were high officials. The husband was the postal superintendent. The wife was the district education officer. They didn't have any children. The DEO who presided over a world of young pupils and teachers didn't have a child of her own! Alas!

It was one of these days that I heard the husband and wife raising their voices in an argument. My wife said: 'That's a usual occurrence. Like in the tehsildar's house there too would be commotion now and then. Is there any home where the husband and wife do not quarrel at least occasionally?'

The postal superintendent would invite the children of the next house over and serve them coffee and delicacies regularly. He would stock food items such as vada, biscuits, plantains, halva, etc. In the evening, he would mix a lot of milk with tea, and make it thick like curd, and serve it to the children along with the delicacies. The norm was that if he was late to return from the office on a certain day, his wife should take his place and feed the children of the neighbourhood. The quarrel today was because the wife defaulted!

From the next day on, I began to pay attention to that house. It was a big mansion. As soon as I woke up in the morning, I went to the terrace and would look towards that house. The house resembled a cremation ground, because, despite my watching the house for hours on end, there would be no movement at all.

Only three times did I ever detect signs of life in that house, except when the children had a gala time. That too after watching the house over such a long period. Once, an old woman was sweeping the backyard. On another occasion, the postal superintendent was standing by the well and peering inside, leaning forward holding on to the rim of the parapet around the well. He held a toothbrush in his right hand. Intermittently, he would move it fore and aft across his teeth and spit out the froth. But he was looking intently inside the well, all the while.

It was seemingly a bottomless well.

One day I woke up from my siesta, hearing a loud noise from the next house. The madwoman had made an unseemly trespass in the postal superintendent's house. She lay down and cuddled with the sleeping man! Hearing the cries of the terror-stricken man we listened intently. The madwoman was saying: 'I will deliver babies yet again.'

That evening, sitting under the tamarind tree behind the house, the superintendent's wife wept for a long time. That time he was not at home.

Noticing my wife leaving, I asked: 'Where are you going?'

'Can't you see? She is sitting there and weeping for such a long time. Let me go and console her.'

'What use is it for you if you console her? God has never asked us to feed the mind. God hasn't even created the mind. God has shaped only the stomach. If she feels hungry, let her come here.'

My wife changed her sari quickly. The only thing she could change quickly was her sari.

Like looking at a wedding photo, in which the husband was long since dead, I kept watching that house. I would see the superintendent looking inside the well, now and then. Some other time, I would see a golden-bangled hand drawing water from the well, and sometimes hands that wore no bangles. For the rest, it would all be silence. I became aware that this world was devoid of all din and bustle only when I watched the movements in that house. What a truism to say that there was indeed solitude!

It was listening to the loud scolding by the madwoman or the cussing from the crowd at the tehsildar's courtyard that I woke up from my divine dreams. But we realized one thing. However much one craved solitude, one cannot live without listening to a din. If nothing, one has at least to listen to the roar of the waves in the sea.

That was how the fourth house went without any residents. The goldsmith Kunjikkelu built this gigantic three-storeyed mansion, after much planning and anticipation. No one in his community had ever built such a big house. And as for Kunjikkelu who built this imposing structure, he was the most impoverished of them all!

He had begun to practise the goldsmith's craft at the age of seven. He would often say that his hammer had fallen only on gold and never on copper all the thirty years of his life. Saving up a fortune through hard work, he built the biggest mansion in the locality. Before he began living in that house, he threw a grand feast. He distributed milk to all the households in the locality. He gave silk clothes to the masons and carpenters who built the house. He put a gold ring on the finger of the master builder. And gave a golden bangle to his pretty wife.

Yet, what was the use? During the very first night of their stay in that house, Kunjikkelu fled. His wife and children followed him. The house was filled with faeces. It was Kuttichchaatthan's—the goblin's—play!

The panchayat road passed through the front of that mansion. It proceeded to the government hospital. All those who passed along that road would hold their breath as they passed that house.

It was not Kuttichchaatthan whom they detested, but his weapon!

That night, when there was no noise to be heard, I got up. I enjoyed observing the surroundings in total silence. When I got tired of lying down, I got up, climbed the stairs in the dark, went to the terrace. I walked stealthily like a thief. I began to be afraid of myself.

The night was ink black. I saw the tehsildar's house, like ink spilled on blotting paper. From the madwoman's house, through the chinks in the coconut-frond thatch, a sliver of light was coming out. I felt as if the house in which the postal superintendent and his wife were sleeping in, was sobbing. It was then that I looked at the deserted house of Kunjikkelu Saraf. The moment I looked at the house, I began to feel the stench of faeces. The wind suddenly swirled and lashed my face. The wind soon surrounded me with waves of faeces. I shivered in horror. I ran down from the terrace. Fear, like a mad dog, pursued me.

As I attempted to descend the stairs, my feet slipped. It was as if I fell into a blind well. I had passed out, to wake up only in the morning. By that time, the deeply bruised spots on my body had all swollen up. I was incapable of getting up and consulting the doctor who was my acquaintance.

It was when I escaped the worst of that pain and infirmity that I realized something. Nature itself can effect such wonderful cures!

But, to go back to the start, it was at the beginning of the dense night of this rain sodden Karkkidakam, a season when old ailments come back in devastating visitations, that I realized that this epiphany of mine was all wrong and misplaced. We had shut the doors and windows dreading robbers. It's just a manner of speaking when I say 'we'. My wife was dead for a year now. During a horrendous Karkkidakam night like this one, she had breathed her last. Though she had died and gone under the earth, she had never left me. She was always with me in this house. When I ate and slept, she guarded over me. I wouldn't do anything without asking her permission. In our bedroom, I always spread two beds side by side. Our bond was so strong.

Yet she was unable to save me. I had begun to experience severe pain suddenly. I haven't read any of those essays about heartache that those who were ignorant about it, wrote. But when I experienced pain in my chest, I knew that it was heartache.

I felt my chest being pressed down as if with a weight much more than the combined weight of all the cement bags that the tehsildar in the opposite house had sanctioned for issue during his entire official tenure. I would explode now. My chest would churn and turn into a liquid. Holding on to the banisters of the bedstead, I bit down my pain. I could hold on only for a brief while. Then I began to howl in pain. I didn't know how long I howled in pain.

I felt relieved when I heard footsteps outside. Someone had come to rescue me. But I was unable to get up and reach the door, to open it.

I saw two raised fists across the window from where I was lying. I could also hear a string of cuss words. 'Son of a...are you crying? Have you become aware that your wife is dead and gone, only now? And are you moaning about it? I will beat you to a pulp! Lie down there quietly, you dog!'

The fists disappeared suddenly. With that, my pain doubled.

I resumed weeping aloud. I grasped the banisters once again. I couldn't remember how long I was in this state of pain. I couldn't remember how many nights I spent like this. The pain was so severe.

Someone was knocking on the door. I recognized the face of the postal superintendent. I got to know who he was as the candle in his hand lit up his countenance.

He was asking so many things. 'Is it proper that you live all alone like this? Shouldn't you keep some links with others? No one can live in this world in isolation. Isn't man a social animal?' He must have been asking me things like these. But nothing was clear. I clearly remembered him laying his palm on my sweaty brow. At the same instant, he withdrew his hand and wiped it on his clothes, like a child.

That was when light spread in the veranda; and voices followed it. The tehsildar, his peon, then God knows who else, arrived.

'Someone should bring the doctor. Quickly,' a voice said.

Then some whisperings. Someone went outside. The blaze of a choottu, the coconut palm leaf torch was moving away. My pain exacerbated.

Someone wet my lips, dipping fingers in water. I felt that finger on my lips like my mother's nipple from the folds of oblivion. I sank into the slumber of extreme pain.

The light from the choottu was nearing. Once again, the weary footsteps, all from outside.

The doctor was indisposed. He said he could not make a house call. He said the patient should be brought to his place if it was such an emergency.

I could recollect only this much. My pain came back with redoubled intensity.

Some people hoisted me up. They started off in the dark. After leaving my house, and passing through alleys, we reached the panchayat road. I became aware of the strength of the superintendent's hands. I heard the voice of the tehsildar. And the comforting words of his wife. Silence prevailed for some time. Then some pieces of advice by the DEO. It was then that I heard the cuss words. Someone was saying: 'They are carrying that demon to his pyre. I forgot about the stick with which I beat children. If not, I should have whacked him hard once across his face.' No sooner than this was said, there was that horrible stench.

No one let go of me. I was amazed that my surroundings and my neighbours were all so loving towards me. I craved to live longer, loving and serving them.

We could only guess it was at the doctor's that we had reached. I heard the DEO complaining that there was neither a nameboard, nor any lamp lighting up his residence.

They lowered me onto a rough bench in the veranda. As soon as I was laid down, I felt an itch which I yearned to scratch. Was it a bedbug? Or was it a bench where eczema patients used to sit? Why was it that I could not remember anything?

My chest was still turning into jelly. It exploded, without anything remaining inside it.

'The calling bell is not working'—it was the voice of the tehsildar. 'Was it the right switch that you pressed? Or was it something else's switch?' asked the superintendent.

Then everyone together began to knock on the door repeatedly.

'At the right time, this demon of a doctor has gone to sleep'—it was the madwoman swearing. It was pitch dark all around.

A little choottu was ablaze. This was the Kuttichchaathan's.

Overarching all these, the long spectral sighs of my wife. Without anyone hearing, she was saying: 'It's time!'

'You rogues! Are you knocking my door down at this unearthly hour? I will stomp you all into a paste!' It was the doctor raving, his words harsh and pungent.

Oh, it was the doctor, all right....

At that moment, an infant awoke and began to wail.

Finally, the door opened.

A faint light spread across the veranda. I saw the doctor's face. He was a horrendous fellow. I felt as if I had got lost in the interiors of some African jungle.

'Put him down here,' the doctor roared, pointing to a bed, about four feet high, by the side of the veranda. A few people lifted me and placed me there.

'This cot is as long as the longest grave,' the doctor said in a thunderous voice. For some time then, he did not say a word. Then like lightning, he hurled a question at me: 'Where is your pain?'

No sooner had I heard that question, than my chest was pulverized and collapsed. It was a freefall into the nether world. I could not speak a word. My eyes felt dim, and they went out. It was then that my internal eyes came alive.

Sitting in some other world, I heard and experienced everything. That was a time in between day and night.

The doctor's fingers fumbled across my chest. Then the cool stethoscope slithered here and there across my cooling body.

'You brought him late. There are so many of you, smart ones, and you bring him only now? Don't keep this corpse here any longer. Remove it quickly.'

As the tehsildar, his wife, the madwoman, the postal superintendent, the DEO, and Kuttichchaathan stood aghast, the sound of the doctor slamming his door shut in their faces, resounded there.

Our party was standing like a ship anchored in the veranda. The cruel doctor was shouting from the inside: 'This living corpse died over an hour ago. Even after that, you demons have come over to disturb my sleep. Take it away! Bury it!'

After that I didn't feel any pain. I didn't perspire. I began to turn cold. Detesting the hands fell on my body.

They began the return journey, hoisting me. The light of the choottu, and the stench gradually turned faint, and went out altogether.

At that moment, I heard her voice from the heavens above: 'Time's up.'

PHOTO

M. MUKUNDAN

Once, two children went to get themselves photographed. It was quite some time since this wish had been born in their tender minds. Photos that were appearing in newspapers with the caption 'Wedding Today' had induced this wish in them. When her mother scolded her uttering curses from the kitchen in between her preparations to go to school in the morning, she would now and then run to the front veranda and look whether the newspaper had arrived. If her father did not get the newspaper along with the morning cup of tea, he was unable to go to the latrine or even to shave. On bandh days, he would pace about restlessly, having been unable to take a look at the newspaper. Though he was not very rich, he subscribed to many papers and weeklies and read them all. She knew in which publications and when 'Wedding Today' would appear. She had clipped some pictures and pasted them inside her bound notebook. She had done that without anyone noticing it.

'Which of these photos do you like?'

On her way to school, she had opened her notebook and shown it to him. His eyes roved over the pictures that had been newly pasted.

'This.'

He touched one of the pictures.

Bridegroom: Satish K. Nambiar, S/o Karunakaran Nambiar, Poykayil House, Kadinjumoolam, Neeleswaram. Bride: K. R. Swapna, D/o K. R. Govindan Nambiar, Theravath House, Koyampuram, Neeleswaram.

'I too like this photo. It'd have been better if the moustache was not there. Why do people have big moustaches like this?'

'Moustache suits some people very well.'

'Would you too sport a moustache when you grow up?'

'Why not?'

Noticing a group of children walking up from behind them, she shut the notebook. They had reached near the school. The road was full of school children. The government higher secondary school where the boy and the girl go to is not far from the St. Antony's Public School. Children with maroon tie and matching skirt or trousers are the ones studying in St. Antony's.

'They are all so puffed up, those children,' she said.

'Don't they have their own school bus? That's why,' he said.

'It's better that they keep their boasting to themselves,' she said.

They had reached in front of the school. Its compound walls, the tops of which were spiked with glass shards, were covered with film bills and graffitis of scrawled slogans. Someone had attempted to scrape away the sign 'Stick No Bills' written in lime. The gate whose latch had fallen off had been removed from its hinges and could be seen leaning against the wall, inside the compound. A crow was perched atop the flagstaff on which the headmaster would hoist the national flag on Republic Day. When its feet slipped, and it lost balance, it flapped its wings and flew up, hovered and alighted on top of the flagstaff once again. Children were playing, dashing about in the compound. Some boys pissing against the walls from the outside.

'Let me just take a look.'

'What?'

'The bound notebook.'

'Oh, no. The children will see.'

'No.'

She looked all around her anxiously and secretly handed him the bound notebook. He quickly hid it in his satchel.

'You must return it in the second period.'

'Yes, I will.'

'Don't show it to anyone.'

'No.'

She ran away into the midst of a cluster of girls studying in her own class, standing around in the compound. Though he knew that the bell might be rung any time, he went into the urinal. There he opened the notebook. There were a lot of photos of newlyweds. Of the pictures she had pasted up the day before, it was that of Satish and Swapna that he liked. He kept looking at that photo until the bell rang. He could hear the noise of the boys and the splashing of urine against the walls, outside. He then put away the notebook back in the satchel and came out. And, yelling along with the other boys, he rushed into the classroom.

'We too must be photographed, like Satishettan and Swapnedathi,' he said as they were returning home after school.

'Oh, but aren't we mere children?' she asked him.

'What's wrong with children getting photographed?'
'I feel shy.'

Her face flushed as she said this. Moving away from the other children, they walked together along the side of the road, towards their homes, talking about the trivia of the day. His home is past hers, and the post office, and five more minutes' walk away.

'I agree,' she said when she reached her home. 'Let's do it tomorrow.'
'Do you have money for it?'
'Money for what?'
'Would anyone take photos for free?'

They walked on together, without talking. He doesn't dare to ask his mother or father for money. He had heard his father tell his mother when the milkman had approached him for money: 'Why do we need so much milk? I have to pay the insurance premium, electricity bill, and so on. I can't bear it any longer. I'll run away somewhere.'

Walking, they reached in front of her house.

'Ask your father for money. Isn't he very rich? Doesn't he go to the office on a scooter?'

Heaving the weighty satchel, she went home past the fence. On the fence, there were tiny white flowers, blossoming in unison. Though she is fond of the flowers, she doesn't stand near the fence. He had told her that there was some kind of a snake that would fly at anyone and bite.

She couldn't muster the courage to ask her father or mother for money. If she asked them, they would ask her a hundred questions. She has a piggy bank. What her father told her when he bought the piggy bank for her was that she could open it when it became full and buy whatever she liked. But however much the coins she put in, it was never filled up. She unravelled the mystery behind it once. Her mother was taking out coins from the piggy bank with the aid of a pliant coconut-leaf midrib! She saw it happen several times. She decided that she also would follow suit. She caught hold of the piggy bank without anyone noticing it, while she was doing homework. She felt as if it didn't weigh as it should. She shook it a bit, to make sure that it was not empty. She heard a faint jingle. She kept in her satchel the few coins she had managed to extract from the piggy bank with the help of the broomstick a very long time.

'Did you get the money?' he asked her.
'Yes.'

'Then, let's go in the afternoon and have our photos taken.'
'Where do we take our photos?'
'In the studio. Why, you don't know a thing, even though you've grown so big.'
'Am I a big girl? I'm only in the Third Standard.'
She walked along by his side, pulling a long face.

He knows that the studio is near Vijaya Talkies. He remembered having gone there once to take a photo along with his parents. The photo was taken then was still hanging on the wall of his house. In the photo, he is sitting in his mother's lap. He had thrown a tantrum demanding that an exclusive photo of him should be taken. But his mother had silenced him pinching him hard on his legs and hands.

They went into the same studio with their school satchels. There was no one else there, at that time. Seeing them, a lean sort of person came out from the interior of the studio. His face was like that of a child with a fake moustache.

'What do you want, children?' He asked, smiling sweetly.
'We want photos taken.'
'Whose?'
'Of us both.'

He looked at them closely. Even when he was doing so, he kept on smiling blandly. Seeing his smile and the innocent expression on his face, the children felt relieved. The fear and anxiety they experienced at first, left them.

'Come.' He called them inside. Putting the satchels down, the children went inside along with him.

'Have you both come after getting the permission of your parents?'
They didn't say anything.

'I knew it the moment I saw you. Never mind. Don't be afraid, children,' he said kindly.

They looked around and stood perplexed.

'Both of you go over to the mirror there and comb your hair. And put a little bit of talcum powder on your faces.'

He adjusted the bulbs fixed on a stand turning them this way and that. The children combed their hair and stood ready.

'Do you want a full or a half?'

The two of them looked at each other's face. They did not understand his question.

'Why don't you say anything, children?' he persisted. 'What type of photo do you want?'

She took out the bound notebook from her satchel and pointed at the photo of Satish and Swapna. The photographer's laughter spread all over his face.

The children sat on the stool. Right behind them, there was a screen with stars and a full moon painted on it. He adjusted their faces several times, turning them slightly, catching hold of their chins and the back of their heads. Then he walked backwards and looked at them through the camera eye. Not satisfied, he once again came near them, lifted their chins, and kept their heads upright and steady. He repeated this exercise several times. The children had no idea that taking a photo would be such a troublesome activity.

At last, directing them to keep still, he switched on all the lights. Their eyes were blinded for a moment. She could not even open her eyes in that intense light.

'All right. Ready. One, two, three....' Click!

He lifted his head from behind the camera and switched off the lights, one by one. The children realized that the photo had already been taken. They felt relieved.

'Mol, you didn't tell me your name.'

'Her name is Sheena and mine is Abhilash,' he said.

'Beautiful names.'

He stroked the heads of both of them with great affection.

'My dear children! You can leave now after giving twelve rupees. If you come the day after tomorrow about this time, you can collect the photo.'

She untied the knotted kerchief, took out the coins and gave it to him. There were three and a half rupees.

'Where is the rest of the money, children?'

They looked at each other's face.

'A fine trick, indeed! Are you trying to cheat me? I won't give you the photo unless you pay in full.'

She began to sob. There isn't a paisa in the piggy bank. Where will they get the balance money from? Whom can they approach?

'Ayyayyo, are you are crying, mol? Don't cry. Just do as I say. You don't have to pay a paisa. I will give you the photo.'

Both of them looked at his face, expectantly. He went on laughing like a child.

'Come. Come right in.'

He began to set the lights right once again. After adjusting the lights, he looked at them and laughed once again.

'I will not ask for even a single paisa. And you don't have to give any, either. Both of you strip and then stand there.'

The children gaped at him.

'Didn't you try to fool me? Didn't you say you didn't have money, after having your photo taken? Just you watch, I'll hand over both of you to the police.'

The children stood without uttering a word.

'Shall I call the police?'

'No,' he said in fear. 'I'll strip.'

He was afraid of even hearing the word 'police' mentioned. He would sometimes see policemen in a dream and start awake from sleep.

'Why are you not taking off your clothes, mol?'

'I wanna go home.'

She started sobbing again.

'Take off your clothes,' he whispered in her ear.

'Aren't we mere children?'

'I feel ashamed.'

Hearing that, he once again put on his contented laugh and switched off the bulbs one by one. Now there was only a dim light. In that light, they couldn't see each other's face. She moved into the darkness and stood there.

'That won't do,' he laughed. 'Remove all your clothes.'

He moved behind the camera and standing there for a very long time did a lot many things. He changed the lenses and switched the lights on and switched them off several times. The children didn't understand what he was doing. She kept saying, 'I wanna go home' every now and then. They heard the clicks from the camera many times. A little later, he lifted his head from behind the camera. His smile could be seen bright in the dim light.

'Now you can go home children,' he switched on the lights one by one. 'There's one thing, but... Don't breathe a word to your parents about what happened. If you do....'

Pulling on their clothes hurriedly and with their satchels over their shoulders, they came out as sparrows let out of a cage. Their enthusiasm drained and heads drooping, they walked home along the side of the road, without talking about anything. The other school children were not there on the road. All of them must have reached their homes. They walked alone, along the road frequented by the grown-ups. They could spot her mother standing outside the fence looking expectantly in their direction.

'Where did you go loafing around?' Mother asked. 'You must come home straight once the school time is over. If not, I'll break your legs.'

As she entered the house with her heavy satchel and walked on in, her mother came after her.

'Why d'you go around with that Abhilash? Don't you have girls for company?'

Without saying a word, she put the satchel on the chair and went into the bedroom. The bed had been shaken, tidied up, and spread out properly. The books and papers on the table were arranged neatly.

'He is a bad man,' she said to herself when she changed her dress. 'A really bad one.'

She couldn't sleep that night. She who used to sleep by the window every day got up from there and lay down in between her father and mother. Her mother mumbled something in her sleep and tried to push her away. When she lay close to her father's cigarette-smelling, rough face, she felt a little relieved. Yet, the click, click sound went on disturbing her in her sleep. She got up in the morning only when her mother shook her awake.

'He will be run over by a bus; just you watch,' she told him when they met.

He was waiting for the children, in a secluded spot beyond the copra mill. There was a bicycle in front of him. He smiled, looking at them, from a good distance off.

'Don't you want to see the photo?' he asked.

Their hearts leapt up. Out of the large pocket of his shirt, he took out the photo. She impatiently snatched it away from his hand. The photo made her extremely happy. She could never imagine that her face was so pretty. His face looked serious as usual. As if he was angry with someone. He gave the children two more copies of the photo.

'We need only two. One for me and one for Abhilash.'

'Never mind. Keep all the three with you, children.'

Carrying their satchels slung across their shoulders, the two of them began to walk alongside the barbed-wire fencing of the copra-mill compound, looking intently at the photo.

'Are you leaving my children? How can you go away like that? Mol, you stop.'

He came after them, pushing the bicycle.

'Mon, you can leave. I have got something to tell Sheena in private.'

Seeing that Abhilash remained there without leaving the place, he asked softly, 'Shall I call the police?'

Breathless, he moved away and at a distance, hid behind a tree.

'Have you seen this, Sheena?' He took out another photo from his pocket and showed it to her. Her mind turned molten. When she made as if to run away, he caught her by her hand from behind.

'I wanna go to school.'

'O yes, you can. Who said you shouldn't? But, mol, you must come with me to the studio before that.'

'No, I won't come even if you kill me.'

'Then don't come if you don't want to. I am going to stick this photo on the wall of your school.'

He got in front of her and walked on, pushing the bicycle. She stood there for a moment, not knowing what to do, and unable to suppress her sobs. At that moment, he took her satchel from her, hung it from the handlebar of the bicycle, lifted her up, and sat her on the frame.

'Hold on firmly to the handle,' he said.

With his usual smile, he tied the dhoti firmly on his waist and mounted the bicycle.

Standing hidden behind the tree, Abhilash looked on until the man disappeared from sight, riding away with Sheena on his bicycle.

THE MISSION
SETHU

'May I call you Uncle Kochunni?'

'Oh, yes. Many call me that.'

'You may not have recognized me.'

'Not necessarily. And besides, I don't try to recognize anyone nowadays. It is always better to avoid the accumulation of unnecessary information.'

'Still....'

'No still. If I don't want to know you, is there anything wrong with that?'

'Uncle Kochunni, it is not that way....'

'What if it is that way for me?'

'I have come from where Achuthankutty works.'

'Have you? Fine, then.'

'It is hot there and it's the children's vacation. I wanted to come home on leave. Besides, the company pays the fare of a first-class ticket.'

'Is it so? Perfect. Where can't one go if one gets a free ticket?'

'Achuthankutty had asked me to specifically meet you before I returned.'

'It is puzzling. Why should this wise guy have such a thought now?'

'Not for any special reason. After all, don't you share the same blood as him? Wouldn't he be anxious to know how you are?'

'Yeah, fine. You must have seen Achuthankutty's blood. And if you must see my blood too, there is only one way. Cut my finger. But since I am diabetic, it will be difficult to heal the cut....'

'Oh no! I didn't mean it that way....'

'Whatever you may mean, you should be careful when you categorically say "share the same blood" or things like that. These days there are machines for everything. Suppose a little blood from each person is tested in a machine, and it is found that the two are of different tribes. The belief in blood relationships handed down to us by our forefathers will be blown to bits.'

'In any case, Achuthankutty cannot but be your son.'

'Whoever is so very sure about it? It doesn't mean that I slightly doubt Devakikutty up there,' he said, pointing to the heavens. 'She was such a meek creature.'

'Achuthankutty has told me everything. We are best friends. He is also the president of the Malayali Association there, and I am the secretary.'

'Is it so? Fine. So Achuthankutty can even become a president, eh? Yeah, perfect. Maybe you can still be his secretary when he becomes the president of India in the days to come.'

'I have to return by the five-thirty train.'

'So, we have fifty-five minutes more to be exact. And leaving aside the ten-minute walk to the station, we have forty-five minutes to talk.'

'Yes, I am rather in a hurry. Moreover, Achuthankutty told me to do certain things...'

'Is it so? Then it is yet another mission....'

'Oh no! Nothing of the sort.'

'Let it be. Where do you hail from?'

'I am from the south.'

'A message from the south. What could it possibly mean? It has come to this: that one should watch the portents signified by the messenger.'

'Uncle Kochunni, you shouldn't consider me thus. I have no special motive in this. I made this trip just because Achuthankutty is my dear friend, and I feel sorry for him when I find him befuddled. I have heard a lot about you, and I thought I should meet you....'

'Earlier many people used to come to meet me. Some have had an image of me, which in actual fact, is composed of a little history and several legends. But for some time now, there is not much fuss. Maybe because I didn't get any pension or the Tamra Patra—an award given by the Government of India in recognition of having participated in the freedom struggle. Don't worry. I am not going to open the baggage of old history.'

'I have heard a lot...'

'If it is Achuthankutty who told you, don't believe it. He is president and all, that's fine. But whatever tumbles out of his tongue is nonsense.'

'You should show a little more compassion to Achuthankutty, your only son, shouldn't you?'

'Oh, fine! The message is perfect. Achuthankutty should now get some compassion from me. Suppose I wrap it in a bundle and send it through you. But it will melt away by the time it reaches him, and it will be bothersome for you to carry the weight. Isn't the journey a long one?'

'I know that you have a lot of misunderstandings in your mind, Uncle Kochunni. Achuthankutty has told me everything.'

'Is it so? Of course, the secretary should believe all that the president says. The organization will have discipline and stability that way.'

'Our relationship is not like that. Our families also are very close. We live in adjacent houses.'

'It is a great quality to be very close to each other, despite living next door. Certainly, you must be a great personage.'

'We are running out of time. What I came to talk to you about....'

'I can very well understand what it might be.'

'You shouldn't say so, Uncle Kochunni.'

'It's an old joke...each messenger believes he is the first one. It could well be the weakness of the tribe of messengers. And to the receiver of the message...oh, let it be. The function of the messenger is to suppress the truth, and sow hints of falsehood in the mind of the receiver. Even powerful messengers like ambassadors say so. I'm not smart enough to come out with its correct terminology in English.'

'A second child has been born to him. It's a boy.'

'Good. A girl and boy and that's exactly what the government say—'

'Uncle Kochunni...I...'

'A postcard would have been sufficient to inform me of this news. You didn't have to take all this trouble. And Achuthankutty has my address. But remind him to write the exact PIN code. Because there are supposed to be more than one hundred villages called Ramapuram in our great India.'

'Uncle Kochunni, you don't let me even open my mouth. It makes me unhappy. Haven't I come all the way to this place to see you?'

'Oh, yes. I forgot. Excuse me. One is duty-bound to hear the messenger. Now I will do one thing. You say all you have to, and I will listen without interrupting. I swear I won't speak a word and will listen attentively. Even otherwise, this thing we call an ear is so very obedient. Whatever one says, be it utter foolishness, this ear will keep on listening without fail. This means that the human ear doesn't have the power of cognition by itself. Yes, go on. But, remember you have to catch a train.

'We have half an hour more.'

'Thirty-three minutes, to be exact. Sixteen and a half minutes for you and sixteen and a half minutes for me.'

'That's not enough for me.'

'Eighteen for you and fifteen for me, then.'

'I need at least twenty minutes.'

'All right. You are a fitting friend to Achuthankutty, giving out very little and bargaining for a lot.'

'I will put it briefly. It is difficult to express my thoughts in an orderly manner. So I will narrate it as it comes to my mind. Of late, Achuthankutty has changed a lot. He is always moody. Something is constantly troubling him. When I ask him what's wrong, he himself is not very sure about it. Sometimes his behaviour is very strange. I'll share an incident that happened recently. A kuravan and his monkey arrived one evening at Achuthankutty's courtyard. They performed several tricks, the usual stuff. But Achuthankutty was captivated, and seeing that, the kuravan too became enthusiastic. The kuravan and the monkey began to display some impossible feats which had never been performed before. At a point it became difficult to distinguish the kuravan from the monkey. As we gaped on, Achuthankutty jumped in with them. The kuravan's child began to frantically beat on a drum. For the residents of the neighbourhood, it was such a strange sight. Soon a crowd gathered. Achuthankutty, the monkey, and the kuravan were doing somersaults together. It went on for a very long time.

'Finally, at the end of the performance, Achuthankutty made a handsome payment to the kuravan and asked him, "Will you give me this monkey, my friend?"

Upon hearing the strange request, the kuravan asked, "To kill or to keep?"

"Not for either. To perform," was Achuthankutty's reply.

"He doesn't know how to perform by himself. He cannot perform without me," said the kuravan.

"Never mind. I am also a kuravan. Give me your old drum and attire, my friend."

'The kuravan roared with laughter. He laughed for so long that his face turned red. "Isn't that a mere fancy, sir? You have to be born lucky to wander about as a kuravan. It is because of the punya I acquired in three previous births that I was able to become a kuravan in this one."'

'Achuthankutty wishing to wander about as a kuravan!' Kochunni exclaimed. 'Hey, what all do I have to hear? Now, your time has nearly run out.'

'There is yet another incident. I will finish soon. Achuthankutty hasn't asked me to tell you all this. But I would have told you nearly everything there is to tell if I narrated this too, and you will get a drift of how things are.'

'The construction work for new buildings in the factory complex was in progress near our compound. When the labourers went on digging, they came upon a small statue... an antique devi idol cast in metal. When the news reached Achuthankutty, he rushed to the spot and took it from the overseer. You will recall that he has always been very fond of antiques. I learned about it only after he had cleaned, polished, and installed it in the showcase in his drawing room. By this time, two or three days must have passed. At the very first sight, I sensed something was certainly amiss about that idol. One of the devi's eyes had fallen off. And in the other eye, at certain times, you could see the glitter of a thousand eyes. Sometimes, the eye would flutter as if it was alive. Achuthankutty and I enjoy a drink at night. On those occasions I was scared stiff even to look at that idol. Something burned brightly in that lone eye. A strange fire! Achuthankutty too confirmed it. He too was frightened out of his wits. She was apparently a fierce deity of ancient times. It was obviously dangerous to have rashly brought the idol inside the house. Additionally, it was troublesome to keep it when the required purity of the surrounding atmosphere was not maintained. I had noted one thing: that Achuthankutty had undergone a change ever since placing that idol inside his home. A disturbing thought began to obsess him. His face was like that of one possessed.'

'And, you didn't see it again?'

'No.'

'I understand. Now, you have taken up a lot of the time. No harm. I shall speak now. You listen. My guru says a lot in a very short time without any hue and cry. I have to speak only about my guru. It may be because I am old. But don't be afraid. It's no evil goddess or evil presence. If you ask me how this guru became my guru, I have no answer. I must have first seen him in a dream. Or maybe I saw him in person. Maybe he came in search of me. Anyway, I am powerless to describe the radiance of his face. What all is reflected in those bright eyes? Compassion, affection, detachment—an entire universe. Just take it that we have nothing else to do but to fall at those feet. He knows everything about me. No need to ask him anything; before that, he will tell me everything about myself. "Kochunni, sit alone for some time. Close your eyes and imagine me within yourself. And say, I am here itself." Other times he will say, "Kochunni, you have been very late in starting this." When I pressed my face to those feet, the only thing I heard was, "Couldn't you do this earlier? You have wasted so much time." My guru knows my reluctance to leave everything behind and set out. But what is there in it to begin and to carry on? Aren't all these within us? Isn't the delay in finding out and becoming aware the main thing? For some, it is easily attained. For others, it comes very late in life. For yet another category, it won't come through even after three incarnations...'

'I don't understand anything, Uncle Kochunni...'

'My guru said, "Let us go", and I too am certain that there is nothing to be afraid of. Yet, some unwanted bonds remain and they serve no purpose whatsoever. All are mere strings. One strong blow of breath and they are gone. Most of them are thoughts like "I" and "mine". You get the dry coconut kernel only after the water dries up. When I said my time hadn't come yet, the guru only laughed. "Haven't our forebears described each phase, Kochunni?" he said. But that's beside the point. The point is that awareness should come from within. It is said that a hundred and one nadis, nerves, rise from the heart, and one of them goes straight into the head. The one who manages to send out life through that nadi will become amara, immortal. For those whose life goes out through the other nadis, the result is rebirth into samsara. It is very difficult for those in the samsara to endure that phase. The guru said one should courageously separate from the body the purusha within, which is only as big as one's thumb. One should do it as carefully as one pulls out the central shoot of the minuscule grass. Which means....'

'I... I...'

'If I go on saying things, there's a lot to say. You must be bored....'

'I...'

'You have to go. Will you be late? Only one saving factor: none of these trains run on time as we think.'

'Never mind. I shall run instead of walking. But you should give me your word about one little thing, Uncle Kochunni. Haven't I come this far, out of my way? Shouldn't I take something back for Achuthankutty?'

'Do you think I have been trying to fool the messenger?'
'No. Never.'
'Then, what do you want now? What should I give you beyond the common courtesy due to a messenger?'
'Only one boon. Your consent for a little thing. Achuthankutty wants to come here just once. He wants to see you. When he meets you, you should recognize him....'
'The only thing you did not mention is that I should "cut a fatted calf". That was nice of you...yes, let him come.... I have never forbidden that. But seeing me.... I don't think that is quite possible.'
'Why?'
'I am on a journey.'
'Where to?'
'Isn't it foolish to ask someone my age where he is going when he is set out on a journey? Just take it that it is a long journey.'
'Then to Achuthankutty...'
'Tell him I am on a journey.'
'If he comes....'
'Tell him I am on a journey.'
'If he wishes to see you...'
'You can still tell him I am on a journey.'

IT'S THE GALLOWS FOR US

M. SUKUMARAN

O those who wistfully think that 'I will never get any punishment, I will sleep at least for a night in the cell where light never reaches inside the stone fortress built for convicts,' you are naive; you are the ones looking for the keys to the fool's paradise! What else to say! I will only commiserate with the old and toothless executioner with shrivelled skin and grey hair when he draws his last breath and when the scaffold erected for my execution is eaten by termites and collapses.

Have you seen that village? Not likely. In the wilderness, under the green foliage, in the atmosphere pregnant with the anticipation of youth, I walked a long way. I heard the wailing of a woman when I reached the peepul tree. Her sobs reached as waves in my ears, like the moaning of the wind blowing past the mountain pass. Why are those who have gathered around, unable to do anything? I halted briefly. I expected a pair of legs would stride forward and kick open the door of that hut. But nothing happened. The uncouth villagers placed their pointed fingers on their noses—a sign of shame, pity, or contempt—and went on talking about something among themselves, their voices low. It was as if the woman's wails sounded like temple bells to them. My blood boiled. When I pushed gently, that palm leaf-braided door opened. I lifted the man, catching him by the scruff of his perspiring neck. I threw the clothes towards the naked woman bathed in sweat. I didn't harm him; I only advised him: 'Why do you rape a woman when there are so many other women in this world who would willingly submit to you? Imagine if this woman were your sister, and I was in your place. You will then never allow me to breathe the air of this world, will you? Go. Immerse yourself in the cold water of the waterlily pond. Let your body and mind cool down.'

In the lethargy of guilt, he tottered out of the hut. I didn't stop there. I did not want the milk and fruits of gratitude the woman would offer me.

As I moved away, my head held high and my arms still at my side, the villagers stood watching me in silence.

Let no one know about this. If the keeper of justice of this village learns about the incident, he will shower me with gifts. He will offer me a silk shawl, a gold bracelet, and a machete with my name engraved on it.

How can someone like me be punished? O those who await my arrival, spreading silk and strewing flower petals on the path to heaven built somewhere in the skies for those who do good down here on earth, I am not coming that way! My path is different!

At a time when those who had sinned threw stones at each other and quarrelled, I, the human being, flew about here and there for the air, water, and light of this world.

When the first bud of memory bloomed....

Father summoned poisonous serpents, made them bite those they had bitten, and had the poison drawn out. The spirits of those serpents who beat their heads on the earth and died, as a result of it, flew about around the taravad carrying the germs of leukoderma. During his leisure times, Father spread out cowrie shells in a ritual of divination, picked out the ghosts and ghouls in their dwellings, and nailed them to the kutaja tree.

My father deserved punishment. He got it when he was fifty years old. When his body turned lifeless, snake poison having spread all over, and sprawled among empty arrack bottles, blood streaming down his cheeks, I became all alone. Father became my memory.

Last night I remembered all this. I do not grieve for my father. I had only thought that, from the many punishments which he might have had to suffer, a greater punishment in the form of death had saved him.

When the odour of the upturned, ploughed soil become dense in the air, the summer sun glance at the earth as if towards a spurned sweetheart. Beginning with the midnight moonlight, till the noon sun was up, he had been plodding on. Any moment he might collapse. I couldn't bear to watch him so. I supported him with my left hand. I dripped tender coconut water through the cracked lips into his mouth. I lifted him in my arms and laid him down on the ground in the shade of the coconut trees. 'Take rest. Get down to the paddy field for work only when you are completely rested and feel fit. Let those four-legged creatures also rest awhile.'

I walked on, parting the waves of sunshine. The horizon would have been alarmed. I walked till the shadow of my erect head fell towards the east.

The raindrops showered by the monsoon clouds kept falling on my head and hair. Seasons changed.

Above me, the full moon lay behind a veil of mist. Trees stood sentinel to the fallen leaves.

The forest dwellers built bonfires under the tent of mist and danced around them. Raising a racket on their drums, they scared off wild elephants and boars. They had not had their supper.

Standing in their midst, I roared with the torch of self-confidence held aloft, 'You are burning in hunger! Guarding the ripe fields on empty stomachs! You, who have sown this field, reap all the grains in the fields through this night, before they reach the yards of those who have not sown them!'

In the moonlit night, braving the cold, they descended on the fields and reaped through the night. All of them had sown the fields months ago, standing in the scorching sun.

When the morning star rose, the paddy fields were empty. Preparing honey and foxtail millet for me to eat, they waited for me, singing all the while. But I had left them far behind—passing the hill, through the dales, marshes, riverbanks.

I did not need a crown. My neck wouldn't bend to accept flower garlands.

For years together, I lived in the veranda of this barn. The cattle shed without a single cow or buffalo, the meadow without oxen or plough, or the barn without a single grain of paddy, didn't afflict me. My hunger was theirs. Their tears had flown through my eyes. Serpents made way for me hearing my footsteps. The mantra to summon them and make them bite the victim and draw back their poison rested unused in my quiver. I restrained myself from stomping, to avoid crushing ants beneath my feet.

That day's dusk was captivating. The paddy fields lay as if in the sweet swoon of early pregnancy. The pond in the middle was holding its breath. I saw the sunset over the hill and following it, the grieving sky. The winds swayed witnessing the intensity of that grief. The flames of the three-wick nilavilakku, the tall brass lamp, squirmed like newborn infants.

I ate the gruel made of broken rice along with tender mango pickle. As I sat cross-legged on the veranda, looking at the trillions and gazillions of stars, my disciples arrived.

They sat around me and asked: 'What kind of people should we become?'

I said, 'Children! Be like a pearl oyster. It may sound like a tale of yore. How it happens is this way: on a chothi asterism, represented by a single star, it will rain at midday, and one of the raindrops will fall inside the oyster. Then that drop turns into a pearl. Therefore, when the asterism rises, the oysters rise to the surface of the water and wait to receive those raindrops. As soon as a raindrop falls into the oyster, it clams itself shut and dives deep into the seabed, to nurture it patiently to the full maturity of a pearl. You should be like that oyster. First, listen to the words of wisdom, then ponder over it, then....'

That was when they came. Four of them. Of equal height and girth.

I said, 'Children, go now. And come tomorrow. Let me ask of them who they are and what they have come for.'

The children paid me obeisance, stepped over the threshold in silence, and departed.

'Come. Come near me.' Darkness had hidden their faces.

Three of them came forward in a column, and the fourth, a little behind them. Their firm muscles shone in the light of the nilavilakku.

'Why have you come, brothers?'

Three of them gnashed their teeth. Their jawbones quivered. Their eyes flashed the embers of rage. The fourth one knit his brow. To increase his imperviousness, he fixed his gaze on the flames on the wicks. His lips moved.

'Come out with us.'

My body didn't shiver. My blood pressure didn't shoot up either. I asked quietly: 'Where to?'

The fourth man came forward slowly. Then he said in a calm voice, 'Come! The justice keeper of the village has summoned you.'

'Me?'

'Yes, my friend! You are going to be punished!'

Then the three men rushed towards me. My arm was crushed in their steel grips. They dragged me. Losing my step, I fell in the yard. They picked me up violently. In a strong wind that blew from somewhere, the light from the nilavilakku went out.

As they dragged me away, I asked them, 'What crime did I commit?'

One of the three men roared, 'Receive the punishment of the justice keeper, first! He who punishes only the guilty is like a god to us!'

The fourth man was walking behind calmly, with an emotionless face.

I was growing increasingly weak. The soles of my feet were bruised, striking against the sharp stones. The skin on my calves were bleeding.

'Go down!'

I went down the mud steps. We were now on the slope of a hill. Facing me was the moon of the twelfth night. I could smell the scent of the kutaja flowers.

'Turn left!'

Two flaming torches came into view. The flames flickered as the winds threatened to blow them out.

They shoved me with great force. I fell flat on the sand-strewn courtyard. In pain, I raised my head. Sitting on the throne, the justice keeper, with long eyebrows and owl's eyes, pursed his dark lips and regarded me with utter scorn. On either side of him, slave girls stood, waving ceremonials whisks made of the tuft of yak's tail hair.

Raising his hand, the justice keeper said, 'According to the traditions of this village, you must first suffer the punishment! Only those who are guilty will be punished! We will provide the charge sheet, later. Get your punishment first!'

The justice keeper dipped the quill in the inkpot. Addressing one of the four men who dragged me in, he said, 'The first one of you, cut off his right hand!'

Blood spouted from my hand and splattered on the face of the first man who stood with his shining sword. I squirmed on the ground. My lifeless right hand lay on the sand soaked in blood. The first one himself smeared the sap of crushed medicinal leaves on the raw wound of the stump. When the blood flow stopped, he supported me and sat me on the ground.

The voice of the keeper of justice, 'Your crime: you forcefully separated a healthy male who was in intimate embrace with a youthful woman in a hut in the village.'

A woman came out from the dark. Her eyes brimmed over. Sobbing, she told the justice keeper, 'This wicked man pulled me away from the man who had come to me to ensure that our lineage, whose roots would have ended with me, would continue through me. It was true that I was wailing and shouting at the climax of the erotic experience. After that incident, that man has never even glanced at me. My lineage is about to be extinct.'

The woman wailed beating her breast and ran away into the darkness.

The keeper of justice roared with laughter. 'It is with your right hand that you picked him up and separated him from her. Therefore, you lost your right hand.'

Oil was poured on to the torches. They blazed forth with renewed vigour.

The keeper of justice picked up his quill once again. 'Now you will suffer the punishment for your second crime. Attention, the second one! Cut off his left hand too!'

Blood gushed from my left hand and splattered on the face of the second man who stood with his sword. When the sap of the crushed leaves was applied, the blood flow from the stump of the left hand too was staunched.

Both my hands lay lifeless on the ground.

He came out into the light. He had draped around him a single loincloth the colour of mud. Bending his body on which his bones stuck out, he told the keeper of justice: 'He supported me with his left hand. He gave me tender coconut water. He laid me down on the sand. I slept there. He must have given tender coconut water to many others like me and pushed them too down into the deep chasm of lethargic sleep. It was past dusk when I woke up. It was then that my senses returned to me. I realized that if the ploughing of the field is delayed, the sowing too will be delayed and that if the sowing is delayed, the reaping also will be delayed. This wicked man's aim was to delay production, bring about a scarcity of foodgrains in the market, and, exploiting a basic urge like hunger, mobilize the villagers against the chief and the justice keeper of this village.'

When he moved away, the keeper of justice said: 'I hope you do not rue the fact that you lost your left hand with which you helped that man.'

The quill of the keeper of justice moved once again: 'Let the third one come forward! As the third punishment, his eyelids should be sewn shut using horsehair. He should not open his eyes and see henceforth. Advising those who sowed to reap the harvest at midnight, anticipating that the grains will reach the courtyard of those who did not sow, he watched to his soul's satisfaction as they reaped in the thick mist till daybreak. He is not likely to have known the fact that the grains reached the courtyard of the village chief at dawn, and since the forest dwellers craved his pardon, the chief had gifted them thick cotton garments. His intention was to create a rift between the amiable village chief and those industrious forest dwellers.'

The sharp needle pierced the tender veins on my eyelids. I didn't squirm. I had grown insensate all over. Though I would not know pain any more, I lost light. In front of me was the palace of darkness.

The voice of the keeper of justice: 'Let the fourth one come forward! I am going to inflict on this man, his fourth punishment! This is for the crimes he may commit if he stays alive. Hang him on the gallows raised on the beach, till he dies!'

The fourth one didn't say a word. I lay on his shoulder like a living corpse. He walked on, carrying me.

His breath fell on my shoulder with soft warmth. The sound of him swallowing hard in utter resentment fell on my ears.

I fumbled in the dense forests of darkness. Where's at least a sliver of light? Will this fourth one be a light for me? Can't it turn out that this one has been born to be my saviour?

I struggled to move my lifeless tongue. I called him, mustering all my strength: 'Comrade!'

'Hmm.'

'Save me! Only you can do something now. You are my saviour!'

He continued walking in silence. The roar of the sea was coming nearer. How far would it be to the scaffold?

I sobbed.

'Save me who hasn't committed any crime, at least now!'

'Don't weep! Tears are the asset of a coward!'

I was startled. His voice was very low. Yet I heard it amidst the commotion raised by the waves.

'I will save you. I will not hang you. I know that you have not committed any crime. You will be awarded a crown and sceptre in the empire of goodness. Be at peace!'

Whatever blood was left in my veins, rollicked with happiness. I would be saved. Till my wounds healed, I could seek the assistance of my disciples. My legs were healthy. I could go away from this village. I could sleep in an inn of some village. I did not have my hands to give them tender coconut water when they were exhausted or point out to them the fields full of ripe grains when they were hungry. But I would advise them to raise their agricultural implements against that class living like the birds of the sky. 'Discover those whose blood is similar to yours. Discern. Organize....'

The sea was right in front. The brine that came flying in the wind stung my wounds.

'Comrade!' the fourth one called out to him.

'Now you are close to the scaffold. I will not hang you. I cannot stand watching an innocent one die. Let us climb those rocks and go over to the other side. What are you going to do from now on, if you escape?'

My voice faltered as I said, 'I will leave this village. I will walk through paddy fields in some other village. I will teach people certain things. Now I have nothing to lose!'

The fourth one stopped.

'Why did you stop?'

'Nothing. Now we are at a great height. Below, is the roaring sea. The waves beat their heads against the craggy creek and die.'

'Hmm.'

'Let's climb down. You are going to escape forever!'

The fourth one stood where he was.

The rocks wept. The seagulls screeched.

Moments became costly.

'Climb down, comrade!'

'I shall.'

My heart and his, beat as if in a contest.... Tik tik...tik tik...tik.. tik....

In the slice of one moment before I reached the surface of the sea, I heard this much: 'Swim and escape. There is a very strong undertow on the western side. Don't swim that side at all.'

THE DINOSAUR BABY
E. HARIKUMAR

'Last night, the dinosaur baby came again,' Rajeevan said. 'It stood looking at me through the window for some time.'

Breakfast time was also story time for Rajeevan. Stories of the dreams he had. When the sunrays fell on the tabletop through the window, he would remember the details of the dreams. Then the stories would come out one after another. Today Mohanan is bound to listen because there is only a single member of the audience! Shailaja is in the kitchen busy making dosas.

'I was sleeping,' he continued. 'The dinosaur baby stood looking at me for some time. It liked me very much. It put out its tongue through the window bars and licked me. Its tongue was very soft. How cute its face was! Like a puppy's.'

This is the second day. On the first day, that is day before yesterday, it came and looked through the second-floor window at Rajeevan as he lay down in bed. It looked in, standing on its hind legs. Rajeevan says it held its short forelegs pressed against the wall. It was twenty feet tall. But it was a baby dinosaur. Cute face. Rajeevan felt like kissing it. But he didn't. He didn't know whether it would like to be kissed!

This was the beginning of a new series. Animals who came and loved him or harmed him were numerous. There were animals ranging from the cat to elephant in that list. But this was the first time, having this big an animal around. As the size of the characters got bigger, the story itself became lengthier. And they lasted many more days.

'Why don't you eat the dosas, hey?' Shailaja asks him. He does not reply. He continues describing the animal.

'Its hind legs have great girth. The forelegs are small. It was standing, dangling those forelegs. Poor thing! It may be hungry. Daddy! What do dinosaurs eat?'

Mohanan doesn't know what food dinosaurs ate. Is it grass? Was there grass on the surface of the earth ten million years ago? He has no idea.

'Aren't you going to eat your dosa?' Mohanan asks. 'The autorickshaw will arrive soon. Don't need to run for it at that time, do we?'

Rajeevan's somnambulistic trip crashed. He began to wolf down mouthfuls of dosa.

'Mummy, did you see my blue pair of socks? Paul sir said he would punish me when I wore black socks to school yesterday. Give me my lunch box.'

'Where is your lunch box? I have told you everyday that you should hand over the lunch box to me as soon as you return from school so I can wash it and keep it ready for the next day. Give it to me now, quick! See! You have two idlis in here uneaten. Why didn't you eat them all?'

From now on, it's mayhem. Till the auto arrives at eight-thirty, Rajeevan will send Shailaja in circles. As soon as the auto has left, she collapses in a chair.

'Gosh! This is the kind of circus I play with just one around! How will it be like to have another four more like this one?'

'Just keep quiet, will you?' Mohanan said. 'There are more important things to think about. Like the food habits of dinosaurs. I must find out before Rajeevan returns in the afternoon. Tonight, he must feed a baby dinosaur. Then I have my own little things too, to attend to. First, I must sell the battery eliminators worth fifty thousand rupees as soon as possible.'

The salesman from Delhi had entrapped him through his sales pitch. The fellow had shown him so many orders he claimed he had received from just two districts in Kerala. There were more than forty-thousand orders! Mohanan fell for it. And got into a sole agency contract with that company. The conditions were all very attractive. The first consignment would be of fifty thousand rupees. After that, they would send him consignments of ten thousand rupees each. It was an item with high demand.

Now, he was shouldering a stock worth fifty thousand rupees and going around shops, trying to sell them.

'Did you say battery eliminator? Oh, we have too much of its stock here already. Items like this would sell maybe occasionally. Do you have transformers? They are in great demand now.'

It went on like this. He had either become a very bad salesman, or the product he was trying to sell had very low demand. Anyhow, those who had lent him money, including the banks, have begun to trouble him for repayment. The due dates of repayment have all been long past.

The next problem is of housing. They had found a small house on rent in the town. But they were expected to pay five thousand as advance deposit for it. The rate of rent was the same as the present one. The advantage was that he could cut down on the commute. That was a great thing. He had given notice to his present landlord. Only when he got a refund of his previous deposit from him, can he pay the deposit to the new landlord.

'Let me drink some tea,' Shailaja said.

As she was drinking tea, she asked me: 'Do you know what to do, Kutty, when you are facing multiple problems? My grandfather used to say: "First of all, sort the problems priority-wise, going by the importance of each subject. Then, start doing the most important one first, and very quickly. Then, attend to the next important one. Attend all the problems, one after another, in this way". It is a very easy-to-follow method. See! Can you fetch me that dosa? And, also pour the batter for another dosa on the tawa.'

He rose, picked up the dosa, and brought it over.

'Aren't I a wonderful man endowed with miraculous powers? Here, I am wasting time cooking dosa for my wife! Your grandfather is unlikely to have faced such difficulties.'

'No. My grandfather used to drink rice gruel for breakfast. Besides, my grandmother's two unmarried younger sisters used to live with them. They used to compete preparing rice gruel and coconut chutney for my grandfather.'

'Tell me! What's the most important of your problems, kutty?'

'Food for the dinosaur.'

'Food for *what*?'

'The dinosaur. A baby dinosaur. It is in Rajeevan's latest dream series. When all the series are over, I will secure a doctorate in that subject. This is the most difficult of them all, so far. I don't know where to turn, to do research on this new subject.'

'Can't you get it done if you go over to the zoo? Ask what they feed dinosaurs.'

Mohanan did not say anything. She was mistaken. She must have confused dinosaur with rhinoceros. Or, she wouldn't have heard about dinosaurs. It was just as well that Rajeevan was not within her earshot right now. If he heard this, he would have laughed, rolling on the ground.

He was apprehensive that Rajeevan was developing into a male chauvinist. It happened last week. Mohanan had just got into the bathroom and was urinating. On the first floor, it was a single bathroom shared by the two rooms—one of them the parents' bedroom and the other, Rajeevan's. When Shailaja had made Rajeevan's bed, and opened the bathroom door, she spotted Mohanan in there. She quickly got out and shut the bathroom door. Rajeevan noticed that. He was aware that Mohanan had been urinating in there. He was observing his mother's movements. He saw Mummy getting into the bathroom and getting out instantly.

He began to laugh. He was laughing away, somersaulting on the bed.

Then when Mohanan again went into the bathroom before sleeping, Rajeevan too came along and asked quietly: 'Did Mummy see you?'

He whispered, 'No.'

'You were lucky, no? If she had seen you, it would have been embarrassing for you, no? It's okay if boys see. But it's bad if girls see, isn't it?'

Saying that, he lowered his shorts, took out his small chilli, and aimed it at the bowl.

'You are right!' Mohanan concurred, without losing the veneer of seriousness on his face.

When they were certain that Rajeevan was fast asleep, Mohanan regaled Shailaja with details of that exchange between father and son. She pressed hard on her tummy unable to suppress her laughter.

༳

Sitting in the reference section of the library, before the book on prehistoric creatures which he had laid open, Mohanan began to think. Something is wrong somewhere. As if everything is topsy-turvy. Whatever he does, turns out to be wrong. When he became certain that the Marwari was exploiting him, Mohanan fought with him, and got out of the firm. The job that fetched him two thousand rupees every month had gone down the drain. He had become a self-styled businessman from that time on. Till now, he had printed the visiting cards of three different companies for himself. He became a salesman of products ranging from iron nails to spare parts of radio. Everything ended in loss. Everything turned out in the same pattern. When he brought a product that was enjoying good demand till then in the market, it turned out to be something with a tardy demand overnight.

'This? We have boxfuls of this in our godown.'

Or, 'Eighteen rupees? Do you want to buy it for twelve rupees a piece? We can sell you as many as you want. We have ready stock.'

Traders yawn when he begins his sales talk. They suggest the names of their rivals. 'Go there. They might be interested.'

Where has his salesmanship gone hiding? His salesmanship which had garnered for the Marwari, orders for machineries worth lakhs of rupees? Something is wrong somewhere.

In front of him he saw dinosaurs that had lived in different eras baring their teeth. When those creatures with horrendous faces, gargantuan monsters which were carnivores and herbivores, walked, the earth shook. Later when the Ice Age came, they perished one after another without being able to get food. He saw the last dinosaur raising its head helplessly and looking, standing in an ice-covered valley. Craving for a little warmth, a little food.

That creature got into a long slumber, to rise again now after sixty million years, to stand guard outside a six-year-old's window to become his pet with a cute face, with a soft tongue. A sleep that lasted countless eras.

For some days now, Mohanan was planning to consult an astrologer. For that purpose, he has kept his horoscope ready. Beyond the rationalism he always vouched for, there were some things happening around him. He was bent on discovering that.

He got out, with a handbag filled with samples of his product. He remembered once going to the residence of an astrologer swami to check a pair of horoscopes for someone for marriage compatibility.

The swami was sitting in the same posture, as then. On leopard-skin. He was wearing a white dhoti. And his upper torso was wrapped in a towel. He wore a sandal-paste mark on his brow. Above his nose, was a golden-rimmed spectacle. An old man and a young man were sitting in front of him. They had obviously come to check the compatibility of a pair of horoscopes.

The swami said emphatically: 'These two horoscopes can never be joined in any way.'

'Swami! Is there no way at all they can be joined?'

'I have followed all that you said,' the swami went on. 'Eight months on, the joining of these two horoscopes will bring in untold troubles. The girl is past twenty-six. That's a fact. But this one won't suit her in any way. There are certain difficult dashaasandhis, troublesome planetary conjunctions, besides.'

They slowly walked away after paying dakshina, a customary offering, to the swami.

'What do you want?' the swami asked Mohanan.

Mohanan roused himself. He opened the briefcase, took out the horoscope, straightened it out and placed it before the swami. A paper in which planetary positions and their fractions were worked out separately. The swami put on his spectacles and studied the paper. As he went on looking at it, the number of lines on his brow increased. Finally, his face twisted.

'Whose horoscope is this? Is it yours?'

'Yes. It is mine.'

'You must have lost your job exactly three years and four months ago. It is obvious that you have fought with your employer and were fired. There's no other way this should have happened. You are unemployed as of now, aren't you?'

Mohanan didn't say anything. The status of being self-styled businessman was no job.

The swami was making calculations.

'For the last four years and seven months, you have been passing through the Ketur dasha, the phase of Ketu. Now a stretch of two and a half years more of it remains. During this period, you cannot expect to make satisfactory progress in anything. Now, currently you are running Ezharaandashani, Saturn's transit in your planetary house that takes seven-and-a-half-years to complete, as well. It's a very bad time for you. You must be extra careful. Loss of property, loss of prestige, anything like that can be expected during this period. For everything that you endeavour to achieve, you are bound to meet with obstacles. You will begin something, trusting that everything will turn out well. But all of it will end in loss. If you invest five, you will lose ten. It's that bad.'

Was the swami reading my mind? Mohanan asked himself.

Once the Ezharaandashani is over then the balance of Ketur dasha remains. It cannot be said to be that bad. But if you want to prosper, it can happen only after Ketur dasha. Ezharaandashani is running for another nine months in your case. Please be careful until then.'

The swami went on. Mohanan was ruminating: so, all these have been written down in the very beginning itself. It has been written on a palm leaf left in a heap somewhere in the recesses where the mysteries of the universe are kept, that a child born in this particular year, under such and such asterism, in such an hour, in such a fraction of a minute and second, would be doing what, would be becoming who or what. Perhaps, even eons before the period dinosaurs and other prehistoric creatures had existed, even millions of years before all that, the creator would have determined that the future of the universe should be such and such.

'Can't you go back to the past as well, like you predict the future?' Mohanan asked the swami.

'Certainly. But you of course know about the past. Like you know, you lost your job. Aren't people eager only to know about the future?'

'I am not asking about the near past. I am asking about a time sixty million years ago, about a time when dinosaurs roamed the earth.'

The swami looked at him keenly. He picked up the specs he had set aside and wore it again. He pored over the horoscope once again. He went on calculating. He put down the specs again and regarded him.

'No! I can't see that you have any mental disorder. Look here! You are undergoing a bad patch right now. Be patient for some more time and do things after much deliberation. Next you are going to have the lucky phase of Venus. That will bring in a lot of prosperity for you. Live within your limits till then. Have darshan of the Goddess twice daily.'

As he left after paying the swami dakshina he thought: the swami has got the impression that he had lost his mental balance. But he had really wanted to know whether the swami could go back beyond eons. Back through the several eras, traversing the primordial chill of the Ice Age, and reach the terrain where mountainous dinosaurs stood raising their heads. One of those dinosaurs who went about grazing then has got the good fortune to be born again after several eras. To become the pet of a six-year-old. To stand guard outside the window of the second-floor bedroom where he sleeps, with a loveable face and a soft tongue, to lick his cheek lovingly.

The swami can never understand that.

Now, he had to meet a trader. He had promised to tell Mohanan whether he will take a certain quantity of his product in his stock for sales. If this trader too were not to show interest, he would throw the battery eliminators worth fifty thousand rupees into the attic.

Luckily, the trader was in his shop. Only that he was pretending not to have seen him. Mohanan reminded him that only the day before the two of them had sat down for half an hour for a sales discussion, and that Mohanan had agreed to sell the item to him at a reduced rate of twenty per cent. Reducing twenty per cent meant he had to lose ten per cent from his pocket. Nevertheless, he would get back at least a part of what he had invested.

Mohanan said: 'You had promised me that you would confirm today whether you would be able to take delivery of my product.'

'Oh, you mean the battery eliminator? It is not in demand nowadays. Maybe you can leave two dozen with me. I will pay you after I sell them.'

Where was two dozen? Where was the stock worth fifty thousand rupees? He turned around and walked off. There was nothing left to look forward to.

When he reached home, Shailaja said: 'Two people had come to have a look at this house, half an hour ago. I have told them to come after you are back, kutty.'

Two minutes later, they knocked at the door.

'I heard you were going to vacate this house. When are you leaving?'

'On the first of the next month.'

'Do you mind if we looked around?'

'Oh no! Please come in.'

'This is the sitting room. The fan has been fitted by the landlord. This is the hall. It's very spacious. The hall leads to the kitchen. It's very convenient. There are racks. And a platform for the gas stove. There's a sink over there. This door leads to the bedroom. I am using it as my office room for the time being. On the first floor too, there are two bedrooms, and a bathroom attached to both. Let's have a look. Come!'

'Water?'

'Running water all twenty-four hours. There is a pump and motor.'

He had come in tired, parched for a cup of tea. When they left, Shailaja asked him; 'Why do you struggle so much, kutty? Why are you so eager and anxious to find tenants for Lonappan Mappila?'

She is right, he thought. In the last ten days, at least eight parties have come to have a look at this house. There were parties ranging from two to ten members. On all these eight occasions, he had narrated about the positives of this property to the parties, like a real estate broker.

Lonappan Mappila's dexterity in controlling me like a robot, sitting five kilometres away, is beyond compare, he mused. He will get back his deposit only if someone takes the house on rent and gives the landlord a deposit. If he didn't pay the deposit for his new house within the first day of the next month, he will lose that house! Therefore, when each party comes, he dons the robe of a real estate broker, and goes on, 'This is the sitting room....'

Rajeevan returned from school with some new suspense as usual.

'Mummy! Can you say what I drew in school? Daddy, please don't tell her.'

His complaint is that Daddy guesses all his secrets. Therefore, his questions and riddles are all addressed to his mother. And a warning alongside: that Daddy shouldn't answer.

Mohanan had already made his guess.

When he realized that his mother had failed, he pulled out a paper from his bag and showed her, without giving Mohanan an opportunity to spell out what it was.

It was a baby dinosaur. A cute face like that of a puppy. Shiny eyes, long neck, thick hind legs, big belly, stubby forelegs, a long tail, trailing behind.

On the whole, the picture was not bad. A figure which was a combination of a kangaroo, a giraffe, and a Pomeranian puppy.

Suddenly, Mohanan remembered that he had become a scholar on prehistoric animals and that he could talk to Rajeevan authoritatively on dinosaurs. He waited for Rajeevan to ask him a question. He was going to get an opportunity to grow in his son's estimation of him.

That was when Shailaja came in with two letters. The first one was from the bank. He had to remit fifteen thousand rupees at once. The other one was from someone who had lent him money. It said that it wasn't polite of him to further delay the repayment of the loan. Therefore, he must pay at least ten, including interest, as soon as he got the letter.

Mohanan had expected that there would be some respite at least, in between. Ketu and Shani were standing opposite him and suffocating him.

Rajeevan came over. He had paint in his hand. Also, brushes.

'Daddy, I am going to draw a big dinosaur. Give me a sheet of paper.'

'Now, leave me alone. Do not disturb me,' he said. 'I have a terrible headache.'

'Just give me a sheet of paper. I won't bother you then.'

A little help, a good word, where to get these from? He sat, supporting his head in his hands. He had not felt so much load of helplessness ever before. He felt angry at himself.

Rajeevan was still waiting for the sheet of paper.

Mohanan suddenly exploded: 'Get lost!'

He roared, 'You and your dinosaur! How did you get such an ugly creature? A likely pet of yours, indeed! Do you know how macabre its face is?'

Rajeevan fell silent, stood listening to what his father said. His face fell. When Mohanan was done, Rajeevan slunk away to the kitchen.

Mohanan could hear his sobs. And also, his complaints.

'My dinosaur is very cute. Why does Daddy say that it is not cute? Look at what I have drawn! It comes at night and licks me. It's licking me because it likes me, doesn't it?'

Nowadays, Mohanan sleeps less and less. Rajeevan's dinosaur is giving him trouble. What he sees when he shut his eyes is a small child walking away along a path in the wilderness, holding in his hand one end of a rope latched around the long neck of a twenty-feet-tall dinosaur. In each footfall of the creature, the earth is trembling. However much he walks, the features of the path don't change. They both are walking away along identical-looking, unending paths. In the midst of all this, the loss of fifty thousand rupees or the state of homelessness from the first of next month onwards do not affect him at all.

Rajeevan is anxious about the new residence. Because it is a single-storey building, it does not have an upper floor. His bedroom would also be on the ground floor. He says that it will create problems for his baby dinosaur. When it bends down to peep in through the window at the ground floor level, it causes pain to its neck, he says.

Mohanan suggests a solution for this. It is a wide expanse beyond his window in the new house, the father assures the son. The dinosaur can lie down, pressing its tummy to the floor. In that posture, it can look through the window, without its neck paining.

Mohanan could not bring himself to reveal to Rajeevan at that point that beyond his window, actually there is a dirty drain in which mosquitoes swarm, and still farther, it is a very narrow street which is always jam-packed with people jostling each other.

'Won't you be afraid to lie down on the ground floor, near the window?' Shailaja asks him.

'Why should I be afraid?' he asks her. 'When such a gigantic dinosaur is standing guard all night outside the window, will the thieves make bold to come near?'

Rajeevan used to sleep alone. One day, he comes over with his blanket and pillow.

'I am sleeping today with you, Mummy!'

'Cche! With mummy? No way!' Shailaja said.

Their plan was all going to the dogs! Mohanan tells Rajeevan, in a mellow, diplomatic tone: 'Mon! Please go and sleep now!'

Rajeevan doesn't relent.

'Aren't I sleeping alone always? Just for this once...'

From age two, he used to sleep alone.

'What's special about today?' Shailaja asks.

'I read the book, *Hardy Boys Mystery* today.'

'Who told you to read that book just before going to bed?'

'There weren't any other books. Mummy, may I lie down here for some time?'

'No, no! Big boys don't usually sleep with their mothers. Do not get into bad habits!'

'Rajeevan, go and sleep now!' Mohanan says sternly.

He is afraid. He goes back to his own bedroom, with his pillow and bedsheet. Tears rolling down his cheeks.

Shailaja says, after lying silently for some time. 'I am not in the mood any more. We could have let him sleep with us. Call him back.'

Mohanan did not say anything. He lies supine, his eyes open. He remembers meeting the swami. He remembers the trader who fed him hope for an entire day, and then thwarted him in the eleventh hour. He remembers the Delhi salesman who cheated him, showing him the bogus orders, he claimed he had received. He remembers the letters and threats of his creditors.

An hour must have passed. Shailaja was asleep. He rose, went to Rajeevan's room, and switched the light on. He was sleeping, hugging a pillow. There were four other pillows, on the four sides. He says it is a fort. When he lies down in the middle, surrounded by them, he says he does not feel fear. He didn't answer the question as to what that pillow was that he hugged. That was his secret.

Near the pillow lay the picture of the dinosaur that he drew. He had attempted to beautify its face further, by painting it over again. He bent over and kissed Rajeevan's sweet face. Then gently licked his soft cheek, once.

He felt envious of the baby dinosaur that stood outside the window gazing at Rajeevan and licked on his cheek when he felt intense love towards the boy. Mohanan painfully yearned to be a dinosaur that stood guard over his son all night long.

WE, TOMORROW'S SHAME
T. R.

There isn't a subject our court doesn't deliberate upon or a law it doesn't pass—the court that *grows* in this garden that never fades, with a lake that never dries up. Sitting apart and quarrelling to no end, we finally parted on bitter terms! In the cold darkness of the night, we hurled expletives at each other and then kissed. We expelled the heat that ripened in our hearts through our lips. The calming kisses of wakefulness and passion; to enjoy the consolation of one's inner being, kissing the lips of gigolos.

How devoid of love we all are if we think about it! That's what became clear tonight. That's what becomes clear every night. Yesterday, something special happened. When we, humans, were kissing and consoling each other, the dirty dogs and enraged wild animals around us began barking. Even as we stay invisible to each other, why do we play-act so perfectly? Then the dogs emitted protracted howls. We thought the dogs barked upon seeing a lamp hanging from the shoulder of someone carrying the corpse of someone among us. Among creatures, only humans bury their dead during the night. The dogs asked: why can't these moving coffins remain buried under the earth for at least some time? It was then that the dogs revealed why they had been startled. It was not because someone had died but because someone was born! Even then, we kept coughing up theories about the purpose of the advent of socialism, the future of poetry, and the violent dance of the stars light years away.

All around us, dogs kept up their long-drawn-out howling. Who becomes right when we are wrong is called the king. Last night the dogs were our kings. What they sang was the truth. The essence of brahmam was their barking. With the onslaught of their howling, the garden's soft surface trembled. Haven't you finished your debates, having talked all day? And are you continuing the deliberations of the court into the night? Are there gardens in distant lands? Are there courts such as ours in those gardens? Devadattan, who was sturdy to look at, said an organization like their court was only found here.

Devadattan rose and looked all around. A willowy mass of darkness billowed around the boundary. The garden, especially its centre, was teeming with crowds. Taking his stance as if he was all alone in the middle of this centre, in this cool and desirable Nandavaadi—Krishna's Vrindavan. He said, 'Be patient for a little longer. The dogs will begin barking in Nandavaadi.' All of those who were gathered knew this. Therefore, no one was surprised to hear this statement. Devadattan had clarified that he yearned to spend his days in hospitals and graveyards.

When we planted flowering trees and tended to the fragrant plants and shrubs, we thought we never had to leave this place. Why were we never ready to get out of the court?

Everything is disappearing behind the folds of darkness. The garden, its centre, the people, and the animals...all are dissolving into darkness. Sounds continue to rise. The court thrived on the lawns and the banks of the lake. Daniel (Cohn-Bendit) argued that brilliant stars existed only in the skies of Marx and Shaw, while the new mayor insisted the stars should be the flowers of freedom. The mayor, Daniel, and their henchmen delivered speeches about the bundles of ideas they carried about. The voices were repeatedly undulating, culminating in endless repetitions and finally crashing. Words writhed. Meanings rose, beating their breasts. The voices of humans and animals dissolved in a single rhythm.

The ringed parakeets who tarried atop the fresh shoots of the foliage whistled tunes of old film songs as if they weren't aware of anything else. A few human voices could be heard distinctly in the garden's dense silence. The birds sang film songs. Life was imitating art. Along with the very first human voices, dogs also barked. They weren't interested in listening to the tunes of the birds. But humans yearned to hear it. However, art should be for birds' sake. The voice that rose the loudest warned the fired-up children that they shouldn't be settling for positions and honours they had previously refused to accept. However, even that voice began to falter. The freedom fighter, who had chained himself to a pillar on a veranda, didn't talk much after that. The children were not trapped in the Saint Neot Margins built for the spokespersons.

Let's now spread into the trees and bushes we planted and tended. Let's now spread into the tender stems of those plants, into the fresh buds put forth by the young shoots. Like the Calcutta that expands in the poems of Mythili, let us spread on these stems...the ringed parakeets continued their song, and the dogs, their barks.

An excited someone sang the story of Sandiakov in a blazing voice. Sandiakov, the one who built a bridge from the Olympus to the Himalayas and remained perpetually hidden for fear of women. The god of love for the Hindu–Muslim–Nepali prostitutes. The breeze that was Sandiakov blew lazily on the banks of the backwaters in Ernakulam. It passed through the low-lying cucumber fields of Vadakkaamcherry. Finally, Sandiakov turned into a sore. A sore that was fifty years old.

Sandiakov and all others within this garden are sores of this garden. All those who lie in hospital beds and shiver in fear, cling to the casuarinas outside the mental asylums, and breathe in numbers in commercial establishments, are the sores of this garden.

'*These are all the sores of this garden,*' sang the old military generals to the new emperor, flattering him and supporting his actions. The emperor and the generals who had collapsed in the snow thrice and lain frozen! First Kyiv. Then Stalingrad. Finally, Moscow. One hundred and forty years before this, Josephine's lover also fell into this false step. A wrong step after the age of forty? Even after forty, when one can see the past and the present to the fullest with clarity! He lost it there. Even Aurelius lost it there! They were sores first and later became the flowers of history. And vice versa. A terrible sight.

The miserable lamentations of those who had chained themselves to the tripod in the corner of the garden could be heard above the ringed parakeets and the court's cacophony. At the tripod's base flashed the cat's eyes of (Herbert) Marcuse, past the age of seventy. Jagadguru, following Herbert, theorized the universe would change only through a change in one's consciousness. Poor Herbert! Poor Ginsberg! By then, the children had fallen into Sandiakov's second slumber. McLuhan's song, 'The medium is the message' had lulled them to sleep.

As piped water supply commenced, public wells disappeared. Public wells were places where people could come together. The bridges collapsed. The state of communications was pitiful. Sandiakov, who had built this bridge, should have heard this song. If Sandiakov, who had made a bridge from Mount Olympus to the Himalayas, had learned about this, what would have become of Marshall? Sandiakov could turn the garden into a fire pit. But Marshall? One hundred houses in Canada. A television company in New York.... Two years have passed since Sandiakov left the garden court. On a night like this one, he left this place. Standing behind the poisonous koda plants in the inner garden, Sandiakov sang the Songs of Solomon at the hour when the moon rose. Then he walked away and disappeared. Sandiakov should have been here today!

Sandiakov asked only one thing before leaving the garden: don't we have a king? Do we have a king? Is it that we do and/or we don't? Sandiakov's question flew like a thousand arrows. The evening echoed the songs of intoxication heard from the hutments of the contractors and the fortresses of the artists. In those places and at commercial establishments and hospitals, the arrows of Sandeepan's (yes, Sandeepan is Sandiakov, according to the etymology of eelmosodorm*) question struck home and were embedded.

Before he parted last night, Devadattan asked the same questions. Every night, some people leave the court; those who part, sing this very same question. Sandeepan, Devadattan, and each one who departed from here sang the same song.

The courtiers shed tears. Devadattan repeated his question and climbed onto the shoulder of the Vetas, onto the ornate bed, in the palanquin, and the coffin. Only a dog followed Devadattan, and he insisted he wouldn't move ahead unless the animal was taken along with them. Devadattan gave the mirror Sandeepan had given him, to Angadharman. Angadharman introduced to the court the mirror and Aabhaasavaad, the theory involving the properties of the mirror. 'The mirror was for me; the Aabhaasavaad was for the court,' said Angadharman. From then on, it was Aabhaasavaad throughout—in battle, art, theory, and lust. In the beginning, Angadharman said he could not do this. Finally, the one driving the chariot made Angadharman fight. The nature of the chariot, racing ahead. The character of the one who drives the chariot. Finally, who lost? War. It's the war that lost. The one who was driving the chariot defeated war.

On whose path was the chariot driven? On that of Red Daniel Bendit, Tariq Ali, or Ivan? Whichever is fine, but none belonging to old men. It's not yet time to forget the fall of Devadattan.

At the entrance to the garden, his feverishness left him. Did Devadattan, who had mounted the shoulders of the Vetas recollect something else? Angadharman didn't understand a thing. Nothing was

---

*A seemingly nonsensical coinage used probably to bring out the absurdity of it all.

reflected in the mirror. Some arguments based on Aabhaasavaad came to be proved. When the Anands of the garden centre argued, some more things became clear. What is the ontological basis of your arguments? The swami who saw Devadattan setting his foot out of the garden and past the gate, was ridiculed by other swamis, who characterized him as 'empirical'. Despite talking for so long and so much, they never reached anywhere. Not even started!

The court was convinced of that secret truth concerning Devadattan only when Angadharman revealed it. Seeing Devadattan pass through the garden's gate and step out of the borders of Time, the dogs had barked and bayed. But why did we bark?

MUSHROOM FOR BREAKFAST
MAYTHIL RADHAKRISHNAN

UNNIMARY

It is at nine in the morning that you leave the house and go out for the hunt among papers. By eight you would have come out of the fragrant womb of the new day after a hot water bath and shave. By that time, Savitha (your wife) would have reached the door, impatient to get into the steam, porous like a sponge, that fills the bathroom. Around eight-thirty, you climb down the stairs and reach the dining hall. By that time Unnimary (the girl who assists your wife in the kitchen) would have set cups, plates, knives, spoons, and forks, and the breakfast items on the dining table. As you take tea in the cup and sip it slowly, Savitha also would have come down bathed and dressed. Then, to the accompanying chant of breakfast, steel and porcelain clanging, the day begins to crawl on its knees upon the shining four tines of the fork. A routine that has the cosy comfort of the myth of childbirth....

But today when you came down at eight-thirty, there is no movement or noise anywhere. Breakfast is not ready on the table. Only a blue and white Chinese soup bowl is there. There is a mushroom in it. An uncooked mushroom. It hasn't opened its parachute yet. How would you react to this sight? How would you interpret it?

I stood for a while, looking at it. That soup bowl, a little bigger than an average saucer, is not an item to find its place on our dining table. Still, certain bowls of this kind were set on the on our table, adding dazzle to our breakfasts and dinners. They are not used to eat from. They are Christmas/New Year gifts received by people who have deposits in a particular bank in Copenhagen. Specially handcrafted for the bank by certain families traditionally engaged in porcelain work. Pictures are embossed on it, like welts, in deep blue. On the brim, the respective years are engraved. Turn it upside down, and you will see the legend, 'Royal Copenhagen' at the bottom, around the figure of a crown. Also, the name of the pictures on the reverse. The bowl lying all alone on the table is from 1982. What is the caption below? In the picture, a little girl looks out a window, standing on a stool. In the snow outside, a rabbit. Inside, a Christmas tree and a teddy bear. And the mushroom is on top of it all! What trick has this Unnimary played?

THE STENOGRAPHER

Sitting in a cabin with glass for walls on three sides, you start telling Aswin Menon, the systems analyst, about that mushroom. At that moment, the stenographer, a young woman, enters the room pushing open the door that closes automatically. Neeraja has come prepared with a yellow pencil, a pad, and some papers. You have forgotten that you had summoned Neeraja. Seeing her through the glass, sitting next to you, the MD remembers something suddenly and rings you up. There is a Chaplinesque effect to it. Two people are talking through a machine, seeing each other and exchanging smiles all the time! As if trying to prove that light passes through the glass, but no sound! There is even some sort of horror in it. Sometimes, it reminds one of the meetings between convicts and their visitors in American prisons. Here are two people talking to each other over telephone, when the actual distance between their lips is the thickness of a glass wall! All the breakdowns that have beset human exchanges are reflected in these glass walls.... The MD is saying: 'Vikram. Excuse me! Can you send that steno girl over here? Right now?'

Before sending Neeraja over, you inform her: 'Neeraja, it is not for giving you dictation that I called you. It's that organization chart. Can't you do it on the computer?'

'Ayyo, sir!'

As Neeraja goes out, Aswin says, picking up the pencil she left behind, 'This is what I call the HB Mentality of pencil pushers.'

∽

As you wonder how you are going to broach the subject of the mushroom if Aswin is going to continue in this vein and enter his pet subject (a discourse on the strategies employed by governments to keep the common man away from computers, fearing the rebellion that is sure to erupt in the spheres of thought and communication if computer is popularized!) a young woman from the computer section comes in and takes Aswin Menon out of the room. As you sit alone, Neeraja re-enters the room.

'My pencil....'

'Sit down.'

'Dictation?'

'No. Not now, either.'

You say that with great satisfaction. The sight of your words (with sound and meaning) turning into some crooked scrawls under her pencil always disturbs you. Is it possible that even the most emotion-charged words you use are imprinted, not only on paper but also in another's heart, in this damned Pitman style? Again, you think about the problems in human communication.

'Sir?'

'Neeraja. I want to talk to you. I would like to know something. Something only a girl knows about. Although I respect the high IQ of people like Aswin Menon, I believe in certain intuitions only girls have access to. So I am telling you this. It is personal. Do you have any objection?' And without even waiting to listen to Neeraja's reply, you start telling her about the mushroom....

Neeraja's explanation is really very simple. 'That mushroom reached your dining table the same way my pencil reached this table. Someone or something intervenes, even as someone is doing something. Excitement. Confusion. Forgetfulness, loss of balance.... There is no magic or witchcraft involved....'

As Neeraja went out, the MD called again, sitting in the glass cubicle. 'Vikram. The trip in the afternoon to Kasturba Distilleries is cancelled. Someone has informed that their MD will reach only tomorrow.' Then, with a laugh, 'You don't have even a single paper to sign, do you? Up to the second! That too, even before the fatigue of that trip to Bulgaria wears off! Do one thing. Go home at one o'clock. After lunch, take a nap. Do you hear? It's an order.' I remembered the dining table when I heard 'lunch' mentioned. Also, Savitha saying she would go to the club at ten o'clock. Her lunch is at the club today. The dining hall would be empty now. I saw in my mind's eye its beauty and loneliness, as in the pictures in a journal on interior decoration. The more attractive the indoors, the deeper it afflicts me in loneliness. Is the mushroom still there on our dining table?

UNNIMARY

There is a reason for you to look for the bowl on the walls when you find out that it is missing from where you saw it in the morning. There is a hole, like on a pearl, on the edge of such gifts from Copenhagen.

Passing a thread through it, you can hang it on the wall. It is to hang them thus, that your old bank sent you those bowls. But, will the bowls climb the walls, breaking the convention of lying on their backs on the table for over a year! Sitting at the table, you gingerly lift the lid of one of the dishes. It is the pungent aroma of a curry prepared in a masala mixed in a typically Christian style, that emanates from the dish. You suppress laughter, thinking to yourself that each step of the printed recipe can be read in it. Unnimary must have hazarded an experiment in cuisine, not expecting you or Savitha for lunch. You feel tempted to call Unnimary and crack a few jokes on this. But the morning's incident will remain between you and her like a leftover. Even Unnimary will feel that an explanation is necessary. It will not be that easy. The interval that stretched and tautened between the incident and its explanation will cause a crack somewhere. It is not for nothing that people compare the smoke billowing after a bomb explosion to a mushroom!

Carefully selecting two pieces of bread, I ladled out a little of curry on to it. When the gravy drained away, the piece that was caught on the bread, like on a strainer, was a whole mushroom. Perhaps, it was the same mushroom which was served for breakfast, complete with its odour of soil and microbes! I sprang up, pushing the chair backwards. The sound of the chair leg grating against the mosaic floor was like a rat's whimper. Although it had not touched the fingers, I washed my hands thoroughly.

At that time something fell on the kitchen floor and broke.

THE WAITRESS

It is four or five days since you reached Bulgaria. You have set up camp in a so-so hotel in Sofia, the capital city. Except for the band led by the clarinettist who plays in the evening the old Spanish song 'Kiss Me a Lot' only for your ears, every moment you spend in the restaurant spins a loom in your abdomen. For you, who is a reactionary vegetarian in food habits, it is impossible to advance adventurously through a Bulgarian menu. Once you are through the American breakfast, you have inevitably chosen the only two items to ward off hunger during the long hours till bedtime. Now, you give your order to the waitress who has come near you in a white shirt, tennis balls bouncing inside: 'Fried mushrooms and beer.' She obliges enticingly, 'Do brey.'

During the past few days, you have seen her near the other tables.

You have also seen her observing you from afar. But it is only today that you select a table assigned to her. Moving away after taking your order, that young woman stops on her tracks abruptly, returns to you and says: 'Even the cooks complain that the Indian guest is eating only mushrooms. Perhaps you like mushrooms so much.' You deny it. 'Then I shall tell the chef to prepare some other....' You stop her, thanking. 'Nema, Nema...merci.'

I know that mushroom is meat in disguise. Vegetarians should never touch it. Mushrooms have the odour and taste of an illicit liaison which draws adrenaline. I blame the non-vegetarians as I can't blame myself. 'I sell you cigars, cigarettes, wine, beer, and champagne. Because all these items are one hundred per cent vegetarian products. Don't put your feet in two different boats, you shameless ones....'

The Bulgarian girl came back with a beer and the mushroom dish. The whole band knows that this is the time when 'Kiss Me a Lot' will be struck up. The clarinettist lifted his instrument, shifting glances from me to the waitress and back, winking. At the strategic moment before the clarinettist started playing, the Bulgarian girl asked: 'Can you give me some US dollars?' Here comes Bulgaria's national question! The question foreigners hear at the rate of once every kilometre, at Warna and Sofia. I said, 'Yes.' Her eyes opened like two champagne bottles. She returned, treading on the champagne's foam. I drank, lifting the glass occasionally to the clarinettist. When I finished eating and drinking, the Bulgarian girl came back running, 'The US dollars you promised...I will come to your room when I finish my shift.' So, that's the foreign exchange rate! I said, 'Not necessary. I will bring it down.' As she cleared the table, a knife or fork escaped her clasp and fell down. If fell into a dish full of tomato juice. The sound of steel and porcelain clashing. A minor explosion. The front of her shirt was dirtied. What a Holi! I turned my head and looked to the side of the band. It seemed the trembling excitement of saving a moment that could easily have slipped into a false note, still lingered on the clarinettist's fingers. At that moment, the Bulgarian girl, leaning against me as if going to pick up something, whispered, 'In any case, I will have to undress.'

UNNIMARY

I slipped into an afternoon nap, hearing that Bulgarian girl burst out laughing, making fun of an Indiski who ate only mushrooms and freely distributed US dollars. Really, an afternoon nap is not meant for me. Its action on my body is ridiculous. When I get up, I will look like a feverish scarecrow. It is to get out of that condition, that I entered the vast compound behind the house. The whole area is left entirely at nature's disposal. Like a dream during sleep, this area is effortlessly filled with foliage, shadows, and hideouts. In the dream I had during my nap, I had wandered among them. Therefore, this walk now is a continuation. A trailing. I used to trail anything that I set eyes on, mechanically as in sleep. I trailed garden lizards, greenhouse lizards, the black cobra—whatever that moved. That is how I began to trail the yellow butterfly I saw now and then. In one sense, I was chasing it. Frequently, it would hang from some twig and turn into a flower. As my footsteps drew near, it would rise and fly again. It is flying low, as it is terribly windy at a higher altitude. Even if it rises up momentarily when meeting with obstacles, it would again fly low the next moment. Sometimes it would make as if to touch the ground. And fly up again, just before touching the ground. Following these repetitions, I practically reached the other side of the compound. I stood stock still when the butterfly suddenly dipped and alighted on the ground, shaking the leaves of a chilli plant touched with a reddish tint. And remembered pointer dogs who act as if to point out something. The soil is upturned at the spot where it is perched. So it is this place where Unnimary plucked the mushroom from! I advanced two steps to see better. Then, the butterfly flew up in a flash, as if its mission was accomplished and disappeared among the foliage. When I stood where it had perched, my feet sank. The soil seems to have been hoed up there. The tool is lying nearby. A stick, its one end cut into a slanted point. Mud is caked on one end. Picking up the stick, I dug some furrows in the mud. Deeper and deeper. The end of the stick struck somewhere, and a noise like at breakfast time was heard. As the next furrow is dug, the blue of the bowl comes into view. Then the different parts of the picture emerge clearly: the girl, rabbit, the teddy bear, the Christmas tree....

You try to recollect. This Copenhagen bowl was not there on the dining table at lunchtime. When you washed your hands, foregoing lunch, something had fallen to the kitchen floor and broken. But that was not this bowl. The broken pieces had not obviously been picked up from elsewhere and buried here. On the other hand, the soil had been dug out, the unbroken bowl was carefully placed in the pit, and hit in the centre with a stone. As everything had been carried out precisely and perfectly like in a ritual, the bowl does not even appear to be broken, at first glance. The stone used to break the bowl is left in the pit itself.

As you cover the pit after throwing the stone away, let me remind you: this is the mystery of the cats. This is how cats bury their faeces and mark their territory with their stench. This is animal language. Even nowadays, animal communications carry on perfectly as before. A special mention is made about this, only because you had occasion to think about the problems in human communication more than once this morning.

THE GARDEN OF THE ANTLIONS
PAUL ZACHARIA

In a piece of land overrun by wild growth, by the shore of a stream, I lived like a chameleon in a bower of leaves, hiding and prowling, camouflaged and contented. My house was like a mound of dead leaves heaped among the vines and green foliage. Along the edge of the courtyard, crowded with weeds and grass, flourished my medicinal plants, as if some unseen power had rescued them from the jungle outside. Only I knew the dividing line between them and the jungle—and once, a little girl thief too!

The old wood of my walls had turned black, white, and green, overgrown with moss and lichen. In a corner of the kitchen were two hearths, a few earthen pots and pans and two plates. On one hearth, I prepared medicated oils and liniments, and on the other my meals. The veranda had not been surfaced and polished with cow dung for years and was filled with dusty holes in which antlions had made their little pit-like wells, at the bottom of which they lay in wait for their lunch and dinner. When a good many wandering insects had vanished without a trace into the fine dust of these traps as if into a bottomless abyss, an occasional antlion would climb out and saunter around. Watching them promenade in their garden—my veranda—I would try to imagine the solitude at the bottom of their dusty wells.

My favourite seat was at the base of a pillar that stood on a length of wood-plank running along the edge of the veranda. The wood had become very smooth at the place where I usually sat, and so had the pillar I leaned against, which gleamed invitingly with oil and sweat. Lounging against the pillar with my legs stretched along the wood, stroking my long beard which hid a stray silver hair or two, exuding a fine aroma of liniments, oils, and salves, I would await my patients. I loved patients.

I could hear each patient and the people who came along from a distance as they made their way through my jungle, whispering, parting the leaves and shaking the branches. I would then get up from the veranda, vanish inside, and watch them through the slit of the closed window as they entered my courtyard.

'O, Vaidyare,' they would call in a low, hesitant voice. I would not answer. They would stand there, looking anxiously at the shut doors. They would call again, but all is silence. They would speak amongst themselves in disappointment and continue to stare at the shut house. I whisper to no one in particular: 'The broken limb is patient; it is the mind that is impatient. Calm your minds, my dear fellow human beings!' I would resume my vigil. They would squat for a while in the courtyard, stand up again, clear their throats and call out, 'O, Vaidyare!' There would be only silence. After a while, one of them would say, 'I don't think the Vaidyar is coming out today. We'd better go!'

Some patients go away with their companions. But a few refuse to leave. 'No, I am going to wait. You can go.'

On one occasion, leaving behind in the courtyard a young man with a sprained arm, the companions of the patient had thus gone away. He stood there, listening miserably to their voices moving further and further away. He waited, lost and fearful, gazing expectantly at the silent house. Then I opened the door and came out.

'Quickly, clap your hands!' I said. 'Clap so that your companions can hear you! Clap and call them back! Tell them that Vaidyar is here!'

For a moment he stood gaping at me. Then, his face registering agony, he tried to raise his sprained right arm to clap, but it fell back limply.

'They have to come back!'

Once again, he raised his sprained arm a little, but lowered it, unable to bear the pain. I clapped my own hands and said, 'Like this! Louder and louder!' He tried painfully to mimic the motions of my hands. Looking at his face and roaring with laughter, I clapped again. My clapping hands lent sound to his agonized mime. I clapped, looking at the rising moon. I clapped so that the yakshis atop the palmyra could hear me. I clapped towards the other-worldly visitors who prowled behind the clouds. 'Come down to these green leaves, to this soil, to this dusk. This is our earth! Come! Here is pain, and here is relief!'

Walking up to the young man, and standing behind him, I held his arms in my hands and made him clap, lifting, dropping and pushing his arms around. Flocks of homing birds glided above. Winds bent towards the sunset, swirled around us. The face of the early moon floated through the clouds like a ritual mask. And I heard, like the grand percussion of many drums, the footfalls of the antlions strolling along the garden of my veranda. I felt the young man's pain-raked body regaining strength in my arms. Crushing him in a bear hug, I led him to the veranda and sat him down. I kissed him on the crown of his head with my beard spreading all over his face. I said, 'You are healed. You can go now.'

Under the moonlight, his body slipped away like a shadow through my herbs. Then I heard a sound from the path beyond the honeysuckle thickets, a message that came darting through the green leaves—a handclap. Jumping down into the courtyard, I, too clapped loudly. His hands replied from beyond the stream. Then, through the distant coconut groves, the farewell claps faded. And I had even forgotten to pose him a riddle! In wonderment, I squatted on the moonlit lawn and burst out laughing.

Except for patients, the only people who crossed the wilderness that was my piece of land were the village schoolchildren taking a short cut. The hushed whispers that rose from the foliage, the soft footfalls over the carpet of moist leaves and the hurriedly suppressed jingling of their tiffin carriers were the only hints of their passage through my dark empire. Sometimes they would suddenly forge a bond of fear amongst themselves, imagining that I was charging behind them with bloodshot eyes and flowing beard, and they would flee in unison, raising a commotion, crashing through the thickets.

One day, while grinding herbs for a liniment behind the shut doors of my house, I heard footsteps in the courtyard. I peeped through the slit of the window. In the dusk outside, among my medicinal plants, stood a little girl. Unaware, she was staring right into my hidden eyes. From my hiding place, I looked at her and smiled. She slowly took a step into the courtyard and looked around her, not for a moment withdrawing her attention from the shut house. I joyfully nodded my head at her from my hiding place. I beckoned to her. I made faces at her, baring my teeth. In a sudden burst of daring, she climbed onto the lower veranda and ran her fingers over the shining smoothness of the place where I usually sat, startling me. She also felt the gleaming pillar with her hands. As I watched breathlessly, she moved back to the courtyard and approached my well. Filled with a strange anxiety, I stood watching her. She picked up a pebble and dropped it into the well. The sharp, distant splash of the pebble hitting the water reached my ears. I was tempted to rush out, but I continued to stand in my hiding place, clasping the window bars, even while I yielded to the thrill of the invitation that the clear, tiny sound brought me.

'Hey, you,' I whispered, 'how dare you to disturb the peace of my home?'

Suddenly, swift as a heifer, she bolted down the courtyard and entered my patch of medicinal plants like a whirlwind. Scooping up the leaves of the kacholam plant with both hands and pulling it out of the soil, she went crashing through the thickets and was gone! I stood stupefied for a moment, unable to contain my amazement. Then I jumped into the courtyard, laughing and shouting.

'Come, one and all! A little girl thief! A little girl thief stealing kacholam! Catch her!' I heard her splash across the steam. I raised the tip of my beard towards the moon which was climbing the sky beyond the trees and danced, roaring, 'O little girl thief, why did you steal the kacholam? To heal whom? Be blessed with the greatest powers of healing, my little thief-doctor! May God protect you!'

Then, as I sat down in my usual spot, which her soft hands had touched, and leaned against the pillar which her tiny fingers had stroked, tenderness and peace floated down the waves of moonlight and embraced me.

The sky visited my dark house as raindrops and sunlight, filtering through the holes in the mouldering palm leaf thatch. The raindrops made craters on the floor, and the antlions dug still more wells in them, spouting fountains of dust. The sun dived into the inner rooms of my home through the holes of the thatch, beamed down from the rafters and danced on the floor in darting circles. My liniment bottles, the bundles of herbs and roots, the torn mat, the blanket and pillow, all would momentarily bear the stamp of the sunlight's swift feet. For the rest, the interior of my house was filled with delicious darkness and my land with the lovely peach of branches and leaves. Seated on the veranda, leaning against the old pillar, I would watch the somnambulist moon in its candlelight procession, the twinkling stars, and the waves of light amongst the clouds that reared their heads in the sky. Like a spider, the life of this solitary Vaidyar wove long webs, stretching from the base of the old pillar to the heights of the bunched-up stars.

I loved patients. I loved them through the melting tenderness of my liniments and the infinite patience of my fingers, understanding the screams of pain of the broken bone and the bruised nerve. Who is a masseur-physician? Even as he inflicts pain on the medicine-anointed body, he fondles it. In the consolation of his hands, as the patient embraces his own body, forgiving it and bearing with its bruises and pain, the crushed bone and fatigued muscles rejoice and grow whole again. The human being hides behind the skeleton and the skeleton behind the human being. Through the bone, vein, and sinew, I seek the human being. Through the nerve, I listen. To the laughter and lamentation of the soul.

How beautiful my solitude was! How wonderful were my disguises! What fine games of hide-and-seek I played with people until they surrendered to themselves!

My crumbling house and cratered floors, my wifeless and childless home and weed-covered land, and the sudden riddles I threw at people, terrified them. The riddle was my last resort. The jungles on my pathless land filtered people like a sieve. The silence of my home bent them like a liniment to my purpose. My riddles demolished their changeless minds. How many trips they had to make through my forest until they accepted against their will—that the broken arm and crushed leg were themselves.

As my thumb probed deep into the bruised nerve, I shouted at the patient, 'The one who makes it does not use it, the one who uses it does not know it, what is it? Answer quickly!'

The patient's face, ready to register pain, stiffens as if it has been slapped. I ask again, 'Do you know what it is?

He answers, 'No, Vaidyare.'

'Think hard, think hard!' I say. By this time, my fingers would have released the tangled nerve. And he gropes in vain in the cellars of his childhood for the answer, alarmed, unmindful of the pain. I shout, 'The answer is: a coffin. You owe me ten points.'

Everyone is afraid of the moment when the fractured bone is set. Every day, before the massage began, the patient would ask, 'Vaidyare, are you going to set the bone today?'

'No,' I answer. Even on the day when I am going to set the bone, I would say, 'No.' When I feel in my fingers the broken parts preparing to unite again, I bellow at the patient, 'Does the pot know the taste of the curry?'

The patient starts and stares at me in helplessness.

'Do you know the answer?' I roar again.

'No,' whispers the patient.

I shout, 'You owe me ten points!'

I ask again, 'Can you sit on the mortar and cry, oh, the pestle is descending?'

In my hands, the broken bone comes together.

'You lose twenty points,' I roar.

The patient, unable to answer, sits gaping at me, thinking of the inexplicable thirty points he owes me.

They feared me as they would a lone tusker. I was invincible. Ha! Ha! Ha! But no one knew that I was a lone tusker only in those gardens of the poor antlions.

So there I was, standing one day in the dazzling sunlight of the courtyard, combing my beard. A passing summer shower suddenly tattooed the dusty lawn. The air was filled with the fragrance of the heady mixture of earth, rain, and sunlight. I stood happily in the courtyard, breathing in the smells, waiting, like my herbs and jungles, for the grand arrival of the rains, thinking of nothing, my mind flying free like a floating leaf. There was a sudden gust of wind. Behind it came a luminous drizzle from the rainclouds that rushed across the sunny sky. I wanted to leap into the joyous wind, the rain and the fleeing clouds.

'Here I come!' I jumped, my arms lifted, to touch the clouds. 'Aha! Aha!' I screamed, 'take me too!'

Suddenly, through the corner of my eye, I saw someone at the far end of the courtyard. In great surprise, I stopped. Without turning around, making up for my embarrassment with gravity of tone, I asked, 'Who is there?'

No answer. I turned slowly. A young woman stood regarding me with one hand on the circular parapet of the well. And the other pressed to a spot on her right thigh. The pain that she had perhaps forgotten as she watched my sky-leaps, now returned to her face. She said, 'I fell down, and something happened to my leg. I can't bear the pain. Could you take a look at it, Vaidyare?'

'Has anyone come with you?' I asked.

'No one,' she said.

'Go and bring someone. I don't usually treat women.'

'I can't walk, Vaidyare,' she said, 'and I don't have anyone to bring along. There's only my mother, she is old and can't walk.'

Hesitantly, I asked her, 'How did you fall?'

'When I climbed the stone wall to pluck musanda, the black mother shrub, for my goat, a stone broke loose.'

I like that. I whispered, 'Black mother, fair daughter. Daughter's daughter, fairest of the fair.' I muttered under my breath, 'You're a smart woman; you've answered a riddle I did not pose to you.'

(The riddle is based on the three-coloured appearance of the wild musanda shrub: the branches and leaves are green (black mother), two-three leaves just below the flower are white (fair daughter) and the flower itself is red (daughter's daughter). The answer to the riddle is: the black mother—which actually makes both the riddle and the answer redundant!)

'Come here,' I said, 'let me see.'

She came limping across the rain-splattered courtyard, through the fresh scent of the rain and sat down at my usual spot. She leaned back on my glistening pillar. Lifting her right leg with both hands, she placed it along the wood plank of the veranda, as I would have done. I wanted to shout, *that's my place, it's I who sit there!* Instead, I continued to stand in the courtyard and watch her anxiously. She began to sob. She sat there and wept in many soft notes which I had never heard before. Her hair, which had come undone, enveloped my shining pillar like a dark cascade. Her tears fell on the edge of my veranda, shattered, and flowed down into the wells of the hungry antlions, carrying the flavour of salt and sorrow. I stood silent in the courtyard, watching her forge a friendship with pain. At the same time, an intense desire possessed me to rush to my place and sit there. I controlled myself and whispered to the antlions, 'My friends, do not swoon in the salt of her tears. Escape to the waters of the springs beneath. Swim away like tortoises.'

After a while, she stopped weeping and wiped away her tears. She gathered up her hair which had fallen loose on her face. Then she rolled her mundu up her thigh and showed me where it hurt.

The tumult of a world crashing filled my ears as I approached her and examined her thigh. There was a black and blue mark.

'Isn't your pain gone?'

'I don't know,' she said, 'I was crying for all of myself, not only for my pain.'

I said nothing. I took the softness of her thigh in both hands and pressed my fingers to it. The sunshine, the wind, the moving shadows, the dancing branches of my medicinal plants, all accompanied my fingers in their journey in quest of the pain. I did not look at her. I turned my face to the clouds in the sky, to the jungle, and the holes of the antlions. Her thigh, which was washed in pain and tears, lay pliant in my hands. O my antlions, I whispered, look at my condition! I saw they were out walking; they sauntered slowly through their gardens of dust like ancient creatures. Suddenly, I came back to myself; I knew I must act. I rolled my eyes. My beard flew up lethally. I stared at her with a hard and cruel look. The nerve that had gone astray beneath that black and blue mark trembled under my fingers.

Keeping a tight hold, I roared, 'Would you like to die, woman?' The words, you lose a hundred points, waited on the tip of my tongue. My eyes awaited the bewilderment, dejection, and defeat that would fill her face. At that moment, wiping the tear stains from her face with one hand, she asked me, 'Did you like to be born?'

I felt suffocated. It seemed to me that her errant vein was squirming out of my grasp. I held on to her thigh as if for support. Someone is answering my riddles! My next roar faltered, 'Are you afraid to die?' And the words, you lose a thousand points, waited on the tip of my tongue.

She asked me calmly, 'Were you afraid to be born, Vaidyare?' Her thigh, with its fine dark hairs, lay in my hands like a sleeping child.

'You owe me a hundred points,' she said. Then, covering my hands with her two palms and pressing them to the quietude of her thigh, she said, 'Heal me, Vaidyare, or else you lose a thousand points.'

∫

Today, in my plot of land where jungles had been, the plants in a vegetable garden toss their heads in the wind and sunlight. My herbs flourish safely behind a bamboo fence. Those who come to consult me sit on benches on the veranda which was once the garden of my antlions. It is long since they have fled from those dusty floors, now polished with the cow-dung mixture. They live on, under the awnings in my backyard. On the rolled-up end of a tiny thread dangled into the pit, I caught one of them and showed it to my one-year-old son. Then I returned it to the solitude of the dust and whispered to my child, 'My son; you'll never know their companionship. Nor will you know how the jungle can enfold and protect you. No girl thief will ever come prowling to steal your kacholam. My son, may God bless you and help you to invent riddles more difficult than those I invented.'

THE HOOK
P. PADMARAJAN

Just below the surface of the stream, a green frog, raising its eyes and hind legs, floated heaving its forelegs on the old man's float. Now and then it paddled its hind legs and played about, clinging to the float.

The line wound around the float went down deep into the water. On the water's surface, in the shade created by the shadows of the tree foliage, the leaves of the uprooted moringa tree that flowed in from the east and the stems of the pathappan bush were lying blocked. In the cold depths below the shade-fallen surface, murrels, pearl spots, and other small varieties of fish lurked around. Most of the time the old man's old hook hung low, lifeless, grazing them.

When the sun rays struck his eyes, the old man spread his left palm, shading his eyes, and gazed intently at the float.

The old man's face was completely disfigured. His lips had caved in. A grey, curly strand of hair grew from his nostrils. His jawbone looked like a mango seed, the flesh on it sucked at and thrown out long ago and lying embedded in the mud.

Thickets of screw pine and honeysuckle growing on either side of the stream extended their heads over the water and spread darkness. The stream that flowed from the east turned abruptly to the north midway and then meandered towards the west. In that bend, in the portion where the current was weak, and the water was deep, a whirlpool formed often. In the whirlpool, the pollen from the screw pine flowers whirled round and round.

The old man was not looking at any of those things. The angling stick shuddered feebly now and then in his right hand. When he dozed off unwittingly, the stick slipped from his grasp, and fell on the water's surface and made a splashing noise.

For the past five days, not even a fingerling had taken his bait. Every day before he set out with his angling stick, his daughter would call out: 'Nothing will come of it. See him going with the expression on his face that says he won't catch anything!'

Even though he failed to catch even a fingerling, he did not possess such an attitude as his daughter had described.

That day there were no children around. Sometimes they would come. If they came, they would cause a lot of nuisance. Before the hook was lowered into the water, they would push the bait further up the hook, exposing its point. If the point of the hook were revealed, not even a fingerling would take the bait.

When the soft breeze from the east blew on him, his tired eyes that escaped the intensity of the sunrays in the shade had closed in a pleasurable lassitude. Flashes of the memories of his childhood sixty years ago, and also the face of his wife who had tended to him till the day she died shone clearly before him. When he felt a slight tug at the end of the line, he started awake and seeing the still float, returned to his earlier expression.

When he set out that morning, his daughter had cursed: 'This is your damned last trip!'

His final journey!

Though he heard those words often, he could discern a particular implication in her words today. A trip from which he would never return! Today what she said would come true.

It was not unlikely that while one was angling sitting on the banks of the stream, one might die. The dead body would lie there. If he died that evening, his corpse with rot setting in, would be found only the next day.

The sun was setting. Waterhens cackled from the high-growing wild grass, and madanta bushes growing like colocasia stems. A long murrel that drifted downstream wriggled into a hole beneath the thickly growing tangle of screw pine roots. It was the hole of the frog. The end of the green frog that was floating on the water was drawing near.

A red water lily came floating down and got tangled on the line. The old man pulled up the line and the hook, and extricated the flower and threw it away. He impaled a fresh piece of meat on the hook as bait.

On the surface, faint ripples formed and disappeared. The frog that was floating on the surface plunged its forelegs into the water and dived deep. It may be speeding towards its hole. Go quickly, the old man said to himself. Death awaits you.

As time passed and the afternoon grew into evening, the old man's anxiety increased. He reminded himself that the curse his daughter uttered that morning could turn futile. He would not die. If he died, who else was there for her? When he thought about his thirty-eight-year-old unmarried daughter, he was adamant that he should not die.

There was a slight movement on the float. It dipped slightly and then came up again. He looked at it attentively. No. Moments of no movement for the float.

The waterhens cackled. A black tortoise rose from the water, caught on to the roots of the screw pines, hauled itself up and moved along the mud.

Scared, the old man looked all around. Darkness was beginning to creep in. Today too he didn't make any catch. He was going to return empty-handed....

The croaking of frogs rose from the hole as if it had descended from the sky. A frog was in the jaws of the water snake. It screamed when it unexpectedly encountered death. With that, the old man's hands turned immobile. The terrible truth of death was lying dormant all around him the whole time. The hook and line in his hand; at its end, the murrels that await death all the time.

The tortoise stuck its head out of its shell, spread its dirty legs and crawled towards him. When he felt fear welling up in him, he picked up a stone and threw it at the tortoise. The stone fell a little ahead of it in the slush, and it sank.

The frog's croak rose louder and intermittently. One or two waterhens came out of their holes, surveyed the surroundings, and returned.

There was another tug at the float. The next death is for the fish. This time, the old man didn't feel like hauling the fish up. He felt as if all movements were depending on that single event.

The moment he pulled on the float with an inward twist, the fish would squirm to death. That same moment, a frog would also die. The only one then left to die would be him. Suppose the three deaths were to happen in a single moment—he imagined the scene in his mind.

A big murrel landed on the mud, describing a wide arc in the sky, he hallucinated. When he felt a faint pain in his chest, the hook and stick fell away from his hand. He felt as if an unknown power was hurling a bigger, sharper hook towards his throat. He shivered and picked up the stick again.

More pulling movements on the float in his hand. The pitiable croak of the frog that was about to die. The tortoise raised its horrific eyes and regarded all around as it crawled into the clump of grass. The waterhens cackled in disquiet and flew away.

His eyes closed by themselves. Was he going to die?

Death was waiting for the murrel just when the hook was pulled. When he realized that he had formed a foolish ruse in his head—what if he could fool death for this once? So, he stood without doing anything.

The darkness thickened. The red-mud farmland beyond the stream and the paddy fields and the white blotches on the boles of the ground-hugging mango trees there became clear before his eyes. His daughter's disgruntled voice and eyes filled with hunger seared through his mind like a lightning bolt.

With that, his awareness of the surroundings returned. Even before a fraction of a second had passed, he twisted the stick in his hand and pulled.

The water was in turmoil. The fingerlings dozing still just below the water's surface, scattered and flashed away scared. The tortoise which had been half-hidden in the grassy clump withdrew its head and legs inside the shell and began its long penance. The waterhens fell silent. The water snake zigzagging away on the water's surface, looked like a long root. The frog which had escaped, though hurt, leapt out of its hole.

The old man gaped and looked around.

None had died. Him included. On the hook, a long fat murrel, its eyes shining. He didn't remember his own fears and the surroundings that had gone crazy along with him as he headed home crossing the paddy fields thick with darkness, carrying a live murrel in his right hand, and the hook and line in his left.

A thought gave him great relief. That day, for the first time in the last five days, he could sleep without listening to cursing.

A DAYTIME IN '53

VICTOR LEENUS

The railway station was a narrow, asbestos-roofed shed. The office was half covered using asbestos sheets. The rest of the open part was the waiting shed. A fence made with spiked iron rods extended north and south to the edge of the waiting room. There was no one sitting on the two concrete benches in the waiting shed.

I peeped in through the small window in the left side wall of the office meant for issuing tickets. The stationmaster was talking on the telephone. When he raised his face, he noticed me and laughed. Through the narrow door, I entered the platform along with Amma. The platform too was empty. Scorching sunlight dappled the gaps in the line of the old mango trees beyond the fence.

There was shade only on one of the concrete benches. Amma sat down there.

I looked all around, standing on the cement veranda on the edge of the platform. Four rails shimmered, snaked and disappeared.

I turned and looked at Amma. She was sitting with her chin in her palm, staring hard at the floor. For some reason, Amma talked very little today. She had been quiet from the moment she suddenly called me out of the class and brought me with her to the station.

It was just at the very moment the teacher had discovered Padmanabhan's baby squirrel that Amma had come to get me. I wonder whether Padmanabhan had taken the squirrel somewhere and dumped it. It was a very tame baby squirrel. It was because we insisted on seeing it that Padmanabhan had brought it to the class that day. It stayed quietly inside his vest. He would frequently take out a bit from a sweet and succulent paalayamkodan banana and feed it to the squirrel. He placed the squirrel in my hand briefly. But it didn't eat the bits of the banana while it sat in my hands.

Disaster struck during the class of Nalini teacher. The baby squirrel was sitting with its head out just below Padmanabhan's chin. Ittoop couldn't remove his gaze from it. Nalini teacher saw that. The teacher asked Padmanabhan to stand up.

'What thing is that?' the teacher asked.

Padmanabhan took it out with great fondness. Sitting in his palm quietly, the baby squirrel looked around.

The teacher shouted angrily: 'Take it out and throw it away.'

Padmanabhan looked at the teacher in great disbelief.

The teacher repeated: 'Why are you gaping at me? Go out and throw it away.'

Padmanabhan quietly put the baby squirrel away once again inside his vest. Then he glared at the teacher, with unmasked rebellion. He didn't move from where he stood.

That was when Amma came to the door of the classroom. Amma held out a chit. Behind her, the headmaster was standing. Nalini teacher came to the door. Amma told the teacher something. Suddenly, the teacher turned around and looked at me. Amma said something again.

Coming near me, Nalini teacher asked me to go along with Amma. The teacher helped me to arrange my books properly before I could pack them.

When I came out, the headmaster asked Amma: 'Isn't it better if I sent someone along with you, teacher?'

Amma said in a soft voice: 'Not necessary, mashe.'

I looked at Amma's face. Amma did not look at me. Her eyes were bloodshot.

The headmaster placed his hand on my shoulder, held me close, and stepped out into the courtyard. The whistling whirlwind came climbing up the hill slope, swirling up dry leaves, bits of paper and dust.

When I looked back, Nalini teacher was still standing at the door of the classroom. Padmanabhan, too, had not moved from where he stood.

Staring at the shining rails, I was wondering: would Padmanabhan have thrown the squirrel away?

I thought I would ask Amma. Then I decided against it. Amma hadn't shown much interest in talking today.

Beyond the rails, granite blocks and granite powder were heaped up. Beyond the heaps of granite were the paddy fields. In the water of the paddy fields, the light green, young tillers stood erect.

On the telephone lines, a flock of small birds alighted. They twittered in unison. Suddenly, they rose up together in the air and flew away southwards. Their wings flapped in unison like the sound of tiny firecrackers bursting.

The stationmaster came out of his office. He walked towards Amma. His white uniform had turned threadbare in places. Two of the buttons on his shirt were missing.

He asked Amma: 'Why are you here earlier than usual this week, teacher?'

We used to go home every week on Friday evening. Today was only Wednesday.

Amma did not say anything, took out a chit from the kerchief bundle, and showed it to him. Reading it, he glanced at me.

I walked away from them as if I was not aware of anything.

Amma's rule was that I should not be within earshot when grown-ups were talking.

I bent down and picked up a stem of lemongrass that was lying on the floor. Then, taking out my kerchief from my pocket, I wound one corner of it around the lemongrass stem. I waved it like the railway guard waved the green flag. Then I converted myself into a train and whistled.... And ran outside as if leaving the station making the sound chuk...chuk...chuk...chuk.... Reaching the next station, I slowed the train. Suddenly extending my left hand to the side, I received the cane loop that the porter would have hurled precisely around my arm.

I had decided that I will take the job of taking that cane loop from the engine when I grew up. But in between there was another job I was equally interested in. That of a lascar in a boat. The job of hurling a looped rope ashore as a boat came alongside the jetty and getting it caught precisely around a mooring stump at the fringe of the jetty. I had not yet been able to choose between the two. I had decided to consult Appachen about it. Appachen would certainly say which of the two was better. Perhaps, he would suggest some way for me to keep both the jobs. Appachen was the smartest person I had ever met. There was nothing he could not do.

I turned around hearing the stationmaster's voice. Standing by the iron fence, he was shouting to someone in the tea shop.

At the end of the path that led down from the station was the tea shop. It was just a shed with a thatched roof. It stood in the shade of a giant mango tree. The bus we had arrived in, which was parked near the tea shop, was about to depart. The bus, with its sides completely open, looked like the skeleton of a long-nosed giant beetle. There were only four or five people inside it now.

Climbing down the hill slope, the bus moved along the red-mud road that wriggled through the middle of the green paddy fields. It disappeared completely in the dust it had raised. I stood watching the cloud of red dust rise and rise, and disappear after climbing the hill. The stationmaster called me. The boy from the tea shop brought three glasses of tea. Till that day, I had not drunk tea, except when Amma had offered me a sip from her glass. Amma had decided that I should drink tea only after I grew up. Immediately after offering me the tea, the stationmaster hesitated. He said, 'O son, I forgot! I should have ordered a glass of diluted milk for you!'

Amma raised her face and said: 'Never mind. Let him start drinking tea. It's time for him to grow up.'

I took the glass from the stationmaster's hand.

After a sip, I lowered the glass. It was really hot. I felt proud when I tasted the slightly bitter taste of the tea. I had a lesson entitled 'Tea' prescribed in my textbook. I had decided to drink tea like the Chinese, without milk or sugar, from tiny egg-shaped cups. Let me just grow up.

When I finished drinking tea, I asked: 'When will the train come?'

'It will take an hour more. I will get your tickets in the meantime,' the stationmaster replied.

Amma untied her kerchief bundle and took out one rupee and five annas. Fourteen annas for Amma's ticket and seven for my half ticket.

The stationmaster walked to the office. A little later, he came back with the tickets. Leaning against the rough bark of an old mango tree, I gazed at the shadows that had been brimming over at the base of the tree. I remembered the lesson that I had studied. I began to recite it in a tone I was used to, without raising my voice, as if I was reading aloud: in a country named Siam, there was a boy called Chiang. He was lame. He was also an orphan.

Crawling along the roadsides, Chiang planted tree saplings. Later, when they grew into big trees and spread their shade, the wayfarers who sought shelter under them used to praise Chiang.

I too felt that I should become like Chiang. But I was not lame. Neither was I an orphan. (Orphan: someone who has no father and mother, I said under my breath.)

The stationmaster said: 'I'll be back. The train is about to arrive.'

He went into the office.

The train appeared in the north, at the bend. I moved close to Amma and asked: 'Is Appachen at home?'

Amma merely hummed. Then she turned her face away. I didn't understand a thing. I prayed that Appachen would be at home when we arrived. If so, he would take me to the cinema today or tomorrow.

The train let out a piercing whistle.

The stationmaster came out with the flags tucked in his armpit, and the cane loop. The engine driver hurled towards the platform, a similar looking cane loop.

The driver expertly caught around his arm the cane loop that the station master threw in, in return.

The train stopped. There was no one to alight.

Amma walked towards the ladies' compartment. And I followed.

Looking at the guard who got down from the train, and waving at him, the stationmaster came running towards us.

Amma was trying to catch hold of me and make me board the train.

The stationmaster said: 'You can get in first, teacher; I will get your son in.'

Amma got inside the train. The stationmaster hoisted me up and put me inside and shut the door.

Amma sat by the window. I stood close to her.

The stationmaster asked Amma: 'When are you returning?'

Amma said: 'I can decide only after I reach there. Anyway, it will be after a week. Shouldn't the rituals at the church be over?'

The guard blew his whistle. The train sounded its whistle and began to move away.

I waved at the stationmaster. He merely laughed. I was wondering why the expression on his face had turned close to weeping. Our compartment had just passed the concrete board at the station limits.

NIRAVATTHU KAYYAANI

C. AYYAPPAN

I had written a story entitled 'Niravatthu Kayyaani' some twenty-five years ago. Although it was a somewhat accomplished work, I could not publish it. Before that could happen, it was lost somewhere. Although there are many stories like mine, which are lost, written or unwritten, I am still somewhat sad that I lost 'Niravatthu Kayyaani'.

I happened to remember this because an image from from the lost story came flashing to my mind—an image of Ottamulachchi, a folk derivative of Kannaki of *Silappathikaram*. With her single breast reaching down to her knees, which she would normally coil around her neck, fancy make-up-like accessories such as her damshtras—protruding fangs—and eyes blazing like embers, she would make quite a dramatic appearance. It need not be night or the midnight hour. Even fulsome dusk is enough and more for her. When you turn the bend in the alleyway or step over a stile, you will feel a scorching breath on your neck. If you are not within an arm's reach, you are saved. Ottamulachchi, thirsty for blood, in her excitement to catch hold of you, would have reached far, far behind because her feet point backwards.

I can't remember the relevance of Ottamulachchi in my lost story, but I'm sure that she was present. Let me retrace my steps, and try to retrieve it.

I think the story began with a brief description of Niravatthu Kayyaani and how the name Niravatthu Kayyaani came about.

A canal needed to be built to direct the water that was collected in the big pond from the stream of the Parutheli paddy fields towards the Niravatthu family's dyke and from there, into their land. The dyke was at a distance of at least three vilippaadu, the distance at which one's call can be heard. The stream was the result of the combined voluntary efforts of the entire inhabitants of the locality. In places, the fifty-metre canal was as deep as two fathoms. At a later time, a road had to be built across the canal. The road and the bridge were built with granite slabs cut from rocks. The slabs were placed across the canal and lumps of earth and grass placed atop them. So, for anyone who stands beneath the bridge and road, in the canal's slush, there's no sky above his head. Only soil. Soil above slush.

'Niravatthu Kayyaani' is about how a girl lost her sky at that spot in the canal where one's feet gets stuck in the slush, and each step has to be wrested out only with great difficulty. At that spot or wherever she is, if she is alive. However, I am sure that her story is still around. That's why I can tell the story once again.

I was startled awake by the loud wailing of a group of people. The sweeping wind was rushing in through the shutterless windows, roaring with laughter. Again a group was wailing. The window was at the southern end of the house. That was where the sound was coming from. Mother, who was struggling to strike a match, cursed both wind and the wailing.

I got out into the alley and suddenly noticed the flames of a fierce fire. Where had it originated? I began running in the darkness punctuated by starlight, but I didn't have to go too far. The entire neighbourhood had gathered there, gazing at a small house that was up in flames—a hut with mud walls and bamboo poles serving as pillars to support its thatched roof.

The onlookers were clearly divided into two camps: those watching with a feeling of helplessness that nothing could be salvaged and those who knew that there wasn't anything much to be salvaged in the first place.

When the hut burned down completely, everyone, including me, went away.

When I reached home, there was still light inside. Father and Mother were talking. They were unbothered about the fact that only two houses away, a hut had been gutted in a fire.

Mother said: 'Let them go anywhere and be damned. The depraved lot!'

Father agreed: 'Right you are!'

That's when Mother noticed me entering the house. In utter anger, she asked: 'Hey! Where did you go in this dark, offering your legs for the snakes to feast upon? Do you think that you have become so great just because you are studying in a college?'

I got in without a word and lay down.

They are Mother's enemies now. It was not like this earlier. Chittaanda, who had come back with his two grown-up daughters, down and out from Mannaankandam, after selling whatever little possessions they had, was Mother's old friend. She was the wife of Father's old friend.

I remember what Mother had sympathetically said one of those days: Ittunnaan had stolen an etha banana bunch at midnight when it was raining in torrents at the height of the famine-ridden month of Karkkidakam (from mid-July to mid-August). He stole the bananas to feed his family who had been starving for days. The owner of the banana tree discovered the theft only after four or five days had passed and was flabbergasted. The etha banana was vowed as an offering to the parish church. Though he couldn't identify the thief, the owner was resolute that the latter should not go unpunished. He plucked the remaining stem, dried it in the rare Karkkidakam sunshine in which one could even dry a wild elephant's skin, and also smoked it to cure it enough before taking it to the church's front yard and burning it there as a ritual of chastisement. On the eighth day, Ittunnaan was struck by lightning and died.

Thus, Chittaanda and her daughters who had become orphans in a far-off land came back to their own land. If severed at the stalk, the fruit will invariably fall at the base!

Back home, she presented herself at the padi—the landlord's gatehouse. Weeping and wailing, she recounted her woes and begged for sympathy and understanding. As she went around renewing her contacts in the neighbourhood and accepting donations, everyone sympathized with the family. It was through the help of many that she was able to build that small shack on the puramboke, surplus land belonging to the government, by the roadside next to the kayyaani.

As months passed, the locality was in turmoil. Hushed whispers about the conduct of the refugees were heard. Many had seen a shooting star passing through the hut's southern yard. Some of them could even divine who the culprit was! The older daughter was a lapsed one! A lord from the landlord's family who went about on his rounds at night, carrying his seven-celled flashlight, concurred with the insinuation.

The next part of the lost story is about the younger girl. When did I see her first? I remember that part very well even now.

I was returning from the library at dusk after borrowing a book. When I reached the bend in front of the Periyappuratthukavu temple, the girl—Chittaanda's younger daughter Shaarada—stood right before me like a star fallen from the sky It was not intentional, but I stared at her unwittingly. When I had spotted her on previous occasions, I was never able to see her fully. She would either hide behind her mother or her sister. Now there was no one with her. That fifteen-year-old was out of her depths.

Suddenly I looked away. She climbed the slope in anxious excitement, and I sauntered forward. After going a couple of paces, I felt compelled to turn my head around and look back. Exactly at the same time, she too looked before hurrying away bashfully. I felt a tinge of shame. Yet once again, I turned after two or three steps, and at that moment, caught her looking again back at me. This time, she lowered her head and summoning all her energy, ran away. I became worried and looked all around in consternation. Had anyone seen us? By this time, she was out of my line of sight. What did this chance encounter mean? Turning the question over and over in my mind, I walked back home at a leisurely pace.

After dinner, as I was reading my book, I overheard Mother narrating a story to Father. I wondered if this was an attempt to make me listen to the tale. The heroine's name was Innooli. She was Chittaanda's aunt, to be exact. Innooli was very beautiful. There wasn't a woman like her in this locality or in the neighbouring places and in any caste. All those who saw her agreed that beauty means black. Many had also seen her when she had been digging for the kayyaani. That feat was accomplished not just by labourers from our village.

Her intoxicating beauty was troublesome not only for the youngsters who became infatuated, but for herself as well. What the Kaarikkal Kaniyaan said about her—that the single child born under the pooraadom asterism wouldn't have a husband who lived long. And miraculously it was true in her case. Though the cause of it was not obvious, the result was as it had been predicted. On the eighth day of the wedding, the groom would invariably return to the other world. The number of parayas who returned thus became five. The proverb which claimed that going as a bridegroom who was adopted by the bride's family is a humiliation equal to death shook off all its figurativeness.

When the five Pandavas were killed thus, Innooli resolved to become Paanchaali. When her skin-and-bones grandfather died because someone had stamped over him, her parents had enough of Innooli. They threw her out.

Those who came forward to look after Innooli during her plight were the leading citizens known for their humanity. The prominent members of the Paruttheli family built a hut for her at the northern bank of the paddy fields. To ensure no one assaulted her during the night, they took turns guarding her like spirits guarding a treasure.

After a year passed, Innooli topped off her service to the community when she offered her own skull as a scarecrow to ward off the evil eye from the vegetable patch in Paruttheli's paddy fields.

Someone had killed her by kicking in her lower abdomen and then sunk her body in the pond. On the third day, the corpse surfaced when the grinding stone tied to its neck got loose. There was no other way than burying her. But the grave that was dug was not deep enough. That's how a jackal dug it up and pulled her head out.

The story had progressed up to this point when Mother stopped talking. But I had heard a few more details.

What was happening to Innooli? Who was her support after her parents and relatives had given up on her? Not even a living being, yet why did she resist all those leading citizens?

Naturally, she became pregnant. No one could be blamed for that. But the question is why did she stubbornly assert that the father of the baby in her belly was Putthenkalam Avaraachen? Couldn't she have left him alone—he who was world-renowned as one unable to father a child? Why wasn't she mindful at least of Putthenkalam's barren wife?

Straining against the chains that bound him, he moaned. Then he caught her leg in obeisance. Then he licked her foot. He even offered to register ten paras of paddy fields as an endowment in her name. In her arrogance, Innooli forgot her status in life and stood firm, resolving that she won't move an inch even if an elephant was to pin her with its tusks.

Now comes the climax of the story. Before that, there is something else that I want to inform the reader. Let not the structural order of the first story be unnecessarily upset.

After the muddy stone bridge spanning Niravatthu Kayyaani ends and the road begins, there's a small bend to the left where there is a stone to wash clothes. It's a ghat for the women who do not have their own wells, ponds, or secluded sheds to wash and bathe. There won't be anyone coming from the northern side of the kayyaani, and if someone takes the trouble to ogle through the honeysuckle branches from the road that ran along the top, they will be caught by the people in the junction. Even someone approaching from the meadows in the south can be spotted from a considerable distance. Then the women who may be in a state of partial undress can spare their modesty by hiding inside the kayyaani under the bridge, where it was dark and at least two women could easily move about.

Shaarada, who was standing in the darkness of the kayyaani, wringing the wet towel to dry her hair, couldn't make out from which side the tampuraan of the Padi had entered and caught her in the evil grip of his strong hands. Her scream, which had distorted itself into some sort of a lusty moan since he had cupped her mouth with the palm of his one hand, aroused him.

As he calmly pulled out his legs that had sunk deep into the slush, he pinched her bleeding buttocks that had suffered from abrasions as it had been rubbed against the kayyaani's laterite wall.

Shaarada stood immobile. Although she noticed the deepening darkness under the bridge and the water flowing through the kayyaani turning into a shade of deep aquamarine, she remained frozen in that stance as if she had no sense of time passing by.

By the time Shaarada reached her hut carrying the wet clothes, she was shaking with a high fever. Without saying a word to anyone, she spread the mat on the floor and lay down. When her mother came and shook her awake for dinner, she felt Shaarada's fever burning her fingers. She prepared a kashaayam with dry ginger and pepper crushed together and shook her awake to make her drink the concoction. Shaarada swallowed two mouthfuls with great difficulty. She once again fell into a delirium.

Shaarada's elder sister whispered in her mother's ear about the blood stain on Shaarada's mundu that had been hung on the clothesline in front of the hut.

'O, my ancestors! Have we been done in?' her mother whispered as she examined the body of her sleeping daughter. She heaved a deep sigh, her chest rising as if to reach to the horizons.

Shaarada awoke from the delirium now and then, looked around, and went on muttering gibberish.

At his insistence, Innooli had reached Puthenkalam's house in the night. His wife had gone to her home. There was no one around. He touched her feet and begged her not to destroy his family. She laughed, and he suspected that Innooli had revealed her damshtras. Though he was terrified, he didn't stop his arguments. 'It's unfair that you blame me alone. If you are so fond of speaking the truth, call out everyone who came to you. I don't mind being one among them.'

She laughed again. This time he turned his head away, unable to face her mirth.

Slowly she began to unravel the mystery. 'It's you who murdered my first husband. I haven't counted the remaining four. It was you who urinated on me for the first time. And the others. Aren't they all your relatives? You are the one who crushed my throat and killed me. It's you alone who buried me. And when the jackal dug up my head, you kicked my skull about with your feet, read the scribble on my head as you laughed, and determined that it will serve as a scarecrow for your vegetable patch.'

As Puthenkalam realized he was a murderer and mistook her for Innooli's ghost, he lost his sanity and tried to push her out. It turned out to be in vain. He then flew into a rage, and dragged her to the door. In that moment, his eyes fell on her pointed breasts that were always ridiculing him. Howling in the mad excitement of a vicious idea that had flowered in his head, he grabbed her left breast, shoved it into the space between the doorframe and the shutter, and slowly began to pull it close.

'You'll tell others, will you?'

She continued laughing, and Puthenkalam certainly saw her two damshtras. He shut the door with all his might.

It was when Shaarada shot up from her sleep, tightly clutching her left breast and screaming, that the two damshtras fell out on to the floor.

Hearing her yell, her mother and elder sister were petrified. They could not discern the source of light flooding their hut. They joined her—the three women crying in unison.

I still try to convince myself that Shaarada must have run away to escape the fire. And yet, how did she fall in the kayyaani? Maybe her feet were pointing backwards as she ran.

Thus had ended the lost story.

SWEAT MARKS

SARA JOSEPH

These stairs are not mine. Neither are these corridors, these overhead beams.... The building, the courtyard...the pathway, the playground, the laburnum tree, the books, the teachers—none of these will consider me theirs. What Chandrika chechi said is true.

Halting at each step, standing there grieving, I climb down the stairs. My slippers are covered with dust. The soles of my feet are sweaty. The heels of my feet are cracked and sore. The distance between the lowly One Lakh Housing Colony* and this college, is really big. Running all that distance, I had somehow reached these stairs breathlessly. At the foot of this ancient, gargantuan staircase, I had stood in awe, like a worm. Before me, my father, mother, or brothers had never seen this staircase. My amazement is theirs too.

A little while ago, I was standing before the admission committee, handing them a complaint. There were eleven members in the committee. They were seated in a crescent formation. Ordinarily, I don't make any complaints about anything at all. It was Chandrika chechi who said that they have done injustice towards me and that I must lodge a complaint. Chandrika chechi is a news agent.

Every day early in the morning, I see Chandrika chechi dashing off on a bicycle with newspaper bundles, while I sweep the courtyard. She talks to me about this and that, without dismounting from the bicycle, resting one foot on the ground. Straightening myself from the bending position and levelling the coconut-leaf midribs of the broom by hitting the base of the handle in the middle of my palm, I too would talk to her about certain things. It's Chandrika chechi who got my SSLC results in advance and told me that I had scored distinction. It was she who bought the admission form from the college, filled it

---

*An innovative scheme of its time, in fact the first in the whole of India, this was a free mass housing scheme meant for the poor, inaugurated in the early 1970s in Kerala, by late Sri M. N. Govindan Nair, of the CPI, when he was minister for Housing. Gradually, a person living in such a house came to be equated with a slum dweller, in the social hierarchy of Kerala.

out, asked me to sign the form, and submitted it to the college, looked up the rank list, and told me the result. When she created a commotion saying that my name has been included only in the Reservation List, and not in the Merit List, I was at a loss—what's Merit List? What's Reservation List? I had only one thought: whatever list it was, I should get admission in the college. I will throw away this broom with which I sweep someone else's courtyard for a living, and walk up straight to the staircase of that college.

'Ass!' Chandrika chechi shouted at me in a rage. 'Your type will never improve.' She was so mad at me that she didn't speak a word further, got on her bicycle, trilled the bell continuously, and pedalled away. She would do the rest of the talking only when she comes back after distributing the newspapers. Therefore, after I had finished sweeping the courtyard, washed the dishes, and scrubbed and swabbed the floor quickly and, wiped my hands dry on my skirt, I waited for her.

'You must not let it go like this. Don't you have pride? You must lodge a complaint,' said Chandrika chechi.

Give a complaint? Me? Won't I get into trouble? Chandrika chechi told me about the rules. 'The admission committee has transgressed the rules. Shouldn't you get justice?'

Who wouldn't want to get justice? But, like everyone else, I, too, was tardy about giving a complaint. Chandrika chechi flew into a rage. She fought with me and left in a huff. She came back. Talked. Went away again. Until I was made aware that the committee had been unfair to me. When I realized that justice had been denied to me, I was grief-stricken. Why did they ostracize me from the fraternity? General Merit List is a fraternity—the fraternity of students who scored the highest marks. I should have been one of the first among them. Chandrika chechi said they put me in the Reservation List, not only based on marks but also based on many other considerations. Many other considerations? What were they? Lineage, complexion, caste, religion, dress, language. I, too, felt I must complain. However much fearful I am, I must lodge a complaint. But it was only because Chandrika chechi went on accusing me a thousand times of not having the least bit of pride, that I finally decided to traverse the distance between the One Lakh Housing Colony and the college, stomping along vehemently on the way. Chandrika chechi did not assist me in drawing up the complaint. 'It's not through newspaper agents that college students lodge complaints,' she said. 'Slog at it.... Write it out yourself, go, and file it.'

So, it was a complaint I myself wrote. Reading my complaint, the admission committee members peered at me as if to say, 'Amazing that you have got such a complaint!' I remembered Chandrika chechi's warning: 'When you see the sahib, you will certainly miss a step.' She was right. I had begun to miss my steps. One of the members said that I should not have written such a complaint. 'How dare you? Aren't you going to study in this college, after doing such a thing? After all, it's we people who are going to teach you. How can you look at our faces? Whose advice are you acting on?'

Then the committee members tried to console themselves saying that I had somehow ventured into such rank foolishness out of naiveté and that it was just all right. But I felt that they were not really convinced. 'How does it matter if you are in Merit List or Reservation List? The important thing is that you will get admission. Isn't that good enough?'

I felt it was not good enough. So, I stood speechless, motionless. My stance before the admission committee was not one befitting the proud winner of top marks in the SSLC Examination. How could I stand erect with pride just like that? Lineage, complexion, caste, religion, dress, language. I am a dark, diminutive girl. Narrow face; emaciated arms and legs. Eyes that betray panic whenever I look at someone. The putrid smell of rancid oil on my hair. My long hair is full of split ends. I always have a book clutched to the chest with both hands. If I have to remove my hands from my chest, I would tremble in fear. My lips and hands are always perspiring and cold like water. Although people are sitting on the throne-like chairs arranged in the crescent shape in front of me, the feeling that I am sitting in the centre of this room, vast and reaching up to the horizon, catches hold of me and terrifies me.

'In the Merit List, you have only the second rank. In the Reservation List, you have the first rank. Which is better?'

They are handing back my complaint to me, with the wily looks in their eyes that flash when they hoodwink a young girl like me through their sweet talk. Before I could answer them, they began their asides, as if this was a discussion that included me as well, which had just concluded. 'If this student is moved over to the Reservation List, one of our students can get into the Merit List. Moving that student, putting this student there and taking away the other student, our student will....'

They smiled faintly looking at me, as if to say, 'Isn't everything okay now?' They pushed my complaint to the edge of the table. They had a lot of work. They plunged into their work, totally forgetting about me. I was afraid to move from where I stood. If I moved away, they would see my footprints on the floor, marked by dust and sweat. When I stretched my arm to take the complaint back, I made sure that none of them was watching me. All the time, Chandika chechi taunted me sitting inside my mind. 'Get away from me! I don't want to see the shower of your tears! You must speak out whatever you have got to say looking at their faces. If not, people like us won't be able to live here.' But neither me, nor my brothers, nor my father, or mother, nor their fathers, or mothers ever had the guts to do such a thing.

From the top of the stairs, Professor Thevan's eyes follow her closely. The footprints on each stair marked by dust and sweat are historical records. That girl who moves away with a bowed head is the continuation of history. These are junctures in history that go unrecorded. He felt it was his bounden duty as a professor of history, to make an intervention here and record it in history. As his thoughts proceed this far, the fingers of his right palm begin to quiver. That is something usual. He is afflicted by such quivering in moments that are deemed to be historical. He can't possibly survive if at least that didn't happen as an expression of the conflict between his mind and body. Professor Thevan yearns to stretch out his shivering hand and beckon back the girl who is slowly descending the stairs. She is climbing down step after step. 'Now, let me climb the steps down quickly and talk to her,' he thinks. 'I will console her saying, "let me see what I can do".'

She keeps climbing down the steps.

'I will ask the watchman Balan Nair, who is coming up the steps, to call her back,' he thinks.

But she has reached the bottom of the staircase, walked along the veranda, along another veranda, still further along a third veranda, reached the farthest end and disappeared.

Only her damp footprints remain on the floor of the veranda. His right hand is shaking, unable to record anything, his head droops into the open history book, as though his neck has snapped. He is sweating. He extricates his feet from the shoes. He takes off his spectacles and rubs his eyes. He is thirsty and longs for water boiled with dry ginger.

At that moment the words of his daughter Namita overwhelm him. 'No redemption for you because of your fear—reasonable sometimes, but mostly unreasonable. I too have got this damned fear in my genes.' Namita had discovered that he is at a loss for words, panicky and withdrawn—in a bus, in the shopping complex, at a wedding reception, in the office, in a hospital, in the temple. Namita thinks that her father is the cause of all her fears—big and small—of darkness, of thieves, of policemen, of snakes, of the devil, of her mother, of God. Why should you be afraid—of whom, what for? Namita always asks. Her father too believes that he got the fear from his fathers and forefathers standing throughout history, bent forward, obsequiously covering their mouths with their palms. He knows what these sweaty footprints are demanding of him. They demand that he should go straight to the admission committee and face it forthwith. He trembles, laying his face down on the tabletop.

After a period of prolonged anxiety, Professor Thevan rises, washes his face, and puts on his spectacles. Walking across the admission committee, he approaches the letter box. As he rummages for letters in the history department box, a question creeps inside his mind. 'Why didn't that girl's name—she is my Namita—figure in the Merit List? Should I ask, "didn't figure" or "wasn't given"?' Professor Thevan dithers, searching for the non-existent letter in the box. The powerlessness that has gripped him now is the same he experiences while looking at his wedding photo. Renuka standing tall, all fair, holding his dark hand, among his dark siblings and their dark offspring. The photo proclaims everything. The fear that has been passed down through generations is reflected in their dazed looks. Renuka, however, stands facing the camera blazing forth in the confidence she has inherited through her birth. Professor Thevan has hidden away that photo to escape from the fear that pulls him down to the depths. However, on critical junctures in the history of his life, his wedding photo looms, erasing all blind spots in his memory.

Therefore, he puts on a smile telling himself that everything is trivial and walks past the admission committee. He draws consolation from the fact that the girl who had stood there with the complaint, in fact, created a juncture in history that called for correction. But, as he opens the door, the footprints she has left behind on the floor of the veranda scare him terribly. 'Tomorrow, yes, tomorrow, definitely I have certain things to question. There's no question of any wedding photo preventing me doing it.'

Watchman Balan Nair asks, in all candidness, 'Are you leaving for the day, Thevammash?' However, Renuka doesn't believe in his candidness. 'Thevammash, Thevammash! He is calling you so on purpose! He calls "Professor" even the boys who joined yesterday. How often have I insisted that you should change the spelling of your name? It's just the question of one letter. If only you replaced the "T" of your name with "D", all shame would vanish!'

Professor Thevan is drenched in his own perspiration.

The smell of sweat will continue in genes. The stench of the ploughed-up slushy paddy field continues in Namita. She insists that she won't trade that stench for all the perfumes of Paris.

THE TWELFTH HOUR
V. P. SIVAKUMAR

That day too he got off the bus and walked home. Like every other day, he thought about resuming the discontinued daily games of badminton from tomorrow and increase his provident fund deposit by ten rupees from next month's salary onwards. The realization that nearly all his days ended the same way was beginning to alarm him. All his attempts at giving life a slightly different turn by going on an excursion, enjoying the occasional drink, and attending a poetry recital were all in vain. He walked towards his sweet home. The day's flame had become extinct in his body. Night approached like a lengthy sigh. He did not mistrust the night even though he sensed something fatal lurking in the darkness. Even otherwise, where else could he rest his faith?

He reached the front entrance of his house and was immediately transfixed—right there was an unbelievable patch of moonlight. What could it possibly signify? His senses became sharp like that of a keen-witted wild animal. Suddenly, he noticed a new neon lamp burning on the street light post. It had not been there till the previous day. His mind relaxed. It was only a trivial novelty. He opened the gate and waited there for a moment to listen to his son reciting a nursery rhyme. He did not like to express his love, not to his son, not to anybody for that matter. It was a song about a Christian called Solomon Grundy. He listened. What a horrible song! Slight and unceremonious like the life of Solomon Grundy, its connotations oozed like a poisonous runoff and seeped into his mind as a creed, as the tragedy of faith, and purely as a sense of the tragic.

Reunion. 'Father!' the son and daughter exclaimed together. They frisked him for any delicacies he might be carrying for them. His wife went inside and came back with an envelope: a telegram from his native place: 'Start immediately'.

She stood silently, waiting for his response.

'I shall go immediately.'

Inwardly, he felt himself growing stronger. This was the only gain from his staggering about over so many years: his ability to tiptoe through any hardship. He rose from the cot and went to the washroom, washed his hands, legs, and face, and combed his hair. Then look at that! He felt like going to the washroom again. He decided against it. In reality, it was just an apprehension. But the pain in his lower abdomen was also a reality. Two realities? That was not right. There would be only one reality ever. What did the psychologist know? Nevertheless, he went again to the toilet and resolved that this toilet hopping should not be repeated.

He could set out on the journey only after the children were asleep. Or else, they would weep and call out to him. His fear of them calling him from behind was not on account of his faith in astrology. The echoes of those tender voices would haunt him throughout the journey. A person like him could leave only after herding together all human relationships inside the gate and bolting it from the outside. The innocent sob heard at the last minute was sufficient to upset the mental balance of one with weak nerves. If they were put to sleep soon enough, he could take the fast passenger bus at 8.30. As usual, his son had many doubts. The boy snuggled close to him. He did not lose his temper. He did not like to make the children cry when he had to set out on a journey. He wanted to travel while remembering their smiling faces.

His daughter, lying to his left, asked, 'Father, will you die?'

He made an affirmative, guttural noise.

'Mother, too?' He affirmed again.

'Brother and I too?'

He felt a lump in his throat. He earnestly yearned to believe his children will not die. But as often happened, his tongue betrayed him: 'You too will die.' It was a cruel answer.

'Only this house will remain then?'

His daughter was smart. She seemed to think about many things. He stroked her hair and caught wilted jasmine in his fist.... A house in the centre of an empty compound in which everything has withered away! A horrendous expanse of barrenness! Our unsatisfied lives will hover forever among the crystalline suns that wobble around inside mirages.... He would usually kiss his son before he went to bed. Now, he was already asleep. Whenever he thought about his son, he would think about his old age and death. His son performing the funeral rites with trembling hands. He extracted his son's hand from his. Those were the hands that would lift him up like a saving grace when he stood alone amid the startling, bluish darkness of the netherworld as thunderclaps boomed all around. He kissed his son's eyes. A causeless sob rose within him. Then he gently got up without shaking the cot. A neon light filtered in through the window, making the room feel like it was all a part of a dream. He whispered: 'Wake up with a smile tomorrow, like a rebirth, full of innocence like a flower....'

He turned energetic like a leopard cub, thinking about the busy schedule ahead of him for the rest of the night. He hurried through dinner. Drank a lot of water and tasted a little of the barfi gifted by the family next door. He packed a bag with all the necessary things, including cigarettes and matches. Then he bid goodbye to his wife and left in a hurry. Stopping under the new neon lamp, he glanced at his watch: 8.30. Oh! No need to hurry now. He could take any bus that was headed for his village.

This was his usual experience. Precisely because of this, he would only walk, even if it was for two or three miles. But that day, his destination was far, far away. He had to take the bus. He leaned lazily against a shop's closed shutters. The streets were turning empty. A dog came close, observed him keenly, and turned away. Three people passed on a bicycle. Only a drunkard hung around the bus station and then fell asleep right there. He considered having a drink. That way, he would sleep comfortably during the journey. No. If Mother died at that exact moment, it would remain a raw wound. The only intoxication he had derived from life was when the intensity of a calamity was experienced in its entirety. It was ten o'clock. Confident that nobody would notice him, he spread his handkerchief on the floor and sat on it. At that moment, a bus roared in. He scrambled to his feet and rushed out, signalling it to stop. The conductor regarded him from head to toe and rang a double bell. He did not feel anger or disappointment. All that time, the night resounded within him. Such an unplanned journey was new to him. He was used to travelling only after reserving a ticket in advance. Just then, an electricity board employee in khaki uniform arrived on a bicycle, got off briskly, and pulled out the fuse of the street lamps. A curtain of darkness descended.

He opened his eyes wide. His mind, that had dozed off in the intensity of the light, awoke from its slumber. The moment's gentle relief touched its delicate walls. Placing his foot upon a high stone, he craned his neck to see the far end of the road. Hoping for a cup of tea, he walked towards a fragment of light he had spotted at a distance. Vapours rose from the molten road. A chill descended from above. Both met within him. When he had walked some distance, he saw a country band practising. They sat motionless like ghosts gathered around a dim light with winged termites flying about. He walked in short steps like a circus clown. Then, when the sound grew thin, his mind was momentarily inflamed by the small breasts of a half-naked woman he saw in a shadow through a window. A long line of women he had looked at with desire formed in his mind. Finally, it ended in a pale face with big eyes. He had forgotten about the bus as he waited for his tea. A tumbler was placed on the table in front of him. The first sip scalded his tongue. He blew on it once or twice for the tea to cool it down.

Suddenly he heard a rumble from the road. A bus that was running out of time! Nobody had told him that there was such a bus. He rushed ahead with his bag, howling like a mad man. Brakes were slammed. He jumped in and the bus roared on.

The conductor said this was the very first trip of a service that had been started along a new route connecting a remote Malabar village to southern Travancore. An experimental route. It might become permanent if there were enough passengers. At that time, the bus was only half full. Some of the passengers were already asleep. He sat in a seat near the driver. That way he could get a little warmth from the engine's heat. The draught was less there. Listening to the driver talk, he guessed that the man was a native of Tiruvalla. He bought a ticket from the conductor and pocketed the change without bothering to count the money. Reclining on his seat, he looked out of the window

An imperious night. It had subjugated the mountains and the wide paddy fields. The road appeared as a bridge made of thread. As the bus rounded a bend, he thought he heard the ancient rolling of a drum. A light appeared every now and then like an unsolicited boon. Whenever people came out on the road against the bus, the driver shouted at least one expletive. He was in awe of the driver's alpha-male, adventurous gestures. The driver stroked his upturned moustache. On one occasion he lit a bidi, removing both his hands from the steering wheel while the bus was in motion. The bus stopped in front of a Pentecostal convention centre. A pastor dressed like a navy man who jumped into the bus said: 'I am going to Tiruvalla, please.' He smiled at everybody. An ordinary person who had none of the pretensions of a pastor. A simpleton who had come after praying for what he thought was best. His mind fluttered. He was so far removed from even a prayer! No.... The pastor started singing hymns all by himself. Time was coming to an end! You should not perish with the world...! A group of college students going for a football match woke up and began to repeat after the pastor. In a strange background in which devotion, frivolity, and derision mixed together, the vehicle flew forward, piercing through the night. The driver seemed to have been carried away; the speed of the bus had increased rather quickly. He felt immensely happy. He felt then what he had felt when was a young boy and he went up high on a swing, as high as a tree. It was the thrill of terror. It was like lightning, beautiful but dangerous. Many times during his life, it had peeped through the cracks of his mind, but never had he experienced it so distinctly and intensely. It burned upwards from his navel. The bus fell into deep potholes, bounced up, and soldiered ahead. He prayed: let this feeling not leave me, no matter what I lose. Lives depended on him. Where would they go? His wife was a person who had never demanded attention for herself. She lay upon the earth with pricked-up ears like a sacrificial victim before a ghastly life. In whose lap would the sleeping offspring seek refuge the next day? It was only then that the possibility of his death and its impact had dawned on him. The howling wind had made him forget everything. The bus was approaching a bend. If it swung a foot to the left, it would plummet down a precipice. What else was there but a lonely road in between sleep and death, two deaths, or a birth and a death? Outside, the hills resembled gigantic statues sleeping on their backs. The pastor had fallen silent. Leaning his head on the shoulders of a child, he slept like a child. All were asleep. He cursed his fellow travellers who could sit straight and sleep as if ensconced in the belly of a python. Why are you not awake to partake in my amusement? He yearned to wake up somebody and shout, 'Look!' His mother lying somewhere, nearing her death, entered his consciousness. She dissolved into the universe—the tragedy of being oppressed in life and rising to immortality after death. The bus rattled frighteningly. He was comforted that there was a road below. He felt as if they had run over a human being. A primordial laughter exploded in him. It spread across his body on which had fallen the rosewater of many springs. His impression that he was the tragic hero who fell dead in the very first act now left him. He realized that he had had a moment of stupendous satiety.

The visions of the nature he saw were steeped in fantasy. They uprooted the rationality of the human eye. Darkness stepped away from the midnight. The big hills pointed towards an unravelled stage of the origin of the universe. Where was that light coming from? It might be another world. There was no other source for the shadow and the light he saw there. He experienced something beyond the three dimensions.... No. That is my world, surely my world, only. Only at times it changes forms like a yakshi. Although she may exhibit cruelty in her weak moments when she cannot suffer or forgive any longer, she is compassionate, she is all-enduring... like the earth. It is there, somewhere inside the dark shadows, that my mother, my wife, and children are lying asleep.... He did not realize the speed at which the bus was going. His mind was empty. To him, they weren't moving at all. No sounds were heard. The wind had sunk to the depths of a strange experience. He leaned back and sat still. He beseeched to God that he might not be set free from this stillness. Life so far had been for this moment.... His heart pounded. He opened his eyes as one who had received the gift of sight for the first time. He first looked at the driver. The man did not blink. He sat like an iron statue, his eyes protruding. He was no longer turning the wheel. Black blood oozed from the corners of his mouth. It wets my feet, he said to himself. Now the bus was racing along. The driver was dead. The sight of the dead driver made a prayer wheel turn in his mind. He retrieved his presence of mind. For the first time, he concluded this was only a beginning. His mind was at the same lofty level. He could no longer see the bus. The prayer wheel turned again. How many names! How many generations flash and fade inside it, he wondered. Nothing is stable! His mother's hands, calloused with love, appeared before him. They stretched towards him. Excitedly, he too reached out, but they began moving away. He waited for his mother's hands to come closer. Suddenly, he could recognize his son's voice. He strained his ears. The call flashed, like the pitiable scream rising from a bus plunging into a gorge.

He was alone again. No grief. He was alone in his world. A hapless mind that came flying through time and space. He closed his eyes to brace himself for the final moment He felt a slight movement somewhere in his mind. And then more...something had woken up inside. A sob in a voice like bursting bubbles. Gradually it became a piercing wail. It rushed upwards as the hard voice that was full of the strength of love. That was a wail for humanity; the wrath of helplessness: a lone and grave protest that rose against death in a solitary human being. That voice reached his lips. But, without forming words, it stood startled seeing the outside world. Tears welled up in his eyes.

Then it happened. With a hideous noise, the bus plunged headlong into a gorge. The moment had arrived when all those asleep were startled into consciousness as a single body. They opened their eyes towards death and closed them again instantly. Fate had simply deceived them without giving them even a moment for a serious mediation on life.

None of those who travelled in that bus survived. That man who had set out on the journey to have a last glimpse of his mother also died. However, that death was not unforeseen as other deaths. It was logical. It was a natural death. The moment the bus plunged into the gorge, his clothes were smeared with a little faeces and urine. One or two drops of semen had been ejaculated in a final ecstasy. On each half of the head that had cracked open, two halves of a smile vertically rested as if proclaiming, 'Look, here was one who was awaiting death throughout his life.'

THE FOURTH WORLD
N. S. MADHAVAN

Once upon a time, there was a Russian and an Indian. Did I say once upon a time? Just my manner of speaking. They live even now.

One day the Russian asked the Indian, 'Have you been keeping a count of the days, Govindankutty?'

'No, I can tell you the month, though.'

Sorry, this is not a joke. I don't know how to tell jokes. This could be because I am the son of a communist. It was after I heard Sandow 'the pugilist' Gopalan talking, sometime before his death, to Father, that I began to think like a communist.

Gopalan said to my father: 'Think about it, comrade, except T. K. Ramakrishnan[*], do we have any other comrade who smiled after Azheekodan[†] was killed?'

⁂

'Govindankutty,' Bakunin said again, 'it's been eighty-eight days since we were shut inside this spacecraft. It will be exactly three months in two days.'

I remained silent. Bakunin got up and stood before the microphone and said, 'Calling Control.'

'Calling Control,' Bakunin repeated in a seductive voice.

For many days now, Control had not established contact with us.

'Calling Control,' Bakunin raised the voice, 'this is Soyuz 24. Can you hear us? Don't you want us any more?'

Bakunin left the microphone and swam towards me like a spermatozoon, wiggling his legs and rotating his head with a jittery motion in the weightlessness of the spacecraft.

'They don't want us. We are lost to them,' Bakunin said, stopping his crazy swirling and sitting down beside me. 'We, the Russians, are people

---

[*]An eminent leader of the Communist Party of India (Marxist) who emerged strong in this group after the split of 1964.

[†]Another prominent leader of the same party, who was suspected to have been murdered by political opponents.

who have lost many things. We lost thirteen days when the calendar was reformed. A big black hole in the history of the Russians. Six days each with a day of rest—ample time for God to create two universes.'

Even as a child, I knew the story of the reform of the Russian calendar. On one of the anniversaries of the October Revolution, I had gone with Father and his young followers to write slogans on the wall. Father told us how the October Revolution came to be celebrated in November. He started shaping a V and wrote 'Victory to Revolution'. Though he was old, no one could beat Father in graffiti writing on the wall. He was the best graffiti artist in Payyalur. The young ones stood transfixed at the magical consonant on the white wall. No drab geometry of straight lines; Father's V looked like the silhouette of a flock of seagulls diving down, pecking at the waves, and then soaring skywards.

When the graffiti was done, Father took me to the tea shop opposite the cinema. It stayed open all night, for tea and crispy pappada-vada. It was at this tea shop that I heard for the first time Father's stories of his past.

'Bakunin,' I called out when the silence inside the craft became unbearable. 'You know my father began his political career when he was ten.'

'Stalin killed my father when he was thirty-six,' countered Bakunin and grew silent again.

Father was ten when he picketed the liquor shops in his native village, Cheranellur. By caste, we were toddy tappers, and many of Father's relatives were in the liquor business. They taunted him: 'You, toddy tapper, what else can you do if you don't tap toddy?' But the boy wore a Gandhi cap and went every day for picketing. When he was older, he joined the nationalist Prajamandalam Party. Father met a communist for the first time in Viyyur jail where he was imprisoned soon after joining the Quit India Movement.

'K. E. Eyyunni, who was running a communist front organization called Trichur Labour Brotherhood used to come to me and drew me into arguments on the untimeliness of Quit India Movement, especially when fascist powers were knocking at our doors. Though I didn't fully grasp what he said, I slowly began turning into a Red,' Father had continued his story.

'When the ban against the party was lifted in 1942, I was given eight annas by the Ernakulam Party Office to go to Payyalur and start a party unit there. That's how Magician Vijayan and I took a bus and came here. Vijayan was already a famous man. When a charlatan from Thiruvilvamala produced some sacred leaves from thin air, Vijayan did the same, but this time it was a cucumber.'

Father and Vijayan recruited sympathizers in their ones and twos. They traversed the neighbouring villages—Chottanikkara, Eloor, Thripoonithura, Thiruvaankulam, Mamala. The soles of their feet blistered. When they ran out of money, Vijayan held magic shows in schools whose headmasters were fellow travellers.

'It was about this time Mathai had returned to Payyalur from Ceylon with some money. Even out there he was flirting with communism. As soon as he arrived, Mathai started an evening newspaper, *Aurora*. He hawked the paper himself, calling out, '*Aurora*, half anna, *Aurora*, half anna', walking around the bus stand and the boat jetty at Ernakulam.'

⌁

Suddenly I recalled going along with Bakunin to Leningrad harbour to see the cruiser, *Aurora*. I asked: 'Bakunin, do you remember the day we went to see the *Aurora?*'

Bakunin's eyes sparkled for a moment. He asked: 'What did you do with the photograph I took that day?'

'I sent it to my father,' I said. That photograph was the only one my father ever got framed. Father would say with pride that it was taken in front of the ship which fired her guns signalling Lenin to take over.

⌁

Father, Vijayan, and Aurora Mathai formed the first trade union among the Pulaya farmhands of the Aayirappara paddy fields belonging to the Kurups of Aaraayil. At the time of threshing, the Pulayas demanded two sheaves more of paddy. The Kurups did not give in. The labourers struck work.

'When Vijayan and I were walking along the fields, the young Kurup of Aaraayil and his men surrounded us. Kurup began to taunt Vijayan, telling him there could be no better time to do his vanishing trick if he could. As for me, he said he would wrap my toddy tapper's body in a mat and send it home. One of Kurup's men hooked Vijayan's neck with a sickle tied to a long staff. It looked as if his head was going to come off! I stood terrified. Then a figure materialized on top of the heap of paddy sheaves in the middle of the field.' Father stopped to draw in his breath.

'Let him go, Kurup, let go of Vijayan,' Sandow Gopalan yelled from the top of the heap. He took off his shirt and threw it on the ground. He removed his coarse cotton vest. Slowly, he undid his dhoti, folded it, and placed it on the pile of clothes he had discarded. Clad only in his blue boxer briefs, Gopalan slid his left leg back while thrusting his right knee forward. His neck muscles bulged as he raised his head, ever so slowly. Like an archer, he lifted his arms to string an imaginary bow. Muscles rippled all over Gopalan's body like waves of sand dunes after a desert storm.

'Kurup and his cohorts fell back. That was the posture which won Gopalan second place in the Mr India contest at Baroda. Next day, Aurora Mathai had banner headlines in his evening paper: "Battle of Paddy Sheaves Won". Anyway, communism spread its roots in Payyalur.' Father ended his story. By then it was two o'clock in the night.

'Calling Control,' Bakunin said in a low voice, standing before the microphone.

'Stop it, Bakunin,' I was irritated. 'If Control has anything to say they will say it.'

'Everyone must be soused in vodka. Pigs!' Bakunin said.

'Don't get us into trouble, shooting your mouth off. Down below, they must be listening with pricked ears.'

'Down below?' Bakunin pointed to the light blue earth above us and smiled. 'Eavesdropping stopped with Stalin and Brezhnev. Now in Gorbachev's time, nothing of the sort happens.'

My thoughts went to the comrades at Payyalur. How they hated Gorbachev. A couple of days before I left; Rajendran, the area committee secretary of the party, Palme Dutt, the secretary at the party office, and a stranger from Kannur dropped in at our house. Father, Aurora Mathai, and I were talking about Iraq, which was losing the war with America.

'This blighter Gorbachev is at the bottom of it,' said Rajendran, the area committee secretary.

'The fellow has orphaned the Third World. Today it is Saddam, tomorrow it'll be Castro,' said Palme Dutt, the secretary at the party office.

'He is anti-Marx,' added the comrade from Kannur.

'Anti-Marx? What on earth is that, comrade?' asked Aurora Mathai.

'Comrade Aurora, haven't you read of the Antichrist? The Bible says his head will be marked with the number 666. Haven't you seen the birthmark on Gorbachev's head, Palme Dutt? What does it look like?'

'What?' Father and Palme Dutt looked excited.

'It's the map of America. The map of America on his head! He who carries the map of America on his head will wreck Marxism. Anti-Marx.'

No one laughed. The comrade from Kannur had not meant them to laugh. He was flushed with anger.

'When are you going, Govindakutty?' Rajendran asked.

'The day after tomorrow. To Bangalore for a medical check-up at the Air Force hospital. Then to Delhi. And from there to Moscow.'

'Is it from Moscow they launch the rocket?' Aurora Mathai asked.

'No, from Baikonur Cosmodrome. There is a six-month training programme in Moscow.'

'Who is going with you?' asked Palme Dutt.

'Captain Igor Bakunin. He is a pilot like me.'

'We have come to remind you,' said Rajendran, 'about the reception tomorrow evening in your honour at the Sandow Gopalan Memorial Library Hall.'

⁜

When Father wrote asking me to donate for a library they were building in memory of Sandow Gopalan, I sent two hundred roubles from Russia. That evening Bakunin and I were walking through Moscow parks where we noticed unsuccessful attempts to erase anti-party slogans scrawled on the pedestals of the statues of Lenin and Marx.

'Back home, they build libraries, hospitals, and party offices in the name of their dead leaders. These are not as easy to destroy as statues.'

⁜

After they had left, Father said: 'It's nice that your reception was held in a hall we dedicated to Gopalan. When you were a little boy, Gopalan would encourage you to build up your body. And that body is taking you to space, ahead of all other pilots in the country.'

When I was small, Sandow used to come to our house every morning with half-sprouted chickpeas wrapped in a piece of wet cloth. As I stood gazing in wonder at the white commas on the sprouts, Sandow would say, 'Don't just stand there looking; eat it up. It is full of protein.' Then we used to jog together. If I slackened to watch the small circles of steam emerging from my mouth in the January mist, Sandow would urge, 'Run harder, become big.'

As solitude spread like smouldering chaff inside the craft, I remarked merely to break the silence: 'Bakunin, was your father a party member?'

'No, my father was a poor violinist in the Leningrad Philharmonic Orchestra. One day the secret police took him away.'

'What crime did your father commit?'

'Crime? In Stalin's time, you didn't have to be a criminal to be picked up. As if there was a clandestine anti-party group in the orchestra. I was six when they took Father away. My mother went out of her mind when she found out a couple of months later that Father was dead. From that day, I wanted to escape earth. I became a pilot to live in the skies.' Laughing mirthlessly, Bakunin went on: 'Govindankutty, it seems that my wish has come true. It is unlikely that we will ever get out of this place. For the rest of our lives, we can live in the skies.'

When his words sank in, I began to sweat with fright. First, solar panels will fail. Then chill will pervade the craft. Even the creases on our corpses' faces will be etched forever. In freezing temperature, Bakunin and I, turned into mummies, shall eternally orbit the earth.

Bakunin stood before the microphone. This time he looked as if he had made up his mind. 'This is Radio Soyuz 24. You are listening to the first broadcast of Radio Soyuz 24.'

Bakunin looked across and asked me in a low voice: 'Can you sing a song, Govindankutty?'

I nodded, glad to be doing something. Bakunin said into the microphone, 'First, a Hindi song by Govindankutty.'

Sare jahaan se achhaa
Hindustan hamaaraa hamaaraa....

After three months in space, that song was turning into my life's credo. I saw through the porthole sunsets on the horizon near Hashimara Air Force Station where tea gardens ended. I sang, rubbing shoulders with the comrades of Payyalur who were taking out a procession, shouting slogans in praise of the party leaders. The intoxicating smell of freshly tapped palm toddy permeated the craft. Those evenings at Coimbatore airbase with friends, sipping palm toddy.... I felt relieved after the song was over.

೧

Aurora Mathai once said: 'There is only one way to ward off madness in solitary confinement, sing, or talk aloud.'

Father, Sandow Gopalan, and Aurora Mathai had all been in solitary confinement. When the party was banned in 1948 after it adopted the Calcutta Thesis, they went underground. A case was also registered against them for sheltering the accused in the Edappally Police Station Attack case.

They hid in attics, bathhouses, hovels of Pulayas, and under thatches of rice boats. Living in hiding did nothing to their minds; it affected their skin, though. The skin of most of the comrades broke out in eczema. On the mats in the hideouts, they tossed and turned in half sleep, leaving behind scabs and pus from their sores. Next day another bunch of comrades slept on the same mats. Eczema spread throughout the movement. Father was caught when he unable to endure the itching any longer, moved in with a sympathetic herbal doctor. Two days later, the police brought in Sandow Gopalan and Aurora Mathai who was carrying on his head the litho-press used for printing his evening paper from the underground. By then, Magician Vijayan had already fled to Bombay.

The police had vowed to crack Gopalan. Inspector Paappaaly ('For thrashing suspects, there was no one to beat Paappaaly,' said the people of the erstwhile state of Cochin) would pick one by one, Sandow's muscles and thoroughly beat him up. Sandow, on his part would hold his breath to harden the muscles. Paappaaly grew desperate. He began whipping Sandow with the tail of a ray fish he had especially ordered from the fishermen of Vypin. Paappaaly's litany would rise: 'This for Constable Velayudhan your men killed at Edappally Police Station. This for Constable Mathew....'

'Hey you, tell me where the Edappally murderer K. C. Mathew is?' Paappaaly pulled the waist cord of Sandow's drawers. 'Tell me where the killer Varuthunni is?'

Paappaaly then discovered a rolled paper in the hem of the drawers.

'Is this the secret of your strength?' Paappaaly asked, crumpling the picture of Stalin he found and flinging it into a corner of the room. Then he began to run a roller over the naked Sandow. Sandow leapt up, throwing off the policemen who were pinning him down. He yelled in Tamil: 'Therefore the working class will never be destroyed. United, they will advance more than ever before. Red salute to martyrs!' Paappaaly didn't understand what Sandow was saying. For a moment, he stood perplexed.

'Sandow was quoting from the cenotaph to the martyrs at the Golden Rock Railway Colony in Tiruchirappalli,' Father explained. 'A superintendent of police of Tiruchi, Harrison, killed several railway workers, to break their strike. Remember Ananthan Nambiar whom we visited on our way to Madurai? He was their leader.'

Paappaaly recovered to strike again. Sandow threatened: 'Paappaaly, I'll kill you the way Comrade Ananthan Nambiar killed the white man Harrison.'

Paappaaly stopped. He knew that of all the deaths, the worst was the one brought upon by Ananthan Nambiar on Harrison. Harrison left Ananthan Nambiar to die after he had collapsed after a severe beating. A superstition that one should not open fire on a corpse saved Ananthan Nambiar from the white man's pistol. A few days later Harrison found Ananthan Nambiar standing outside his window. Another day, when his snow-white stallion tethered in the yard changed into Ananthan Nambiar, Harrison shot at it. The horse reared up with a neigh and fell down, blood gushing out of his breast and a red flag fluttering in Ananthan Nambiar's hand.

Nambiar stalked Harrison even to the bathroom. When he stood before the mirror, he saw his image fading out with a dance only to re-emerge as Ananthan Nambiar. After that, to destroy his enemy was easy. Harrison committed suicide.

Before long, Father, Aurora Mathai, and Sandow were transferred to Viyyur jail. In windowless cells, they spent several weeks in solitary confinement—unable to tell day from night, in an eternal twilight. Madness seeped into the cells irresistibly like diluvial waters. The party sent a message through a warder: 'Don't keep quiet. Talk to yourself loudly. A trick told to us by our leader A. K. G.'

⌁

'Tra lala tra lala'. Standing before the microphone, Bakunin was conducting an invisible orchestra, waving his hands in the air and singing aloud.

'Do you know which symphony this is, Govindankutty?'

'No.'

'Symphony No. 7 of Shostakovich. He composed this during the 900-day siege of Leningrad by the Nazis.'

The siege of Leningrad still evoked ardour in Father and other comrades of Payyalur. Whenever I came home on leave during training, they gathered around me to hear about life in the Soviet Union. Last time I went home, I said to them, 'Now in the Soviet Union, Stalin is as hated as Hitler.'

'Has this man conducted an opinion poll in the whole of the Soviet Union?' asked Rajendran, the area committee secretary, angrily.

'What's the use of snapping at him? Blame him, that Khrushchev. He started all this,' Aurora Mathai said.

Father stood up and began to speak in an oratorical tone: 'Who held out for nine hundred days when the Nazis were set to capture Leningrad? Stalin! Who in '42 engaged the Nazis in Stalingrad, razed to naught by the German bombs, fighting them man to man, in trenches, in sewers, and on rooftops? Stalin! Who made General Zhukov kill two thousand Germans, recapture Stalingrad, and win World War II? Stalin!'

'And despite all this, some people blame Stalin,' Aurora Mathai added. 'Tell me, if Stalin's five-year plans had not made the Soviet Union what it is, would this lad, Govindankutty from Payyalur, ever go to space?'

Stalin's posters began to multiply at processions in Payyalur. With the immutability of a mathematical formula devised by Father and his companions, the comrades of Payyalur carried more pictures of Stalin in their processions. For every five Stalins, three Lenins, and every three Lenins, two Marxs, and for every two Marxs, one Engels.

⌁

When Bakunin's long silence became unbearable, I asked him: 'What happened to Shostakovich's Symphony No. 7?'

'Govindakutty,' his voice faltered. 'My father was among those who performed the symphony for the first time. By then, half the population of Leningrad had perished—with no bread to eat; no coal to warm them. The dead included my grandfather and my father's elder brother. The symphony kept my father going. Finally, Father and other violinists lined up in the unheated Philharmonic hall, in thick woollens, their bodies pressed close together for warmth. They clutched the violin bows with their gloved fingers, not letting them slip even once, and played the symphony. The entire city listened; they needed to. When the Germans in the trenches heard the broadcast over the local radio, it dawned upon them their siege was doomed.'

Bakunin fell silent again. I guessed that he might be thinking about his father and colleagues, men of determination, but who were later on herded off and murdered by the secret police. I glanced at his face. It looked as if he was going to cry. But instead, he went through the entire symphony, with renewed vigour, humming different sounds.

When the symphony was over, the radio receiver suddenly came alive. We heard someone clapping.

'Calling Control, the is Soyuz,' Bakunin said.

'What Soyuz?' a girl asked in Russian.

'Soyuz 24 of the Soviet Union.'

'Soviet Union! It is withering away. Now we have a bunch of republics. Let that be. Now, what is your name?'

'Captain Igor Bakunin.'

We heard fingers typing on a keyboard. 'There is no such name in the computer. Where are you from?'

'Leningrad.'

The girl laughed. She said: 'There is no such city either. Mayor Sobchak changed its name. It is called Saint Petersburg now.'

'We want to return to earth.'

'You are a liability to the Soviet Union. Whether or not the republics should take you on will be decided by the parliament of those republics. And what do you mean, "we"?'

'There is an Indian with me. A symbol of friendship between the Soviet Union and the Third World.'

'The republics cannot take on the international obligations of the Soviet Union, either.'

'Tell us what shall we do now to come down to earth?'

'A lost property office has just been opened at the United Nations. I shall register your names there. Perhaps someone may claim you,' and the girl burst out laughing.

I was standing looking through the porthole. Chunks of the Milky Way swirled into snow-white stallions, Ananthan Nambiars, and violinists of Leningrad Orchestra. The girl's laughter did not stop. Suddenly, I became Bakunin, his history, my own wounds. Shoving Bakunin aside, I stood in front of the microphone. At first, I felt such stage fright that I could say nothing. Then I shouted the words which came rushing to me—in Tamil: 'Therefore the working class will never be destroyed. United, they will advance more than ever before. Red salute to martyrs!'

The sound of a frightened girl snapping shut the microphone echoed through the spacecraft.

Bakunin put on his spacewalk suit. He began walking towards the door of the spacecraft.

'Here I go, Govindankutty,' Bakunin said over the small mike inside his helmet. He opened the door and swam out. The metallic cable connecting him to the craft grew taut.

I went to the door. Outside, the solar panels of the spacecraft were spread like the primeval wings of a pterodactyl. Bakunin was about to unhook the latch of the cable and plunge himself free.

'Bakunin, what will happen to me, this Third World, if you go?'

'Are you asking me this question, to this Fourth World, Govindankutty?' I saw through the visor of the helmet the flicker of a smile in his moist eyes.

Bakunin unfastened the latch and surged. He floated away, his jagged route making sentences in Russian. When the saw-toothed Cyrillic letters ended, Bakunin rested his chin on his knees and began making his orbit on a linear path.

CIVICS AND PHYSICS PRACTICALS
MAANASI

It maybe because we live in a locality which can be described as somewhat 'civilized' within the that many of us had not seen a leopard cub. That was the reason why we were so very curious when we heard that a leopard cub roamed our apartment building and the areas around it. We didn't meet anyone who had seen the cub. But if we believe only what we see, we will have to refute even the existence of God. Not only that. Neither Ganesh Bhatt nor Sharma would spread a false rumour about the leopard cub. When those who saw it said it had rudraksha-like red spots all over its skin, Ganesh Bhatt joined his palms together in devotion. For us who lived in the city, in the narrow, closed-in rooms devoid of proper ventilation and light, with dark, moss-covered minds that couldn't be spread out in the sun and dried at least now and then, the rumour of the cub arrived like the freshness of a cool breeze.

'Bhagavan incarnated in Kaliyuga, riding such a leopard,' Ganesh Bhatt told us when we got around him to hear the story. 'Bhagavan must have been convinced that in these times when injustice and untruth abound, the ignorant people must be shown some signs. Aren't they, after all, His own creations?'

For us, the ordinary folks who were vexed by the daily occurrence of ominous happenings, avatars and their siddhis were important matters. And for quite some time, we were awaiting someone who could look into our minds. Because it is a great solace for us if there's a man (or a woman) endowed with intellligence and verve and the courage to manage things. Our everyday world is filled with things like the court verdict that proclaimed the house bought with hard-earned money was situated on an illegal plot of land, municipality authorities would arrive anytime with a bulldozer, police who lack the fortitude to give evidence against criminals, but who, nevertheless, turn off drinking water to the neighbourhood, the stinking water that daily spills over to the road from the choked sewage pipes lying uncleaned for years together, the local dadas who swoop down to levy 'maramat hafta' as soon as one so much as digs the yard to plant a drumstick tree and the like. Cleverly enough, we had long ago stopped making appeals for justice or putting forward our arguments. We would keep quiet, giving whatever is demanded. If the question is, 'Isn't there the police?' the answer that comes to my mind is: 'We had already acquired, as racial memory, a contempt for all such uniforms.' Anyhow, none of us would ever approach the police for anything.

'So much of money and dignity will be lost.' Even Menon Saar, the one with the greatest trust in justice and truth would say, 'No. We don't want to do that, in any case.'

It was through the mechanic Sharma that matters escalated from the leopard cub to the one with the Matted Hair. Sharma, while returning from the factory at midnight after the second shift, would usually take out his wristwatch and put it in his vest and chant the name of Rama as he reached the corner by the side of the drain where the hooch distillers were encamped. That day, the distillers or the water that spilled over from the drain were not to be seen on the road. Instead, Sharma was welcomed by a gigantic, matted hair fluttering in the wind and blocking the path. In the light from the crescent moon, the three-line forehead mark above the third eye glittered like silver. It was then the leopard cub had come into Sharma's view, who had prostrated at his feet with Om Namasivaya instead of Rama Rama on his lips. The sewage water had rushed through the drains free of dirt and refuse! Sharma had heard the disembodied voice wafting over the fragrance that rose from the rushing waters!

'I am the forerunner and the saviour.' The utterance was in pure Sanskrit. 'Follow me.'

When he opened his eyes, he was lying across the doorway of his house, in a raging fever.

'He is terribly frightened,' Menon Saar said, cooling Sharma's forehead by sprinkling water. 'Wasn't it at midnight? The mind should cool down gradually.'

When the three-line forehead marks began to appear continuously on the door of Vibhuti Mukherjee, we, the neighbours, looked at each other in amazement. Vibhuti, who was writhing in hellish pain after the surgeon had carelessly sewn up, his stomach and left a napkin inside during the surgery, sat up, forgetting everything. The arrogant Dr Pednekar, who extracted cut-throat fees from all, fell at Vibhuti

Mukherjee's feet who sat immobile as if in meditation. 'Pass the verdict of any punishment on me.' Forgetting that the dust on the mud floor in Vibhuti's house would soil his immaculately white safari suit, Dr Pednekar touched his forehead repeatedly on the floor. 'You can ask for any amount of money. This humble servant will send it here.'

In an excitement that knew no differences of caste, creed, or language, the thought of the power that brought no less a person than Dr Pednekar to his knees, brought tears to our eyes. It was like a crowd lifting a victor bodily off the ground and shouting his praises that we greeted this power. That presence spread among us like the fragrance of virtue, morality, and a sense of security.

In that atmosphere charged with the intoxication of devotion and hope, Savant suddenly began to quake and weep. Wailing, saying that he was a great sinner and craving forgiveness, he rolled in the dust. With that, our suspicions that it was he who had raped the eight-year-old daughter of the sweeper Manohar was confirmed. Neither did Savant refute it. Sharma and Bhatt did not tarry any longer. Within days, above the dilapidated, abandoned pavilion, the flying matted hair and the shining third eye were installed. Acolytes with the three white marks across their forehead, wearing yellow armbands, began acting as mediators in strife and quarrels.

'That piercing gaze touching this body, raises horripilation,' said Bhatt. 'Let alone telling a lie; nobody can ever dare to think up one.'

To erect the image, renovate the pavilion, and then convert it into a hall for holding darshans, money flowed in like water. Many among us felt that it was the building of a dam against the inundating injustice and violence. But when one of neighbours, Mr Joshi, who was a senior official of the municipality, took the initiative to demarcate the public property around the pavilion, fence it in, and put up a pandal there for the devotees to escape the sun, I grew apprehensive.

'Isn't that the playground allotted for the school?' I asked the teacher Meenakshi, who was my neighbour, when I saw the people planting posts along the demarcation and putting up a fence.

'Yes. But isn't it going to be used for a better purpose than the originally intended one? Is playing games greater than divine affairs?'

'Teacher, shouldn't the pandal have been in your courtyard?' Samuel said unexpectedly, tying a rubber band around his ponytail-like long hair reaching down to the neck. 'We could then see whether God, or the courtyard you paid for dearly, was greater for you.'

'If it's to be so, I'd consider it my great good fortune. It's a rare luck to have God at your doorstep. What else is?'

To the acolytes who approached Samuel to distribute the yellow armbands, with the complaint that he is not seen at the pavilion for making the darshan, it was heard that he said, 'Can't God, who can see the whole world sitting where He is, see my mind although I am sitting here?' Samuel didn't buy the yellow armbands either.

'Not buying them isn't the right thing. You wouldn't lose anything if you took those bands and kept them at home.'

'But shouldn't I feel like buying them, If I were to buy them at all?' Samuel's face flushed. 'No one needs to stick a yellow band on my mind.'

'Luck comes by!' Samuel continued, after hawking and spitting out. 'Isn't God at one's doorstep? And yet God will learn that Joshi's daughter is getting married only if the news is blared out over loudspeakers. Is God hard of hearing?'

Samuel was alluding to the bhajans blaring out of the loudspeakers during the last three or four days. Mrs Menon had informed us that it was in connection with Joshi's daughter's marriage.

Samuel continued in his sarcastic vein, 'Isn't it fortunate to be suffering the loss of eyesight and hearing too?'

The picture that rushed to my mind was that of Suraj who had curled up in exasperation with three or four cushions against his ears as I returned from office yesterday.

'You are sleeping day and night,' I said to Suraj sternly. 'Exams are around the corner. I sweat blood to raise money for your education.'

What I said was literally true. For a lower middle-class person like me, my children's study was not a trivial matter to be negligent about. A good amount of money was required for their private tuition, coaching classes, transport expenses, food, and the like. Besides, there were medicines meant for maintaining their power of concentration and increasing their memory and consultation fees charged by doctors. If Suraj who is in the twelfth standard gets one mark less, the thousands of rupees spent like this would be futile. In addition, there was mental tension of the children, their frustration, anxiety about donations to be given to secure college admission, and the depression stemming from struggles. Dr Rao's daughter who lost one and a half marks during the

last examination still locks herself in her room like a nutcase.
My stomach was ablaze.

'Can't you hear this din, Mother?' Suraj was on the brink of tears. 'How can one study, sitting here?' It was only then the fact dawned on me that in spite of Suraj closing all doors and windows, the bhajans from the loudspeakers had completely filled the room.

'Going to that park far away and sitting there is one way out,' I told myself, plugging my ears and Suraj's with big balls of cotton wool. 'Or, we could go to Sarita's house as a last resort.'

'Mother would be discharged this evening,' Samuel said, taking his hand away from his long hair and rubbing his face vigorously. 'Let Joshi come. I will see whether it can be stopped or not.'

Only four days were left for Suraj's exams.

'I will try and persuade Joshi,' I told to placate Samuel. 'You sit with your mother, Samuel.' Samuel's mother is a heart patient. If she comes here from the hospital, she would not be able to sleep at all. Samuel's worry is understandable. He walked about restlessly.

I was certain that matters will become only worse if Samuel and Joshi met. Samuel is one who is easily provoked. That's why I decided to meet Joshi, come what may.

I waited at the window until Joshi's car drew near and came to a halt.

'And a woman, at that!'

'My son is also with me here,' I said, like giving an explanation, pushing Suraj forward. As soon as I said it, the anxiety at self-justification in my statement filled myself with revulsion.

'Suraj's exams are at hand,' I made my voice grave, to hide my embarrassment. 'And there are sick people in the neighbourhood. Don't others also have many things to do? This din for the last three-four days....'

'Mine is a house where a wedding celebration is underway. There's likely to be singing and noise until the wedding is over.'

'What I am beseeching you is to lower the volume. What will the others do if everyone decided to celebrate one thing or the other like this? The exams....'

'What of the others? Only you have complained. Certain things done by people who have money and circumstance won't be understood by those who don't have access to such affluence.'

The barb in Joshi's retort must have really struck me. My voice rose more than was necessary.

'Is it by distressing others that a gentleman celebrates his daughter's wedding?'

'Madam, the loudspeaker is an integral part of a wedding celebration.' The muscles on Joshi's face quivered and twitched. 'This is the way gentlemen celebrate weddings. Try and see if you can stop that.'

More faces appeared in the doorway. Maybe because our voices were raised that the doors of the flats opposite and on the floors above had opened. 'Come, Mother.' Suraj pulled me away by my arm and tried to climb down the stairs. 'Okay, Uncle! So long!'

As we got down the stairs and reached home, the loudspeakers blared even more loudly. Suraj was laughing, looking at my face.

My fear was whether my eyes would brim over, feeling foolish and embarrassed.

'Didn't I tell you at the very outset?' Suraj tumbled on to the sofa, slamming the door shut with a backward push of his leg. 'But Mother couldn't....'

I was piqued when I took the phone from the table without looking at Suraj's face.

⁂

'It is a marriage celebration going on there, madam,' the police said from the other end of the phone. 'Aren't they your neighbours? Aren't song, dance, and bhajans customary for weddings?'

'If people hold their weddings in this fashion, the neighbours would be hard put, officer. For the last three-four days....'

'Stopping the singing of devotional songs will amount to injuring religious sentiments,' the officer said. 'Sorry, we can't do that.'

'The law is not for one individual alone. The others also are to live here.'

'Oh, you are an atheist! Isn't it better for all concerned not to disrespect the Three-eyed One?'

I put down the phone suddenly. My mind burned like the palms of the hand cupped around live embers.

I didn't speak to anyone until I returned home from work the next day. But I was stupefied when I saw a crowd in front of our house. The yellow armband bearers and acolytes were all there. Oh my God! What is it now? Only weariness was left in my mind. Suddenly I saw Samuel, red-faced, trembling in rage. Standing next to him, Menon Saar was trying to calm him down. Samuel was driven to a frenzy when he was not able to hear what was being said from the hospital about his mother's condition over the phone. 'Only we will rule this place,' Joshi's son exclaimed as he drew near to Samuel. 'We are calling the shots here!'

'We?' Samuel's face reddened like a flame. I realized the dimensions of things were mutating very fast. The first thing I did was scrutinize the crowd to ascertain whether Suraj was standing around there. He had told me in the morning itself that he was going over to his friend's house.

'Yes,' Joshi's son continued to bark at Samuel as he advanced. 'Those who don't want to listen to these things can get out, whenever they wish!' The yellow band on Joshi's son's raised hand shone in the evening sun. 'They can also come back as and when they like!'

'What's going out will be the loudspeakers.' Samuel was really flaring. 'I'll have no one commanding me when to stay in my house and when to go away!'

'Aha! What'll you do if I command you?'

I was aware of the consternation seeping through like the muffled rumble of a stream rushing into a pool. The crowd was spreading like the ripples in water where a stone had fallen. And Samuel was not likely to cool down.

Suraj, approaching from the outside, pulled me by my hand as soon as he spotted me.

'Aren't you satisfied, Mother? I am scared. Come away.'

'Leaving these people here like this?' I stared at Suraj as if I heard him speak some obscenity. 'It's only a just demand that the loudspeakers should be stopped. That's what we want too!'

'Come, Mother,' Suraj was not prepared to let me go. 'I have got a lot to write.'

Menon Saar's raised voice, the threats of Joshi's son, and Samuel's shouts together swirled like a whirling vortex.

No one was clear about who had stopped the loudspeakers, or when was the wire connection from the main switch snapped off. I only saw Joshi's son's hand descending on Samuel's head. I held Suraj's hand tightly. Next, I saw Samuel's face sprawled on the ground, through the gaps between the legs of the people standing around the scene. In the jostling melee, Menon Saar fell on his back and lay still. I was at a loss to decide whether to leave the spot or remain there. As the yellow-banded ones kept running here and there, the onlookers had begun to withdraw from the scene, one by one. Open doors and windows were shut one after another. The other end of the loose wire trailing on the ground was coiled around Samuel's neck, and his eyes popped out on his blood-red face.

'Free him; if not, he'll die now,' I yelled, pushing away Suraj who had begun to scream, covering his face with my pallu. My voice was drowned in the din from the loudspeakers that had begun to blare again somehow.

Next, I watched a heavy blow fall on Suraj as he ran towards home, screaming.

With the one blow, the books in Suraj's hand were scattered all over the place. As if in a dream, I saw Suraj curling like a worm on the hand that fell on him.

Lying where I was, I wound myself around Joshi's son's leg like a wet cloth.

'Leave Samuel alone,' I begged, forgetting all sense of shame. 'It's I who phoned the police. My son's having his exams.'

When I was sitting in the car on the way to the hospital with Suraj's head in my lap, there was no one else from our neighbourhood to help me, except two yellow-banded ones.

⁓

In the compound that lay empty like a festival ground after celebrations had ended, there were no loudspeakers or electric wires or the crowd. And Samuel too was not there.

Even Suraj didn't talk to me much after he regained consciousness. No one visited Suraj or me in the hospital either.

Therefore, it was from the yellow-banded ones who came to assist me that I heard, several days later, about Samuel slipping and falling into the sewage canal and disappearing, while running away to escape the crowd.

'Samuel didn't run at all!' I said when I heard the story. 'How could he have run when an electric wire was fastened around his neck?'

'But I saw it when I was returning from Jitu's house,' Suraj said. 'He fell midstream, when he attempted to jump across.'

The interior of the house was covered with dust. Mrs Menon must have neatly piled up on the table all the books that were scattered from

Suraj's hand that day. I noticed that Suraj stood gazing at them.

'Not a single person turned up in the hospital,' I said, sitting on the sofa with Suraj's head in my lap. 'Not even Mrs Menon.'

'Uncle Menon has gone back to Kerala,' Suraj said. 'It is unlikely that he will ever return.'

Another story. Like Samuel falling into the sewage canal!

Looking at Suraj's face I said, 'I saw with my own eyes the wire around Samuel's throat!'

'Mother!' Suraj sprang up from where he lay, startled. 'Can you keep quiet, Mother?'

'It is our duty, the duty of people like us, to tell the police about this, Suraj.' I bolted the door and shut the windows tightly, and stroked Suraj's head. 'Such underhand deeds....'

'I saw with my own eyes Uncle Samuel slipping and falling into the sewage canal,' Suraj said. 'Even the police know that. What if you say it's not like that, Mother?'

I stared at Suraj, with a faint scream that slipped from my throat.

'Did the police say that?'

'It was from the corner at the bend in the canal that Uncle Samuel attempted to jump across,' Suraj went on, twiddling the yellow band that the children had tied around his arm. Taking my hand away from Suraj's head, I looked at the phone right in front of me and then fixed my gaze at infinity, at the other possible end of the line.

'Do you want to ring up someone?' Suraj asked in a measured voice. On top of the consternation in it, the rumble of water rushing through the open sewage canal, and the waves of the bhajans rising from the renovated pavilion, stagnated without moving or flowing.

Like a flame that blazes forth from the fire on embers, my mind retches up Samuel's ruddy face.

'You may not have remembered it, Mother,' Suraj said, stroking my head softly like a rather mature person, 'but today was my Physics practical.'

A LETTER TO A FRIEND PLUNGED INTO DESPAIR

U. P. JAYARAJ

This is a letter 'V' writes from the city of 'T' to his friend 'C', who lived in the city of 'B', in deep melancholy, having been plunged into despair as he was dismissed from his job and was subjected to torture for the 'crime' of sympathizing with the people and attempting to live together with them (participating in their struggles, victories, and hardships alike). That is: this is an incident narrated by my friend who was active underground as a revolutionary for about six years, and then was snitched on by a betrayer and served time.

Once, when the pursuit by the hounds had turned extremely intense and the might of white terror tormented ordinary human existence, this friend somehow got hold of my address and knocked on the door of my rented accommodation in the city. When I opened the door, at first, I was dismayed to see him looking like a bag of bones and with a distraught face. I then shuddered remembering the terrible circumstances prevalent at that time. My friend, on the other hand, betraying no trace of fatigue and offering me a disarming smile with a mischievous twinkle in his eyes, said: 'I have somehow reached here, dodging my horrendously relentless pursuers. The conditions are utterly hopeless. Most of our comrades have been either eliminated, neutralized, or imprisoned. Somehow, we have to rip through this status quo. I intend to spend the night here, and set off on a journey tomorrow morning. Within this time, you must provide me with the money to travel by train over one thousand kilometres, and also with a pair of North Indian clothes.'

As I watched him getting ready to curl up on the cement floor without paying the least attention to me or waiting for my response, I was filled with intense displeasure towards him. What do such types think? It is a fact that all of us aspire for the revolution. But surely, it is not my sole responsibility to maintain it through my financial support. Is he aware of the fact that, as a result of helping out one of his comrades in a similar fashion, I had to live on snacks instead of proper dinner for the past month. I have been leading a miserable life on a half-filled stomach, suffering cold, boredom, and melancholy thoughts.

'Look,' I said, 'long live the revolution! But you and your companions must please stop ordering me about as if it is my personal responsibility to help you. Considering the facts, you seem to be much better off as you somehow get your daily needs fulfilled here and there, and go everywhere and demand this and that on account of the revolution. It's people like me who are undergoing extreme hardships and making the hardest sacrifices. But when it comes to reckoning, I am termed as a coward and a vacillating petit bourgeois, and you all are heroic soldiers of the revolution! Isn't it ironic?'

My friend who was now lying on the floor with his eyes closed, proceeded to sit up as if slightly amazed—his face bore an expression as if my words had greatly amused him—and said to me:

'Your words are so right and fitting. They assure me that I can spend the night here completely trusting you. Anyone who is having the mentality of any other class can never talk so guilelessly.'

Then, he thrust his hand in his soiled shoulder bag scouring for a bidi. Putting it on his lips, he squatted in front of me.

'I will narrate an incident from my life. It happened about four years ago. I had been only one year into my underground life by then. At about that time, when I began to read books voraciously to satiate my youthful curiosity. I wanted to find answers to questions such as why people live as slaves, why do they undergo hellish suffering, why only a minuscule minority manages to turn the earth into their paradise? But then, the police began to become unreasonably suspicious about me. You too know that the police, through their 'timely' intervention, had helped convert into resolute revolutionaries, those who otherwise would have for pure thrill and romantic pursuit, remained teacup revolutionaries and roamed around for long without touching base anywhere, and would finally have ended up serenely in the bedrooms of their fathers-in-law's houses. In my own case, too, what had happened was something similar. After my initial experiences, which were rough and brutal, I began to grasp things doubly fast and went underground before long.

'One of those days, I was deputed to travel to a distant place with an important mission, as per the direction from the top command. During that journey, which I carried out with the utmost caution, I witnessed sights, scenes, and pathetic incidents which were strange, beautiful, and heart-rending as I had not seen before; I cleverly escaped from mishaps more than once; and reached my destination with a precision unique to our operations. After I had safely handed over the records and the details of the mission, the comrade whom I had met took me to a village on the bank of the river Krishna, to wait and rest before my return journey. I do not want to elaborate on the river Krishna and explain as to what kind of a river it is, and where it is, as I suppose that you know all about it. Krishna is one of the reddest rivers of south India.

The incident that I am going to narrate happened after this. My stay was arranged in the hut of an old woman. A grandmother who, though grey all over, was vigorously engaged in one task or the other every minute, and who laughed innocently showing her toothless gums. When the comrade returned without introducing me, I was alone in that hut. After giving me potatoes boiled with red chilli to eat, she sat guarding the sorghum that was spread to dry on a torn mat in the courtyard and started a conversation.

'Why are you so deeply immersed in thought, my son?' the old woman asked me, looking at me and laughing, showing her bare gums. 'I don't see you laughing at all. How horrible our life will be if we do not laugh and be happy!'

I felt sympathy towards her.

'The terrible experiences of my life have caused me to lose the ability to laugh,' I told her. 'What we see and experience is a life totally different from what you see. There is nothing in it to laugh about.'

'It may be true,' she said, trying to shoo away with a bamboo cane, a crow that had tried to land on the sorghum. 'For you all, life may be terrible, isn't it so?'

'Absolutely terrible!' I said. 'We live at the most dangerous levels. We witness the terrible. We fight against evils and cruelties. Blood and death have become constants in our life. We manage to advance forward, although we aren't sure at what moment we are going to go down!'

Listening to my words, the old woman's face turned dark and wracked with thought. Gradually her face turned into one full of tender fondness and affection. She looked at me with eyes shining with their wetness and laughed.

'Certainly you darlings are suffering extreme sacrifices for us all!'

At that moment, with the newborn confidence of gaining validation for my own importance, I asked her: 'How do you live in this hut all by yourself, grandma? Don't you have anyone?'

'I have no one. Yet I have everyone. Grandchildren like you,' the old woman said. She laughed once again, showing her toothless gums as before. 'After my husband was killed in 1948, I have been alone more or less all the time.'

Startling awake to the news, with a shudder of cloudburst in my nerves, I asked: 'What! What was that again? Your husband was killed?'

'Yes.' The old woman said in a deep yet soft voice as if she was cruising by herself through her memories. 'In 1948, during the Telangana struggle, they shot my husband dead.'

I was shocked and sat still like a statue.

'Don't you have children?'

'Yes. I had. The eldest, Basavayya, was murdered in the police station. Though in the newspapers it was reported that he was killed in an encounter, that's not true. The entire village had witnessed Basavayya being picked up by the police from his hideout and being taken away in their vehicle.'

'Wasn't Basavayya your eldest son?' I repeated what she had told me, halting mid-sentence, with a face from where sweat drops emerged and steam came out.

'Yes. The eldest was just like his father. The younger one, Nagayya, is rumoured to be in jail; and some say he is no more. But our comrades say that he is alive and is in jail.'

When the old woman stopped speaking, I sat with my head lowered like a criminal, in shame and self-loathing. At that moment, laughing, showing her gums, with a face radiant in fond affection, the old woman said: 'Oh, listening to me talk, you have stopped eating! Eat, my son, eat! It doesn't make much difference if we the old ones eat or not. We have wasted our entire lifetime without doing any grand things. But you, our grandchildren, our darlings, must eat to your fill and grow strong!'

Finishing the narration thus, my friend who was squatting before me, threw away the bidi that had gone out and said: 'This little incident taught me the real meaning of life, struggle, and sacrifice. Never afterwards had I to look back while I've had to traverse obstacles.'

Yet, this is the letter 'V' writes from the city of 'T' to his friend 'C', who was living in the city of 'B', in deep melancholy, and with an oscillating mind:

For each fighter who collapses, there's another one who

resurrects like the head of Ravana. Each brave fighter who takes the struggle forward, multiplies in their thousands, like the arrows of Rama.

The sunlight is dappling the outside. Memories are rising. The crows are cawing. The wind is blowing. The trees are swaying. The canopy of the woods is undulating.

Exploitations are multiple.

Exactly for the same reason, the struggle continues.

TWO HISTORIANS AND A YOUNG WOMAN
GRACY

They were immersed in history. Dusk had fallen. Exactly at the centre of the table, like a thick candle, an empty vodka bottle dispersed the memories of their several past lives. With that, the elder historian untied his imaginary kuduma, the mane of hair tied into a bun, as was wont by ancient scholars. Then he rubbed the imaginary, red-stoned stud in his unpierced earlobe. Holding, with the thumb of his left hand, the imaginary sacred thread worn diagonally across his torso as Brahmins do, he was immersed deep in thought for a moment. Then he cleared his throat.

'Can you forget this face that easily?'

The younger historian roused himself from past memories and raised his face towards the Namboodiri Brahmin melshaanti, the chief priest, of Perinjanam temple in the kingdom of Kochi. The chief priest who had a wife and five children, had married a twenty-two-year-old antharjanam, a Namboodiri woman, as his second wife. Reaching his illam, the ancestral Namboodiri home, once a week from the far-off temple where he presided over the pujas, he experienced ratisukham, conjugal bliss, with his second wife. But he was not enough for this beautiful young woman.

The chief priest had been making very good earnings from the temple. He used to keep all that money in a copper pot and bury it in the temple courtyard at night, without anyone seeing it. The night before his weekly departure to his illam, he would transfer the contents of the copper pot to a towel and make a bundle of it. Setting off with it before dawn the next morning, he would reach his illam, hand over the money to his second wife and make her happy. During a night after enjoying carnal pleasures with her to his surfeit, he shared with her the secret of the copper pot. And enjoined upon her not to breathe a word about it to anyone. The chief priest continued to collect the takings from the temple weekly from the copper pot, make it into a bundle, and carry it home at the next daybreak. But when the Namboodiri dug for the copper pot one night, he could not find it in the spot he used to bury it. Though the Namboodiri spent the rest of the night sleeplessly thinking about the thief who stole the copper pot containing his money, he did set out towards his illam at dawn as usual. When he told his second wife about what had happened, she beat her breast and wailed. Anyhow, the Namboodiri lodged a complaint with Shaktan Thampuran, the legendary king of Kochi. The first thing that the Thampuran asked the Namboodiri was whether he had told anyone about the copper pot. He told the king that he had not shared the secret with no one else, but his second wife. Lost in thought for a brief while, the king promised the Namboodiri that he would certainly catch the thief. The king then presented the Namboodiri with a bottle of a very special kind of attar. He sent the priest off, with the instructions that he could use it personally sometimes, and never to give it to anyone else. When the Namboodiri visited the king the next week, the latter did not even mention the thief. Instead, he disguised himself in the uniform of a Nair soldier and took the Namboodiri along with him for the pooram, an important temple festival, at Aaraattupuzha. With the consternation wrenching his mind as to how the king was going to catch the thief if he went about celebrating the festival, the Namboodiri nevertheless tagged along with the king, looking at the various spectacles in the festival grounds.

When the king approached the merchant who sold dates and puffed rice, the special fragrance of the attar which he had given to the Namboodiri struck his nostrils. The king, who became aware that the fragrance was wafting from a youth who was purchasing dates from the merchant, drew his sword from his waist and raised it against him. As the youth trembled in fear, the king interrogated him and learned that he was a Nair, the mahout of the elephant at the illam of the Namboodiri's second wife. The mahout confessed to his crime before the king, prostrated before him, and sought his forgiveness. The king immediately instructed the Namboodiri to make arrangements for the smaarthavichaaram, the special ethics court of the Namboodiri community to try the erring antharjanam woman.

The elder historian, who was relishing his own narration of the events of his former birth as if it was someone else's story, commented to the younger historian, continuing from where he left off in his memories: 'It is that second wife who has been reincarnated as the second scholar who has joined the research programme under my supervision. We both are in love with her. Since I have revealed the secret about my relationship with her in my former birth, isn't it right and fitting that you should withdraw from your affair with her?'

The younger historian laughed, as he retched and released outside the aftertaste of the pickle he had licked after downing his vodka. 'Thirumeni, O exalted Brahmin, when, after the Smaarthavichaaram, she was ostracized and cast outside the gatehouse of the illam, I and my elephant were waiting outside on the lookout for her. The elephant shook his tusks and swished his trunk at the people of other castes who had gathered to grab her as she emerged from the gate; the elephant further trumpeted and chased after them and they fled. Returning the elephant to the illam, the antharjanam and I left the kingdom of Kochi and sought refuge in the kingdom of Travancore. We had four children during our wedded life together. So, who is her real claimant?'

The elder historian lost his footing and tottered at the climax of the story. Then he immediately roused his self into action, narrating an older story of his previous birth with renewed vigour.

Cheraman Perumal, one of the Chera rulers who reigned over all of Kerala, had four wives in four different swaroopams or subsidiary kingdoms. The most beautiful of them all was the Kettilamma, the leading lady and the king's sister, of the royal family of the kingdom of Kolathunaadu. The king's chief minister was an extremely handsome man with the highest martial arts prowess. His physical charms made the Kettilamma lose her sleep. The minister had to take out all his manoeuvring skills to evade the Kettilamma's snare. Left with no choice, and her mind enthralled by his charisma, she opened her mind before him. But that gem of a man was not without conscience as to accede to the desires of that woman. The Kettilamma, blinded with the rejection and thirsting for revenge, made the charge before Cheraman Perumal, her husband, that the minister had attempted to rape her, and she, who is sworn to lifelong fidelity to her husband, had managed to escape because of the grace of God. She succeeded in convincing her husband, who issued the command to have the minister beheaded immediately. The Perumal began to have second thoughts right after the execution. Therefore, he decided to have the character of his wife subjected to a test. The Perumal sent to Kolathunaadu his most trusted pageboy who was a strikingly handsome young man with a robust physique, with the instruction that he should report all news regarding the Kettilamma promptly. Seeing the young man, the Kettilamma was filled with desire for him. The young man kept on updating the Perumal as to the extreme difficulty with which he had been dodging the moves of the Kettilamma. Finally, stricken with remorse that he had executed an innocent man listening to the words of such a woman, of the lowest moral standards, the Perumal gave up his kingdom and became a mendicant.

'You know that I was the Perumal, and the Kettilamma was this young scholar. Don't you remember who you were in this story?'

The younger historian, with a mysterious smile, nodded his head with a smile and said with fake humility:

'I was that trusted pageboy who went to Kolathunaadu, on the Perumal's mission. And all the details I gave the Perumal about the Kettilamma were true as well. But you must realize one thing. To reject the entreaty of a lust-filled woman would attract consequences that are worse than injuring a cobra and letting it go. Therefore, it was by playing the role of a humble slave of the Kettilamma, and she herself playing the self-same role as a submissive lover for me, that I kept sending those reports to you. It was the Kettilamma herself who told me that the Perumal was not so despicable as to murder a woman, and that at the most he would only forsake her. Though I had made use of all favourable circumstances, since the Kettilamma was a barren woman I could not leave a trace of myself with her.'

'Oh, my fate! The one I entrusted to watch over her, himself became the betrayer!' The elder historian wiped his nose and mumbled, utterly shattered. 'You, the worst of sinners! This young woman scholar whom we both are in love with, is that barren Kettilamma! Even after becoming a mendicant, I could not find peace, and I therefore decided to punish myself. The only way to do it, is to hold that same woman to my bosom once again.'

Suppressing a laughter that retched up from within him, the young historian disguised it as a hiccup and then said: 'There may be punishments in hell like cuddling a red-hot iron statue. But aren't we here, on earth? Not only that, do the rulers of yore eat leftovers? Aren't those meant for serfs like me?'

Undoing the costume of the Perumal, the elder historian was in a dilemma as to what role to assume next. He picked up the masala peanuts from the plate and threw them into his mouth one by one. The younger historian said: 'Now it is my turn. Let me place a past life episode of mine alongside a historically famous moment.'

After King Marthanda Varma of Travancore overran the kingdom of Kayamkulam, his avarice found him contemplating annexing the kingdom of Chempakassery. Marthanda Varma who arrived with a massive army at the eastern side of the bund at Thottappally that separated the sea from the backwaters, encountered the battle-ready Chempakassery army. When the king realized that they were all Brahmins, he was in a dilemma. As the terrible sin of brahmahatya was unbearable for him if he were to commit it, Marthanda Varma turned back with his army. Captain De Lannoy, the commander of the Travancore army, could not in any way agree with the king's decision to withdraw. The Dutchman gave him his word that if the king permitted him, he would certainly defeat the Chempakassery army. Thus, the Travancore army once again marched towards Chempakassery. They disembarked from the warships at Purakkaatt beach. De Lannoy seeing a mighty fort there, issued the command to attack it. The Chempakassery army that rushed out of the fort, unleashed a withering counterattack on the advancing Travancore army. As several soldiers died, De Lannoy realized that it was not easy to conquer the fort. Despite the best efforts of the Travancore army over a week, De Lannoy failed to achieve any progress. Meanwhile, Marthanda Varma had sent some spies over to Chempakassery. One of them contacted the most trusted aide of the Chempakassery king, a certain Kurup, bribed him with money and extracted from him a crucial secret concerning the fort. Though the fort at Purakkaatt looked like a granite-built one, it was actually built with teakwood palisades driven to the ground, with reed mats draped over, and expertly painted to appear like granite rubble work. De Lannoy at first refused to believe it. Therefore, Kurup swore he would pull out a teak post from the palisade and show it to the Travancore army at the time of attack. As De Lannoy became convinced of the truth, he ordered one corner of the fort to be set ablaze. The Travancore army stormed into the fort through the other side and the remaining Chempakassery army fought to the death. Following this the king of Chemapakassery was captured as a prisoner of war. With that, the kingdom of Chempakassery ceased to exist and was merged with Travancore.

Kurup's wife detested her husband who betrayed his own country and king, and therefore left home and wandered aimlessly. Even in those times, patriotism was a priceless commodity. She, however, landed unawares in front of De Lannoy, by a quirk of fate. The Dutchman, who was a bachelor, fell in love with her, and made her his wife.

The young historian who stole a furtive glance at the elder historian made a surprise move.

'It is so surprising that you have not been able to detect De Lannoy from my quartz-coloured irises. It will be enlightening for you to learn how your erstwhile wife encountered with her body, my stuttering Malayaazhma (the Malayalam-Tamil-mixed patois spoken by the Travancore royals). She quenched her thirst by thrusting her swelling breasts in my mouth and filled the skin of my body with the fragrance of her mouth from the chewing of paan with exotic ingredients. She kissed my quartz-eyes with her fulsome lips and imprisoned my sleep. She willingly bore me a son. It was not her fault that my son was stillborn. She is this young scholar whom both of us love. I don't think that proud woman will accept back someone whom she had rejected once with all her heart.'

The incensed elder historian pulled from the tabletop a sword visible only to him. The angry young historian too pulled out another invisible sword. In the swish of that sword, the vodka bottle that had stood so far with an inscrutable smile, lost its neck, and was knocked over. Ignoring the shards of glass shattered on the floor, both the historians continued their sword duel until daybreak, and then fell back to both sides, in total exhaustion.

A PATH IN THE MOONLIGHT
N. PRABHAKARAN

Moonlit nights are surely a reality even in these times. Scattering spangles of intoxication among the wakeful beings, some human beings are filling themselves with it like fabulous Chinese jars.... No. In my case, nothing of the sort happened. I was in conversation with a friend, full of levity and with the equanimity of an ordinary human being. We must have been in the portico of his house.

This friend with a moon face and a handsome body was a television repairman. Except for a clandestine infatuation with music, other desires of the soul were alien to him. Literature, the graphic arts, politics, etc., would never peep into his thinking. Though fully aware that straight paths are seldom found in this world, he was never worried about it. He lived as though there was no one who could spread thorns across his path. The flow of this faith enveloped all his actions like the morning sun. 'A man full of grace,' I used to call him inwardly.

It was an exceptionally moonlit night. Although out of context, I remembered something. It hadn't been many days since I was elected to the district council. It was a stiff contest, and I had managed to scrape through with a margin of sixteen votes. I was relieved, and my friend was jubilant that I won. We talked for a long time about many ordinary and trivial matters. All that time, his sister was sitting next to us in a cane chair, reading a novel.

My friend and I are around thirty-five. His sister is past thirty. She is the wife of a bank employee and the mother of two children. However, it was as a young girl, dressed in a light top and a white miniskirt with small saffron flowers printed on it, that I saw her now. Her countenance, though grave, was serene and pretty. Once upon a time, I had loved this girl furtively and had somehow managed to utter one or two words hinting at my love.

When the conversation between my friend and I reached a juncture where it remained sluggish, she stopped reading, stood up, and started singing an ancient Chinese song in a most dulcet voice. That song was filled with the heartaches of a young woman called Linging who had loved a hunter named Wangchou without his knowledge. When the song was over, I stood up and congratulated her rather formally. Then I told them, 'I am going now. See you two months later.'

'Two months! It is good that one can forget a politician at least for two months a year,' she said.

I should have been pained by her remark but I pretended to laugh it off like it was an ordinary joke. Then I got out and walked away.

While walking through a clean alley on whose either side resided high-ranking officials and rich merchants, my mind drifted to the song. None of us knew the Chinese language. Then how could she sing that song? How did I grasp its meaning? How could I visualize with my mind's eye an orchard in the Fukian region? It is all so very strange. I can say with certainty that I am not dreaming. It is unlikely such a logical strain of thought can be present while dreaming.

I stood still for a moment, firmly resolving to have my doubts cleared. With a strange tremulousness in my soul, I began to move forward. I turned a corner and saw that the path had become very narrow. The wall on the left had been slightly pushed forward. It had only been two or three days since the wall had been rebuilt. The cold smell of cement and mortar was still in the air. The plot beyond that wall belonged to Koneri Damu, a land broker. It was Damu who had steered my election campaign. I had heard many things whispered against Damu. I was not at all interested in appointing him as the chairman of my election committee. But the party had insisted. Or it was Damu that made the party decide.

One of these days someone would surely complain to me about the encroachment of the public pathway, and that it would necessitate a confrontation with Damu. If presented straightforwardly, Damu will scoff at the matter. Subtle manoeuvres must be set in motion. Similar incidents will recur if he is not subdued in time. Damu, who used to be a nobody within the party and in public life, had emerged as a centre of power centre before one's very eyes. Many approached him for favours. A group of acolytes had formed around Damu. Student activists, youth leaders, and even leaders of teachers' organizations were busy imitating his ways. Grooming their hair Damu style, laughing like him, hawking and spitting noisily like him.... From now on, things cannot be allowed to go on this way. In my capacity as a councillor, I can do certain things. I can also look forward to the support of the idealists in the party.

Ruminating and turning many bends, I arrived in front of Kuppuswamy's ashram. This ashram was one of the cornerstones of civic life in my division. It is rumoured that while Kuppuswamy was still alive, several dubious incidents including prostitution and murder had taken place in this ashram. Now the head of the institution was Yoginiamma, one of Kuppuswamy's old handmaids. She may have a name of her own. But everyone calls her Yoginiamma.

I had gone to the ashram along with Damu to meet this woman. I wanted to avoid such an audience with her, but Damu had not budged. 'You ask me whether you should meet her? Any doubts about that? There are three hundred twenty-seven votes in that woman's hand. That is not a trifle as far as this division is concerned. If you go and bow your head before her, she will bless you. They have a notion that we will win. The ashram's politics is to stand firm with the winners. If we do not meet them, they will act with vengeance.'

I do not know whether Yoginiamma helped us or not. Nevertheless, she had treated us with great affection when we visited her. When that woman, clad in a saffron sari and reclining in an easy chair, had raised her withered hand above my head in benediction, for some reason I felt a sensation of fear.

But now, clad in a gold-bordered garment, she is strolling among the flowering plants in the ashram's courtyard garden with the sprightliness of a Thiruvathira dancer. The middle-aged man walking behind her, like a dwarf with a very long tail, was chewing something. I burst out laughing, noticing his tail trailing behind on the ground.

When I passed the main gate, another astonishing sight caught my eye. The ashram's wall had grown across the path and had touched the wall opposite, completely blocking the alley. 'This is sheer roguery; I am not going to allow this at any rate,' I must have said to myself. My body must have quivered all over, and I must have gnashed my teeth, and the blood must have rushed to my eyes. When I suddenly lifted my head and looked up, I saw Piandre sitting on the wall, wearing a sports blazer and cowboy hat and smoking his pipe serenely. Piandre, the agent of an arms manufacturing company in the United States, is a well-known figure. Although we hadn't met each other before, Piandre smiled at me like one would at an old friend. For my part, I engaged him in conversation about a profound subject.

'Poetry is pain; it is an all-consuming thirst; it is a fire-flower that blooms in the dark valleys of solitude,' I said in one breath.

Piandre nodded his head in agreement. Then he proffered his hand in perfect amity. Hanging on to that sturdy hand and lifted high in the air, I fell on the other side of the wall. Immense glee filled my senses. Whose hand did I catch hold of? Who lifted me off the ground with a single hand? How did I merit such luck?

For what length of time did I stand transfixed on the path beyond the ashram, immersed in the headiness of blissful oblivion! The first thing that caught my eye was an extensive coconut grove. Thousands of coconut palms laden with coconuts growing luxuriantly. At a single glance, one can see that they are the high-yielding variety. Somehow, I felt I should get hold of that grove by any means. I should continue in politics for another five or six years. Then I should put an end to all that and come and live here with my family. Money for the asking, as much serenity as you want, and above all, the much-celebrated existence in perpetual communion with nature. In this grove there is a way to reach the fullness of life. For the time being, some funds should be organized to make a token advance payment for this land. It could be easily managed if Piandre would give it a thought.

Koneri Damu should be the agent. In my knowledge, there is no another man as experienced as Damu when it comes to land deals. Let us forget for the time being that he had extended his wall far out into the public road. If there are any allegations rising against him in the party, they can be silenced in an appropriate manner. These days it is always better to be friendly to everyone. Even Gorbachev, who is so much more diligent and worldly wise than I am, is thinking along these lines. Above anything else it is maturity and equanimity that are important. Everything else will automatically follow. In the meanwhile, I have learned some lessons. If I sufficiently put my mind to the game, I can proceed with confidence. Yes, here I am, close to the threshold of success. All circumstances are in my favour. Nothing is likely to go away. A careful step... just a single step!

Perhaps the inordinate excitement had caused me to tightly shut my eyes. When I forced them open, I saw my friend's sister right in front of me. She came running and caught hold of my hands and kissed them all over. Then, leaning on to my shoulder she told me, 'You should not have forgotten me; you should not have hidden your love.'

Watching the public exhibition of her love or hearing her emotional words—I am not sure which—young men sitting on the platform under the peepul tree had laughed aloud. 'What a savage thing to do,' the expression on their face seemed to say. The youths ranged from workers of a communal party with roots in my division, to some extremists. Their sarcasm was beyond the limits of my endurance. I was overwhelmed by an intense desire to save myself from humiliation. I wanted to demonstrate that I had no part whatsoever in this love affair.

'Hey! What nonsense is this!' I pushed her aside with a theatrical flourish and marched forward. But I faltered on my very first step. I slipped and fell into a deep chasm.

I must have lain unconscious for quite some time. When I opened my eyes and looked around, I saw a green grassy expanse. Her last words enveloped me like the fragrant air from a distant valley.

I do not know when, but I saw a man dressed in a long, flowing Arabian gown and a headdress of golden lace. There was a big watermelon in his hand. He moved in at a leisurely pace, tossing the melon high in the air every now and then and catching it in the palm of one hand. When I ran up and reached his side, he wheeled around abruptly. His hairless face, though pleasant, was quite pale.

'Where are you going? Where are we?' I asked him with perplexity.

'You started off from the world of the dead. Although you went astray in between, you are now back in the same world.' He handed over the watermelon to me and walked away, disappearing from my sight.

Again I was alone—the primordial sky, the boundless expanse of green, this watermelon, and I. Enough...it is enough. There is no meaning in continuing with this story.

There is no golden seed or anything wondrous resting inside this watermelon. Only the red flesh and faintly sweet juice that quenches thirst, revives, and gives one the joy of life for at least a little while. There is only thing that I can say: this fruit had grown hugging the earth, learning the secrets of sweetness under the soil. I hope that there is at least one reader who has followed me all this way. I give it to him.

POMEGRANATE TREES BLOSSOM STILL
C. V. BALAKRISHNAN

'Aren't you alone? Don't stay here, Father. Until now you lived only looking after Mother. She is gone. Who else is here now? You know without me having to say this, but Ramani and I can't live here and look after you and the house, Father. So....'

As the son continued speaking in that strain, he stood motionless looking at the pomegranate trees in the courtyard. The son could not see his mother looking for blossoms on the pomegranate branches. As usual, she was clad in white. The father walked quietly towards the pomegranate trees. *Did you hear what your son said? He wants to sell this house! Then he would go to the city and take me with him. There, if I fall ill—now that I am so old, I may fall ill anytime—the Medical College Hospital is near his house. They have several expert doctors. Even if it is a disease of the heart, lung, brain, or anything else, there is nothing to be afraid of. Excellent treatment will come my way. That is, one does not have to die... ever. We can live as an immortal being. Hasn't our son said that you are gone! Who is here then? But I have a doubt...maybe because I am not as wise as he is. Which way did you go? Can you go just like that? Aren't you here itself?*

'Father, you haven't said anything yet,' the son prompted.

The son saw only the father. His eyes were fixed on the pomegranate branches shaking lightly in the wind. He stood recollecting something and then trying to forget what he recalled.

The wind kept blowing.

On the road to Thirunavaya, the son watched the father's reflection in the rearview mirror. The father sat reclined in the back seat, his eyes closed. To his left was the urn containing the ashes from the pyre.

He slowly opened his eyes and saw a peepul tree on the boundary of the paddy fields. Beyond that, he could discern a dark temple wall. Inside the wall, was the gopuram that served as a haven for doves.

He asked his son to stop the car: 'I shall go inside, offer my prayers, and come back soon. Come along, if you feel like it.'

'No, Father, you go ahead.'

The son lit a cigarette and watched his father walk towards the fields. Father is like this. Has always been. Obstinate. Father wants to win always. But he suffered only one defeat. Mother departed first.

When it came to being stubborn, Mother stood second to none. As soon as she was discharged from the hospital, she declared: 'Straight homeward'.

Everyone tried persuading her, but there was no change in her resolve...she was as stubborn as a child.

Suppressing his anger, he had taken Father aside and stood looking at his face for some time. Finally, he said: 'Mother is ill. Let her be. But won't you at least understand, Father?'

'I don't understand what you mean,' his father had answered in a subdued voice. 'Haven't you heard what Mother said, Father?'

'I heard. What of it? Your mother only said she wanted to go home, didn't she?'

'Go home?' the son exclaimed. 'How can the two of you live so far away alone. Everyone would blame me for being a careless son. It would look like I did not let you live here with me.'

'Don't worry. Isn't this your mother's wish? Let it be. Poor thing, she has had only a few little wishes like this.'

'All right. Agreed. But I can't come and visit every now and then. I have tours and conferences. Even if I want—'

'You don't have to. Come and see us whenever you have the time and the opportunity, free from all busy affairs. Both of us will be there, each being the other's helper. Isn't it better this way? Your mother and I would not want to burden anyone. If we are to live with you, it will be an inconvenience for your wife and children. We can avoid all that.'

'Why are you deciding for yourself that it will be inconvenient for us, Father? Has anyone said so? You and Mother can stay with me without any problem. Also, Mother needs her check-up every now and then.'

'Now there is no need for check-ups any more.'

'Is it for you to decide, Father? Dr Menon said—'

'What can Dr Menon, Dr Pillai, Dr Thomas, Dr Bhagyalakshmi, and all the rest do now? Isn't your mother dying? Haven't they washed their hands off her and said she no longer requires treatment? How much time did they give her? Three months? Six months? Let it be. I will look after her until she dies. You need only to let her die in peace. Nothing more.'

The father's voice was choked, and eyes his had become moist. As the son stood stupefied at the outburst, he had hurriedly wiped his eyes and with a smile, patted him soothingly on the shoulder and walked towards the mother.

The mother was now sitting in the back seat. The father was walking through the paddy fields, returning after offering worship.

⁂

Throwing the cigarette away, the son waited for the father to return to the car. He was holding a plantain leaf with a little prasadam. Sandal paste, tulsi leaves, and flower petals.

'Let's go,' and he shut the door.

The son started the car.

After a little while, the mother was seen sobbing, pressing her face on the father's shoulder. Holding her close, the father whispered: '*Do not weep. Aren't we going home?*'

The bits of bones picked up from the pyre are kept in the house. They should be immersed in Rameswaram or Kasi. Only the portion for water remains. A nilavilakku burns in the mother's room. Pouring oil and drawing out the wick a little, the father closes the door behind him, leaving a small gap through which the flicker of the lamp can be seen.

Paruamma comes every day and sweeps the room and the courtyard. Crows caw. The wind blows through the pomegranate blossoms. The father takes up the hoe and clears the foot of the trees. His body perspires. The son can see his father's bare back shining with beads of sweat. He can see his father's moving muscles, his damp brow, and his dimming eyes.

The father is ruminating over something. He steps back a little, slowly stretches his tongue to one corner of the mouth, and touches his grey eyebrows with his fingers.

Those pomegranate trees had been planted by the mother. The son believes that the father is remembering her. The cow moos in its shed. When the father was with the mother in the hospital, the cow was in Paruamma's house. When the son had suggested that Paruamma tends to it, the father had only smiled.

The father cleans the cowshed himself. Looking through the western window, the son can see the father holding cow dung in his palms. The father scoops the entire pile, puts it in the nearby pit, and covers it with straw soaked in dung and urine. The father comes out, the pungent odour of the cow shed lingering around him.

The father takes a dip in the pond and rises. Sitting on a stair leading to the water, the son looks at the father. The father disappears again. The son searches intently before the father resurfaces at another spot in the pond.

The father, lost in darkness, reaches up to the water's surface. The son sees grey strands of hair and the shining scalp in between. The father plunges into the darkness. The son's eyes are looking. Nothing is visible. Suddenly he hears the father's voice, reciting a shlokam from the Gita. The son listens carefully. Silence, once again.

'Father,' he calls out in fright.

The father answers comfortingly:

'The atman is without birth, without death.
It doesn't become existent after previous non-existence;
nor does it cease to exist after previous existence.
It is birthless, changeless, and eternal.
It does not die when the flesh dies.'

'Father!'

Only an echo answers. Nothing more to be heard. Darkness spreads everywhere. When he wakes up, there is a crow at the window.

A cold wind entered the room. There was mist outside, the sunlight yet to arrive. Mist, like thin smoke. The father was near the pomegranate trees, walking around them in wonder and happiness. They were in bloom.

Seeing the son's face through the branches, the father beckoned to him, waving his hand like a child calling his friend. To come closer and watch those blossoms.

HOW MANY JENNYS ARE THERE IN ANTHIKKAD?

ASOKAN CHARUVIL

This story does not have much of a connection to its title. I have written it here just as an adornment. John Abraham, who exists amongst us like a question mark, first living and then dying, has written a story titled 'How Many Mathais Are there in Kottayam?'

The theme of that story, as indicated by its title, is an enumeration of the people named Mathai in Kottayam. The author scours telephone directories and voters lists for this purpose. Here, there is no relevance to such a quest. The question as to how many girls in Anthikkad are called Jenny is not the core of this story. (It will be of interest to the reader to know that Jenny was the name of Karl Marx's wife. Anthikkad is traditionally a predominantly communist-dominated village.)

But in Anthikkad—a green and white countryside west of Thrissur, located between the Kole paddy fields and a river—there are several Jennys. At Kaanjaani or Peringottukara, you can ask any slim, fairly dark girl who stares at you with arching eyebrows. Whatever name she says, without any bashfulness and with a hint of insolence, you would certainly hear 'Jenny'.

This is not a question of your hearing. The locals of Anthikkad have no line separating dream and reality. For an entire kilometre, you'll find chattansevamadhams—centres of sorcery—and toddy shops. Each family owns a separate sacred grove and kalari. The worshipped deities are Karimkutty (a ferocious form of Kuttichattan, the dwarf goblin), Teechchaamundi (the fire-dancing Devi), Muttappan (ancestor god of the Tiyyas), and Brahmarakshassu (the ghost of a Brahmin who had met a violent death). Every dawn, it was only after lighting lamps of oblation at the site of worship that the communist leaders would proceed to the party office at Thrissur.

Dark, fearsome sacred groves dedicated to serpents can be seen among the coconut groves. The paddy fields appear intensely green. The alleys and pathways are pure white. Small ponds covered in weeds lie steeped in silence. The soft sound of the wind blowing in the screw pine thickets is heard. A small house with a thatched roof made of braided coconut palm fronds and a courtyard covered in white sand. The base of the coconut tree is darkened by the ash used to scour vessels. The water collects in mud jars covered with coconut shells. This is Jenny's house. On the front veranda, her father sits with his legs stretched out into the courtyard. He is generally known as Secretary Shankarettan. Presently, he is not the secretary of anything. He used to be a toddy tapper. Now he is too weak. Contracting jaundice multiple times has made him feeble. His eyes are yellow and his cheeks sag. His joints and feet are inflamed. He wears a small raw cotton mundu as a loincloth. He sits looking at the bright sun that has come out after the rains have stopped.

This scene is an old one—ten years old. It exists now in Sateeshan's memories. He is the protagonist of this story. This isn't Jenny's tale but Sateeshan's. In his mind, there are several old pictures with faded colours. Yet, this particular scene is fresh.

*

Sateeshan is standing on a street in Moscow, frozen and silent but teeming with crowds. He is a hawker. Expensive watches, pens, shoes, calculators, cameras, torches, albums, and porn video cassettes—these are his merchandise. It's been ten years since he had arrived in Russia.

Suddenly, Sateeshan remembered having strolled along this very same street in the company of a Jenny from Anthikkad. As he tried to intertwine his fingers with hers, she said: 'My palm is quite rough, Sateeshan.'

He looked at her face. She continued apologetically: 'Don't you remember we had studied about the princess who dipped her palms in the snow and made them soft?'

Sateeshan's recollection begins in front of a store where toddy was measured out. He had got off a bus at that spot to go to Jenny's house. The small markets of Anthikkad surround such toddy stores. He remembers seeing movie posters, flags and hoardings of political parties, a banner announcing Ashtamangalyaprashnam, and the news bulletin board of the Shastra Sahitya Parishad. Heaps of river fish for sale lined the streets. Bustling stores sold meat, vegetables, dry fish, and groceries. People had formed little groups after they measured out their toddy into the storage jars. In their hands were empty jerry cans. Inside the store, newspapers were being read aloud, and discussions were in progress.

When Sateeshan had enquired about Jenny's house, they were confused. Which Jenny's house?

'Jenny, the daughter of Vishwambharan Mash, Jenny, the daughter of Shivaramettan, or Jenny, the sister of Karunan.'

'Shivaramettan's daughter is not Jenny. She's Natasha. Her younger sister is Nadia.'

Suddenly recognition dawned on one of them.

'I can say who this is. Isn't it the girl who's going to Russia? Secretary Shankarettan's daughter. The girl who is studying for her M.A.'

Although monsoon was over, water ran through the alley. The bottom of Sateeshan's trouser legs were wet and muddy. Grasshoppers and the scent of maangaanaari, the mango-smelling plant, drifted from the mud bunds. Some of the screw pines had bloomed. A soft breeze swept over the ripe paddy fields

'A guest is coming towards our house, my dear!' Shankarettan exclaimed, sitting on the veranda. He looked at the visitor intently. His vision had lost its sharpness. He was able to discern people only as shadows.

'Jenny and I study together,' Sateeshan introduced himself. By that time, she had come out to join her father. She was breathless with amazement.

'Achcha, this is Sateeshan I have told you about. He's the one who is going to Russia with me. He is the student leader in our college.'

'Yes, yes. You told me. But it hasn't stayed firm in my memory. My intellect and consciousness have all gone!' Shankarettan said.

Sateeshan took some time to untie his shoelaces and then sat on a bench

'I never expected you'd take the trouble to come here, Sateeshan. Leaping across these paddy fields and streams. It's such a hassle for you!'

'I loved taking the trouble.'

'I heard that you were not well,' Sateeshan asked Shankarettan.

'I have become too weak. I was admitted to the Thrissur civil hospital for a month. Between life and death. Now I live as if I am dead. I can't work any more. I don't think I can climb coconut trees. I have given away the tapping business to someone for half the returns. It was when I returned from the hospital that I got to know about her trip to Russia. Oh, when I think of her going to Russia, my heart shudders.'

'Why should you be worried? Aren't we all with her? Isn't it to

Russia that we are going? What difficulty will anyone face there?'

'Of that, I am confident. Isn't she going to Russia? Lenin's Russia?' Shankarettan's dark face immediately lit up

Jenny invited him inside, 'Come, Sateeshan. Don't you want to see our home? Be careful, mind your head so it does not hit the door frame. Aren't you really tall?'

Inside the house, the walls were only half the normal height. The floor had been polished with cow dung and charcoal. Sateeshan descended into a small lean-on adjacent to the kitchen. Jenny's mother was busy arranging food—tea, ada (stuffed rice cake), and Avalos (a powder made from rice flour and coconut scraps). She had a pallid complexion and seemed anxious—it was her second nature.

'Have you been to Russia before, son?' she asked.

'No. This is my first time.'

'Don't you have to change many planes to reach there? I am scared even to think about it. I have made an offering of five ladles of oil to Muttappan. That's my only solace....'

'What all do you get to eat there? Jenny absolutely refuses to eat her meals unless she gets fish curry in which kokum is added,' Shankarettan said.

'Sateeshan is a Namboodiri, achcha! In olden days, Vedic yagnas were organized in their illam.'

'Is he? That's very good! My only Namboodiri acquaintance is Eeshan. You'd have heard. He would be positioned at the base of the coconut tree when I was tapping toddy at the riverside above the terrace. He would wait there, eager to make me join the union. We gave him the slip and scuttled away whenever we spotted him. But when Eeshan found out about our tactics to avoid him, he employed a special ruse. How could we escape if he waited for us at the base of the coconut tree we were tapping toddy from?'

Sateeshan burst out laughing.

'Then what happened? I joined the union. If one joins the union, it should look one has really joined it. I was the secretary at number 14. The police vehicle came with a whoosh and first caught hold of me. Their kick landed in the centre of my belly. Can't describe what happened later.'

'Oh, all that's just fine,' Shankarettan continued. 'Though I got kicked around by the police, the times have changed. Look. Now my daughter is studying for her M.A., and she is about to go to Russia in a plane. Isn't it true that Lenin's dead body is still preserved there?'

'Yes. It is kept embalmed. We will go and visit the mausoleum.'

'Oh, my gods!'

Shankarettan looked heavenwards, joined his palms together and wept, overwhelmed.

⁘

Let me describe another scene which is not in Sateeshan's memory. The next day, Jenny was walking towards the toddy store bus stop to catch a bus to college.

P. R. Kumaran, popularly known as P. R., said to her: 'We were waiting for you, dear!'

'What's special, Kumaretta?'

P. R. laughed. There were others with him—Bhaskaran Mash and Sardar Narayanan. Bhaskaran Mash was a CPI member, while Sardar Narayanan was the branch secretary of CPI (M). P. R. didn't belong to any party. He had withdrawn from political activities since the Communist Party split in 1964.

Bhaskaran Mash began talking:

'We heard you are going to Russia next week. We are proud of that. It's for the first time that a girl from a family of us toddy tappers in Anthikkad is going to Russia. This is a big event.'

P. R. continued: 'My dear! Maybe you are not aware of the gravity of this occasion. When a girl from Anthikkad goes to Russia, they don't consider it as an extraordinary matter. But this is our great dream come true. The people of Anthikkad had gone through such ordeals of fire, only with the constant thought, "There's a country called Soviet"*.'

'I am aware of this, Kumaretta. I will tell the Russians, in whatever language possible, about how Anthikkad and its people are steadfast in their Soviet dream.'

Sardar Narayanan did not say anything. He was as usual twirling his grey, upturned moustache. But his eyes were shining with tears.

Bhaskaran Mash said: 'We have arranged a farewell meeting for you at the Gurusamajam on Sunday. Our people will all be there. You

---

*A catchy communist slogan of the 1950s, dreaming about the 'Promised Land' of the communists, the USSR, when they were languishing in 'the capitalist, bourgeois hells' elsewhere.

must speak a few words!'

Sateeshan recollected how just like that, Jenny had refused to hold his hands and they strolled along this very street ten years ago. He had never met her after that. She went back along with the other members of the delegation after spending a month in Russia. Sateeshan joined a course in medicine in Moscow. The story of his life began from there. I don't intend to record it here.

Sateeshan was wearing a woollen overcoat, trousers, and a cap to escape the cold. Yet, the cold made him tremble. He sauntered up and down the footpath, thrusting his hands in his pockets to keep them warm. This street in Moscow has become very famous. Lots of tourists roam about.

Sateeshan quietly approached an African-American who was standing apparently aimless, and asked softly: 'Can I help you?'

MAN-IN-WATER

AYMANAM JOHN

Man-in-water is the seventy-year-old memory of Manalepparambil Mathaichen, who was our neighbour at our family home called Akkaraveedu—the house on the other shore.

First Akkaraveedu, then Manalepparambil Mathaichen, and finally Man-in-water—I will narrate this story in that order. (Only those who have enduring patience may read it.)

Though Akkaraveedu was the family home, it did not actually belong to our family. The house and compound had been owned by a neighbouring family who moved to town three or four generations ago when their wealth burgeoned. The complex had been entrusted to our care. As they became powerful dealers of rubber and pepper, it was as if they had all but forsaken that house and compound in the rural outback which was not a prime property at all. Our family's hold on the land became stronger. Meanwhile, since almost all our landed property had been sold, only Akkaraveedu remained which we could call our family home. However, when the younger generations of our family later acquired their own properties elsewhere, the need to have Akkaraveedu as our family home had almost been obviated. But, Father's elder sister Mary-ammachi who was widowed in her youth, opted to return and live alone in that house when she had passed her prime. She did not want to be a nuisance to her brothers. She spent nearly all her time reading the Bible...reading and praying...praying for her only son Josettan who was in the military.

Akkarapparampu, the compound where Akkaraveedu was situated, was almost an island that lay isolated among the small canals and paddy fields. In that compound, there were plenty of living creatures that dreaded the proximity of man...monitor lizards, garden lizards, moorhens, yellow rat snakes, green whip snakes, owlets, and bats. In that land which had not been hoed and cultivated and lay overgrown with grass and creepers, fruit trees mingled with sapwood trees, including the itch-inducing cherumaram—the black varnish tree. Among the wild growth, giant ants and red ants scurried hither-thither all the time. In the darkness of the thick canopy, cicadas kept up their racket without being able to distinguish between day and night. Looking up, the sun appeared like a spider who had built a web in the sky.

Half-eaten ripe guavas left behind by birds, fallen mangoes that no one wanted, the varikka jackfruit which the crows had pecked holes into, the golden kernels of a shattered anjil fruit scattered on the ground...a rich imagery that invoked childhood. That's why we loved Akkaraveedu more than our own home and always yearned to go there.

Mary-ammachi, who had a striking facial resemblance to our father, and whom we loved like our mother, would come to our house at the beginning of school vacation and take us with her one after another. Turn by turn.

We went for an afternoon boat trip around the bird sanctuary along the backwaters. Alighting at the Seminary Jetty, we walked along the elongated, rectangular mud bunds of the paddy fields filled with grasshoppers and crickets, climbed over the coconut trunk bridges connecting them...the joy of that one-and-a-half-hour journey which was an inseparable part of every summer vacation hasn't altogether disappeared from my memory even now.

Manalepparambil Mathaichen was a model farmer whose fame had spread far and wide. Whatever would sprout once planted was found in the Manalepparambil compound. As soon as the pre-monsoon rains were over, the locals flocked there for seeds and saplings—tapioca stem, elephant foot yam, pepper vine. Rice boats filled with the seeds and produce from his farm crossed the backwaters and travelled to distant lands. Mathaichen become rich enough to send his two sons for higher education in faraway cities. Those who knew the early history of the Manalepparambil family said Mathaichen grew immensely popular since he had grown so affluent despite being born in a poor man's hut.

Akkarapparambu and Manalepparambu, positioned on either bank of a narrow stream that flowed amidst the thickets where moorhens lived hidden, appeared like antitheses. Akkarapparambu nestled in the deep, green canopy of ageing trees; Manalepparambu, where square farms were full of tender shoots. We sat under the cool tree boughs with playmates from surrounding areas until the midday sun rays began to slant. We watched the farming activities at Manalepparambu and the arrival and departure of boats at the landing attached to the compound. That's how the words, the glances, the gait, and the stances of the famous

Manalepparambil Mathaichen became deeply imprinted memories like footprints on upturned fresh soil.

When we swam across the stream and went foraging under the cashew tree on the compound's boundary ('Children, don't trample the germinating elephant foot yam and the purple yam!') during our mischief in the waters of the bathing ghat ('My children, don't go to the deep pools of the stream, it's full of whirlpools…') when he came over at dusk to pick up his wife Thresia-chedathy who would be hobnobbing with Mary-ammachi ('My children, isn't my wife sitting there? Call her over, will you?'), we met and were acquainted with Mathaichen.

Finally, when Mary-ammachi on her way to Akkarapparamu taking one of us along for the holiday, took a short cut through Manalepparambil's front yard, Mathaichen, reclining in the easy chair on the veranda and chewing paan would send his spittle in a long jet into the yard, laugh aloud, and say: 'Oh, the locusts have come.' When we turned our faces away hearing that good-humoured, derisive taunt on account of our picking and eating all the fruits in his farm, he would call out to our disappearing backs and ask, as if to make amends: 'Have you passed your exams, my children?' Even if it wasn't the exam season, it was a question he would ask whenever he saw us. Did he believe that life was a relentless series of tests and passes?

Only one of those days when we took turns keeping vigil in the cold darkness, waiting beside Mary-ammachi as she lay on her deathbed, did Mathaichen appear before us with the face of one who had discerned the futility of success and failure. He stood for a long time, his hands crossed across his chest, looking at Mary-ammachi's face as she struggled to keep her eyelids open. Finally, he leaned over to the bed and called in a soothing voice: 'Marykuttye.' Even though it was so very soft, that voice was enough for Mary-ammachi to open her eyes for a fraction of a second. Immediately after, the sheen of the lamp's flame was reflected in the wetness spreading in her rheumy eyes.

Mary-ammachi's death was indeed the death of Akkaraveedu. The descendants of the old owners reached soon, put up a high stone wall around the compound, installed a tall gate, and locked it with a giant padlock. Yet, it's heard that following a dispute with their extended family, Akkarapparampu lies forsaken even now. There was no one to sell or buy.

We, who had frequented that compound and climbed the farthest boughs of the trees, didn't like to see it once it was thus incarcerated. Moreover, since there was nothing there that was not readily available in our village, there wasn't even any reason left for us to visit. Paddy fields, coconut trees, plantain trees, the river, and the distant vignettes of the backwaters—all of these were there in our village too.

Later, we weren't able to meet Manalepparambil Mathaichen much; only once during the rush following fireworks at the feast held at the Attirambu church and then during the Tirunakkara temple festival when he was bargaining with timber merchants. Just a few fleeting meetings. Even those meetings had stopped over the course of time. Our relationship with him was reduced to the greetings he passed on through several coconut merchants, plantain farmers, and those who cut and gathered plantain leaves that were sold to hotels to serve rice-meals. These farmers would travel all along the length of the canals and call at all the landings of the routes they travelled.

It was through these people that we found out about Mathaichen's two sons being in high positions abroad and that as he grew older, he had his entire farm planted with rubber and had entered a retired life.

Backed by titbits of old news and without any other reliable information, I decided to set apart a day to see Manalepparambil Mathaichen. It was during this visit that he told me the story of the Man-in-water.

I was somewhat depressed by the thought that it was so long since something exciting had happened in my life. As those melancholy days wore on, the decision to create a rather dramatic occasion arose in my mind. So came about the idea of a reunion with Manalepparambil Mathaichen.

When that pre-planned holiday arrived, I told Leela and the kids a suitable lie and went in search of Manalepparambil Mathaichen. I caught an early morning boat. When I alighted at the granite steps of the Seminary Jetty, I noticed that the old path along the mud bunds and the coconut trunk bridges had disappeared. I began to walk along a mud road across the paddy fields, following the trail like a red tape that would lead me in the direction of Manalepparambil. On either side of the road, in the old paddy fields that had been left uncultivated for long, weeds grew abundantly. Beyond those barren lands from which rose the stench of dirty, stagnant water, I could see big houses that resembled foreign luxury liners. They stood under the shade of young coconut trees in farm compounds reclaimed from the paddy fields. Beyond the long rows of these houses where the view began to fade into the slanting skyline by the backwater, a tourist resort could be seen dotted with multicoloured decorative umbrellas. At the windows of cars that blew their horns to shoo me away were faces of strangers. As they drove past me, I was struck by the leftover tunes of music from their stereos. The route seemed so outlandish and as I advanced, I grew frightened thinking that I was being subjected to a magic trick. Yet I moved on with a false sense of bravery my resolute mind had given me.

Soon I recognized the old mud bund that branched off from the path and had fallen into disuse. Landmarks from my memory loomed all around: the pala tree grove at the point where the mud bund met the land and the sacred grove for serpents at its base. Right from there, I could see the rubber trees of Manalepparambil. They had comingled with Akkarapparambu's old trees across the sky above the stream, forming a dense canopy.

When I reached the pala tree grove, I halted for a while and rested as if I had just finished an ocean voyage. Then I continued my slow walk, sensing the absence of Mary-ammachi's soft footfalls beside me on the dry leaves that had fallen by the side. It felt like the scent in a house where someone had died had been infused into stillness that surrounded me. The new path that skirted around Akkaraveedu's boundary wall took me towards Manalepparambu. When I peeked over the wall, Akkaraveedu, overgrown with creepers and plants, appeared like a film set long abandoned by a movie company. Plants grew outwards from walls that were falling apart.

It was only when I saw Mathaichen lying in an armchair on the veranda of Manalepparambil House, with his legs up on the armrests, continuing in that same posture that began so many years ago, that the melancholy thoughts began to depart from my mind. There weren't any visible changes to the house. Even the vessel containing umikkari—charcoal for cleaning teeth—hung from its usual corner rafter. When I walked on the gravel in the courtyard, the cadence of the same old crunching sound was heard.

Mathaichen taking a midday nap—which he was not accustomed to enjoy back then—laying his head on the backrest of the easy chair. Beside him on the floor, Thresia-chedathy was enjoying a deep sleep on a grass mat. The usual midday film was playing on the TV and a love song was nearing its end. As I stood watching those senile bodies marked by the multiplication and division symbols of old age, I was tempted to continue enjoying the irony of the situation to the accompaniment of those meaningless couplets. However, following an unstoppable inner urge, I woke up Mathaichen immediately. He was startled awake, followed by Thresia-chedathy. As if from behind a bramble bush of oblivion, Mathaichen looked up at me in consternation and huffed: 'Who's it? What'd you want?'

Now presenting the dramatic 'reminding' scene that I had secretly rehearsed and kept prepared days ago. I stood before Manalepparambil Mathaichen, as the 'locust' of olden times.

Rising and standing up with the old laughter whose resounding effect had not diminished even a bit, Manalepparambil Mathaichen ushered me on to the veranda, clasping my palms in his shaking ones. Thresia-chedathy stood filled with amazement and glee.

'The wonder of it! Who thought one would be able to see you in the form of a grown-up parent-like man!' Looking at my face, Manalepparambil Mathaichen too was enjoying the joke that life really is!

I sensed a guest was coming to that house after a very long time. Mathaichen's effervescence and Thresia-chedathy's tea and snacks hinted at that. When all that noise died down, the distance that had been imposed by the long lapse between our last meeting had now began to shrink, and soon, it disappeared. For the first time, Manalepparambil Mathaichen began to speak to me like an adult. He started by speaking about his sons: the eldest one was an engineer in Kuwait and the second one, a PhD, was in Germany.

'Let those fellows live wherever they like to live,' Mathaichen continued, throwing a glance each at the ageing coconut trees and the forest of rubber trees. 'If they plan to live by tending to these useless trees and gazing at the sky, won't they go starving?'

Then, about the recent earthquake. 'Only that was lacking.... Now that too has come to pass.'

About the tourist resort: 'The spot these fellows celebrate as the tourist resort—that's where I was born and raised. If someone wanted to see it, they should have seen it then. The young coconut trees were in full bloom, like the rising sun. Ah the western horizon...how beautiful was the afterglow seen through the coconut fronds! And the people of those times? There was hunger, sickness, and hardship everywhere.

What of it? The people were more gentle and noble than the ones we see around now. Any number of men with their bodies shining like polished rosewood, the ones who enjoyed tender palm toddy along with boiled tapioca and karimeen could be found in our place. In those times, a man was a real man! It was such a captivating sight to watch them going about, their bare broad chest without a stitch on. What's the use of saying all this? In those times, people did not eat the pesticide-saturated rice, the mackerel brought from Pondicherry, and the smoke ripened mango that you get from the market. Not to mention the sardine they sell now at forty rupees a kilo! The sardine we used to dump as manure at the base of the coconut trees during the chakara season was far better. The fishmonger was telling my wife yesterday, "Chedathy, please don't buy the fish the local fellows give you saying that they caught it from the river. They poison the water to kill the fish the easy way." What do you say to that?'

About TV programmes: 'The damned concoctions that they call serials and mega-serials. Are they anywhere near our real life, son? When I was young, there was this man called Man-in-water in our place.'

That's how Manalepparambil Mathaichen began narrating the story of Man-in-water.

⁂

A summertime beyond the memory of Manalepparambil Mathaichen. Smallpox had been sweeping across the countryside. Every day, many people died. Kith and kin were afraid not only of those who had contracted the disease but even of the dead bodies of those who had succumbed. As the numbers grew unmanageable, the people dispensed with the cremation or burial of the dead and funerary rituals loaded the corpses onto big rice boats, carried them to the middle of the backwaters, and dumped them in the water. When a particular stage was over in the disease's progress people didn't wait to confirm if the sick were actually dead. Instead, they began to carry away the dying ones too and sank them alongside the dead. Man-in-water was one such person who had been submerged in the backwaters before death had arrived. Yet he was miraculously revived owing to the water's magical qualities and returned to life. Realizing the cruelty of his kin who had attempted to kill him alive, he refused to go back to the land where they lived and decided to live in the backwaters that brought him back to life.

He must have chosen the isolated, uninhabited islets as his habitat. They were scattered far across the backwaters that appeared like the other bank of earth and life. It was rumoured that the water plants and creatures became his food. The snakebirds and cormorants became his companions. Together, they swam in the water. He swam as best and as long as he could and then latching on to the stern of the rice boats of friendly boatmen, he travelled to new islets. He didn't respond to the queries of the boatmen. He only screamed in a tone that didn't convey any emotion—like a bird's call. Apart from letting him hang from the stern, Man-in-water didn't accept any charity from the boatmen—no food, a plug of tobacco, or even a bidi butt.

Each rice boat that returned after a long trip carried the paeans of Man-in-water. Imbedded in Mathaichen's seventy-year-old memory, like a miracle that never flowed away from a child's mind, is the unforgettable day when Man-in-water appeared right before his eyes, diving and surfacing so near to him where he could have even touched him.

Mathaichen was eight or ten years old. At midday, the river was in spate with muddy, turbulent waters brimming over the banks. Mathaikutty was walking alongside his older brothers. He was their helper as they went hurling the baited hooks aimed at the olive barb fish and boal fish which were shooting upstream in exhilaration of their anticipated mating. Suddenly, he heard a great commotion from the far end of the vast paddy fields. It was followed by hooting and howling from both banks of the river. People were shouting. Shankunnippanikken, who was bathing on the rubble stairs leading to the river ghat, caught the wondrous news first.

'O, hear, hear my boys...Man-in-water is coming near!' Shankunnippanikken hollered at the top of his voice.

Running behind his brothers who had thrown the hooks and baits into the screw pine cluster and dashed forward, Mathaikutty also reached the spot where he heard the commotion. It was the meeting place of many streams. There in front of the copra yard was a moored riverboat. He jumped aboard and stood on the bow of the boat. The amazing form appeared before his eyes, swimming like a race boat. As the crowd stood watching, Man-in-water neared the rice boat on which Mathaikutty was standing. The commotion died down. Man-in-water cut through the water with his hands, like sharp strikes of a sword, splashing all around before whooshing forward towards the rice boat. Along with his brothers, Mathaikutty too jumped off board on to the bank in great dread. He took refuge behind the wall of people.

At that moment, like someone who was spent at the height of excitement and tension, Man-in-water began to pant in great heaves. He clutched the rice boat's bow and hung limply. Careful not to let his gaze fall on the faces of those looking at him with bated breath, he was straining his eyes to find an escape route towards the backwaters. It seemed that he feared and hated people living on land—he was anxious to get away from the flabbergasted crowds. Man-in-water looked like a soaring bird who had been suddenly trapped in a cage.

Stuck to his black, overgrown hair and beard were shiny green water weeds. His stare was as intense as that of a gaur. Were those tears or water streaming down his bloodshot eyes?

When his panting subsided, Man-in-water watched the varying speeds and the directions of the rapids in the downstream current, and discerning exactly which stream led to the backwaters, he let go of the bow and dived back in while emitting a roar that couldn't be compared with any known sound. The stupefied crowd stared at the vortex that had formed at the spot where he disappeared. They waited for Man-in-water to resurface after that gigantic dive they had witnessed. He came up to the surface at a distance where it was difficult for prying eyes to reach and making lightning strokes with his arms, faded away from sight. Only five or six people saw him disappear. By the time they could holler, 'There he goes, there he goes,' the water had already hidden Man-in-water.

Mathaichen stopped his story, making it clear he was one of those lucky five or six people who had witnessed the last sighting of Man-in-water as he disappeared before their very eyes.

Then Mathaichen proceeded to take out a tender betel leaf from the box he kept on the arm of the chair, cleaned it, scooped up the lime stored in a coconut shell, and drew a big dot on the back of the leaf with his finger.

He sat for some time, chewing betel and carefully observing my face to ascertain whether I could grasp the spirit of his story. After that pause, sending his spittle in a long arc into the courtyard, Mathaichen added: 'That's how life should be lived, son. If one hates life on land, then live in water. Just like that. If kith and kin forsake you, one should have the guts to sense for oneself that the sky and earth are there still for you. One must make others also feel the same way. Or, does life merely consist of going to work and coming back with military precision, reading newspapers, and making political comments, watching serials, and frying in Kottayam the fish caught in Pondicherry? Oh, what's the use of saying all these things at this time when people rush to commit suicide just because they failed in an exam or the bus didn't stop when one showed one's hand? Whatever is said and done, it is only Man-in-water who is our—that is, of the people of Aattirambu who are my age—supreme hero. This was the greatest passive resistance that we witnessed. Gandhiji and all comes later.'

I conclude Mathaichen's story here. I thank you for your enduring patience.

What's so special in this story that I chose to narrate at such length and detail? Is that what you ask? There's nothing. It's just an episode from the mega serial called life. At a time when the rice boats which used to bring back to land such stories like that of Man-in-water have stopped their long journeys and now exist merely as spectacles in tourist resorts, such tales are swallowed by the pythons we call mega serials. Just that.

THE SHIP OF BUTTERFLIES

THOMAS JOSEPH

A ship which had begun its voyage years ago, traversed different latitudes and longitudes and dropped anchor near the shores of the island of butterflies which had remained isolated for thousands of miles from anywhere, in the middle of the ocean.

Butterflies rising from the bursting pupa of life hovered over the glittering and dancing waves. As the boisterous conversations and mirthful ditties of the sailors floated in the atmosphere towards the island, the butterflies, like newly arriving guests, rose and flew down towards the ship. All those spots in the ship the butterflies reached, far removed from their instantly put-out flashes of lives, were the esoteric forms of man, a mixture of dream and blood, all mutated beyond recognition. The ship sat squat in the ocean, steeped in its own destiny, freezing under thick billows of mist.

Here, a limitless world is revealed in which the resounding roar of the breakers pervades, and sundry human forms scamper up to the top of the rocks. Amid all this, the ship lay motionless on the surface of those great depths, like a giant, many-winged butterfly. The captain who stepped out on the deck intermittently, dressed in his uniform, with silver stars and the ribbons of his rank sewn in, stood in brooding majesty throwing his daring gaze across the ocean over the endless waters. He lit his pipe and smoked standing still for hours on end. The butterflies were motionless sitting here and there on the ship, their wings unfurled, practically invisible to anyone. Keenly watching the captain's countenance which had blanked out in deep thought, they now joined his seemingly endless voyage as the sentinels of a foreboding that foresaw devastating events of the future. The captain's face was covered with worry lines accentuated by sleepless nights, and caused by portents of oncoming events.

He stood peering at the limitless expanse of the ocean, with a searching look only he had specialized in, directing it past the numerous mountains and valleys, reaching his own native place. In front of their house, in the garden, his wife Susanna was sitting, sewing in butterflies on a silk handkerchief.

For many years the captain had, through his thunderous commands barked at his sailors, steered his ship through perilous, dreadful currents to reach unmapped territories. He would remain steadfast, even as he had lost all his weapons at a fierce engagement with the foe and everything around him lay scattered, in ruins. At the last moment when everything had seemed to collapse and was on the brink of being immersed into the drab grey waters of death, the surface of the ocean would blossom into a fountain spraying serenity. And the ship would buck and leap forward, the foam and spray falling gaily on the foredeck. At a time when they were plunged into despair thinking that it would take months, nay, years to strike land again, the ship would suddenly swim up to a wharf where shafts of light fell like an array of swords falling on their sides. The waterfront would echo with the joyous shouts and loud talk of the sailors, coming out of the portholes of the ship. And the captain would remain standing erect on deck, in the floodlight of resurrection, his dress uniform flapping in the wind, looking like a huge bird.

In all the ports the ship had docked, wide streets lined with bars and restaurants hosted the captain and his men. He got back to the ship after enjoying his drinks and buying fine gifts from the shopping district. Alone at night, as he lay in bed, enveloped in the darkness of his cabin, his eyes were filled with the sights he had witnessed during the day. The bad guys with guns and knives tucked away under their belts, lurking in the alleys of the suburbs. He shuddered to recall that the faces of some of their victims, lone, isolated people, had indeed looked familiar to him. He also dwelt on his own visage at midday that day, as he roamed in the sweltering sun in strange city corners, in search of exactly what he could not say.

Finally, the ship, buffeted by mountainous breakers tossed up by tempests conjured up by hot ocean currents, had miraculously reached the island of butterflies. It lay anchored, at rest and peace, looking forward expectantly to the next leg of the voyage. The days filled with the turbulent waters of the ocean and dreaded waves had now been replaced by soft sounds flowing in from far away and faint whispers all around, the hot sun warming up the whole thing together.

Although the captain thought he could hear Susanna's caressing voice raised in prayer and her calling his name gently, which had seemingly been rising from the moving waters outside, he knew it was unreal and that knowledge pushed him into a depressed mood. And yet, he was unable to avoid hearing that voice. From across the ocean currents and the mountains and valleys far beyond, the vision of a Sunday morning appeared in his mind. Susanna and he were climbing the steps of a church that was serene but tense at the same time. Hovering around their beautiful bodies, butterflies were floating and dancing in the golden sunlight.

Suddenly, when Susanna toppled down, fainting, the captain held her. When they arrived back home, a telegram awaited them, ordering the captain back to the ship immediately.

As he lay in the darkening cabin, fresh meanings seemed to attach themselves to events of the recent past. He thought he had caught Susanna's silent figure, immobile, staring at the endless ocean, behind the several hands that rose and waved farewell as the ship bounded out to sea on an evening when the waves were rolling menacingly, and a chilly wind was blowing in with great force. Memories glimmered as he peered through the telescope; they flashed and died over the mirages of the seething ocean.

As he lay upon a bed of butterflies in that ship anchored in that remote spot, he could see Susanna, floored by despair, sprawled among the broken pieces of crockery and flower vases in their house. Her face was marked by deep creases, her dress soiled and smelly, and her feet dirty. He then dreamt that he had arrived at her side instantaneously, caught her by her hand and pulled her out of the grime and fumes and, they had together flown away into the far reaches of the cosmos.

He dreamt that in an instant, he had reached the borders of his faraway land lined by barbed wires and gazed into a magical but alien country filled with people, vehicles, and apartments built in concrete. His clothes and bones were filled with the boom of the ocean and the blood of the creatures inhabiting it. He turned back, failing to find a beautiful house on a riverbank. Susanna's radiance spread on and off through the rooms and the flowering plants of his garden. He woke up shuddering, thinking that his ship was shooting forward into a tumultuous strait. As he rolled on the bed he heard, like the faint murmur of raindrops on the waters, Susanna's prayer rising, meant for sailors washed away in distant seas. Then he sank into the bottom of sleep—the deep ocean.

The butterflies that took flight from Susanna's prayers and from the silken kerchiefs she made, usually disappeared for some time, to some place, after presenting to the earth rare demonstrations of their magical beauty. They lost themselves in the exploding rays of the sun and the soft moonbeams. Those butterflies that vanished into the inner murmurs of an esoteric realm, could have been transformed by invisible, beautiful fingers, into embroidery on gowns and coats. Sitting in the front garden, Susanna would be lost in this otherworldly task.

The captain, standing upon the deck, observing the ominous upheavals in the ocean, could not extricate himself from the octopus-like stranglehold of loneliness, nor from the silent weeping of Susanna. During those dark days and nights of inner turmoil, he would sometimes dash among his sailors and shout at them; other times he would yell and emit hideous laughter, partaking in their rough and ribald jokes and hard toil. Then, singing a melancholy song in a sorrowful, deep voice, he would steer the ship crossing the steaming currents of the future. Passing shorelines where waterlilies floated and heaved on the waves, he would disembark on coasts of snow-white bears and penguins, after dropping anchor.

The captain strove to feel happy by pulling out the gifts he had collected for Susanna over the several years of his absence and kept in chests and drawers. He would touch them all over and breathe in the smell of garments and undergarments Susanna was fated never to wear. He drew smoke from his pipe and sent his kissing lips and a beaming smile flying for Susanna borne over the blown-out smoke that travelled beyond the infinite horizon of the eyes. Getting to know these secrets of the captain, the butterflies fluttered their wings. The captain's ramblings and sighs flew into their wings along with the wind, and large numbers of butterflies rose into the air. Filling their wings with the extraordinary beauty of winds, they alighted on the revolvers and cartridge-boxes. One or two of them crept down the barrel of a gun, in a strange adventure, as if they were descending a deep well. Their wings collected the scent of gunpowder and smoke, and they were enveloped by an invisible presence of death.

The captain disembarked on the coast of the island of butterflies and ventured further inland. He was taken inside through a door into a darkened space akin to the cavernous depths of a bar. One more night of the butterflies for the captain. Amidst darkness and mysterious conversations, someone delivered to him a chalice full of blood. He sat still, unfamiliar glances and languages flying around him, as glasses were being filled and emptied. Upon the lips and hands of the people, there were the images of butterflies, waxing in the faint light. A butterfly sat still on every wine glass. As the captain abruptly departed, the butterflies unfurled their wings, rose from the tables and chairs, and trailed behind him.

The captain arrived at a street with many shops on both sides. Everything was available there. To the shock and amusement of the shopowners, he bought large quantities of women's and children's garments and slung the bundles over his shoulders. He also bought all kinds of sweet fruits available and portraits of beautiful women and many other paintings at exorbitant prices. Carrying it all on his back, he wandered around the shopping district, his revolver thrust under his belt. Hearing the mirthful voices of women and children after a very long time, strangely, he felt deeply sad. In his drunken delirium he had visions of Susanna accosted by merchants in their own house for some unknown business and of thieves who took away money and ornaments. He fell upon his face. He was covered in layers of dust like the scales of an ancient beast. Mud, like fruits of the earth, filled his eyes and mouth. He kept kissing the slushy mud.

Back on the ship in a daze, the captain lay on a bed of butterflies; when he came to, at midnight, he looked out and detected a faint shadow floating on the ocean. He noticed that it was the body of a woman as it floated abreast of the ship; her hands were crossed upon her chest, her body was enveloped in a white shroud and her head was covered in a white veil. It was indeed Susanna's body as he had feared. Trembling in shock, he felt as if her face, and the pupils of her eyes filled with tenderness, were rising, and floating towards him. He noticed that he was crouching near Susanna's body in a vast cemetery, with his head between his knees, amongst cenotaphs and broken crosses.

In the ship, he was lost in strategizing a battle against himself. He wore his armour, his ribbons and medals and got ready. He took out a blood-stained sword, the figure of a butterfly carved on its hilt.

As he got down from the ship and reached the shore with the naked sword raised, he noticed that the pre-dawn white light had spread in the east. The captain's form, as he climbed the rocks, was bathed in the early morning sun's light. He seemed to flutter in the wind. Then he began his soldierly battle dance. His sword rose in the air and flashed about. The pupils of his eyes reflected the sharp point of his sword.

Increasingly, he began to turn the sword's point towards his own body. Eyes and cells of life began to open all over his body, like a bloody memory. The butterflies soared above the rocky peaks, keenly watching how destiny played out in the case of this unique human guest. The great sharks and fish that surged above the ocean's surface, witnessed the captain's battle against himself before they sank back.

The whisper of flying wings rose and grew like the noise of a whirlwind over the island of butterflies. Flying out of the earth's life crevices and the clumps of grass, the butterflies swam into the realm of the soul's laments where blood glistened in drops. The captain, fighting with himself on his way up, reached the crests of the rocks touching the clouds. The blade of his sword appeared like a cascade as he thrust it down into his body. A fountain of blood spouted from the wound. He tottered on the rocks and his body took a free fall all the way down into the open hands of the ocean. Where he fell, blood spread across the water as a trace of his immortal memory.

The captain's body lay floating on the bloodied waters, bathed in serenity. The number of butterflies gathered around his body had increased suddenly. Swarms of butterflies flew over the captain's body, alighted on it, and sat in repose.

In the course of time, the captain's body was washed up on the shore of that hidden territory unmarked in maps. Plants and butterfly wings began to sprout on the body that lay enveloped in grass and earth.

REINDEER
CHANDRAMATHI

O sky traveller! Why did you tell stories that you should never have told?
My Krishnashila idol shattered because of your words.
The one who carried the compassion in his silken voice.
The one who asserted that his action would never move along the path of evil.
O sky traveller! Your story trod over the poetry in my mind.

The story begins like this. Once upon a time, a reindeer adorned with a garland of ringing bells around its neck and shiny snowflakes on its hooves leapt out of the pages of a Russian folk tale and entered Varsha's life. During her vacation, Varsha frequently visited the children's library in Soviet House.

Noticing that she read the same story every day, the secretary asked, 'I don't understand why you are so obsessed with this reindeer. Our spotted deer is so much more beautiful than this dirty animal!'

Sometime later, the Soviet House was shut down, and it was decided that all the books in the library would be gathered in a heap and burnt—a decision that angered many. Varsha was worried the beautifully illustrated book with the story of the reindeer too would be destroyed.

As time passed, she summoned the reindeer in her dream.

Reindeer: What a wonder! Do you still remember me?

Varsha: I have not forgotten you. Only if I forget you does the question of remembering you arise, doesn't it?

Reindeer: You had indeed forgotten me. In your teenage and youth, when you wandered looking for new pastures, I wasn't found anywhere in your mind.

Varsha: You were there. I swear you were there—right in the corner of my mind.

Reindeer: Only thoughts that are of no use are stowed away in the corner. All right. Let's not argue any more. Tell me. Why did you conjure me now?

Varsha: To give you a piece of news that will make you happy, I'm coming to meet you.

Reindeer: Come.

As the reader, you must have noticed the disinterested nature of the reindeer's words. Indeed its attitude had disappointed Varsha—she was still unaware that even if an entity existed within one's self, it wouldn't necessarily know everything about one.

However, she went to the cold land where the reindeer lived.

Listening to the story of her dream, Philippa said: Father Christmas is the troublemaker here! He makes the reindeer haul him to tropical countries! But we, the compatriots of reindeer, do not even think about that animal.

Varsha felt that Philippa would be able to take her to the reindeer. She presented her with a small souvenir that she had brought with her.

Philippa: Thank you, friend. But haven't you arrived today? Isn't gifting a memento to your host something you do at the end of your trip?

Varsha: I do things in a topsy-turvy manner. In fact, in our language, there's an adjective 'topsy-turvy' which we use for both the genders, like 'he'-topsy turvy or 'she'-topsy-turvy!

Philippa: That adjective perfectly suits you! Or else why will you dream of a reindeer while living in a tropical country where there are so many strange and colourful animals?

Philippa's joke ensured there remained no walls between Varsha and her.

Philippa said that in the zoo's open section where animals were allowed to roam free, there were reindeer. But they rarely came out of the green thickets.

Then Philippa narrated the story of a friend who had visited India to see elephants. This friend—who felt that the shining black Indian elephants were 'manlier' than their African counterparts with their fan-like, spread-out large ears, flat face, and grey hair—had managed to reach India after spending all the savings she had accumulated through three years of hard work. On seeing her first elephant in India, she blossomed into arousal like a beloved before her lover. But soon after, she began seeing elephants everywhere—drinking water on the wayside, breaking coconut palm fronds for fodder, in front of houses and inside their compounds, bearing the weight of the deity in temple processions, carrying tree boles in the logging areas, and rolling balls in circuses.... Finally, she returned to her land feeling nothing but a deep sense of detachment owing to the satiation of her desires.

'But such instances are not intended to diminish the value of the reindeer in your mind. Let me see whether I can show you a reindeer,' Philippa said laughing innocently, displaying a set of faintly saffron-tinged teeth.

One of those days, as she lazed in her room nursing the blazing fire within her, a phone call came.

'I am Philippa. I rang the hotel for something and found out that you alone did not step out of your room What happened? Are you homesick? Or is the weather too cold? Do you need a coat, pullover, stockings, or some medicines?'

'I need nothing,' Varsha answered. 'My body is well-protected. But I don't suppose you have any power to heal the mind?'

'If I did, I would have healed my mind first.'

There was an interval of silence indicating a deep mutual understanding.

'All right. I'll come within half an hour. Come down to the reception and wait for me. The lovely daylight hours are not to be wasted indoors.'

'No,' Varsha resisted 'Today I am not in a mood for anything. Let's do the outing later.'

'My dear friend! Philippa doesn't take no for an answer. I *am* coming. You *are* going to go out with me. I will introduce you to one of my elderly lady friends.'

'Why should I meet her?'

'The two of you have something in common—reindeer!'

So, Varsha went down and sat on a sprawling sofa close to the fireplace in the dining hall, waiting for Philippa. Her mind was filled with fantastical thoughts. Would Philippa's friend be keeping a reindeer? Perhaps she might be an eccentric millionaire. Perhaps she must have written a book on reindeers. Perhaps she may have a son or a daughter or grandchildren who are crazy about the animal. Perhaps she might have been the chief of a zoo. She might know a lot of things about reindeer. Of all those possibilities, she liked the first one the best. A family of happy reindeer living in the garden of Philippa's elderly friend. Mother, father, and a fawn.

As she sat daydreaming, Philippa arrived with her father. She looked attractive, the deep blue scarf that Varsha had gifted her snugly wrapped around her neck.

Philippa's father raises his head: My dear Indian lady! We meet finally!

Sitting in the empty underground train, Varsha narrated to her friend the story of the magical reindeer that had come out of a Russian folk tale, its hoof falls resounding in the sky, and how they had gained entry into her mind.

'Which folk tale is that? What's its title? I haven't read or even heard about such a story.'

'I too have forgotten its title. The story is about a beautiful girl in the grip of poverty. She has a legal obligation to czar, to whom she must give a certain quantity of gold every day. If she fails, death awaits her. The night before she has to present the gold—a night of tears and terror—a reindeer appears from the clouds in the sky. It swoops down, lands in her snowy courtyard, gallops around three times, and then disappears. The wondrous sight makes the girl forget her fears. As dawn arrives, she notices something incredible. Wherever the reindeer's hooves that touched the ground, the ice had turned into gold bars. The girl collects them and hands them over to the emperor and escapes death. Nevertheless, the czar's greed could not be curtailed. He began to demand pearls and diamonds. But on every occasion, the reindeer came to the girl's rescue. He gambolled in the snow and left her with all that the emperor desired.'

'Enough. I can imagine the rest of the story. Wonderstruck at her magical ability, the emperor marries her. It's the wont of such oppressive male figures to immediately possess a woman if she exhibits a hint of talent and then stamp out that flame, isn't it? The poor reindeer wanders off into infinity, in utter solitude!'

'The story can end differently. The reindeer could be a prince or a gandharva under the spell of a curse. He can be set free from the evil spell and marry her later.'

'We have done away with those wonderful endings long ago,' Philippa observed 'The endings in snowy countries are much more pitiful. The emperor will marry her. Then she wouldn't have to produce gold or diamonds. She would merely have to produce offspring for him and live in the harem.'

'It's an Indian ending as well.'

The train had reached the station. As they walked, Varsha noticed the sheen of the maple leaves in the chilly light of the sun. The biting cold penetrated her coat and sweater like the onslaught of many needles.

Philippa predicted that autumn would come early, and it might begin snowing before Varsha returned to India. She began talking about Selma Echmann who was past seventy. She cherished the cold. She never closed the windows of her house, unless it was extremely unbearable. The rooms would be of the same temperature as outside. Philippa was afraid whether Varsha would be able to bear that kind of cold for long.

Now Varsha was more convinced than ever before. Surely that enigmatic old lady was rearing a reindeer! A reindeer that could transform the snow in her garden into pearls and gold!

When Philippa got into a department store and bought a bottle of champagne, Varsha thought that it was a gift for Selma Echmann. How would she know its real use unless we reached the right page?

Selma Echmann's isolated mansion stood amidst a cluster of rocks. Beyond the lake, one could see the proud outline of the city with its towering skyscrapers. When she opened the door, Varsha found an old woman with a shrivelled, contorted face, like a dried-up loaf of bread. Her grey hair was tied into a bun atop her head. She appeared somewhat familiar, as an eccentric, old woman whom she had met in the pages of a folk tale. Mrs Echmann welcomed them inside.

'My friend is going to get chilly inside your house, granny Selma! Will it be discourteous if I shut these windows?'

'It will be completely discourteous! Instead, ask your shivering friend whether I can get her something hot to drink? There are liquors here that burn like liquid fire...they'll burn the oesophagus. Let's swallow those flaming torches to ward off the cold!'

'We can do that. But not Varsha. I have brought something that would suit her.'

Philippa opened the champagne after giving the bottle a thorough shake. Varsha watched in amazement as the cork shot towards the ceiling, and a stream of golden liquid cascaded and fell like abhisekha water on the animal head mounted on a marble stool

'O, my Indian girl! We meet for the first time!'

Who made Varsha hold the glass of bubbling champagne? Where did the heat come from that burned in her nerves?

In Varsha's eyes, there was only a head with antlers and tawny hair. In that head, there were two holes where its eyes had been. Perhaps following Varsha's gaze, Selma Echmann said: 'It's I who shot this bastard. One night on the ice lumps on the ground, he trampled my husband to death. My poor, dear Bremer. I emptied Bremer's gun into that devil. Down to the very last bullet. I stood watching him collapse on the same snow on which Bremer had died, and writhe and wriggle until life ebbed from his body.'

Varsha's eyes refused to look away from the animal's hollow sockets. Is the reindeer's blood red? Do lumps of ice become ruddy like ruby when blood is spilt on it?

'Philippa, your friend seems to be in some other world.'

'She is stunned listening to your heroic tale. In her dreams, she saw a reindeer that produced gold with the mere touch of its hooves.'

'Ha ha ha!' roared Selma Echmann. 'How easy it is to dream! Especially about someone or something one has never seen about!'

That was how Varsha was saved from her dreams. Or rather, the dreams were saved from her.

✧

'What an imagination!' This was another Philippa speaking. Not the Philippa of the story.

'The reindeer is a meek and mild creature. It will never trample a man to death. I have only one doubt: is this contorted imagination conjured by the characters or is it that of the work of the writer?'

The writer's silence aroused yet another suspicion.

'Wasn't it a mere reindeer, after all?'

The writer remained silent still.

ACKNOWLEDGEMENTS

I wish to acknowledge with a deep sense of gratitude, the kind support of the following individuals in the execution of this project:

Mini Krishnan, the matriarch of the tribe of literary translators in our country, who convinced me to take up this daunting project.

Professor K. S. Ravikumar, former pro-vice chancellor, Sree Sankaracharya University of Sanskrit, Kalady, Kerala, for wholeheartedly supporting me from the very beginning of this project. He sent me the hard copies of many of the stories which were not available to me in Delhi. I have also made selections from his landmark anthology, *100 Varsham, 100 Katha*, (100 years, 100 Stories). I have also selected a few stories from *Malayala Kadha—60 Kadhakal* (The Malayalam Story—60 Stories, 2017), compiled and edited by N. S. Madhavan.

Anvar Ali, Anitha Thampi, N. G. Unnikrishnan, P. P. Ramachandran—all friends and poets; Sanjay Gupta, *Indian Literature* Section, Sahitya Akademi, New Delhi; filmmakers Rajiv Vijay Raghavan and Sajeev Pillai and many more who helped me retrieve crucial texts—both originals and my translations.

Numerous friends and their contacts who made it possible for me to reach each and every author/legal heir, especially A. V. Sreekumar, Publications Manager and Asha Aravind, Rights Manager, DC Books, Kottayam, Kerala; Radhakrishnan Varier, Publications Manager, Sahithya Pravarthaka Cooperative Society, Kottayam, Kerala; Nayana Thara, Publications Manager, Kerala Sahitya Akademi, Thrissur, Kerala; Anvar Ali, and Lekshmy Rajeev—both friends and poets; V. C. Thomas, Proprietor, VC Thomas Editions, Kochi; Noushad, Manager, Publications, Mathrubhumi Books, Kozhikode; K. J. Johny, Manager, Current Books, Thrissur; and Ajith, Proprietor, Logos Books, Perinthalmanna, and many others.

My wife, Prema, and daughter, Aparna, who have been veritable towers of strength.

∽

Grateful acknowledgement is made to the following copyright holders for permission to translate and reprint copyrighted material in this volume:

'Wooden Dolls' by Karoor Neelakanta Pillai. Reprinted by permission of B. Saraswathy Amma.

'The World-renowned Nose' by Vaikom Muhammad Basheer. Reprinted by permission of DC Books.

'The Oath' by P. Kesavadev. Reprinted by permission of Jothydev Kesavadev.

'Dhirendu Majumdar's Mother' by Lalithambika Antharjanam. Reprinted by permission of DC Books.

'The Speaking Plough' by Ponkunnam Varkey. Reprinted by permission of P. Rajen Varkey.

'The Farmer' by Thakazhi Sivasankara Pillai. Reprinted by permission of DC Books.

'On the Riverbank' by S. K. Pottekkatt. Reprinted by permission of DC Books.

'The Fair Child' by Uroob. Reprinted by permission of DC Books.

'The Shade Trees' by K. Saraswathi Amma. Reprinted by permission of DC Books.

'Chankraanti Ada' by T. K. C. Vaduthala. Reprinted by permission of Chandrahassan.

'The Omen' by Kovilan. Reprinted by permission of Amitha V.A.

'Fear' by Paarappurathu. Reprinted by permission of John Mathew.

'Allopanishad' by Pattathuvila Karunakaran. Reprinted by permission of Anitha Venu.

'Humans and Animals' by Nandanar. Reprinted by permission of DC Books.

'Candle' by N. P. Mohammed. Reprinted by permission of C. Imbichi Pathummabi.

'Lunch' by V. K. N. Reprinted by permission of DC Books.

'The Hanging' by O. V. Vijayan. Reprinted by permission of DC Books.

'The Apology' by Rajalakshmi. Reprinted by permission of Aarati Mohanram.

'Chidambaram' by C. V. Sreeraman. Reprinted by permission of C. S. Hrithwik.

'The Death of Makhan Singh' by T. Padmanabhan. Reprinted by permission of the author.

'Your Story (Mine Too)' by N. Mohanan. Reprinted by permission of Sarita Mohanan Varma.

'Vision' by M. T. Vasudevan Nair. Reprinted by permission of the author.
'Scent of a Bird' by Madhavikkutty. Reprinted by permission of DC Books.
'The War Ends' by Kakkanadan. Reprinted by permission of Radha Kakkanadan.
'Dimensions' by Anand. Reprinted by permission of the author.
'Pempi' by P. Vatsala. Reprinted by permission of the author.
'The Court of King George VI' by M. P. Narayana Pillai. Reprinted by permission of DC Books.
'The Society' by Punathil Kunjabdulla. Reprinted by permission of DC Books.
'Photo' by M. Mukundan. Reprinted by permission of DC Books.
'The Mission' by Sethu. Reprinted by permission of the author.
'It's the Gallows for Us' by M. Sukumaran. Reprinted by permission of DC Books.
'The Dinosaur Baby' by E. Harikumar. Reprinted by permission of Lalitha Harikumar.
'We, Tomorrow's Shame' by T. R. Reprinted by permission of Valsala Ramachandran.
'Mushroom for Breakfast' by Maythil Radhakrishnan. Reprinted by permission of the author.
'The Garden of the Antlions' by Paul Zacharia. Reprinted by permission of DC Books.
'The Hook' by P. Padmarajan. Reprinted by permission of DC Books.
'A Daytime in '53' by Victor Leenus. Reprinted by permission of DC Books.
'Niravatthu Kayyaani' by C. Ayyapan. Reprinted by permission of T. C. Lalitha.
'Sweat Marks' by Sara Joseph. Reprinted by permission of the author.
'The Twelfth Hour' by V. P. Sivakumar. Reprinted by permission of Geetha Sivakumar.
'The Fourth World' by N. S. Madhavan. Reprinted by permission of DC Books.
'Civics and Physics Practicals' by Maanasi. Reprinted by permission of the author.
'A Letter to a Friend Plunged into Despair' by U. P. Jayaraj. Reprinted by permission of DC Books.

'Two Historians and a Young Woman' by Gracy. Reprinted by permission of the author.

'A Path in the Moonlight' by N. Prabhakaran. Reprinted by permission of the author.

'Pomegranate Trees Blossom Still' by C. V. Balakrishnan. Reprinted by permission of the author.

'How Many Jennys Are There in Anthikkad?' by Asokan Charuvil. Reprinted by permission of the author.

'Man-in-water' by Aymanam John. Reprinted by permission of the author.

'The Ship of Butterflies' by Thomas Joseph. Reprinted by permission of Rosily Joseph.

'Reindeer' by Chandramathi. Reprinted by permission of the author.

NOTES ON THE AUTHORS

Karoor Neelakanta Pillai (1898–1975) was one of the most distinguished storytellers in the Malayalam literary tradition. He has twenty-one collections of short stories, eleven collections of children's stories, three novels, three collections of one-act plays, and a collection of essays to his credit. A founding member of the Sahithya Pravarthaka Co-operative Society, Pillai received the Kerala Sahitya Akademi Award for Children's Literature in 1960 for *Anakkaran*, a tale of a boy and his elephant, and the Kerala Sahitya Akademi Award in 1969 for his short story collection, *Mothiram* (The Ring).

P. Kesavadev (1904–83) is the non de plume of P. Kesava Pillai. A genre-defying author and social reformer, his novel *Odayil Ninnu* featured a rickshaw-puller as its protagonist, thereby ushering in an era of progressive Malayalam literature characterized by ordinary characters, experimental prose, and themes drawn from the struggles of everyday life. He has nineteen novels, seven collections of short stories, seven plays, and a memoir to his credit. He won the Sahitya Akademi Award for his novel, *Ayalkaar* (The Neighbours).

Vaikom Muhammad Basheer (1908–94) was a freedom fighter, novelist, short story and screenplay writer who revolutionized Malayalam storytelling through the inclusion of marginalized voices, satire, black humour, and pathos in his stories. Themes of love, poverty, hunger, and humanism featured frequently in his writings, as did Basheer's defiance of grammatical conventions. He developed his unique style of language free of traditional baggage, a first in Malayalam literature. Fondly known as Beypore Sultan, he received the Padma Shri in 1982 and the Vallathol Award in 1993. He was a fellow of the Sahitya Akademi, New Delhi.

Lalithambika Antharjanam (1909–87) was a social activist, poet, and novelist at the crux of whose revolutionary writings was an outspoken contempt for the hypocrisy and violence meted out to women in the upper-caste Namboodiri Brahmin community. Antharjanam's works such as *Mulappalinte Manam* exposed historical disenfranchisement and advocated vehemently for women's emancipation. She has produced six collections of poetry, nineteen collections of short stories, six collections of children's literature, and multiple essays. She pioneered feminist writing and was later joined by K. Saraswathi Amma. She received the Sahitya Akademi Award in 1977 for her iconic novel *Agnisakshi*.

Ponkunnam Varkey (1910–2004) began his writing journey with a collection of highly-appreciated poetry titled *Thirumulkazhcha* before steering into Malayalam prose. He believed in the power of the written word in the fight against social injustices and corruption, and his writing spoke of the complex lives of ordinary people and their relationship with the echelons of power, nature, and rural life. Two of his short stories, 'Manthrikkettu' and 'Model', were banned in 1946 by the state of Travancore, leading to a six-month imprisonment on the charges of treason.

Thakazhi Sivasankara Pillai (1912–99), fondly known as Kerala Maupassant, wrote more than thirty novels that brought to life the trials and tribulations of the oppressed classes and the socio-political pitfalls of mid-twentieth century Kerala. He authored *Chemmeen*, an epic love story that went on to become the first post-colonial Indian novel to be translated into English. In 1978, he wrote *Kayar*, an extensive and celebrated generational history covering 200 years of change in the region of Kuttanad. He is the winner of the Sahitya Akademi Award and the Jnanpith Award.

S. K. Pottekkatt (1913–82) is often considered to be the pioneer of travel writing in India. A seasoned globetrotter, he emerged as the most distinguished practitioner of the travelogue genre in Malayalam literature. Pottekkatt's works have been extensively translated into English, Italian, Russian, Czech, German, and other Indian languages. His short story, 'Kadathuthoni', was adapted into an award-winning short film by M. T. Vasudevan Nair. He is the winner of the Sahitya Akademi Award and the Jnanpith Award.

Uroob (1915–79) is the nom de plume of Parutholli Chalappurathu Kuttikrishnan, an exponent of progressive Malayalam literature and children's fiction. An advocate of gender equality, his writing frequently featured impactful women protagonists. 'Neelakuyil', his short story about untouchability and feudalism, was adapted into a neo-realistic film that became the first feature film from the region to win the All India Certificate of Merit for Best Feature Film at the second National Film Awards. He has also won the Sahitya Akademi Award.

K. Saraswathi Amma (1919–75) was a feminist writer whose stories have been celebrated for breaking the mould and vehemently criticizing patriarchy, female subservience, and oppression through satire and dark humour. She has produced over twelve collections of short stories, a collection of essays entitled *Purushanmarillatha Lokham* (A World Without Men), a play called *Devaduthi* (A Messenger of God), and two novels, *Premabhaajanam* and *Ponninkudam* (she was known as Ponninkudam Saraswathi Amma). Her attempts to shatter the illusions surrounding love and traditional gender roles have found her a special place in the annals of Malayalam literature. Her untimely demise at the age of fifty-six cut short a potentially rich literary career.

T. K. C. Vaduthala (1921–88) was one the earliest writers of Dalit fiction. A freedom fighter who participated in the Quit India Movement and later joined the army, he subsequently held positions in All India Radio and the Cochin Port Trust. His short stories were among the first to depict Dalit life in Kerala, his magnum opus *Changalakal Nurungunnu* shedding light on the life of the Pulayar community. From 1986–88, he was a member of the Rajya Sabha.

Kovilan (1923–2010) was the nom de plume of Kandanisseri Vattamparambil Velappan Ayyappan. The recipient of multiple accolades including the Kerala Sahitya Akademi Award, Muttathu Varkey Award, Ezhuthachan Puraskaram, Sahitya Akademi Award, and Mathrubhumi Literary Award, his novels such as *A Minus B, Ezhamedangal, Thazhvarakal,* and *Himalayam* heavily drew upon his experiences in the Royal Indian Navy. *Thottangal*, a story about the delirium of an elderly woman, was serialized by Doordarshan. He was a fellow of the Sahitya Akademi.

Paarappurathu (1924–81) was the nom de plume of Kizhakkepainummoodu Easo Mathai. Known as the 'Storyteller of Onattukara' after his birthplace, he authored twenty novels, fourteen collections of short stories, and fifteen screenplays. His significant works such as *Ara Nazhika Neram, Panitheeraatha Veedu, Ninamaninja Kaalppaadukal,* and *Makane Ninakku Vendi* were adapted into critically and commercially successful films. He won the Kerala State Film Award for Best Story twice, in 1970 and 1972, as well as the Sahitya Akademi Award.

Pattathuvila Karunakaran (1925–88) was a Malayalam film producer and modernist writer. Best known for his collections of short stories such as *Vimarsam, Bourgeois Snehithan,* and *Muni* (selected for the Sahitya Akademi Award), Karunakaran's works often explore themes of personal identity, sacrifice, and betrayal. He was a part of the esteemed Kozhikode Cultural Circle which included Vaikom Muhammad Basheer, M. T. Vasudevan Nair, G. Aravindan, and N. P. Mohammed and was involved in the making of *Uttarayanam*, a film that influenced parallel cinema in Kerala.

Nandanar (1926–74) was the nom de plume of P. C. Gopalan, who served in the Indian Army for two decades and was famous for his short stories and novels often set against life in the barracks. His writing explores the different manifestations of longing, such as the nostalgia experienced by army men for their families and the youth's desire for love. He authored an iconic book for children, *Unnikkuttante Lokam*, a poignant tale of a little boy and the wonders of his world. He has written ten collections of short stories and six novels of which *Aatmaavinte Novukal, Anubhootikalude Lokam,* and *Ariyappedattha Manushyakjeevithangal* are the most celebrated. He won the Sahitya Akademi Award for Novel in 1964. His suicide at forty-eight cut short a bright literary career.

N. P. Mohammed (1928–2003) was a pioneer of the modernist literary tradition in Kerala, ranking alongside O. V. Vijayan, Kakkanandan, and Madhavikkutty. His celebrated works include five collections of short stories, eight collections of essays, and novels such as *Arabi Ponnu* (co-authored with M. T. Vasudevan Nair), *Hiranyakasipu, Daivatthinte Kannu, Ennappaadam,* and *Muhammad Abdurrahman* (published posthumously). He served as the president of the Kerala Sahitya Akademi and was honoured with several prizes, including the Sahitya Akademi Award, the Lalithambika Antharjanam Award, and the Muttathu Varkey Award.

V. K. N. (1929–2004) was the nom de plume of Vadakke Koottala

Narayanankutty Nair. Known for his highbrow satire and layered humour, his stories offered scathing criticism of social evils, particularly the class divide and libertinism of the affluent. He has eleven novels to his credit, including *Pitaamahan, Adhikaaram, Kaavi, Syndicate, Arohanam* (translated into English by himself as *Bovine Bugles*), *General Chathans*, and *Kavi*. In 1982, he was awarded the Sahitya Akademi Award for a collection of short stories, *Payyan Kathakal,* alongside being the recipient of the Muttathu Varkey Award and M. P. Paul Award.

O. V. Vijayan (1930–2005) was a political cartoonist and pioneering author from Palakkad, best known for writing one of the most popular Malayalam novels and what is considered a masterclass in magical realism and a turning point in modern literature, *Khasakkinte Itihasam*. He received the inaugural Muttathu Varkey Award in 1982, the Sahitya Akademi Award in 1990 and its translation prize, and in 2003, was conferred the Padma Bhushan by the Government of India. Significant works by Vijayan include *Gurusagaram, Madhuram Gayathi,* and *Thalamurakal*. His cartoons and political commentary have appeared in *The Statesman* and *The Hindu*.

Rajalakshmi (1930–65) was a novelist, short story writer, and poet. A postgraduate in physics, she was known for her nuanced expression of intense emotions and the delicate portrayal of female characters. Her notable publications include a collection of poetry entitled *Ninne Njan Snehikkunnu* and three novels: *Oru Vazhiyum Kure Nizhalukalum* (winner of the 1960 Kerala Sahitya Akademi Award for Novel), *Njaanenna Bhavam,* and *Uchaveyilum Ilam Nilavum*. Her writing career which showed great promise was cut short by her suicide at the age of thirty-four.

C. V. Sreeraman (1931–2007) was a prolific Malayalam short story writer. He worked in the rehabilitation department of the Andaman and Nicobar Islands for seven years, an experience that became the backdrop for many of his short stories. His famous works include short story collections such as *Anaayaasena Maranam, Railway Paalangal, Oru Puthiya Samararoopam,* and *Entosy Valyamma*. The unique visual quality of his writing enticed notable filmmakers such as G. Aravindan and K. R. Mohanan who adapted his stories into acclaimed films such as *Chidambaram* and *Purushaartham*. The several honours he has received include the Kerala Sahitya Akademi Award and Sahitya Akademi Award for *Vaasthuhaara*.

T. Padmanabhan (born 1931) began writing at the age of nineteen and to date, has produced nearly 200 short stories loved for their lyrical language and layered understanding of emotions like loneliness, longing, and helplessness. His celebrated works are *Prakaasham Paratthunna Oru Penkutty, Gauri,* and *Oru Kathaakritthu Kurishil.* He consistently refused to accept awards including the Sahitya Akademi Award, but later agreed to receive them, beginning with the Muttathu Varkey Award and then the Ezhuthachan Puraskaram, the highest literary honour conferred by the Government of Kerala.

N. Mohanan (1933–99) has published nearly ten collections of short stories, the notable ones being *Ninte Katha, Dukhathinte Rathrikal, Poojakkedukkatha Pookkal,* and *Nishedha.* In 1988, he received the Kerala Sahitya Akademi Award for his novel, *Innalathe Mazha.* He was the son of Lalithambika Antharjanam.

M. T. Vasudevan Nair (born 1933) is hailed as one of the masters of literature to have emerged out of India after Independence. At twenty, he won an award for the best short story written in Malayalam at the World Short Story Competition conducted by the *New York Herald Tribune.* His seminal novels include *Naalukettu* (winner of the 1958 Kerala Sahitya Akademi Award), *Asuravithu, Kaalam,* and *Randamoozham.* His writing adroitly captures the complex dynamics of the quintessential Malayali family and the intricacies of the region's culture. Among the numerous awards he has won are the Sahitya Akademi Award, Jnanpith Award, Ezhuthachan Puraskaram, and the inaugural Kerala Jyothi Award in 2022, the highest civilian honour conferred by the Government of Kerala. He has been awarded the Padma Bhushan.

Madhavikkutty (1934–2009) was the one-time nom de plume of Kamala Surayya, one of the fiercest feminist writers in Indian literature. Her oeuvre covers an admirable expanse, including short stories, poems, an autobiography, and newspaper columns. Her brave writing delved into subjects like femininity, individuality, sexual desire, love, and the anguish of betrayal. She was the recipient of the PEN Asian Poetry Prize, Sahitya Akademi Award, Valayar Award (for *Neermathalam Pootha Kalam*), South Asian Literary Prize, and Muttathu Varkey Award. She was nominated for the Nobel Prize in Literature in 1984. She was the daughter of the celebrated Malayalam poet Nalappaat Balamani Amma.

Kakkanadan (1935–2011) was the nom de plume of George Varghese, an unforgettable architect of the modernist tradition in Malayalam literature. His writing signified a radical break from the past, utilizing subversive language, new narrative techniques, and apocalyptic imagery to explore the darker, often violent lives of those on the periphery of society. His works were considered cultural milestones for the Keralan youth of the 1960s and the 1970s. His short story collection *Aswathamavinte Chiri* won the Kerala Sahitya Akademi Award in 1980 while his collection of stories, *Jaappaanam Pukayila*, was awarded the Sahitya Akademi Award in 2005.

Anand (born 1936) is the nom de plume of P. Sachidanandan, a prolific essayist, novelist, and short story writer from Thrissur. His works are characterized by a distinct humanism, articulate yet economical use of language, abstract imagery, historical elements, and a palpable undercurrent of resistance. He is a recipient of several prizes, including the Ezhuthachan Puraskaram, Muttathu Varkey Award, three Kerala Sahitya Akademi Awards—for story, novel, and scholarly literature, and the Sahitya Akademi Award.

P. Vatsala (born 1938) is a social activist, novelist, and short story writer who received the Ezhuthachan Puraskaram in 2021, making her the fifth woman to receive this literary honour ever since its inception. She has produced seventeen novels and over twenty-five collections of stories, with *Nizhalurangunna Vazhikal* winning the Kerala Sahitya Akademi Award in 1976 and 'Nellu' being adapted into an award-winning film.

M. P. Narayana Pillai (1939–98) was a celebrated journalist and short story writer whose works are considered an inseparable part of the trajectory of modernist Malayalam literature. He was associated with the *Far Eastern Economic Review* and *McGraw-Hill World News*. His notable achievements include novels such as *Parinamam* (for which he was awarded the Kerala Sahitya Akademi Award) and *Hanumanseva*, sixteen collections of short stories collections of which the most famous are *George Aaraamante Kodathi* and *Murukan Enna Paampaatti*, eight collections of essays, and a memoir.

Punathil Kunjabdulla (1940–2017) was one of the most notable practitioners of avant-garde in Malayalam literature. A practising doctor, his profession greatly influenced his fiction which often revolved around themes of medicine, the lives of medical students, and death. He was awarded the Sahitya Akademi Award in 1978 and the Kerala Sahitya Akademi Award thrice—for his novel *Smarakasilakal*, for his short story collection *Malamukalile Abdulla*, and a travelogue entitled *Volgayil Manju Peyyumpol*.

M. Mukundan (born 1943) is one of the foremost writers of modernist Malayalam fiction. His first novel, *Mayyazhippuzhayude Theerangalil* (On the Banks of River Mayyazhil) has emerged as a cult classic, continuing to captivate readers even today and leading to the moniker 'Mayyazhiyude Kathaakaaran', meaning the 'The Storyteller of Mahe'. He has twenty-two novels, five novellas, two short story collections, a book of literary criticism, and a memoir to his credit. He has been awarded the Sahitya Akademi Award, Vayalar Award, JCB Prize, Crossword Book Award for his novel *Keshavante Vilaapangal* along with translator A. J. Thomas (translated as *Keshavan's Lamentations*), the Muttathu Varkey Award, the Ezhuthachan Puraskaram, and the Chevalier des Arts et des Lettres from the Government of France.

Sethu (born 1942) is the nom de plume of A. Sethumadhavan, an acclaimed modernist writer who has published more than thirty-five books. He has been awarded the Kerala Sahitya Akademi Award, Sahitya Akademi Award, Muttathu Varkey Award, and in 2022, the Ezhuthachan Puraskaram. His distinguished works include novels such as *Pandavapuram, Niyogam, Navagrahangalude Thadavara, Vilayaattam, Marupiravi, Adayaaalangal* and short story collections like *Doothu* and *Pediswapnangal*. The English translation of his selected stories, *During the Journey and Other Stories*, is another notable work.

M. Sukumaran (1943–2018) was renowned for his powerful novels and short stories that depicted his strong political convictions. He received the Kerala State Film Award for Best Story twice, for *Sheshakriya* and *Kazhakam*, and the inaugural Padmarajan Award for *Pithru Tharpanam*. In 1976, he was awarded the Kerala Sahitya Akademi Award for his collection of short stories, *Marichittillathavarude Smarakam*, and the Sahitya Akademi Award in 2006 for another collection, *Chuvanna Chihnangal*.

E. Harikumar (1943–2020) was born to the noted poet and playwright Edasseri Govindan Nair and E. Janaki Amma who translated Tagore's works into Malayalam. He won the Kerala Sahitya Akademi Award in 1988 for his compendium of short stories, *Dinosarinte Kutty*, and the Padmarajan Award in 1997 for 'Pachhapayyine Pidikkan'. He has produced nine novels, seventeen collections of short stories, and two memoirs.

T. R. (1944–2000) is the nom de plume of T. Ramachandran, a standalone name in the high modernist phase of Malayalam fiction. He gave up a career in banking to teach literature at the college level, beginning his journey in short fiction in 1969. His notable works include *Korunnyotathu Komutti, Naam Naalayute Nanakkedu, and Jassakkine Kollaruthu*. His well-known collection of short fiction, *Chitrakalayum Cherukathayum*, is a rich study of the art of writing and painting. His untimely demise at fifty-six cut short a brilliant literary career.

Maythil Radhakrishnan (born 1944) is a journalist, poet, and writer of both fiction and non-fiction from Palakkad. Celebrated for his unique narrative voice and original perceptions of life, his oeuvre covers a surprising range of subjects—from computers to insects. His famed works include novels like *Sooryavamsam, Chuvanna Vidooshakarute Anchampathi*, and *Hitcockinte Itapetal*, two poetry collections entitled *Penguin* and *Bhoomiyeyum Maranatheyum Kuricchu*, and short story collections such as *Sooryamalsyathe Vivarikkal, Dylan Thomasinte Panth*, and *Sangeetham Oru Samayakalyaani*. He refused the Kerala Sahitya Akademi Award in 2016, citing his distrust of academics.

Paul Zacharia (born 1945) is an eminent Malayalam fiction writer and essayist noted for his ever-renewing style across different phases in the development of modernist, after-modernist, and postmodernist fiction in Malayalam literature. He was awarded the Sahitya Akademi Award in 2005 for a short-story collection, *Zachariyayte Kathakal*, and several other prizes such as the Kerala State Film Award for Best Story, the Vallathol Award, the Muttathu Varkey Award, and the Ezhuthachan Puraskaram. In 2013, he was a Distinguished Fellow of the Kerala Sahitya Akademi. His works that have been translated into English include *Bhaskara Pattelar and Other Stories, Reflections of a Hen in her Last Hour and Other Stories*, and *Paul Zacharia: Two Novels*.

P. Padmarajan (1945–91) was a renowned author, filmmaker, and screenwriter. In 1972, he was conferred the Kerala Sahitya Akademi Award for his novel *Nakshathrangale Kaval*. He is a six-time recipient of the Kerala State Film Awards and a two-time recipient of the National Award for the Best Feature Film in Malayalam, for *Peruvazhiyambalam* and *Thinkalaazhcha Nalla Divasam*. His career spanned only for a brief period of sixteen years, cut short by a cardiac arrest at forty-six.

Victor Leenus (1946–92) was a journalist and writer who like T. R. can be considered a lone star in modernist Malayalam literature. He has produced a few, but brilliant short stories, collated in a single volume entitled *Victor Leenusinte Kathakal*. His extraordinary talent could never reach its potential as he passed away under mysterious circumstances when he was only forty-six years old.

C. Ayyappan (1946–2011) was one of the most prominent practitioners of Dalit fiction in Malayalam literature. Known for utilizing intense narrative techniques to portray the lives of the oppressed, his landmark works include *Uchayurakathile Swapnangal* and *Njandukal*, both compilations of short stories.

Sara Joseph (born 1946) is the prolific leader of a talented generation of women writers in Malayalam fiction. An outspoken feminist and advocate for creative freedom, she founded Manushi, an organization that brings together women activists. She has written ten novels and fifteen collections of short stories, with *Aalahayude Penmakkal* being awarded the prestigious Vayalar Award. She has won the Crossword Book Award, the Sahitya Akademi Award in 2003 (which she returned in 2016), the Muttathu Varkey Award, the O. V. Vijayan Puraskaram, and the Padmaprabha Puraskaram.

V. P. Sivakumar (1947–93) was a celebrated writer and translator of the high modernist era, known for his powerful narrative language, sense of humour, and the use of irony even in the most dismal situations. He has translated works by Jorge Luis Borges and Eugene Ionesco into Malayalam. The prestigious V. P. Sivakumar Memorial Keli Award was founded in his honour.

N. S. Madhavan (born 1948) is a forerunner of the after-modern tradition of Malayalam storytelling. He has authored several short stories, essays, a novel, and two plays, and is the recipient of the Crossword Award, the Kerala Sahitya Akademi Award, the Muttathu Varkey Award, and the Mathrubhumi Literary Award. His well-known works include a novel, *Lanthan Batheriyile Luthinivakal* (Litanies of the Dutch Battery)and short-story collections such as *Choolaimedile Shavangal*, *Thirutthu*, *Nilaavil*, and *Higuita*.

Maanasi (born 1948) is the nom de plume of P. A. Rukmini. Her writing defies conventions associated with female portrayal, especially those laid down by men, and explores the darker aspects of a woman's psyche. Her short story 'Punaradhivasam' was adapted into an acclaimed feature film that received the National Film Award and two Kerala State Film Awards. She won the Kerala Sahitya Akademi Award for Story in 1993.

U. P. Jayaraj (1950–99) is remembered for his hard-hitting stories, strong political viewpoints, and his accurate portrayal of the turbulence faced by the youth in Kerala in the seventies and eighties. An early proponent of the after-modern story, his promising literary career was cut short by an untimely demise. He has produced three collections of short stories.

Gracy (born 1950) is noted for her sharp feminist voice in fiction. She is the recipient of several prestigious literary prizes like the Lalithambika Antharjanam Award, the Thoppil Ravi Award, the Katha Prize for the Best Malayalam Short Story, and the Sahitya Akademi Award for Children's Literature. Her stories have been translated into English, Hindi, Tamil, and Odia.

N. Prabhakaran (born 1952) is a prolific writer, essayist, educationist, editor, and columnist. He began his literary journey in 1971, with the short story 'Ottayante Pappan' (Mahout of the Lone Tusker). To date, he has produced forty-eight books across genres, and his works have been extensively translated. He has won the Muttathu Varkey Award and the Sahitya Akademi Award twice—in 1987 for his play, *Pulijanmam*, and in 1966 for his short story collection, *Raatrimozhi*. *Pulijanmam* was translated by Jayashree Kalathil and won the Crossword Award in 2020 and the first prize at a state-level competition organized by the Kerala Sangeetha Nataka Akademi.

C. V. Balakrishnan (born 1952) has more than sixty literary works to his credit, including but not limited to, twelve novels, thirty-three novellas, and eighteen collections of short stories. The prominent themes in his writing include mass culture, sexual politics, the lives of those belonging to marginalized communities, and the nuances of religion. He is a three-time recipient of the Kerala Sahitya Akademi Award and has been conferred with the Padmaprabha Puraskaram and the Muttathu Varkey Award.

Asokan Charuvil (born 1952) has penned eighteen collections of short stories and received several esteemed prizes during his literary career. These include the Kerala Sahitya Akademi Award, Edassery Award, Padmarajan Award, and Muttathu Varkey Award.

Aymanam John (born 1953) is a significant name in after-modern Malayalam storytelling, having based several of his short stories in the quaint village of Aymanam, made popular by Arundhati Roy's *The God of Small Things*. He has written three collections of stories and a memoir and received the Odakkuzhal Award in 2017 and the Kerala Sahitya Akademi Award.

Thomas Joseph (1954–2021) was known for this highly visual narrative style, his language reminiscent of contemporary paintings. He has produced two novels and six collections of short stories, and his novel *Marichavar Cinema Kaanukayaanu* won the Kerala Sahitya Akademi Award in 2013. He is also a recipient of the V. P. Sivakumar Memorial Keli Award and the K. A. Kodungalloor Award.

Chandramathi (born 1954) is the nom de plume of Chandrika Balan, a writer, translator, and critic who writes both in English and Malayalam. She has four books in English and twenty in Malayalam to her credit, including impactful short stories, essays, and memoirs. She is the recipient of fifteen literary prizes, including the V. P. Sivakumar Memorial Keli Award, the Kerala Sahitya Akademi Award, and the Katha Award.